Praise for the Planetside Series

Planetside

"This was a brisk, entertaining novel. . . . I was reminded a bit of some of John Scalzi's Old Man's War novels."

—SFFWorld

"A tough, authentic-feeling story that starts out fast and accelerates from there."

—Jack Campbell, author of *Ascendant*

"Not just for military SF fans—although military SF fans will love it—*Planetside* is an amazing debut novel, and I'm looking forward to what Mammay writes next."

—Tanya Huff, author of the Confederation and Peacekeeper series

"*Planetside* is a smart and fast-paced blend of mystery and boots-in-the-dirt military SF that reads like a high-speed collision between *Courage Under Fire* and *Heart of Darkness*."

—Marko Kloos, bestselling author of the Frontline series

"The book was an enjoyable read and would likely sit well with any fan of military SF looking for an action-thriller to browse while lying in the sun at the beach."

—Chris Kluwe for *Lightspeed Magazine*

"*Planetside*, the debut novel by Michael Mammay, is an easy book to love. . . . [A] page-turner and an extremely satisfying read."

—Washington Independent Review of Books

"If you like military SF you'll love this or if you like SF mysteries or probably just SF in general. It's a highly impressive first novel that left a real impact."

—*SFcrowsnest*

Spaceside

"Highly recommended for military SF lovers, who will savor his perspective and probably want to buy the man a drink."

—*Library Journal* (starred review)

"*Spaceside* is a worthy sequel to *Planetside* and Mammay once again successfully delivered another highly entertaining page-turner. The cleverly mixed mystery and military sci-fi element made this relatively small book packed with a strong impact, and I highly recommend it to readers who are looking for a fast-paced mystery/sci-fi read."

—Novel Notions

"This is another wonderfully addictive, fast-moving book from Michael Mammay. Corporate intrigue, interplanetary politics and military action are blended into a cohesive whole that is both satisfying and great fun."

—*SFcrowsnest*

"Wow, just wow. This was another exceptional book from Mammay, who has once again produced a fantastic science fiction thriller hybrid with some amazing moments in it. . . . *Spaceside* is an incredible second outing from Michael Mammay, who has a truly bright future in the science fiction genre."

—Unseen Library

Colonyside

"Highly recommended for readers who like their heroes cynical, their mystery twisted, and their SF thought-provoking."

—*Library Journal* (starred review)

"A fine read clearly informed by the author's own military background."

—*Amazing Stories*

Darkside

"*Darkside* is Mammay's best yet. Nearly nonstop action interspersed with ratcheting tension, humor, and scenes that provoke a fist-pumping YES! Highly recommended."

—Craig Alanson, author of the Expeditionary Force Series

BLINDSIDE

Books by Michael Mammay

BLINDSIDE

A Novel

MICHAEL MAMMAY

HARPER Voyager
An Imprint of HarperCollins*Publishers*

HarperCollins books may be purchased for educational, business, or sales promotional use. For information, please email the Special Markets Department at SPsales@harpercollins.com.

Harper Voyager and design are trademarks of HarperCollins Publishers LLC.

hc.com

FIRST EDITION

Library of Congress Cataloging-in-Publication Data has been applied for.

ISBN 978-0-06-343379-3

Printed in the United States of America

26 27 28 29 30 HDC 10 9 8 7 6 5 4 3 2 1

A NOTE FROM THE AUTHOR

Due to the growing length of the Planetside series, I wanted to provide recaps of previous books for those who want them. The first three books aren't necessary for the enjoyment of *Blindside*, but may help with some references and callbacks. *Darkside*, the immediate predecessor to *Blindside*, has a lot of carryover to this book and is a better start point than jumping directly into *Blindside*.

Obviously, these summaries contain **massive spoilers** for the previous books, so if you haven't read those yet, consider this your fair warning to turn away.

Which is more warning than Butler usually gets . . .

—

PLANETSIDE

Colonel Carl Butler is nearing retirement when he's called in by an old boss (and friend), General Serata. The military brass need him to travel to the distant, war-torn planet of Cappa to investigate the disappearance of Lieutenant Mallot, who is not only a soldier, but the son of a high councilor. It's a difficult mission but seems like a straightforward one.

Of course, it isn't.

Cappa Base is anything but friendly to Butler's inquiries, and more than one person is hiding something. The military commander is covering his ass, the hospital commander, Dr. Elliot, stonewalls Butler, and the special forces commander, Colonel Karikov, won't come up off the planet. Not to mention the witness who goes missing or the critical data that disappears.

Butler, along with his security guard, Mac, goes down to the planet's surface in search of answers, but they're hard to find. After a battle, Butler learns of a medical experiment that blended Cappan and human DNA, allowing humans to better tolerate cybernetic appendages. Except a flaw in the process means that patients who undergo the procedure need constant treatment, or they start to go insane. Butler and his team are attacked by human-Cappan hybrids led by Mallot, the man Butler had come to find. They need a leader, and since Butler himself has a cybernetic appendage, they want Butler for the job. Small problem: He has to undergo the medical procedure first. Butler is captured and taken to a medical facility where he's restrained until Dr. Elliot shows up. Elliot won't operate on an unwilling patient, and while she and Mallot are arguing, Butler steals a pistol and shoots Mallot in the face. Realizing the damage she's done, Elliot shoots herself.

Back on the orbiting base, Butler learns that in their dealings with humans, the Cappans have acquired fusion technology that will allow them to spread the war to the rest of the galaxy. He suspects that the powers that be who sent him to Cappa knew that all along, and part of the reason he's there is to deal with it while providing those leaders with plausible deniability.

Butler, being above all else a soldier, understands the mission. Despite serious misgivings, he fires weapons of mass destruction at the planet, ending the Cappan threat but killing millions in the process. He turns himself in to be arrested for what he sees as a war crime.

SPACESIDE

Carl Butler doesn't go to jail due to a political deal, which is pretty messed up in his mind. It does end his military career, however. He quickly lands a cushy job doing minimal work for a defense contractor, but his personal life is not as good. His wife divorced him, he's suffering from PTSD, and he's seeing Cappan-human hybrids everywhere. Half the galaxy considers him a pariah, the other half as a hero.

When someone breaks into the network of a rival company called Omicron, Butler's boss asks him to investigate so that their company can eliminate any vulnerability that might make it susceptible to the same thing. Butler uses his contacts to set up a meeting with an Omicron executive, who later calls him and says he's found something big. The contact is killed before Butler can get the information.

In part to battle his own demons Butler pursues one of the Cappan hybrids he thinks he's been seeing and finally confronts them. He learns that not only has he not been hallucinating, but that a large number of Cappans escaped their home planet and perfected the hybrid process, eliminating the insanity side effect. Brought face-to-face with a Cappan leader, he learns that Omicron is trying to steal that technology for commercial gain. Butler teams up with the Cappans to try to put a stop to it.

He hatches a plan, along with a computer genius named Maria Ganos, to break into Omicron. Unfortunately, he's captured, relocated across the galaxy, and forced to collaborate with Omicron's mercenaries to extort from the Cappan refugees the final pieces of information that Omicron requires to exploit the technology. After they get what they need, they intend to nuke the settlement from orbit.

Following a battle on the surface, Butler kills the leader from Omicron and makes his escape back into orbit. He convinces the crew of the ship to let him target the missiles, as he's already got one genocide on his record. While planning the attack, he uses a subtle trick to minimize the damage to the Cappan colony, and the ship leaves, convinced that everyone is dead.

COLONYSIDE

Carl Butler has fully retired to the idyllic backwater of rural Ridia, enjoying his time gardening and generally not being shot at. That comes to an end when General Serata, also retired, shows up and asks him to do another job. While Butler remembers how Serata set him up in the past, the job itself is to find someone's missing daughter. Having lost a daughter himself in the past, Butler can't say no. That the client is a CEO named Drake Zentas, one of the richest men in the galaxy, is a drawback, but Butler reluctantly signs on anyway.

Butler, along with Mac, Ganos, and a captain named Fader,

arrives at the mostly undeveloped colony in the jungle on the planet Eccasis, where he finds an understaffed military, an incompetent governor, and a corporation called Caliber running roughshod over both. When someone tries to blow him up, signs point to a protest group that is trying to save the planet and hates Butler for what he did back on Cappa. But he has no shortage of enemies.

Butler's chief suspect gets shipped off planet before he can question him, but he finds information that brings the circumstances of Zentas's daughter's disappearance into question. Initially, it had appeared that she was killed by the planet's alpha predators: large green apelike creatures called "hominiverts." But it could have been more sinister: Someone at Caliber has found a way to control the animals and drive them into a rage, causing them to kill.

As Butler works to get to the bottom of the mystery, a sting operation goes sideways and he's captured and taken to an underground facility. There, Caliber is scheming to have hominiverts overrun the entire colony, an excuse to allow Caliber to exterminate them (which is illegal, especially after Butler's "genocide" of the Cappans) and move on to full-scale mining operations. Caliber forces Butler into service, and he fights against the raging beasts using an army of killer drones before turning the tables on Caliber and stopping the hominivert attack.

Realizing what he's done, Zentas tries to execute Butler, but Butler escapes, subjecting himself to the hostile atmosphere of Eccasis in the process. Mac leads the cavalry to the rescue, and Butler exposes Caliber for their crimes.

DARKSIDE

A young girl seeks out Carl Butler in his hometown to ask him to find Jorge Ramiro, her missing father. Carl doesn't do that kind of thing, but she has raised money to pay him, and she won't take no for an answer. Carl starts to look into the situation and finds enough to get him off planet to the mining colony on Taug, a moon that orbits a gas giant in his solar system.

Ramiro worked for Dr. Whiteman, a famous archaeologist, but Butler can't find either of them when he reaches Taug. What he does find is operations run by two corporations he knows: Omicron and Caliber. That both of those companies have tried to kill him in the past is a little too big a coincidence for comfort.

As the investigation progresses, it becomes clear that Ramiro is dead. What's not clear is why, or who's behind it. To find answers, Butler and his team head for the archaeological dig site on the dark side of the moon, but they are forced to turn back when an unknown enemy attacks them and destroys one of their vehicles. Butler isn't one to give up when things get difficult, so he talks the military into launching a mission to the dig site. His transport gets shot down, leading to a protracted battle between the military and multiple forces of corporation mercenaries.

Following the battle, Butler finally makes it to the excavation site where he discovers what the archaeologist—and the corporation—have been hiding: the remnants of an alien starship that pre-dates known space travel by millennia. There is no evidence of the crew who crashed it on Taug, but the technology it holds has incredible implications for the entire galaxy.

Butler returns to base with the information, but the battle with the corporations continues. He can't see a way out where he makes them pay for their crimes, so instead, he turns them on each other and leaves, contenting himself with taking news of Jorge Ramiro's death back to his family—his original mission.

BLINDSIDE

CHAPTER 1

Butler

W E'D BEEN BACK from Taug for six weeks when I heard about Justin Parnavic's death. He was—or, had been— the commander of the base on the moon where we'd recently seen action. Because of how my life has played out, I'm probably a bit more inured to death than most people, but this one struck me pretty hard. Maybe because I'd seen him recently or because it came unexpectedly. Taug had always been peaceful until recently, and I'd thought that when I left there, we'd put it back together so that would continue. Apparently not.

As with a lot of my information, I got the news from Ganos. She knew everything, often before it hit public media. In this case, her sources had been mainstream—in her words, "mundane, but effective." Parnavic had gone down in a crash that the military had categorized as a mechanical failure. Four dead—everyone who'd been onboard the small craft. I thought about it constantly for a day or so, but like most things that happen far away and don't affect us directly, it didn't stick with me much beyond that. Other things came up and pushed it back into the depths of my mind with all the other death and bad things that lurked there. If I let that stuff sit at the surface, I wouldn't be able to function.

Not that I found myself overly busy. My normal routine at home on Ridia 2 consisted of going to Mac's gym two or three times a week, working in my vegetable garden, and reading a lot of books. The garden was mostly a dig up and replant job since we'd missed harvest for a lot of the produce during our trip and stuff had rotted on the vine. Or the deer got it. But in this case, anything they ate, I didn't have to clean up, so I'd give them a pass.

My big event of the week came on Wednesdays at four in the afternoon when I met Mac for drinks at Moop's. It probably sounds like a boring life, and maybe it is. But boring is nice sometimes. Nothing exploding, nobody trying to kill me. Or, if they were, they were at least being subtle about it.

So it came as a surprise when I woke on a Saturday morning to find that something had tripped my new security system in the night. Mac had immediately upgraded everything I had when we returned from Taug. I'm pretty sure we paid extra for rush installation. It was mostly legal—which was saying something considering my recent life—though it probably skirted the edges of some of the rules on lethal force. And maybe taser drones. Mac had become obsessed with those after he'd seen Alanson operate them on Taug.

The system hadn't woken me, which meant that it hadn't assessed the threat as serious enough for that. But any incursion was enough to mess with my head, and I'd promised Mac that I'd act with an abundance of caution when it came to security matters. I called him, first thing, even before I made my coffee. I'd just finished it twenty minutes later when he came through the back door without knocking.

Mac had on running shoes, shorts, and a stretchy t-shirt with Mac's Gym on the front that might have been half a size too small, muscles bulging. I couldn't make fun of him for it. It made for good advertising.

"You get to finish your run?" I asked.

"Nah. I broke it off at the five-kilometer mark when you called."

"Sorry." Saturday was his distance day. He'd probably planned on fifteen.

"Don't worry about it. I work in a gym. I'll make it up later—this is more important." I had my doubts about that, though I'd shared them often enough with Mac that I didn't feel the need to raise them again now. On the other hand, given how little running I did these days, maybe security *was* more important.

"Did the cameras pick anything up?" asked Mac.

"I didn't look. I figured I'd wait for you, and we'd check it together."

"Let's fire it up." Mac moved to the far side of the living room and pushed the camouflaged activation button. A section of wall slid up and a terminal folded down. He entered a six-digit code on the keypad along with his thumbprint and the metal casing that protected the screen slid away.

I'm pretty sure I mentioned that my security system might be a bit over the top.

Mac played with the interface for a bit while I went to the kitchen to make him a cup of coffee. I didn't need to watch over his shoulder—I'd hate if he did that to me, and he'd show me whatever he found anyway.

"Here it is," he called. "Zero two twenty-one. Someone breached the perimeter."

"Someone? Or something?" I walked over to him and set a mug of black coffee on the side table. It was a reasonable question. The AI in the system was supposed to screen out animals, but it wasn't perfect, and the deer messed with the sensors almost as much as they messed with my garden. I hate deer. They're basically giant rats with better PR. I'd asked Mac if we could set the system up to terminate them on site, but he'd said no. Sure. He picks *that* to show self-restraint about. That was fine. I'd been joking about it anyway.

Mostly.

Mac sat back so I could see the screen. A dark figure stood in the trees, clearly silhouetted from a streetlight in the distance behind them. Not a deer. "Definitely someone," he said, emphasizing what I could already see for myself.

"He . . . they . . ." I corrected myself. It was too dark to determine gender. "They came in from the front? How much did video capture?"

"Running that now." It would take a few seconds, because the system would pull from all thirty-five cameras and piece together the entire incursion.

I let out a sigh. Just what I needed. While the intruder might not have meant me harm, we absolutely had to treat it like they did, which would be a giant pain in the ass. I didn't even have to watch the video to know that much.

"Here we go." Mac stood so we could both get a good view of the screen at the same time.

The dark figure entered the tree line about thirty meters west of the driveway. It was difficult to judge height or weight without something to compare it to, but the system would produce that as well, so I didn't worry about it. A brief moment of light caught their face, hidden by a dark facemask—the kind that people use in the winter. Winter was around the corner, but the weather last night hadn't been nearly cold enough to merit a face covering. They walked mostly straight toward the house, only varying course to pick their way around trees and the small bits of brush that had grown back since the last time I had it cleared. They stopped between two larger trees and stood there for at least a minute, not advancing any farther, which would have triggered more active defense measures—not just sensors and cameras. I couldn't say for sure, but they seemed to be staring at the house. At least in that direction. After a bit, they turned and left the same way they'd come in.

Once it finished, we stood there for a few seconds in silence before Mac reached forward and shut the screen off. We weren't done with it, but we didn't need it for the moment.

"What do you make of it?" I asked. "Could just be someone who got lost."

"Dressed like that?" asked Mac. He was right, of course. "What worries me is that they seemed to know your system. Knew how far they could come in without triggering active countermeasures."

"That might be a stretch," I said. "We can't say that for sure."

"No," Mac allowed. "Not for sure."

But, again, his assertion felt correct. "So what's the point of it?"

"They could be casing your place. Evaluating your defenses for a later attack."

"If so, why show themselves so blatantly? It just gives us warning. It looked like they almost *wanted* to be seen. They didn't do anything to try to avoid the cameras."

"They didn't," Mac said. "Maybe they were tracking them—figuring out where the cameras are so they could avoid them in the future."

"But you're going to move them," I said.

Mac shrugged and nodded. "True." He moved them regularly even *without* a specific reason.

"Which any pro would know, so either they're a total amateur, which makes them less of a threat, or they've got a different purpose."

"Sending a message?" asked Mac, more to himself than to me.

"What's the message?"

He ignored my question. "Maybe they dropped something out there. We'll know more once we comb the area."

I nodded. I didn't want to make a big deal of this, but no chance Mac would let it go, so I might as well ride with it. "You going to bring in help?"

"Yeah. I'll call Castellano. Maybe another guy. Get them to help me go through the woods and see if the visitor left anything behind."

"Pull up what the system has on the intruder. I'll fire it over to Ganos to see if she can do any magic with it."

"Roger." Mac flipped the screen back on and keyed in some requests. "1.71 meters tall. 76 percent likely they're male."

"That only describes about twenty percent of the planet," I said.

"It tells us something, though," said Mac. "For a system as good as yours to only have seventy-six percent confidence . . . that's not an accident. The intruder purposefully worked to conceal that information."

I frowned. "You sure?"

Mac gave me the look that noncoms give officers when the officer asks a stupid question.

"Right," I said. "Of course you are. So, a pro."

"At least in that aspect. It's worth looking into."

"Sure. I'll have Ganos run a search on anybody who might be on planet who fits the bill." It seemed like a search for the letter O in a field of zeroes, but it didn't hurt to try. If anybody could turn nothing into something, Ganos could.

"I'm going home to change," said Mac. "Do me a favor, and don't wander outside of your security system until I get back?"

"I won't," I promised. I actually meant it.

CHAPTER 2

Mac

DON'T LOOK FOR trouble. I can see why people might not believe that, given how often it finds me. And that's fair. I own it. I've made some decisions in my life that ensure that trouble and I . . . well . . . we're never too far apart. Funny thing is, when I joined the military, I was trying to get *out* of trouble. That worked out *great*.

And then there's Butler. Look up trouble in the dictionary, and there's his mug staring back at you. But I love the guy, and here's the thing: While I don't *look* for trouble, I learned my lesson that first time. I don't run from it. I also know it when I see it. When someone came onto Butler's property two nights back, *that* was trouble. Butler didn't see it that way, but there was nothing new in that. He has the luxury of looking past stuff. Because he has me.

And that was trouble of a different kind. At least if you listened to my therapist, which I mostly did. He said that I needed to figure out who I was outside of the military. Outside of Butler. That I used my dedication to Butler as a coping technique to avoid spending time with myself. He might have been right. He had a lot of fancy diplomas on his walls and seemed pretty smart. On the other hand, he'd also told me that you can't solve every problem in life by punching someone in the neck.

So clearly some of his advice was suspect.

Right now, I had to focus on the current trouble: we hadn't found anything to add to what we knew the first morning after the intrusion onto Butler's property. Ganos had even looked into it and come up blank. Nothing. She and I had never really seen eye to eye—we're too different. And things had become extra weird between us since I left her behind on Taug and she got kidnapped. Sure, I'd saved her after that. But she had scars, and I blamed myself for them. But whatever baggage we had, she's the best there is when it comes to finding information. So for her to come up blank? That meant something. For now, it meant that I needed to keep looking. Something would show up. It always does, even if you don't see it until it blows up in your face. But I still had a gym to run, and right now that meant a completely different kind of trouble in the form of one of my regulars: a fit-looking woman named Judith Strand.

Judith was a forty-something woman with blonde hair and a fully paid-up membership. And not one of the discount specials we ran at the beginning of the year to entice people with ill-conceived new year's resolutions. She'd joined about a month ago and paid full price. Her husband had a membership too, though he'd never been in. Judith came in five times a week and had a smile for everyone. She addressed even the part-time staff by name. Today, she was staring at her leg press machine like it owed her money. That might not sound like trouble, but here's what I know about running a gym: if you want to keep it running, you better keep your forty-something-year-old woman clients happy. They've got the time and money to spend on memberships, and if they like you, they tell their friends.

I was working alone at the moment—Sandra had needed the morning off and wouldn't be in for another forty-five minutes—but I left the front desk unattended and made my way past the cardio machines to where Judith sat on the press machine.

"Something wrong?" I asked.

She looked up at me. "Oh. Hey, Mac."

"Workout going okay?"

She looked at the unmoved weights. "Yeah . . . I'm not really into it today."

"That doesn't sound like you. Something wrong? Anything I can help with?"

She sighed. "It's nothing."

It was definitely something, but I didn't know how hard to push. If I kept at her and got her to open up, she might end up telling me about some problem that she had with Mr. Strand. As much as I wanted to keep my clients happy and coming back, I didn't want it enough to get involved in *that*. "You sure? It's not like you to short yourself on leg day."

She gave me a half-smile, but it seemed forced. Something was really bothering her. "Janie didn't come home last night."

"Oh . . . I'm really sorry." Janie was her oldest daughter—seventeen or eighteen, if I recalled correctly. "No idea where she might have gone?"

"None. This isn't like her."

I nodded. In my experience, a lot of upper middle-class parents didn't have a great handle on what was and wasn't like their kids, but I knew better than to say that. Besides, I didn't know Janie beyond the couple of times she'd come to the gym on her mom's guest pass, so who was I to say anything? But then, I was standing there, and I had to say *something*. It was too awkward not to.

"Anything I can do?" I regretted saying it immediately. What was I going to do?

She scrunched up her face, probably wondering the same thing: how a muscle-headed gym owner could help with a kid who stayed out overnight. "You know anybody who finds people?"

"Uh—" I mean . . . I did, in theory. But not the way she needed. Finally, my brain caught up with my mouth. "Can you hire a private investigator?"

"My husband said I was overreacting and that we didn't need to hire one. Said she'd come back on her own."

Guy sounded like a dick, but maybe I didn't have all of the story. Still . . . probably a dick. Just playing the odds. "What are you looking for?" Another dumb question, but she seemed distraught, and I couldn't walk away.

"I don't know." She wiped her face with her towel, though she wasn't sweating. Drying her eyes. "I'm not very smart about stuff like this. I just want to know that my daughter is okay."

I took a few seconds. It *really* wasn't my business, and I had the whole thing with Butler's intruder to deal with. But I found that I didn't care that it wasn't my business. "I might know someone who could look into it."

"Really?" Her face lit up, and I have to admit that when it did, it warmed my cold, dead heart just a little.

"Sure. Off the books. I'll ask them to poke around and see what they find. If they find her, great. If they find that something's wrong . . . not that I expect that," I added quickly, "then you'll have the information, and you can decide if you want to take more drastic action."

She considered it for a few seconds. "Thanks, Mac." She looked like she wanted to hug me. I took a step backward to forestall that.

"Of course. No problem." I left her to her lift and when I got back to the register, I called Butler. I'd signed up for the job, but he had the skills and contacts for this, and he owed me enough favors where I'd never run out.

"Hey boss. I need a favor."

"Of course. What is it?" He probably thought I was going to ask him something about the intruder. Surprise!

"I need help finding a girl."

"Wait . . . what happened to Cassie?"

"Very funny," I said. Cassie was my girlfriend, and nothing was wrong with that as far as I knew. "Another girl."

"Okay, but Cassie isn't going to like it."

"Can we cut the dad jokes for a second?"

"Ouch," he said. "Something serious?"

"Maybe. The daughter of a client is missing."

There was silence at the other end of the connection for several seconds. "Okay . . ."

"Nothing like that," I said. "I just want to see if you can ask Ganos to dig around and see if she can drum up something on where the kid might have gone."

"Oh. Right," he said. "Why didn't you call Ganos?"

"She'll be more inclined to do it if it comes from you."

"You think?"

I didn't think. I knew. He did too. "Yeah. Either way . . . could you do it?"

"Sure. What can you tell me about the kid?"

"Name's Janie Strand. Daughter of Hank and Judith Strand. They live at 14 Everlight Circle in Brockton."

"Nice address."

"Yeah. Her dad's a physician, I think. Surgeon, maybe. I mostly know the mom. She's here at the gym now. Leg day."

"Ganos isn't up yet, so this may take a bit."

"Sure. I'll meet you at Moop's this afternoon. Let me know then."

"Will do."

MOOP'S WAS ALMOST empty when I arrived—four people at one table, two women in the corner booth, and one loner at the bar. The slack patronage didn't surprise me since I showed up at 3:50 on a Wednesday afternoon. Butler hadn't arrived yet—he'd be there in ten minutes, almost on the dot. The colonel was nothing if not punctual. I took a stroll around the room, surreptitiously checking faces on the people there. I didn't know the foursome, but I recognized them as having been there before. Locals. Jake was at the bar. That left the pair of women as unknowns—one in her thirties, one mid-twenties, both in business clothes. Definitely not from around here. Normally I'd have marked them as low threat, but the incursion at Butler's had me on edge. Not that I could accost two random women. Moop liked us, but not enough to tolerate us harassing his customers, even if they clearly didn't belong here.

I took a seat in our normal booth, facing the door but still able to watch the suspicious women, and signaled to Martha behind the bar for a water. I'd wait for Butler to order real drinks. We'd probably have beer unless he was stressed, and then he'd buy the good whiskey. I'd call it top shelf, but Moop didn't even keep Butler's stuff on the shelf. It was under the bar. This wasn't the kind of place that casually served up whiskey from Ferra 3. It was a bit beyond the clientele, and they didn't want to make people uncomfortable or put on airs. But they kept it for us, because Moop's good like that.

I caught a glance of Butler through the window, and he came through the door nine seconds later. "How're you doing, Martha?" he asked

"Right as rain, Carl. What're you drinking?"

"Two beers." He didn't bother with a brand. Martha knew.

"Coming right up."

He slid into the seat across from me.

"What'd you find out?" I asked, unable to wait. I'd been thinking about Janie most of the day. Not worried, exactly, but not comfortable. Once I decided to get involved, it had stuck with me. Unfortunately, I'd *have* to wait, because the older of the two women got up and came toward our table. Because of *course* she did. We were going to need to find a different bar. I should have trusted my instinct and ran them out of the place. Instead, I stood and blocked her path before she could reach Butler.

"Mac," he said, a hint of warning in his voice. "It's okay."

I didn't move. The woman took the hint and stopped, but she leaned around me in an exaggerated fashion that was almost comical. I took the chance to look for weapons. None that I could see. I glanced at her partner, but she had her head in her device, not even watching us.

"Colonel Butler?" she asked, as if she didn't know.

"That's right," he said.

"I'm Elizabeth Young. I work for Meridian Resources. Can I sit?" She glanced at me. "Your man can frisk me, if he wants." She could have made it sound silly, could have even made it sound suggestive, but she didn't. She was legitimately ready to let me pat her down.

Butler looked at me expectantly.

"She can sit," I said. "Just keep your hands on the table."

"I will," she said. And she did. "I'll get right to the point," she said, as I took the seat across from her, next to Butler.

"I'll get to a point of my own: I'm not a fan of being approached in bars," said Butler.

"I understand and respect that. We messaged. Multiple times. We even sent standard mail. You didn't respond to any of it."

"Maybe that was a hint." He smiled as he said it, mostly joking. But not totally. "You didn't come to my house recently, did you?"

"Absolutely not," she said. "That seemed even more over the line than walking up to you here."

"Okay," said Butler. "Just checking. What can I do for you?"

"Recently my company—"

"Meridian Resources," said Butler.

"Right. We've started working with some old friends of yours."

"That so? Which friends?" From his tone, he was thinking the same thing as I was. We had some *friends* who often proved somewhat less than friendly. I adjusted myself in my seat so I could get up faster.

"A group of Cappans."

Butler didn't say anything. He just studied her. I didn't have to say anything because that's not my job, which was good, because it stunned me as much as it appeared to stun him. The silence got a little awkward, and after a few seconds she continued, "We thought that if you came to work with us, we could do a lot of good together."

"I'm retired," he said. He kept a straight face. I mostly did too. It was funny though, the idea of him being retired.

"You don't have to stay that way. Give us a chance. Come see what we do—I think you'll be interested."

He considered it—or at least pretended to. I couldn't say for sure which. "I'm going to pass. Thanks."

I stood, and Elizabeth Young got the message and stood too. "I'll leave you my card. We're pretty resourceful. Reach out if you change your mind."

"Sure," he said.

She put it on the table. "I'm serious—it doesn't have to just be about what we want. Anything we can help you with, you get in touch."

He looked at the card, but didn't respond. After a few seconds, she went back to her table. The other woman stood as she approached, and the two of them promptly left.

"That was weird," he said.

"You think they had anything to do with the intruder on your property?" I asked.

"I don't like coincidences, but when she denied it, my gut says she was telling the truth." He thought about it a few seconds longer and then must have decided he'd discussed it enough and shifted gears. "So, Janie Strand. It's not good."

I immediately forgot the uninvited woman. "Not good how?" With Butler, that phrase could mean anything from 'hiding out on her parents' to 'mauled by a bear and dead in a ditch.' He was the king of understatement.

"Looks like she ran away. She's almost certainly left town."

"Oof. That *is* not good. We sure?"

"Pretty sure. Ganos broke into her home computer and found a record of her talking to someone about getting a ticket to Cranston."

Cranston. The closest metropolitan area to our small town—about a million people in population. Though close was relative since we lived in the middle of nowhere. It was about three hundred kilometers, and not a straight shot. About a four-hour drive. "Ganos say who Janie was talking to?"

"Yeah. Guy named Frank Green—but that's not his real name. Just what he used to talk to her."

"Scammer?" I asked.

"Lowlife. Real name, Frank Figeroa, also known as Figs."

I nodded. Yeah. The mix of suburban girl and city lowlife wasn't good. "What kind of lowlife?"

"Hard to say. Multiple arrests, only one conviction. Suspended sentence for possession of a controlled substance."

"Ganos found all of that already?"

Butler shrugged. "She's Ganos."

"Remind me never to cross her." *Or to never cross her* again.

Martha arrived with our beers, and Butler lifted his in acknowledgment of my wisdom. "Did Ganos say why Janie took off to meet him?" I asked.

"Romantic meet-up, probably. They'd been chatting for a couple of weeks."

"So, this guy chats up a well-off suburban girl, lures her to the city . . . could be legit." *Probably not.*

"Could be," Butler allowed. He didn't believe it either.

"Fake name, criminal record. It probably isn't."

"Probably not. What are you going to do?"

"Tell the mom, I guess. Though I'll have to talk around how we got the information. She might not like that Ganos broke into their home network."

JUDITH TOOK IT better than I expected, though when I think about it, I'm not sure what I expected. I thought maybe she'd yell, or cry, or . . . at least something. Instead, she stood there, the two of us alone in a corner of the gym, and didn't react at all. It caught me so off guard that I wondered if she'd heard me. I was debating with myself whether or not to repeat the information when I recognized the signs: she was in shock. I'd seen shock enough in combat, but I never associated it with something like this. I guess learning that your daughter, who had probably lived a very safe life protected in her parents' wealth, had not only run away but now faced potential danger—that could do it.

"What are you going to do?" I asked. I hadn't wanted to speak, but I really wanted her to say something. Let me know she was okay.

"I . . . I don't know." She stood there for a few more seconds, leaning back on the wall next to a seated row machine. "I have to go after her."

I started to respond, tell her that was a good idea, but then I hesitated. *Was it* a good idea? A suburban housewife going to the city to deal with who knows what? "Are you sure that's a good plan? Do you know people in Cranston?"

"No," she admitted. "But what else can I do?"

"Tell your husband?"

She shook her head. "He'll blow up. Blame me."

"How's he going to react when you tell him that you're going?" Seemed like the obvious question, if he was the dick I thought he was.

"Oh. Right." She thought about it. "Those friends of yours . . . the ones who found her. Are they for hire? I can pay. Could they go get her and bring her back?"

I should have said no. Because they—*we*—really didn't do that kind of thing. But in the moment, looking at a mom in distress, I couldn't bring myself to voice those words. "Sure," I said.

CHAPTER 3

Butler

WHEN MAC TOLD me about his conversation with the mom from the gym, I didn't react. His sheepish tone said he already knew what I thought. It surprised me a little that he'd agreed to go. I'd always thought of him as more cautious than that, that he'd avoid getting entangled in someone else's business. But who was *I* to judge? It's not like I'm a walking fount of good choices.

Of course I was going with him. He hadn't asked, but he didn't need to. After all he'd done for me, how could I not? Besides, it was Cranston. It wasn't like we were going into combat. Plus, I liked to visit the city from time to time anyway. Our small corner of the woods lacked for quality eating establishments, and I looked forward to getting a couple of good meals and enjoying drinks somewhere other than Moop's.

When I arrived at Mac's condo the next morning, however, I had to reassess my thoughts about not going into combat. He had cameras, communicators, a couple of drones. And guns. Lots and lots of guns.

"Do we really need this kind of weaponry?" I asked, trying to imply with my tone that we absolutely did *not*.

"It's the city. We'll keep the long guns packed away in the travel safe and mostly use the stuff we can conceal."

I couldn't tell if he'd missed my point on purpose to mess with me or if he meant it. "Why do we need weapons at all? We're not storming an armed position."

"Concealed carry is legal in Cranston," he said, as if the legality was my question—it wasn't. He *was* correct, of course. This part of Ridia 2 had pretty lax gun laws. Most of it was rural enough where that made sense. A little less so in Cranston these days, but tradition died hard.

"Not the question," I said.

"The guy she went to see is no good, right? Who's to say he's not armed?" asked Mac.

"We're not going to have a gunfight with him over the girl."

"Not intentionally," he said.

I shook my head but moved toward the armaments on the table. Better to have it and not need it than the alternative, I guess. I picked up something the size of a deck of cards that appeared to be made of Kevlar. "What's this?"

"Palm gun. Pulse. Three shots when fully charged. Codes to your prints so only you can fire it."

I turned it over in my hand, examining it. It had grooves on the bottom to fit my fingers. I could see the appeal of it. You could keep it in your pocket, and it would look like a wallet, not a weapon. I didn't want to know what we'd paid for the pair of them. "Range?"

"Less than a pistol. Probably wouldn't try it outside of fifteen or twenty meters."

I nodded. In the city, that wasn't likely to matter. It's not like a regular pulse pistol would give me much more than that. I put it in my pocket.

"Grab a pistol, too," said Mac, but I'd already moved on to study the surveillance equipment. There were two flexible tablets and a laptop, which would ostensibly let us see the drone feeds. I started to consider the various uses of such things. The drones seemed impractical, given the limitations of a city environment, but a remote camera to cover the outside of wherever we ended up staying had at least some benefit. In the end, most of it would stay in a suitcase anyway, so I didn't argue much. Compared to what we spent on my security system, this was a drop in the bucket.

Castellano arrived and loaded all our kit into Mac's SUV, and then the three of us were off. We took a wheeled vehicle—everything in the rural areas ran on wheels. In the city we'd see more hover tech and self-driving options, but out here, the infrastructure didn't support it. We'd both agreed on bringing C—more out of preference than need. Mac and I both liked the kid, and I was happy to throw some money his way to keep him around. We hadn't talked about it, but I assumed I'd foot the bill. I had the bankroll. It also made sense to have a driver so Mac and I could get out and ask questions without having to find somewhere to park. That last bit might have been mostly in my head. I have this thing about cities and finding parking. I don't know why.

WE MADE GOOD time to our hotel—if you could call it that. More of a motor lodge, really, with a single story and room doors that opened to the parking lot. It lay outside of the city proper, leaving us a twenty- or thirty-minute drive into the city center, depending on the time of day and traffic, but it fit with the nature of what we were carrying. Laws or no laws, a swanky downtown hotel probably wouldn't look kindly on three guys toting in an armory. Here, nobody would blink an eye at it. Not that we were advertising our stash, but still.

We took two rooms, side by side. I offered to pay for three, but Mac and C wanted to bunk together so that one of them could stay there and keep an eye on our kit. That kind of put a crimp in my plans for a nice dinner, but sometimes you've got to sacrifice for the job. Hopefully we could still get some decent takeout. It probably sounds like my priorities were off, but in my defense, I didn't see this as much more than a visit. We'd find the kid—or more likely, we'd hit a dead end—and we'd be back home in a day or two.

We *did* have a better plan than just walking around and looking, at least. Ganos hadn't been able to locate Janie—she'd left her device at home, probably because she knew her parents would track her from it. Frankie had his, though, and while we shouldn't have been able to track that, should and shouldn't didn't really apply to Ganos. Conveniently, he was out and moving around, so once we got checked in and settled, we loaded back up and headed into the city. Mac kept the tracking program up on a flexible tablet and rode shotgun, telling C which way to go. I looked over his shoulder and punched the location into my own device so I could scout it out.

I didn't know the city neighborhoods, but even a tourist could tell that our destination wasn't in a good one. If I hadn't known from the map, it became clear enough as we got closer and passed by a series of low-rise apartments in varying degrees of decay.

The few businesses—convenience stores, pawn shops, liquor stores—all had bars or cages over the windows. Armoglass—which is virtually unbreakable—came with a price tag beyond this part of the city. A few pedestrians moved along both sides of the four-lane street, but none of them lingered, walking fast with heads down. We passed one larger group—kids horsing around as they moved slowly on the sidewalk—but even then, they stayed together. Safety in numbers.

"Here's our boy," said Mac, gesturing ahead to a lone figure leaning against the corner of a dirty two-story red brick building with a small liquor store on the ground floor.

"Convenient that he's by himself." We didn't have a live picture of him, just a dot on a map.

"Drive past him. We'll do a U-turn a couple blocks up and come back on his side of the road," said Mac.

"Roger," answered C. He didn't slow as we passed the young man, but I took what time we had to check him out. Ganos's info said he was twenty years old, but he had that ubiquitous look that young people had where he could have been seventeen or twenty-five. He was skinny and wore a dark fabric jacket against the cold. If he noticed us passing, he didn't show it, leaned back against the building, smoking some kind of vape.

"What's he doing?" I asked.

"Maybe working," offered Mac.

"You think he's selling something?"

"That or he's waiting on someone. No real other reason to be sitting out there on a windy street corner in this cold."

"Never know," offered C. "Might be he doesn't have a place to go."

"No sign of the girl," I said.

"We couldn't get *that* lucky," said Mac. He was probably right, though by my estimation, the universe owed me some luck, given all the crap it had put me through. "I just hope it's actually him."

"What's the play?" I asked. "Hard or soft?"

"Soft. We pull up, and I'll ask him where the girl is. His reaction should tell us everything we need to know."

I didn't know about that. I doubted that he'd willingly part with that kind of information. Three guys pulling up and asking about a girl was pretty suspicious in the best of circumstances. He might run away out of simple survival instinct. We wouldn't be able to draw any concrete conclusions from that, but I didn't have a better idea, and I much preferred a soft approach to a hard, which might end with Mac beating the shit out of a man on a public street.

C pulled us up to the curb and Frankie pushed himself up off of the building and sauntered toward us. He was definitely working. Mac rolled his window down, and I followed suit in the back seat.

"Can I help you gentlemen?"

"We're looking for a girl," said Mac.

Frankie smirked. "Not my line of sales. But I know a guy . . . I can give you directions." Mac started to open his door, but Frankie put a hand on it, blocking him. "What the fuck are you doing? You don't get out of your vehicle, asshole."

Mac forced the door open, causing Frankie to stumble back. I hopped out as well, though in the moment I didn't know if I was trying to help Mac or hold him back. This had the potential to rapidly become *not soft*.

"You fucking crazy, man?" Frankie asked as he gained his balance. He glanced both ways down the road, maybe looking for an escape.

"Girl's name is Janie. Came here a couple days back from out of town."

Frankie smirked again. He had a smarmy way about it that had definitely gotten him punched in the face before. "Oh." He chuckled. "Yeah, I might have seen her. You her dad?"

"I'm a friend."

Same smirk. "Friend. Right. Banging her mom?"

"Her mom and dad are still together," said Mac, his voice flat, giving nothing away about his emotional state. His restraint in not laying hands on the kid impressed me. So far.

"Right. Sorry. Her family situation didn't come up. Except her dad's an asshole." Frankie looked at me. "Hey. You're that military dude, right? That colonel?"

I didn't respond. I got recognized on occasion, though not as often as I used to. But Frankie here didn't fit the news-watching demographic, and it struck me as strange that he might know me.

"Look," said Mac, "we don't want any trouble. Tell us where to find the girl and we'll be out of your business."

"And why would I do that?" asked Frankie.

Mac started to speak—probably a threat—but I cut him off before he could get it out. "I'll pay you," I said.

Frankie came up short at that. I'd caught him by surprise, apparently. "Maybe we could work something out."

"You tell me where she is, I'll give you a hundred right now."

"He's just going to lie about it," said Mac. Frankie didn't deny it or even seem to take exception to Mac's accusation.

"Or," I said, forestalling any brewing argument, "you bring her to us, and I'll give you a thousand."

"A thousand," said Frankie.

"A thousand. Unaffiliated transfer stick." That would matter to him. He could use it anywhere. It was the closest thing we had to cash in our cashless economy.

"You have it on you?" he asked.

"You have the girl on you?"

He snorted. "Give me an hour. Meet me back here."

"You going to bring her?" I asked.

"That's the thing," he said. "I don't know for sure where she is."

"But you have an idea."

"I know some people who might know. And for a thousand? You can bet your ass I'm going to try to find her."

"That's good," I said.

"Yeah. Whatever. You just be back here in an hour with that stick."

WE DIDN'T GO back to our motel. By the time we made it there, it would be time to turn right around and come back. Instead, we drove a couple klicks, found a parking garage, and pulled inside to wait.

"You think he's actually going to bring her?" asked Mac.

"Hard to say," I said. "I think for what I offered, he's got to at least be thinking about it."

"For all he knows, you might want her for less than honorable reasons," said C.

"For some reason I don't think *that* matters to him in the slightest," said Mac.

"I think we learn something either way. If he brings her, great. If not, we've got a track on him right now and we see where he went. It gives us another lead."

"You're setting a bad precedent, paying to get someone back," said Mac.

"Maybe. But we don't think they physically took her, right? She came to the city of her own free will."

"That's what the mom implied," said Mac.

"What if he brings her, but she doesn't want to go with us?" asked C. Another good question. Made me glad to have him along.

"Hopefully when she sees that her boy Frankie is willing to ditch her to make a buck, she sees reason and is happy to get out of here."

"If not?" asked Mac.

"We'll wing it," I said.

Mac snorted.

WE ARRIVED BACK at the designated corner at one hour on the nose. No Frankie.

"He's not coming," said Mac.

"You expect someone like Frankie to be punctual?" I asked.

Mac got out of the vehicle and looked up and down the street. After a few seconds, when it became clear he wasn't getting back in, I joined him.

"Feed has him four blocks away. Looks like he's inside a building—entered twelve minutes ago," said C.

"Let me know if he starts moving," said Mac. "If he won't come to us, we'll go to him."

Two men were walking up the sidewalk from the south, talking to each other, taking their time. They were the only pedestrians, and the street had only a smattering of vehicle traffic.

"He moving yet?" I asked C.

"Nope."

The door to the vape shop opened a crack, barely wide enough for a person to fit through it, and Frankie slithered out. Shit. Guess he left his device behind. Maybe he realized we had a track on him. Maybe he was just cautious.

"You find her?" I asked, but even as I said it, I sensed that something was off.

"Gonna need you to hand over that money stick," said Frankie, confirming my assessment. He glanced to his left and I followed his eyes. The two young men were about thirty meters from us, still approaching, and no longer on a casual stroll. They weren't visibly armed, but both wore dark jackets, so I couldn't say what they might be concealing. I looked the other way and found that another guy had materialized—a monster of a youth, younger than the others, but with at least thirty kilos on any of us.

Mac had a pistol in his hand—I'm not sure when or how it got there, but when I looked back, he had it pointed at Frankie. "How about your friends stop right where they are."

Frankie, who should have been sweating despite the cool weather, looked as relaxed as a man on vacation. "You're making a mistake, brah."

"One of us is," said Mac.

"Pulling a gun with all the cameras around in this city?"

"And here I thought that you picked this corner for the *lack* of cameras," said Mac.

Frankie sniffed, but then nodded to the group of two guys, and they stopped. One of them pulled his coat to the side to make sure that we saw his sidearm. In case we had any doubt. This was going nowhere good in a hurry. The guy approaching from the other direction stopped as well, and for a few seconds, we all stood there looking at each other. "Four of us, two of you. I don't like your odds, brah."

"You might want to consider your own chances. If this gets messy, I put your odds of survival at exactly zero," said Mac, his pistol held close to his body and still trained on Frankie.

"This ain't the military, brah. You're not going to shoot me." Frankie seemed a lot surer about that than I was. Mac might shoot him just out of spite. "Besides, you need me if you want to find your girl."

"Like I said, you tell us where she is, we're out of here, and you can go back to your life," said Mac.

"This is *your* last chance. You set your gun down . . . and that thousand . . . and I let you get back in your vehicle and drive home to whatever backwater hole you came from. I'll pass on your message to the girl. She can follow you if she wants."

"So, you *do* know where she is," I said, stalling as much as trying to get information. I put my hand into my front pocket as if retrieving my wallet and grasped the palm gun, making sure I got my hand aligned to activate it. If things were going to get stupid, I definitely planned to be a part of it. Hopefully to defuse it. Dead bodies in the street—whether ours or theirs—seemed like a really bad way to announce our emergence into city society.

Mac and Frankie stared at each other for several long seconds, neither of them willing to give a centimeter. I had to give the guy credit—I didn't know many people who could stare down Mac, let alone Mac with a loaded sidearm, and not blink. I shifted my eyes to the other three as best I could given their spacing and them coming from two different directions. If something happened, I'd go for the group of two. At least one of them had a weapon, making them the bigger immediate threat.

Frankie lifted his chin and then wrenched his body sideways, making as small a target of himself as he could. Time seemed to slow. It's a feeling I'd only had in combat before this moment, but each fraction of a second stretched and I took in more information in that instant than should be humanly possible. His three friends began closing, reaching into their coats for weapons as they started to move.

I pulled my palm gun.

A pulse blast shrieked, piercing the din of background city noise like a rooster on a quiet morning.

Everybody stopped.

For a second, I thought Mac had fired at Frankie, but it had only been me. My pulse weapon had left a half-meter-long black scar on the sidewalk right between baddie one and baddie two.

I guess everybody else had been bluffing. Whoops. I not only called, I raised. That's the problem when you're playing in an unfamiliar game: you never know who's in it for fun and who's playing for keeps.

The guy on the left had a pistol out, but he hadn't gotten it raised, and it sat there in his hand, pointed down at the ground.

"Nobody has to get hurt," I said, trying to forestall further rash action. Somebody had to say *something*. I could only imagine what Mac was thinking. He was supposed to be the hothead, and then I went and did *that*.

We stood there for several more seconds before a siren cut in from down the street, forcing a decision. The four locals turned and ran.

"Stay or run?" Mac asked, still cool, no panic in his voice.

"We stay. Toss your weapon into the vehicle. C, you get out of here. No sense in all three of us getting run in." This had gone to shit in a hurry. We didn't need to make it worse. We'd worry about Frankie—and more important, Janie—after we sorted this out.

Mac complied without hesitation, and I tossed my palm gun through the window of his SUV even as C hit the gas. It took the authorities another twenty seconds to arrive in a heavy-duty hover vehicle, and by then our car had disappeared around the next corner.

"We could have made it," Mac said, before anybody exited the vehicle.

"Nah. This is the city. They'd have picked up our vehicle on traffic cameras, and if we ran, we'd look guilty."

"We aren't exactly *not* guilty."

"I wouldn't lead with that in your statement," I said.

Two law enforcement officers exited the vehicle at the same time, leaving the lights on. A tall, dark-skinned man came around from the driver's side while a pale, red-headed woman with square shoulders and a strong jawline got out onto the curb.

"What happened here?" asked the woman. Her nametag read Donato. I didn't know their exact rank structure, but she had two chevrons on her sleeve, and he had one, making her the senior in rank as well as age. He was in his twenties, while she might have been a fit forty.

"Four guys tried to jump us," I said. "They took off in three different directions. If you hurry, you might be able to catch them."

Neither officer moved to take me up on my suggestion. Oh well. I tried.

"This isn't exactly a tourist spot. What brings you two gentlemen here?" asked Donato.

"We were looking for someone." I didn't plan on lying to the authorities, but that didn't mean I had to tell them *everything*.

"I bet you were," said the male officer, but the woman glared at him, and he fell silent. I didn't blame him. The kinds of things people might look for in a spot like this weren't exactly savory.

"How'd you get here?" she asked.

"Somebody dropped us off."

"You want to tell me about that scorch mark over there? Looks pretty fresh," she said.

"I'm no expert, but it looks like a pulse weapon mark," I said.

"That it does," she said. "Want to tell me how it got there?"

"I don't." Like I said, I wasn't going to lie. I also didn't want to incriminate myself.

She stared me down for a few seconds. That might have worked on some suspects but wouldn't get her anywhere with me, so she shifted her gaze to Mac. She got even less reaction from him. After a few more seconds, I guess she realized the futility of it. "IDs, please."

Mac and I produced our IDs, and the woman disappeared into their vehicle while her partner continued to mean mug us. He didn't have his weapon out, but he rested his hand on the butt of it, as if daring us to make him use it. Neither Mac nor I responded. I was proud of Mac. Our adrenaline was up from the confrontation, and he had to have been steaming. She reappeared a couple minutes later.

"Colonel Butler," she said. "Sergeant McCann. We're going to go ahead and take you in." She didn't say she knew anything beyond our names, but something in her demeanor told me she'd just learned our backgrounds.

"This is bullshit," said Mac, apparently having reached his tolerance point. The tall cop took a half step closer.

"What are the charges?" I asked, trying to forestall further confrontation.

"Let's call it a courtesy," said Donato. "You don't have a ride, and you don't want to be walking through this part of town."

"We're fine walking," said Mac, but I put a hand on his forearm and gave Donato a slight nod.

"We're going to pat you down before we put you in the vehicle," she said. "Standard procedure. You understand. Help us out. You armed?"

I looked over at Mac. I'd seen him toss his pistol, but I knew better than to assume that was his only weapon. He shook his head slightly. "We aren't," I said.

The male officer took Mac to the other side of the vehicle while Donato searched me. I definitely got the better end of that deal. After a cursory search, she deposited me into the back seat. I didn't buy the courtesy angle at all, but at least they didn't cuff us. That's so uncomfortable.

We rode the seven minutes to the station in silence, though Mac fumed, barely able to sit still. I wanted him to relax but didn't want to talk in front of our audience, so I gave him a hand signal.

He ignored it.

They didn't bring us to the front of the building—a large three story made of gray faux-stone with a lot of big windows—instead opting to take us through the gate in the fence that surrounded the free-standing structure. We parked in a lot with a bunch of police vehicles in spots shaded by solar collectors, and the officers hooked up the vehicle to charge before escorting Mac and me through a back entrance. We weaved through a couple of hallways and out into a bullpen where a dozen or so officers worked at twice as many desks.

"Sergeant Kinlaw," said Donato. "You have time for the case I called in?"

A stocky tanned man of about fifty looked up from one of the desks—apparently Kinlaw—and gave us the once-over. "I need about ten minutes. There's a private cell they can share."

"Don't do us any favors," Mac said, under his breath.

"What's that?" asked Kinlaw. "I can throw you in the tank, if you'd rather."

"No, thank you," I said, speaking before Mac could. "We would be grateful to take you up on your initial offer."

Kinlaw stared at Mac, who thankfully let it go.

Thank the Mother for small victories.

CHAPTER 4

Butler

TRUE TO KINLAW'S initial estimate, Donato returned in ten or fifteen minutes to retrieve me from our cell. Mac and I hadn't talked much. For one reason, too much chance that someone could be listening in, and we didn't want to give them free information. I'd share what I knew with the police, but only if I thought it might get me something in return. For another, Mac didn't seem ready for a conversation, and I could respect that.

I held off on calling for my attorney. Since Frankie had clearly ditched his device before trying to jump us, we were fresh out of ways to find Janie. Maybe one of the officers here could help us. Once I brought a lawyer into the equation, any chance I had to negotiate for intel got a lot harder.

Donato led me to Kinlaw's desk, where I took a seat next to the side of it. They still hadn't cuffed me, but Donato stood over us, I guess in case I got out of hand or something. I had no plans for that. Mac, on the other hand . . . well, they'd deal with that when they got to him.

"Coffee?" asked Kinlaw.

"I'm good. Thanks." He was trying to establish a rapport, but I didn't need a stimulant this late in the day. I have enough trouble sleeping as it is.

He nodded. "Before I waste a lot of time and send you for biometric processing, you want to tell me what happened?"

"Four guys jumped us," I said. "When the sirens came, the guys took off. So thanks to your officers for that."

"The officers responded because sensors picked up the sound of a pulse weapon discharge," said Kinlaw. "So how about we don't bullshit each other?"

"What do you mean?" I was only half-disingenuous with the question. Sure, I was hiding information, but also, I really couldn't tell where he was going.

Kinlaw frowned, only half of his mouth turning downward, as if maybe he had some sort of impediment on the other side. "Guy like you doesn't end up in that part of town on accident."

I didn't follow his logic. People got lost all the time. But he was right, in that we hadn't, and it seemed best to be at least a little honest. "Fair. I went there intentionally. But I didn't instigate the altercation, nor was that my intent."

"And you were there . . . looking for something? You have to know that there are better ways to go about getting whatever it is that you wanted."

I suppressed a laugh. "I was looking for something . . . someone . . . very specific. I had reason to believe I might find them there."

"Who are you looking for?"

"I can't say."

"Can't?" asked Kinlaw.

"Won't. What are the charges against us again?"

Kinlaw thought about it, maybe considering his next question, trying to figure out what might break something free from me.

I decided to take us in another direction, see if I could gain something useful. "I can tell you the name of the person I met there."

"Go ahead," said Kinlaw, his voice noncommittal, as if he didn't care if I shared it or not.

"Frank Green. Goes by Frankie Figeroa. Or Figs." I looked at Donato as I said it. It was her beat, so she was more likely to know the guy than Kinlaw.

Seeing my gaze, Kinlaw looked at her too.

"Frankie," said Donato, giving a snort. "Yeah. I know him."

"He likely to fire a pulse weapon inside city limits?" asked Kinlaw.

"Not his usual style," said Donato. "But with Frankie I'd hesitate to rule anything out."

"Other than that corner, you have any idea where he hangs out?" I asked.

"See," said Kinlaw, not letting Donato answer, "it's a question like that that makes me think that you were looking for *him*. Makes it a lot harder to let you walk, if you understand."

Looking for Frankie wasn't illegal, but that probably wasn't his real point. "Would you believe I'm just curious?" I smiled as I asked it, trying to get things back on the right side of friendly.

Kinlaw shook his head and rolled his eyes. "Take him to biometric processing. We're going to have to do this the hard way."

"I'm sorry, I've already forgotten—what were the charges again?"

He ignored me, and Donato gestured for me to stand, so I did.

"Sergeant . . . if you wouldn't mind," I said, before Donato could lead me away.

"Yeah?"

"If you could contact my attorney and tell her that I'm here? Maxine Stoddard. Her number is in my device—if you hand it to me, I can get it for you."

Kinlaw stared me down. "Really?"

I shrugged. I hoped he didn't take it personally and decide to throw me in the tank to spite me for being difficult, but he was the one who brought up "the hard way."

Kinlaw sighed. "Take him back to his cell and call the lawyer," he said to Donato. "No sense in processing him until she arrives."

"Come on." She led me away. I thought maybe I heard a smile in her voice—that she might not be nearly as annoyed as Kinlaw. There was something there, but I couldn't immediately figure out what it meant. Regardless, it wasn't the right time to push it.

AN OFFICER I hadn't met—a short, pale-skinned guy in a brown suit, not a uniform—came and got me from the cell Mac and I shared about forty minutes later.

"He comes with me," I said, nodding to Mac, who stood up from the wooden bench attached to the back wall.

"Ms. Stoddard said she represented you. She didn't mention McCann," said the officer.

"She'll be representing him about thirty seconds after I start talking to her. It'll be easier if you bring him along, but we can be official if you'd like, and you can come back and get him then."

Brown Suit didn't hesitate. "Come on, then." He led the two of us out through the pit and back toward the way we came in but took a turn away from the exit and around another corner to a hallway where doors branched off each side at regular intervals. Each door bore a sign with the words "Interview Room" and a number. The officer led us to Interview Room 7, opened the door for us, and ushered us in.

Inside, it looked like every other interview room, complete with table and chairs, all bolted to the floor, and one mirrored window that took up most of the side wall. What made this one unique was the blonde woman in the very expensive gray pants suit leaning on the edge of the table.

"Carl. I didn't expect to see you today. Or this month. I didn't know you were in town."

"Thanks for coming, Maxine."

"I'd have been here sooner, but I'd quit for the day. I had to get dressed."

"You didn't need to do that," I said. "You could have come in civvies."

"Would you go into combat without your body armor?" she asked.

"Good point."

"And I was being polite. I also had to look up where this jail was. Can't say I've ever had cause to come here before."

I smiled, trying to turn on the charm. "Another point taken. This is Mac. I'd appreciate it if you'd represent him as well."

"Well . . . that's kind of an issue. I can represent him, and I'd be happy to take more of your money, but I'm not a criminal defense attorney."

"That's great. Because we're not criminals."

She didn't smile. "You know that's not how any of this works." She looked to Mac. "If you find yourself in need of tax advice, especially as it might relate to a legal settlement, definitely give me a call."

"Wait . . . are you saying there's more than one kind of lawyer?" I asked.

Still no smile. Okay. I'd misread the situation. At a minimum she was annoyed. She might even be pissed. I hadn't spent a lot of time with her—just enough to handle the many legal settlements that bankrolled my life. She'd made a lot of money on those herself, and I guess I presumed that that bought me some leeway. More likely, I was being an ass.

"Seriously," I said. "I understand that. But you're the only lawyer I know in the city. On this planet, really. I really appreciate you coming."

"You *do* pay me a pretty hefty retainer. It was the least I could do. So why don't you tell me what happened, and I'll recommend a colleague who fits your needs."

"That would be great." I looked at the two-way mirror. "Is it safe to talk in here?"

"This isn't a spy vid, Carl. Nobody is listening in on privileged conversation." She raised her voice a bit. "Because I'm a *very* expensive attorney, and if they did and I caught them, you'd own half this city by the time we were through, and everyone here would be out of a job."

"Just in case," I said.

"Right. Have a seat." Maxine took a seat on one side while Mac and I sat on the other and filled her in on our day up to that point. I told her everything—why we were there, how Frankie had set us up, and what went down when his friends showed up. She took it in without comment, and when we finished, she stood.

"This seems simple enough. I should be able to handle it without calling in help," she said. "I'll go talk to them and see what I can do."

"Tear them a new one," said Mac.

"On the contrary. I'm going to be as pleasant as possible, because while carrying a weapon isn't a crime, discharging it inside of city limits is. In this case, since nobody was hurt, it's probably just a fine. But that's not our issue."

"What's our issue?" I asked.

"According to your story, when they ran your IDs, they immediately started treating you differently. That means they know exactly who you are. The last thing we need is for any of this to hit the news feeds. Unless you've changed your stance on public attention in the last few months and haven't told me about it."

"No, no change. You're spot on. Do you think we can keep it quiet?"

"I'm not sure. But any chance we've got requires a lot of goodwill from everybody involved, so it's in our best interest to play nice." She looked at Mac. "Can you handle that?"

"Yes, ma'am," he said, chastened.

That gave me another thought. "We're in a similar challenging situation regarding whether we involve the authorities in helping to find our missing person. We can ask, but as soon as we do, then Janie's name is public. We have no control of how it gets spread."

"Might even put her in additional danger," said Mac.

"You two hash that out," said Maxine. "I'm going to go explain to the officer in charge why this is all a misunderstanding and that they should let the war hero go without public record."

"I'm no war hero," I said.

"Let's hope they disagree," she said.

WE WALKED OUT of the station eight minutes later, and judging by the mood of the officers, there were no hard feelings. But we wouldn't know immediately whether they'd kept it quiet, or somebody leaked our involvement in a potential crime to the press.

"Thanks, Maxine," I said, as she walked us to the back entrance where C was waiting with the vehicle.

"You're welcome. I told them you're leaving town as part of my plea for them to let you go. Please don't make me a liar."

"We'll leave town right away," I said.

She stared me down in a way that said she didn't believe me, but eventually left. She was definitely worth what I paid her.

"Where to?" asked C, once we were in the vehicle and moving.

"Hotel," I said.

Mac turned in his seat so he could look at me.

"What?" I asked with fake innocence. "Technically our hotel is out of town. It's getting late. Nobody would expect us to drive all the way home in the dark."

"Next time you call for a lawyer, she's going to send you a public defender."

"That does seem likely," I said. "Hopefully it won't come to that. I don't plan to need a lawyer."

"Nobody *plans* to need a lawyer."

C dropped us at our rooms and then went out for burgers from a local joint that had good reviews. I can confirm those reviews. It was a good burger. Mac ordered grilled chicken. Dude never takes a cheat day.

Meal finished and whiskey open, the three of us sat in their room, discussing our options. More accurately, C and I sat. Mac paced, staring at the tablet in his hands as if he expected something to change.

"We've lost our track on Frankie," said Mac. "Totally disappeared."

"He left it behind before they ambushed us. Feels like he knew how we were tracking him," I said.

"Probably. But can we have Ganos take a look? Who knows what she can accomplish?"

"Right. I'll get in touch with her." Mac didn't want to call her himself. There was something going on there, but I didn't want to push right then.

I messaged her, as that's the only way she'd pick up a comm, and soon I had her on speaker.

"He's gone," she announced.

"Can you get him back?" I asked.

"His device? No chance. When I say gone, I'm talking threw it in a bucket of water or put it in a lead box gone. No sign of it since a few minutes after your altercation."

"We kind of figured that might be the case," I said.

"Y'all really fucked this one up, didn't you? I delivered him right into your hands."

"Yes, you did. We are not worthy of your brilliance," I said.

She hesitated at that, maybe unsure if I was mocking her or if I really meant it. I didn't clarify.

"Is there any way we can find him now?" I asked.

"No easy ones. I'd have to sift the net in the entire area and try to pick up some digital sign that I had the right guy and then tie that to something with a pinpoint location. You don't happen to have a voice sample, do you?"

"No," I said. That a voice sample would help her made me reconsider the notion of using my device for calls, even though as usual, I didn't really know what she was talking about. "On a scale from one to ten, how hard is this?"

"Seven or eight," she said. "Difficulty isn't the issue though. Time is. I could find him with some level of confidence eventually. But the odds that I could do it in a timeframe that helps you—or saves the girl if she's in danger—are pretty slim."

"Any other options?" I asked.

"I could get into all the city cameras in the area around where you made contact, but that's only going to give me a ping on his location at a given moment in the past, and the visual recognition software isn't going to be a hundred percent with those kinds of cameras."

"Yeah, maybe," I said, though it didn't seem worth it given the lack of probability weighed against the legality of it.

"Your best bet is probably setting up local surveillance. Guy was there on that corner for a reason. That reason probably didn't go away. Unless you *completely* spooked him, he'll probably pop up again somewhere nearby."

"Okay. Thanks. We'll give it a shot." I thought about what she'd said about the city cameras some more. I couldn't believe I was about to ask my next question. "Would you get into whatever cameras you can and see if you can get a hit on the girl? It would be good to know she's still here in the city."

"Smart," said Ganos. "If it's a pure human trafficking thing, they'd probably move her far away. Even off planet."

"Let's hope it's not that," I said.

"Right. I'll get on it. And you get yourself some digital facial distorters and something for the plates on your vehicle. The same cameras I use to find her can see you doing whatever shady things you're up to. I can overnight some to you if you don't have a way to get them."

"That would be great," I said.

She cut the connection. Finding this girl was getting expensive, and I didn't owe her parents anything. But now that I saw the potential trouble Janie was in, I couldn't turn away from it. It seemed important to Mac, too. I turned to him. If he said we should leave, we would, but I didn't want to ask it as a leading question and risk influencing him. "How do you see this?"

"We have the location of the device before they ambushed us. That's a potential place to check out."

"There are at least four of them, and they're armed. If they're all there, even checking it out might run us into a fight," I said.

Mac nodded. "Could be a stronghold. We'd have to verify that."

"Even if they hang out there, I'm not sure what it does for us. It's not like we can storm the place."

Mac raised his eyebrows at me. "Not with only the three of us."

I didn't know if he truly meant it or if he was joking. I chose to ignore it. "Regardless, it seems like our next step is surveillance, right?"

"Sure," said Mac.

"You think Alanson would come if we called?"

"I don't know. We got him blown up pretty good last time. If he's smart, he wants nothing to do with us."

"Get him on the line and ask. See if he's well enough to travel and find out how fast he can get here. And Mac?"

"Yeah?"

"If he's coming, tell him to bring everything he's got."

CHAPTER 5

Mac

I CALLED ALANSON. I expected him to be reluctant, but he seemed all in on trying to get revenge on the people who injured him. They weren't here, so I doubted that would happen, but that apparently didn't matter. He also went on for a bit about coming with an armed drone, which I didn't encourage. But I didn't exactly *rule it out*. Butler said to have him bring everything. He definitely didn't mean armed drones, but you never know what you might need.

Alanson arrived the next morning, and C and I picked him up from the airport. He walked down the ramp, and if I didn't know to look for it, I wouldn't have noticed the slight limp. Either way, he looked good for someone who we'd carted off of a distant moon six weeks ago in a medical suite. There'd been a time not too long ago where I doubted that he'd walk again. Happy to be wrong about that one.

It was good to see him. I'd brought him and C in for our escapade on Taug, and both of them had performed way beyond the call. Alanson put his body on the line, getting wounded not once, but twice. The second time he'd thrown himself into the crosshairs of a high-end hit man to buy me time to act. That alone made him okay in my book. That he came with two footlockers of high-tech gear in baggage made him more than okay.

"How you feeling?" I asked, as we waited for his kit to come off the plane.

"Still a little ginger," said Alanson. "Body doesn't heal like it used to. I'd prefer not to get shot again, if we can avoid it."

"No promises," I said. Alanson didn't laugh, but C did, so it was worth it.

"Where's the boss?" he asked.

"He stayed at the hotel. Ganos is sending us a package, and someone had to be there to receive it."

We mostly made small talk after that. I wanted to save the important stuff until we reached the privacy of our vehicle. I didn't think anyone was following us, but you can never be too safe about security.

Once we reached the SUV, we went into full operations mode. "What do you have with you?"

"Pretty much brought everything I own," said Alanson. "But we'll need more. I only keep so much on hand because this stuff is expensive. So mostly I've got the . . . hard to get . . . stuff."

"You mean the illegal stuff."

"What is legality, really?"

I laughed. Another reason why I liked him. "Any place in particular we need to go to purchase stuff?"

"What's the mission?"

"As much surveillance as we can get on two locations. One's on the street—a corner and a store. Maybe the surrounding intersections as well."

"Easy enough," he said.

"Second one's tougher. We've got an address. We need to see who comes and goes from it, but we also want to know everything we can about the inside."

"Better off pulling the building plan for that," said Alanson.

"We're doing that. But the place has forty apartments, and we don't know which one—or more than one—our targets are using. Or if they're using them at all."

"We have access to the building?"

"Not yet. But we can probably manage that," I said. "You want to get into the halls?"

"If we want video, we've got to get something in there, yeah. What about mobile? Overhead?"

"Like drones? It's illegal to fly them in the city."

"Again, with legality?" Alanson asked, shaking his head. "It's only illegal if we get caught."

"You have something that won't? We've probably used all our favors with the local authorities. Almost got arrested yesterday." They didn't charge us, so in my mind, it didn't count as a full arrest. Details matter.

"Nothing's foolproof. But yeah, probably. We'll have to be judicious, but I have equipment that's almost invisible. It wouldn't fool the military, but local authorities usually aren't out there doing active sensor sweeps for drones. If they do catch one, I cut the digital tether, and they can't tie it to us without a lot of luck on their part. We're just out the cost of the tech."

"We can live with that." Easy for me to say, since it wasn't my money. That we intended to launch a full intelligence gathering campaign in a civilian city against a nebulous enemy is a thing that I probably should have given more thought to before we started.

This might not come as a surprise, but sometimes I act first and think later. Butler usually thought enough about things for both of us. It felt wrong to leave everything to him, though, since I got us into this situation.

WE DIDN'T GO back to the hotel, instead hitting up two stores for Alanson's shopping spree and then heading out to set up our systems. Part of me wanted to go back to pick up the facial distorters that Butler probably had for us by now, but another part wanted to get this handled. After yesterday's fiasco on the corner, I was determined to go back to the boss with a mission accomplished. Hand him the results and let him do his thing from there. That's where he excelled. We'd get him the information, and then he'd put it all together and see things in it that other people couldn't. But *we* had to get the info.

I couldn't emplace the sensors. Frankie—and maybe a couple others—knew my face, and they might have people watching out for me. I sat in the vehicle in a parking garage while Alanson and C went to install things. Alanson had a tethering tracker in his pocket that linked to an almost invisible drone that would fly overhead while keeping its camera locked on them. I watched the feed on a tablet. I had limited controls—mostly zoom in and zoom out—but it let me keep the illusion of being involved. They also had earpieces and throat mics, so we could communicate while they worked, and I could warn them of trouble.

We tackled the easy job first, installing surveillance around the area where Butler and I got into it with Frankie the day prior. Alanson had done an initial drone pass through and picked his spots. For street level, he had mini cams, each about half a centimeter thick and as big as a thumbprint, with digital outer skins that he programmed to match each surface he planned to attach them to, making them nearly invisible. They'd install bigger cameras with more capabilities on the tops of buildings to look down on different intersections, giving us a constant bird's-eye view.

It was early afternoon, and the foot traffic had increased compared to the previous day. That helped my team not to stand out as much but made it harder for me to monitor potential threats from above. I mostly watched from a zoomed-out perspective, only focusing in occasionally to look at the faces of men, searching for anybody I'd seen previously. We started a block away from Frankie's corner and would place cameras in four or five spots at each intersection to give us full coverage. Alanson could fine-tune each one via remote later—for now we just needed them in place.

At the first intersection, Alanson and C stood on a corner, pretending to talk until traffic cleared around them. C slapped a camera slightly above head level on a faux-brick wall of an apartment building. Nobody around them reacted in any way. They crossed the street and did the same thing, and before long, they'd moved on down the block to the next intersection.

Right after they put the first camera in, though, something happened. At first, I didn't know what. Just a feeling—a sense of change in the pattern. Then I saw him. A big man walking down the sidewalk across the street from my team. There was nothing that indicated he'd spotted them, or that he had any specific reason for being there. But I knew that guy. The big bastard from the day before. It could have been a coincidence—it probably was. Alanson and C hadn't been out there long enough for someone to spot them and react.

But still.

The problem was, if I aborted, then coming back later made them even more obvious. Not to mention that we were up against a running clock trying to find Janie and needed the cameras *now*.

I opted for a half measure. "I've got a potential bogey inbound. Turn left, go down a block, and then turn right. Do it now. Move fast but don't run."

They started moving immediately, and as they did, I watched the big man. He reached the intersection, and turned to cross the street, headed straight to the location that my team had just vacated. The light was against him, and even though there was a break in the traffic, the man waited for the signal before crossing. He didn't *look* like someone chasing after a target. By the time he reached the other side of the street, Alanson and C were gone, already around another corner and hidden by buildings.

I tried to read the guy's body language. Was he angry? Frustrated? Problem was, the drone was still tethered to Alanson, so if I zoomed in, it showed me them and I lost sight of my bogey. For me to get a more detailed view of him, they'd have to move closer, which I didn't want them to do. I could break the tether on the drone, but Alanson had the AI set to fly on auto with the tether, and if I broke it, I'd either have to operate it manually or reorient the AI, which I didn't know how to do. I opted to stick with what I had and observe from a distance. Not ideal, but it beat accidentally smashing a drone through someone's apartment window.

Big Man stopped at the corner and waited. I took that opportunity to do another wide scan, looking for other potential threats. It would suck if I got so focused on this one that I let my boys run straight into something else. But I didn't see anyone. C and

Alanson walked down a narrower street—a one way—clear of foot traffic.

"Bogey stopped at the intersection you just left. Continue to work, but stay out of sight of that location."

"Did he find our camera?" asked Alanson.

I focused on Big Man. He wasn't looking at the walls of the buildings. In fact, he didn't seem to be doing anything other than waiting. "Negative."

"Roger. We'll hit intersections away from him. Let us know when he clears."

I continued to observe, making sure to back out and check other directions on a regular basis. Initially, I didn't see the second guy at all. On the surface, he was an average-sized guy walking down the middle of the sidewalk—nobody I recognized. But everybody gave him space. Nobody passed him from behind, and people coming the opposite direction spread wide to either side, making a lane for him. From above, that stood out. He was walking perpendicular to my team—to reach them, he'd have to turn back and then turn down a cross street—so he didn't present an immediate threat. At least not to us. To the other pedestrians, he was a shark in a fishpond. They knew him and they stayed clear.

"Second bogey. Not moving toward you. Continue mission. I'll know more in about thirty seconds." Or at least I thought I would. The new predator was walking right toward Big Man. Second Guy stopped, and he and Big Man appeared to chat for several seconds. Two other men who passed by each gave them a wide berth. And then the two separated, each going off in a different direction, perpendicular to each other, with neither going back the way they had come.

There was something here, but I couldn't put my finger on it. I got out of the vehicle and did fifty pushups on the garage floor. Probably seems strange, but it helps clear my head. It worked. By pushup thirty-seven, it hit me—I finished my set, though, because you always finish your set. When I recovered, I could visualize where each man had come from and where they headed. It fit a pattern. They were walking sentry—patrolling the area. It wasn't the same as the military, but it was similar enough. Once I figured that, it got easier to find other potential threats. I found a third man working the same grid of about twenty blocks. Four by five. And I was able to direct Alanson and C to avoid the three sentries and get the rest of their street-level cameras emplaced. But discovering the patrols alone was at least as valuable. If we knew their pattern, we could exploit it.

C and Alanson met me back at the garage after they finished. "That was a little more tense than I expected," said Alanson. "My heart didn't need that kind of workout. What's next?"

"I've been thinking about the four roofs where we want to put cameras and how we get at them," I said. "I don't know how we get up there unobserved."

"We should get a pizza," said C.

I checked the time. "Yeah, I guess I could eat."

"No. As a disguise. I'll pretend I'm delivering pizza and use that as a cover to get into the buildings."

I didn't know if we could get roof access that way, but it was worth a try. "Great idea. Let's get two."

"I think as a young guy, I fit the profile of a pizza delivery man a little better," said C. "Maybe I handle this one alone?"

"Totally agree. One of them is to eat."

Alanson took charge of overhead monitoring while C did his work. It took time, because he had to enter four different buildings, which meant four separate pizzas. He couldn't walk out still carrying one. It gave me a lot of time to do air squats and think. I kept coming back to the men on patrol. They were organized, sure, but that wasn't the part that concerned me. What worried me was that nobody stopped them. That meant authorities either didn't know what was going on, or they didn't have the ability to stop it. Or they didn't care. I guess technically there was nothing illegal about people patrolling a neighborhood. But it did give me some doubts about how much assistance we could expect from the police if we found Janie and she needed help. And why they needed sentries.

I came to a single conclusion: We were going to need more people.

I started making calls.

CHAPTER 6

Butler

I DIDN'T RECOGNIZE THE city—not all of it anyway. Parts of it seemed vaguely familiar, but not so much that I could place myself. I needed to get somewhere, though even that seemed nebulous. The man—or maybe men—following me . . . those were real. I didn't know what they wanted, but they definitely meant me harm. I stood outside a building, but when I tried the code on the door, it didn't open. Not the right place. I hurried away, trying to reach the next corner before my pursuers caught sight of me.

It grew darker around the corner, so much so that it felt like a different place altogether. Somehow, my pursuers were closer, and I'd gone the wrong way. Dead end. A muscular man all in black grabbed me by the neck with one hand, and impossibly lifted me from my feet—

I woke in a sweat, disoriented for a moment, light coming from unfamiliar places in the room. It took me several seconds to remember I was in a motel, several more to calm myself enough to realize the entirety of the situation. I checked my device for the time. 0445. I considered going back to sleep. This was a new dream—not part of my usual set of nightmares—and it frightened me a bit to consider that it might come back if I closed my eyes again. But I needed the rest. I'd stayed up late collating all of the information we'd gathered, figuring out a plan.

I didn't get up, and I eventually dozed off again, though I don't know how long I lay there in the dark thinking before that happened. When I woke again, it was 0630. A much more reasonable time. Mac wouldn't bother me for at least another hour, so I grabbed a shower. I wanted coffee, but the cheap room didn't have a maker, and I didn't want to venture out into the unknown, so I sat down in a passable chair at a worn desk and got back to work.

When targeting in the military, delivering an attack was never the hard part. We had an abundance of ways to service a target. So many that the art became picking the best method for the specific target. No, the hard part was finding the thing you wanted to hit. Your enemy knew what you wanted to attack, so they did their best to hide it from you. They put it under cover or made it appear like something innocuous. And they had all kinds of ways to do that. Physical or electronic camouflage, false signals broadcasts, or simply putting things in places you wouldn't expect them to be.

Here, I had the opposite issue. With what Ganos found from her searches and from the cameras that Mac and the boys had put in, I had almost *too much* information. Ganos's cameras confirmed Janie's presence in the area. A man and a woman escorted her, the man gripping her arm tightly. The camera wouldn't have identified her if she hadn't looked back over her shoulder, right at it. Almost like she knew it was there, and somebody might find her from it. I couldn't say for sure, since we didn't have any sound with it, but it sure *looked* like she was under duress.

Mac's cameras picked up the same man and woman entering the building that we'd tagged via Frankie's device on our first day in the city. Further analysis of video showed that all the people— five different men and one woman—who fit the patrolling pattern that Mac identified all started and ended at that same building. This confirmed what we thought: they had a headquarters. We didn't have video specifically tying Janie to that location yet, but it seemed likely she was there. If she came or went, we'd see it. Hopefully we'd catch it in real time, but we didn't have enough people to watch that one feed constantly when we also had to gather input from all the others.

At least not yet.

Mac had called for reinforcements. I don't know where he got them, but he'd assured me they were ex-soldiers and people we could trust. I didn't trust them, of course. Not completely. Not after what had happened with Barnes back on Taug. But we needed help, and the tasks here weren't nearly as dangerous as what Taug had presented, so we could keep an eye on the newcomers. We just needed help monitoring all our inputs. At least for now. Mac wanted to move, to attack. Part of my job now was to rein him in. For him, knowing that Frankie and crew had a headquarters would be enough to launch an operation. Me? Not so much.

My hesitation was twofold. First, I didn't think we had enough information or enough firepower. We didn't know what they had in that building. They might be using multiple apartments. They'd be watching the front door, and we didn't know how. We had blue- prints, so we knew where the doors and windows were. Knew how many apartments with how many rooms on which floors. But our adversaries could be in any of them or in all of them. We needed eyes on the inside, and a fake pizza delivery wouldn't do it this time. No way could we send C—or anyone—in there alone. Too risky.

Second, and more important, I didn't want to engage in all-out warfare in a civilian city. We'd be breaking the law, and not in a little way that could be overlooked. We'd be breaking the big ones, where any rational person who looked at it would say: *Yep. That's a crime.* Those are generally laws you don't want to mess with.

Even if I put aside the legality of it, which—despite my reputation—I couldn't, we didn't know our enemy. There could be—and almost certainly were—innocents in that building, and we couldn't risk catching anybody in the crossfire. Even with those we currently saw as enemies, we had limitations. We couldn't kill people other than in self-defense, and even then, we really didn't *want* to. That's a pretty big detriment when most of your primary team has been trained for most of their lives to kill people. Add it all up, and there were too many obstacles for us to consider direct action at the moment.

But Mac wasn't going to let this go. This thing with Janie meant something to him personally, and while I didn't understand exactly why, I understood what it meant. Leaving her here wouldn't stand with him. It didn't stand with me either. But I was thinking about it differently—as two distinct problems. Yes, I wanted to find the best way to extricate her. But I also needed to forestall my own team from taking rash action. Two problems meant four times the complexity. At least that's how the math worked in my head.

Luckily, I had one solution that addressed both: I needed to go to the authorities.

That presented its own set of complications. I didn't have any trusted contacts here and, more, I didn't know the relationships between the cops and Frankie's crew. I couldn't rule out the possibility that the authorities were complicit, or more likely turning a blind eye to some of the criminal activity. Gang members were patrolling the streets. The police mostly weren't. If I talked to the police, I risked harming rather than helping our efforts. Or maybe they'd take offense to me involving myself and detain me again on the spot.

Despite the risks, going to the police was the best of a set of less than ideal options. For starters, I felt that the kidnapping—or at least unlawful detention—of a girl would go beyond what law enforcement would accept. If they were turning a blind eye, there would be lines, and in my mind, this crossed most people's. My gut also kept going back to my read on one of the officers. Donato struck me as straight, and with nothing else to go on, I'd trust my instincts when it came to people. In the few hours I'd spent around her, I found I liked her. If nothing else, she was a beat officer, so she might worry less about where I got my information than her superiors, which mattered if I didn't want them to arrest me for Ganos hacking into the city's cameras.

I cut the pieces of video that I wanted to show her, and then I got dressed for the day, glad to have a plan.

Now I just had to convince Mac.

I went with him to get coffee for everyone while Alanson and C stayed back at the room, so he and I could talk alone.

"When do your new people get here?" I asked.

"This afternoon. Might take a minute to get them kitted out—this isn't exactly a standard equipment kind of thing, but they'll—"

"I'm going to the authorities."

Mac didn't respond immediately, which was good and bad. He didn't get on board, but at least he didn't flat out say no. Finally, he said, "You think that'll help?"

I wanted to say that it beat illegally attacking an enemy strongpoint undermanned and underprepared, but that would only get his back up. "It's worth a shot."

"Cops might warn them that we're coming."

"I'm not going to *tell* them we're coming."

Mac snorted. "Okay, I guess not. Doubt it'll do any good, but it can't hurt."

That was as much as I could hope for from him, so I took it. "I'm going to approach Donato. Got a good vibe from her."

He snorted. "I'll bet you did."

I looked at him, confused. "What do you mean by that?"

"She was into you."

"What? No, she wasn't. She was doing her job."

Mac shook his head. "For someone who notices everything about everyone, it amazes me that you can be that oblivious. She kept *looking* at you."

"People do that," I said.

"Not like this they don't. Trust me. I think it's great. You should definitely meet up with her."

"It's not a *date*."

"Not yet." He smirked.

He was in my head. Had I really missed the signs? "She's too young for me."

"She's in her forties. Might even be forty-five."

"I'm almost sixty."

"How many years have you spent in cryo?" asked Mac.

"Maybe fourteen."

"Right. To her, you're forty-six."

"I don't *feel* forty-six."

"So maybe lay off the burgers." He flexed one bicep and patted it with the other hand. "Clean living."

"Whatever. I'm going to go see her."

"Just be careful. As the officer closest to the scene, she's the most likely to be on the take."

"Or the one who's the most fed up with the system."

He tilted his head. "Yeah, maybe. You see what you get from her. I'll get working on how we get eyes inside that building."

I appreciated the change in topic. "I've got Ganos working it, too. With a specific location, that cuts down her search area. She thinks she can reestablish a tail on Frankie or one of his associates. Something about him probably buying his new device near his location cutting down on the number of activations she has to sift through."

"If we could snatch one of them outside of their building, it would make things a hell of a lot easier."

I chuckled, but it was more discomfort than humor.

"What?" asked Mac.

"Listen to you, plotting straight up crimes."

"It's not a crime—"

"That's *kidnapping*. What are we going to do from there? Torture?"

"I mean . . . not *per se*."

"We're definitely going to jail." At least we were unless I could find a more rational way out of this.

I MET DONATO in front of the precinct building as she came in for her shift, which was easy enough to do since Ganos provided me the manning schedule for the precinct. My bill for her work on this job would be significant. With all the people Mac hired—and all the equipment Alanson had lugged along—I would need to check in with my accountant after this and see if I still had anything left.

If it surprised Donato to see me, it didn't show in her expression. She wore a loose workout suit in dark green with her red hair up in a bun.

"Colonel Butler." She smiled, which made me think back to what Mac had said—and hating him for it. Asshole was getting in my head. "I have to admit, I didn't expect to see you here. Kind of thought you'd have been smart enough to get out of town after our last encounter."

"People make that mistake about me all the time," I said.

She laughed. "I'm sure this isn't an accidental encounter. What can I do for you?"

"I wanted to talk to you about a crime."

"Yours, or . . ."

Now it was my turn to laugh. "Not mine. As far as you know."

"You can report it at the desk inside," she said, though her tone said she knew that wasn't what I meant. I guess she wanted me to say it.

"I was hoping to talk off the record. See if there's anything you can do about it before I make it into something formal."

"If it's a crime, it's a crime," she said.

We both knew that was bullshit, but if she wanted to play the game that way, I could. So, I said, "Might be true. But still. Humor me."

She stared me down for a few seconds, assessing, and then she checked her device. "I've got forty-five minutes before I have to roll. Give me five to get into uniform and then meet me inside at my desk."

"Any chance we can talk somewhere less official?" She looked skeptical, so I continued, "I don't want someone overhearing and getting excited. I mostly just want your opinion."

Another stare. "Yeah. Okay. I'll meet you right here. We'll walk around the block."

True to her word, she came back in five and we started off at a mild pace. I waited for a pedestrian to pass by before I started talking, and then Donato beat me to it. "I assume this is about Frankie and his friends. I'm going to tell you right now, it's hard to pin anything on them."

"How come?" I doubted she'd implicate her department in corruption, but I had to give her a chance.

"They're smart. They don't do anything obvious that we can prove."

"Frankie out on the corner isn't obvious?"

"You can search him ten times. He doesn't have anything on him."

"He's just setting the transaction," I said.

"Right. He gets the money. The buyer gets their goods—"

"Drugs?" I asked, just to be sure.

"Yeah. They pick up from a runner at another location and time."

"That's a lot of trust from the buyer."

"They've got a good rep."

I nodded. "You could track the buyer. Make the bust when they get their package."

"We could. We have. But it's not worth doing it on a regular basis. The mule is inevitably an underage kid—hard to prosecute. And if we go after the buyer, we get them for possession, which is usually a fine and doesn't even get them in front of a judge."

"So it's a lot of work for not much payoff."

"Right. And the stuff they're moving—it's not dangerous. Illegal, sure. Mood enhancers, low level amphetamines, muscle relaxants. None of the hard stuff. Nothing that hurts people. Like I said, they're smart. Not greedy. They don't cross lines that make us go after them."

That got my attention. "What else are they into besides drugs?"

"Protection, probably. Though nobody will say so, which means they keep the price low enough where merchants don't have enough incentive to complain."

"Anything else?"

"Prostitution."

"That's legal though."

"Legal if you're licensed and in a licensed facility. That's a barrier to entry that a lot of sex workers can't manage." That was a potentially dark path, but worth following up on. For now, I tucked it away.

"Frankie's boss must have pretty good control to keep his people from going into business for themselves. Who is it?"

"Guy named Jinks."

"Not the big guy, is it?"

"No. That's Marvin. He's definitely not the brains. Jinks doesn't rule by muscle. He grew up in the neighborhood, and everyone has known him forever. Story goes that even as a kid he was a leader. People naturally listen to him."

I took a second to think. If Jinks was more businessman than criminal, if I could talk to him, maybe we could cut a deal. That was a big *if* though. I doubted I could simply set a meeting. I kept it to myself for the time being, because while my gut still said to trust Donato, I didn't want to go too far with that. "What if they did cross the line?"

She sighed. "What have you got?"

"Potential kidnapping. Unlawful detention."

"Fancy words. Tell me what's really happening."

"Girl from out of town gets lured to the city by Frankie. Jinks and his folks are keeping her against her will."

She frowned. "Doesn't seem likely. Not their style."

"What do you mean?"

"What would they do with her? If they ask for ransom, that's a major crime." She paused. "Have they asked for ransom?"

"No."

"So then . . . what?"

"Sex work? You mentioned that they ran prostitution."

"Not a chance. No forced labor. In fact, it's exactly the opposite. Jinks *protects* sex workers. Anybody messes with them, tries to force them to do something they don't want? They end up on our front door. Often bloody."

"You sure?"

"I'm pretty fucking sure. Jinks's *mom* was a sex worker. Yeah, they take a cut for the protection. But it's a fair cut for services provided."

"Honorable criminals."

"I wouldn't go that far. But yeah," she said. "Comparatively speaking, at least."

I pulled out my device and queued up the video clip from the traffic camera of Janie being manhandled. Donato watched it quietly.

"That's the girl?"

I appreciated that her first question wasn't "How did you get that?" "Yeah."

"Have to admit, she does look like she doesn't want to be there. But it's not enough. That could be her dad, dragging her in for being out when she shouldn't be. Could be a lot of things."

"Could be. But it isn't."

"You seem sure."

"Her dad doesn't know where she is." I *was* sure. I'd had Ganos track his comms to make sure we hadn't blundered into a parent versus parent situation.

"Still. No way I get a warrant from this, even if I could use this footage, which . . . I probably can't." She didn't ask me to confirm that, as doing so would be admitting to hacking the cameras. The more we talked, the more I liked this woman.

"That's why we're talking unofficially. All we want is the girl back."

She stopped, so I stopped with her. She considered me for a few seconds. "You're working for the family."

I shrugged. "In a manner of speaking. It's complicated. But

I promise you, I've got nothing but the girl's best interests at heart."

"I believe you . . . well . . . I should say that I believe that *you* believe that. I'm not sure it's your place to define her best interests. Kid leaves home, sometimes they have a reason." Something in how she said it led me to believe that she wasn't talking about Janie. I wanted to ask, but it didn't feel like the time or place.

Either way, she had a point, and while I'd considered it and done what I could to check, I didn't have an infallible view of her home life. "So you're saying that Jinks and crew are *protecting her*?"

"No. I'm saying you can't say that they're *not*."

Another good point. We'd have to confirm that before we took any kind of action, assuming I couldn't talk Mac out of that altogether. "Any chance you could look into it?" She looked like she might refuse, so I held my hand up to forestall that. "Not a search. Just ask around. See what you hear. Specifically, around 1474 Brighton Ave."

She snorted. Obviously she recognized the address. "I can ask a few questions. But like I said, what you're saying they did *really* doesn't sound like them."

"Someone else then?"

"At 1474 Brighton? No chance it's somebody else."

"Thanks, Donato. That's helpful."

"Call me Steph."

"Okay, Steph. I'm Carl."

"You're welcome, Carl. Now . . . I've got to get to work. When you showed up, you said you wanted advice. Wanted to know what I thought you should do. You still want it?"

"Sure." What did I have to lose?

"If the girl's really missing, file a report. Let the pros handle it. Go home. Here's my number." She handed me a card. "Call me if you need anything."

"Thanks." *Go home.* It was good advice. I wish I could have followed it.

CHAPTER 7

Mac

I DID A DOUBLE take when I saw the name on my incoming call. Ganos. I had her in my device—because of course I did—but we never texted, let alone *talked*. I almost didn't want to answer it, figuring it had to be a butt dial. Or a prank. I guess in the darkest part of my mind, maybe I thought she was calling to let me have it. But that didn't seem like her. If she wanted to get back at me, one day all my credit would evaporate, and my identity would be missing from the net. Or I'd be registered as a sexual predator. That was more her style. She kept things inside, and she *never* called anyone. But since she did, I had to answer.

"Mac here."

"Where's the boss?"

"He went to talk to the cops."

"He's not answering his device. I texted and I called." She sounded pissed. More than her normal level of simmering anger.

"He wouldn't ignore your call without a reason. Maybe he's tied up in a discussion. It *might* be a date." It almost certainly wasn't, but I had to tell *someone*, and Ganos was the only other person who would appreciate the significance.

"I've—" She broke off her prepared thought. "Wait. What? Never mind. I've got something hot. That data you sent me—the locations of the patrols and what you figured out about the sentries—that was gold."

I didn't respond. Couldn't. I don't think she'd ever given me a compliment. "Uh . . . thanks."

"Right. I've got your boy's new device. Frankie."

"You can track it?" I asked.

"Yeah. You want it? He's on the move right now. Not sure how long we'll have it. He might change equipment again, now that he knows we're trying to find him."

"Yeah. Of course. Send it."

The line went dead for about two seconds. "Done."

My device vibrated. "Got it. Thanks."

"No prob. Tell the boss to get in touch."

"Will do," I said, but I think she'd disconnected before she heard it. I opened the app on my device and studied it.

C picked exactly that moment to enter the room. "I heard you talking. Was it the boss?"

"Nope. Ganos."

He stood there for a second, trying to work it out. "Really? On the comm?"

"I know, right? She found Frankie." I showed him my screen. "He's on the move."

"Oh. Shit. What are we going to do?" He stared at me like he expected me to know. Alanson too. Guess that meant it was my call.

I wasn't afraid of making a decision. I'd done it plenty of times in the military. Stuff at my level and even some above that. I never hesitated. But this was different. This was officer shit, for one thing, but more than that it was *Butler* shit. He'd know what to do in half a second. I really wanted to call him. But Ganos said he wasn't answering, and more important, *I* had gotten us into this crap, and calling him was just another admission that maybe I shouldn't have. That I couldn't handle it.

I thought about what Butler would do, and he'd start with facts. What did he *know*. I could do that.

Fact 1: If we didn't act now, we might lose the chance to act at all. Frankie could disappear again, and we wouldn't get to question the guy most likely to be able to tell us exactly what we needed to know.

Fact 2: If we *did* act, it might mess up other options—potentially better options. And that's if we got him. If we tried and missed, we might fuck things up beyond measure. We were considering kidnapping a guy, after all. Not only would his own people be pissed, we'd be breaking the law. And not in a little way. This wasn't discharging a weapon in public. I wondered how much Butler's lawyer cost. Probably a lot. That didn't matter. *Focus!* Okay, if we tried and missed, that would be bad. We couldn't miss.

I had the facts, but still couldn't figure out what to *do* with them. In the end, I took the coward's way out. I called Butler.

He didn't answer.

Because of course he fucking didn't. Well . . . I tried. That option exhausted, I came to the same decision I always did. It's better to fail taking action than to fail doing nothing.

"Let's roll."

WE FOUND FRANKIE right where my device indicated, walking a patrol like the guys I'd spotted the day prior. Alanson was driving—he was still ginger, and I needed C to help me snatch our target. Frankie might recognize the vehicle, so we approached from behind him. He was walking alone, and there was no pedestrian traffic nearby when Alanson drew alongside.

C and I jumped out of the vehicle before it stopped moving. Frankie didn't respond for a second. Maybe he felt a sense of security because he was normally a predator, not prey. Hard to say. Right before I got to him, he saw me, froze, and then recovered himself and bolted. Asshole was prey *now*. C took two sprinting steps and tackled him to the ground. He outweighed his target by twenty kilos or so and had way more training. Frankie had no chance. I reached them a second later, and the two of us dragged him toward the vehicle.

Realizing our intention, Frankie started to thrash, kicking out with his feet and twisting. I almost lost my grip. Slippery little fucker.

"You're coming with us," I growled, giving him my best "don't fuck with me" voice. "The only question is whether I slam your head into the door on your way into the vehicle or not."

He hesitated at that, maybe thinking through his options, but by the time he figured it out we had him inside and Alanson pulled out into traffic. C zip tied his feet while I secured his hands behind his back. Once we had him trussed, I put a cloth bag over his head. Yes, I had a black bag with me for this kind of thing. Never know when you might need it.

"You guys are dead." Frankie shouted the words, but his voice shook. Pure posturing. I got that. Probably hadn't been grabbed and bagged before. I mean . . . who has? Okay . . . I know a few people. But that's not the point.

"I think we'll be okay." I couldn't help but respond. Kind of felt bad for the guy, all scrawny and scared.

"You grabbed me off the street. The *cops* are going to get you even if my boys don't. They've got your faces on camera."

That wasn't as much of a problem as he thought since we had the distorters that Ganos sent, but I let him keep his illusion. He had a point about the police though. We couldn't take him back to the hotel. The cameras wouldn't recognize us, but there'd be no way to hide a dude with a bag over his head. The hotel had a reputation for discretion—or, more likely, didn't care what people did—but a bound prisoner might be too far even for them.

"We need a new place," I said. "Something without cameras."

"On it." C got on his device and started scrolling. We drove for a few more minutes before he handed it to me. It was a rental by owner—one of those sites that had become really popular for some reason that I didn't understand. They dubbed the place as a cabin, but if this was a cabin, a swimming pool was a bathtub. It was huge, but more important to us, it sat on a large property with a private drive, surrounded by woods. Nice and isolated. It also cost eight hundred a night, but that was Butler's problem, not mine. He should have picked up when I called.

"It's perfect. Nobody will hear a gunshot at a place that re-mote." I said that for Frankie's benefit. I probably wouldn't shoot him, but if he thought I might, maybe he'd cooperate better. "How far?"

C inclined his head toward our guest before saying, "Not too far. I'll book it with my card, so they won't find it if they search for names they know."

"Good thought." C was a little paranoid. I appreciated that. "Send the address to our new friends so they can join us there."

"Wilco. What about the boss?"

"Someone will have to go pick him up and explain the situation. If we just send him a new address, he'll probably worry."

C snorted, getting the joke. Butler was *definitely* going to worry. Shit, it worried *me* a little, and I'd come up with the plan.

As if summoned, my device rang. Butler. I had to answer. I didn't *want* to. I put on my best innocent voice. "Mac here."

"I missed your call. And Ganos's. I returned hers first."

"How much do you know?" I asked.

"Tell me you didn't do what I think you did."

"I'd tell you that, but I don't like to lie. Best if I explain it in person."

"Yeah. Probably is. You going to come get me, or do I need to call a vehicle?"

"We need to finish this up before we come back into the city. C can be there in an hour. We changed residences." I could almost hear him rolling his eyes.

"Yeah. Okay. Tell him to get me from the bakery across from the police station. I'm going to get some coffee. Got a feeling I'm going to need it." He disconnected.

Well . . . that went about as well as it could have. For now. We'd see when we got face to face.

FIFTEEN MINUTES OUTSIDE the city we turned onto a narrow, winding country road which we followed for about ten klicks before turning again onto an even smaller road, which wound back into a patch of woods. We found a dirt and gravel driveway that matched the address from the ad, and Alanson took us slowly down it. We couldn't see the place itself until we rounded a curve in the drive.

Cabin my ass.

C and I went in to scout the place using the code provided by the rental site to open the front door. The entryway had a rustic hardwood floor, and a wide staircase led to the second story. The kitchen had a spacious eating area with a sliding door that led to a large, wooden porch, complete with outdoor kitchen. There was one bedroom downstairs, four upstairs, and each had their own ensuite facilities complete with plush towels and fancy soaps. This was the kind of place they showed on those dream house vid shows.

More important for our purposes, the house sat in a clearing in the woods, with a lot of privacy. I'd have liked to have had a little more than the fifty or so meters of open lawn between us and cover. Better fields of fire. Not that I expected it to come to that, but we *did* tend to attract the unexpected. "I wonder why this place was available."

"Cost?" said C. "It's not the best location—there's not much near here for entertainment—and if you can afford this, you could stay somewhere *really* nice in the city and be closer to everything."

"Well, it worked out for us." I signaled Alanson to bring in our guest, which he did after cutting the zip tie around his ankles so Frankie could walk, which he did. The fight had gone out of him.

I yanked the bag off of Frankie's head as soon as he got inside, and he blinked, dealing with the light, even though it wasn't that bright. "Put him in a chair. Don't do anything stupid, Frankie. You'll regret it."

C sat him down hard in a chair, zip tied his legs to the chair legs, and then cut the ties on his hands before putting new ones on that secured him to the chairback. "I'm going to head out to pick up the boss."

"Yeah. Hurry back. Once this guy talks, we might need wheels." Not having a second vehicle had been a mistake. One we'd rectify when our reinforcements arrived. Hopefully they'd get here before Butler, so I'd have a chance to brief them.

Butler couldn't be too mad at me. I was following his example. I didn't know what to do, so I took action to shake things up and see what fell out.

That was my story, and I was sticking to it.

I turned my attention to Frankie. "You going to tell me what I want to know, or do I have to beat you first?"

Frankie gave me a sneer, which impressed me, given his situation. If things had been different, maybe we'd have been friends. Probably not. Still, bravado aside, he talked. "What do you want to know?"

"Same thing we asked yesterday. Where's the girl?"

"Lotsa girls. Have to be more specific."

I took a step toward him like I was going to punch him in the face but held up once he flinched. "Don't make this harder than it already is. Janie Strand. Short red hair."

"Oh. *That* girl."

"*That* girl. Where is she?"

"At the apartment."

"The one at 1474 Brighton?"

His eyes went wide. Guess he didn't think I knew about that. "Yeah," he said, after a few seconds.

"Which apartment number?"

"If I tell you, you going to let me go?"

"If you *don't* tell me, I can promise you I won't. How about that?"

He thought about it. "Seems like me knowing might be the only reason I'm still alive." He had a point. If I planned to kill him, that would be the information I needed before I did it.

"What am I supposed to say? You're not going to believe me anyway."

"Look. You're in over your head," said Frankie. "How about you let me go and we pretend this never happened. Drop me at the nearest bus station. You can even bag my head again, so I don't know where I was."

I chuckled. The balls on this guy, sitting there tied to a chair, taking a lecturing tone, trying to dictate terms. "I'm going to bury you in the woods up to your neck, just your head sticking out. See what kind of critters are out here."

He stared me down, maybe trying to figure out if I'd really do it. He couldn't know, because I didn't. I didn't *want* to do it. Digging a hole is always more work than you expect. I didn't even know if this place had a shovel. Finally, his shoulders sagged. "Apartment 214."

"There. That was easy enough, wasn't it?" The number matched one of the two rooms we'd tracked people to, which gave me some confidence that he wasn't lying. "What's she doing there?"

He snorted. "What do you *think* she's doing there? Girl's a freak."

I didn't hit him. That took a lot of effort. "She's seventeen."

"Eighteen," he said.

Was she? I'd thought seventeen, but why did I think that? Or maybe she'd lied to Frankie. He was nineteen but could have passed for fifteen. "She staying there?"

"Yep." He smirked as he said it. "Not like we're going to let her leave, now, is it?"

That I didn't know. And I didn't know what to do next.

I put the bag back on Frankie's head and made my next decision:

I waited.

Butler would know what to do. He always knew.

CHAPTER 8

Butler

I HAD NO FUCKING idea what to do. I resisted the urge to grill C on the drive out to the country house, which is how he described it. I did get the basics from him—that they couldn't get in touch with me and that they'd grabbed Frankie. But it wasn't his fault, so chewing his ass for it didn't serve any purpose. I'd save that for Mac. I had plenty of time to think about it, rehearse what I wanted to say in my head. C seemed to get it, remaining unusually silent.

It would probably be okay. Sure, it was kidnapping, which was a felony. But we probably wouldn't get caught, and if I'd learned anything from my time searching out illicit dealings, it was this: if you didn't get caught, you didn't face consequences. Not that I wanted to live my life that way. But we'd already *done* the crime, so we couldn't put that toothpaste back in the tube. It helped that nobody would fill out a missing person report on Frankie, and nobody in law enforcement would come looking for him if someone did. Even Frankie himself wouldn't go to the police.

Nope. The law wasn't our biggest threat. That was Jinks. Mac's action probably threw a wrench in any plan I had to talk to him . . .

at least amicably. And while I didn't know exactly how much of a threat he presented, I also didn't think he could project that threat outside the city. His operation seemed to be confined to a few blocks. We could fix this. We could take Frankie back, drop him off somewhere near transportation, and get out of here. We didn't have Janie, but hopefully Donato would shake something loose on that front.

We turned off the paved road and wound our way back through a well-kept forest to a big house. Another vehicle—an SUV—sat at the end of the drive. Mac stood on the front porch talking to two people I didn't know. Once C stopped beside the other vehicle, I sat there for a few seconds, gathering my thoughts. The three people on the porch faced me, waiting for me to approach. No sense putting it off, I guess.

"Sir, this is Dae Kim and Zac Clement," said Mac, as if we had all gathered at this lovely house for a weekend getaway. Kim was a bit shorter than Mac, with tan skin and jet-black hair. Clement was dark-skinned and tall. Maybe fifteen centimeters taller than me. He looked to be about thirty. With Kim, I couldn't put a number on it. "Kim was an engineer. Clement was a grunt."

"Kim. Clement," I said, as way of greeting.

"Sir," they responded together.

"What was your specialty, Kim?" I asked. These were soldiers. I didn't want them there, but I could at least be polite.

"Explosives," she said, her face flat and unexpressive, as if she was telling me her address. *Explosives.* Because of course it was.

I nodded. "Where'd you serve, Clement?"

"Two tours. I saw the most action in the year on Falania."

I'd been there, but probably before his time. Not exactly a

garden spot. "You know a sergeant major named Davenport? He served there."

"Just by reputation. He left maybe six months before I got there, but people still talked about him."

"We saw him recently on Taug. He's still doing the thing."

"Good man," added Mac.

I was done being pleasant. "If the two of you would excuse us for a few minutes, Mac and I need to have a chat," I said.

Mac opened the door for them. "There are two empty rooms upstairs. You can stow your kit there. Meet back downstairs in fifteen."

They both gave a roger and moved out. Mac stood there and waited for me to lay into him. He met my eyes and didn't flinch, but he stood a tiny bit smaller, knowing what he had coming. But since he knew, I had no reason to berate him for his decisions. It didn't add anything. We did need to discuss it though. "So . . . what are you thinking?"

He hesitated, as if maybe suspecting a trap. It wasn't. You play the hand you've got, not the one you wished you had. I hadn't asked what he *had been* thinking, but what he was thinking *now*. Everything that had happened up to this point was already on the books. We'd kidnapped a dude. We had to move forward from here.

"When you didn't answer, I had to make a decision. I didn't know which way to go, but I figured that it's better to force the action, see what comes from it."

I couldn't really argue that in theory. I'd done the same thing often enough. "You kidnapped a man. We talked about that, remember? It's pretty illegal."

"Yeah, but he's a dick."

"Not a crime," I said.

"It should be."

I chuckled at that, though I shouldn't have. This was serious, but I'd been in so many worse situations, I couldn't bring myself to give it the gravity it deserved. Yeah, we'd done the wrong thing. But nobody was dead. We could recover. "Fair enough. I assume you've still got him."

"Yeah. He's inside. Told us what we needed to know. Only had to break a few bones to get it." He was fucking with me. Probably. Either way, I didn't react to that.

"He told you where to find Janie?"

"Yeah. She's in one of their apartments."

"Okay. So, what now?"

Mac hesitated. "That's where you come in."

"How so?" I knew what I wanted to do, but I needed Mac to say it. To ask for help. He'd been the one who accepted the job to go look for the girl, so he had to buy into this.

"This is the part where you fuse everything we've learned and come up with a plan."

"My plan was to let the authorities handle it."

Mac considered that for a few seconds. "You think they will?"

"With this new information? They might. Donato might. We have to tell her."

He didn't look so sure. "I trust you. If anybody can read her, you can. If you think that's the best way, let's do it."

In truth, I wasn't sure either. I believed Donato would ask around. I didn't know that she'd find much, and if she did, I didn't know what she could do about it if she didn't specifically see someone detained against their will. "I'll call her."

"Right. Before you do, though . . . what if she won't?"

I didn't know, but I didn't want to say that. He expected me to know, and I wanted him to trust that expectation the next time he considered violating someone's personal liberties. "Let's just see what happens." I took the card from my pocket and punched in the number. Even before I hit send, I felt the despair. Almost like I knew what she'd say. It was like standing on train tracks, seeing the train coming, but not being able to move out of the way. I'd have liked to have hope, but I'm not naïve enough.

She picked up right away. "Carl. When I gave you my card, I didn't expect to hear from you so soon."

"I've got new information. The girl we talked about is being held against her will in or near apartment 214. Same address we talked about."

"And you know this . . . how?"

"I can't tell you. But it's solid. Can you go by and check it out?"

"You already know the answer to that. No source, no warrant. No warrant . . . what do you want me to do, knock on the door and ask 'Hey, is anybody in here committing a felony right now?'"

"Right. It was a long shot. I thought maybe with a stronger indication, you'd be able to do something. Wring something out."

"I wish I could. I really do."

"Okay. Thanks."

"Carl?"

"Yeah?"

"Tell me you're not going to do anything stupid."

I wish I could. We already *had.* "No, of course not," I lied.

"Okay. Thanks. Take care of yourself."

"You too, Steph."

Mac was standing there, waiting as I disconnected. He probably got the gist but had the courtesy to ask, "Is she going to do it?"

I shook my head. "No."

"We can't leave that girl there." He waited for me to say something, but I didn't. "We've got to act, right?"

It didn't *seem* right. But I didn't have another answer, and neither one of us could live with ourselves if we left her there in trouble. "What if she wants to be there?"

"Even if there's a chance that she's there on her own will, there's a bigger chance that she's *not*. Frankie's attitude suggested she isn't, but like I said . . . he's a dick. We can't trust him." He shrugged. "If she wants to stay, we let her stay. Maybe ask if she'll write a note to her mom saying that she's okay. Or call her, if we're really lucky."

I knew it was a bad idea even as I talked myself into it. "Any chance you can let this go?"

To his credit, Mac thought about it for some time before answering. "I don't think I can."

I nodded. I couldn't either. "Okay. How do we do it without killing anybody?"

"We've got a bunch of non-lethal weapons. Beanbag guns. Stun sticks."

I flinched at that. Stun sticks and I have a bad history.

"I know," said Mac. "We'll be careful. I've got gas grenades, but I don't want to use them in case it leaks into another apartment."

"Why do you have . . . you know, never mind. Don't tell me."

"Right. I won't tell you. What I don't know is how we get in there without being seen. They've got sentries, and they've got monitoring systems outside the building—at least I assume that they're theirs. *Someone* certainly has a camera out there. They won't be able to ID us with our distorters, but they'll know somebody is coming."

"Ganos might be able to knock it out."

"I thought about that," said Mac. "But if the camera goes out, they're going to be suspicious. That would warn them as sure as if it picked us up."

"Good point." I thought about it for a few seconds. "Maybe she can take the power out to the whole building. Or even the block. That might seem more natural and wouldn't necessarily make them suspect the camera."

"Can she do that?"

"Only one way to be sure," I said. "But if I've learned anything, it's not to underestimate her."

"See if she'll do it. We'll go tonight. Late."

"I'll get my kit set up. Body armor or no?"

Mac winced.

"You don't want me to go."

"It's not that we don't want you . . ."

"Yes it is." I smiled. I understood.

"It's a four-person job. Me and C along with Kim and Clement will run the stack. Alanson will do overwatch with his surveillance assets."

"And I'll . . . what? Drive the vehicle?"

"I was hoping you'd stay here. With the prisoner."

"We can't hold this guy," I said.

"We can't release him. He'll warn them that we're coming."

"How about this? I take him in the other vehicle and wait for your call. As soon as you're clear of the target, I drop him off on the other side of the city."

Mac considered it. "That could work. Though I'd really like to hold on to him in case he's not telling the truth."

"You think he's lying about the girl?"

"Doesn't *feel* like a lie. But it could be, right?"

"I think we need to risk it and let him go. We can't double down on this."

Mac nodded. "Okay. I'll defer to your judgment."

I snorted. Mac could afford to be deferential. He'd already gotten everything he wanted.

"YOU WANT ME to do *what*?" Ganos was less than enthused about our plan to knock out the electricity around the target.

"Can you do it?"

"It's not a matter of *can I*. It's a matter of *should I*."

"Since when has that mattered to you?" I'd seen her do way riskier things for less reason than this.

"This is the kind of thing that *I* bring to *you,* and you tell me not to do it."

"And then you do it anyway."

"And the fact that I'm saying it's a bad idea should tell you exactly *how* bad it is. If I hit the building, maybe it's not such a big deal. Somebody owns that and they'll be pissed, but it's probably a corporation, and given the demographics at the address, they probably don't care all that much. But taking out a block? The government's going to treat that like a terrorist attack. You want to know why?"

"Because that's what it looks like."

"That's what it *is*. Turns out they don't love it when somebody goes after the utilities grid. They'll put a lot of assets into finding the person responsible. And I'm not talking city assets. It'll be bigger than that."

Clearly I hadn't thought it all the way through. "Okay . . . if you can't do that, what's our next best option?"

"I didn't say I couldn't do it."

"Right. You can do anything. Sorry. I meant if you won't do it."

"I didn't say that either. Just that they'll come after me, and eventually they'll find that I did it."

I could almost hear the gears turning in her head, so I let her cook. Eventually she said, "We'll make it look like a system glitch. I'll hack the AC system in the server room of the power station—threaten to overheat the servers that control the generators that power the block. Then I'll . . . you know what, never mind. I got this. Will three minutes do it?"

I looked at Mac, who was listening in. He nodded. "Yeah. Three minutes will work, as long as we know exactly when the timer starts."

"Pick a time. Don't make it a round number, though. Pick 1:42 AM and 14 seconds, or something random like that. Then be ready. Because that's exactly when it's going to happen. And whatever you do, don't text me the time. Nobody on location contacts me at all once we start, either."

"They can trace that?" I was genuinely curious.

"They absolutely can. They may or may not in real time, but after the fact they definitely will if they're looking for foul play. And let's face it: if the high-level law enforcement folks come in and suspect it was a hack, I'm going to immediately be a suspect.

There are only a handful of people on the planet who'd try this, and with you involved, I'm an easy link."

She was right. I always forgot my own notoriety, and that people interested in me knew more about me and my contacts than I'd prefer. It's hard because I don't *feel* notorious. "Got it. The time you said will work. 1:42 and 14 seconds."

"Bank on it." She cut the connection.

I looked at Mac. The ball was firmly in his court. He wanted to do this without me, and he was going to get his chance. This was bad. But I wasn't naïve enough to think that it couldn't get worse. Everything can get worse.

"You've only got one shot at this. Don't fuck it up."

CHAPTER 9

Mac

B UTLER TOLD ME not to fuck it up. On the surface, that wasn't a big deal. He said it a lot. Except this time, it hit hard. Probably because I felt like I *was* fucking it up by us even *being there.* We were kitted out for a combat mission while driving the speed limit and obeying the traffic rules in a mostly peaceful city, getting ready to assault a civilian building. What part of that *wasn't* fucked up? Part of me wondered if Butler thought I didn't know that. That I didn't for a minute think this was a good idea. But it beat the only other idea I had, which was to leave. I couldn't do that. So there we were.

We'd left ourselves plenty of time, and now we waited, each of us sitting silent in the second rental vehicle, lost in our own thoughts. We'd been over the plan, walked through it, and even rehearsed stacking on the door and entry into the apartment, who would cover what angles, all that. I didn't worry about that part— hitting the objective. I had three pros with me, and while we didn't have anything lethal with us, we *did* have a few surprises in the form of toys that I hadn't mentioned to Butler. He'd have just worried. We'd go in hard and fast, get the girl and be out of there before these amateurs knew what hit them.

They wouldn't see themselves that way—as amateurs. But compared to my team? That's what they were. I don't know if that's arrogance on their part or inexperience, but it's human nature. People with a little skill overrate themselves. They underestimate the gap between a decent amateur and a true professional. Until they met a professional. Then they learned how big the difference was. Tonight would be an education.

It probably sounds like I was overconfident. That I thought nothing would go wrong. Nope. Something could always go wrong—something always *did*. I just had to look over at Alanson to remind myself of that. But he *was* here, and that's where my confidence came from: the people I had with me and their abilities. That when something went wrong, we had the skill to react and overcome it.

We parked in a surface lot with a bunch of other vehicles. We didn't want to register ours to park it, so we picked a stickered lot that went with two apartment buildings. Nobody would check decals this late in this neighborhood. We were close to the target, but not too close. We didn't want to spend a lot of time walking on the street, but we also didn't want to get so close that somebody made us before we even started. Alanson would stay with the vehicle. With his eyes in the sky, he'd point out observers and sentries. Where possible, we'd take them out on the way. Where it wasn't, we'd avoid them.

It simultaneously seemed like no time and forever until we started moving. We walked in pairs, casually, not even trying to avoid being seen. Night owls, out on the town. We all wore dark clothing, but nothing tactical. Stuff you could mistake as everyday wear. Our obvious weapons we kept in backpacks or bags to hide the silhouettes.

Alanson's voice whispered through my earpiece. "Patroller, grid 1-3, at the corner. Currently stationary." The blocks were square, so we'd made a four-by-four grid of the area as a reference scheme. It beat trying to remember street names. 1-3 sat right on our current path. We'd have to take him out or go around him.

"Let me know which way he moves." If he went north or south, we could keep our route and miss him.

"Second sentry. Moving east from 4-2 toward 3-2."

"Roger." That one wouldn't be a problem if we stayed on pace unless we detoured around the first one. Number two was north of our route. If these were the only two, then we'd take out number one. "Anything else moving?"

"Group of three near 4-4. Appear to be in dresses. Moving erratically. No pattern. Likely not connected to our target. No other movement."

"Roger. Continuing planned route. Bogey one is the focus. Let us know if he moves." We were two blocks from him and closing. As the lead pair, Kim and I would reach him first.

"He's coming straight at you," said Alanson.

"Roger. My target." We'd intersect with him a block and a half from our destination in about fifteen seconds. I stumbled, faking at being drunk, hunching over.

"You two are out a little late." The man said it in a gruff voice, matter of fact, no condemnation in his tone, but with a hint of warning. As if our response mattered.

I came up from my hunch and fired my modified pistol. The ball from it slammed into the man's gut and discharged its fifty thousand volts. He froze in place, twitching, and Kim hurried forward and auto injected him with a strong sedative. We each got under one of his arms and half walked, half dragged him to an alcove where we let him slide to the ground, mostly out of sight. I'd have rather not used the weapon, as I only had the single charge, and it would have been useful to keep it to use on the objective, but we had to get there. C had one as well, but after that, we'd be tapped out. We'd have to use our other options.

KIM AND I hurried now, picking up our pace. We were half a block from the door when the block went dark. Once it did, we ran. "Night vision on," I ordered. Kim slapped an opener on the door—it carried its own charge to get power to the door while simultaneously disarming the lock. Strictly black market, probably stolen from or sold by emergency services who kept them to get into buildings specifically during a loss of power. Once again I was reminded that this was not a cheap venture.

When the door popped, I opened it a few centimeters and tossed in three mini drones. "Drones in," I announced across the net.

"Roger," said Alanson. C and Clement reached us, and we all waited for a report. "Hallway clear," said Alanson.

That was fortunate. I entered first, a fifty-millimeter beanbag gun in both hands, ready in case the drones had missed something. They hadn't.

"Someone's coming down the stairs," said Alanson. "Armed."

"C," I said.

C hurried around me and took up a position where he could observe the bottom of the stairwell. We were using time we didn't have. A few seconds later he fired, eliciting a grunt, and then the sound of someone falling down the last few stairs.

"We've gotta move," I said.

"Second floor hallway clear," said Alanson.

"Go. Full speed." I didn't wait for a response, sprinting toward the stairs. I passed C, who had stopped to inject the downed man with an auto-injector full of sedative.

"He had a pistol. Slug thrower," said C.

That wasn't unexpected, but it still sucked. We didn't have anything lethal with us except for what C had taken off of the enemy. Our targets definitely did. One less now, though. Still. Going through that apartment door would be a significant risk if they knew we were coming. Nothing for it now but to move.

We stacked on the door to apartment 214. Kim slapped a micro-charge on the lock. Nothing high-tech this time. At her signal, we turned away and she triggered it. Fuck! I forgot how loud those things were. We'd just woken the entire building. The door now hung from a single hinge. Job done.

"Flash," said Clement, and I muted my night vision sight and closed my eyes as he tossed a grenade into the room. We'd decided against using a flash bang to disable our enemies. Too public of a place. The explosion to open the door was the only one we'd use. Instead, we used a modified version that made an intense flash that would blind and disorient anybody unprotected in the room.

Clement and C entered first, and without watching them I knew that they'd go left and right inside the door staying along the wall. I entered immediately behind them, third in, and swept the room with my beanbag gun. Three targets. One was fumbling in their waistband, possibly going for a weapon. I fired a beanbag into them and slid left one step to make room for Kim behind me. I hit my target center of mass, and they flew back, hit a chair, and went down in a heap. I looked to the other two targets, trying to determine if they were armed. If I'd been carrying something lethal, I'd have taken another half second to assess whether my first target had had a weapon before engaging. That was one of the risks with non-lethal munitions. Mentally, you tended to hit the trigger faster, subconsciously knowing that you probably wouldn't kill the person. Sometimes too fast.

Kim hurried past and slapped a stun stick to one of the other people. That was more effective and would leave less damage than the beanbag. C was already circling the room to reach the door to the bedroom while Clement covered it in case someone burst through. I moved to the third bogey in the room.

"Get on the floor."

The youth—he couldn't have been more than nineteen or twenty—raised his hands away from his body. He glared at me for two or three seconds before going to his knees. "Calm down, brah. Nobody's fighting back." Sure. They weren't now.

"Anyone in the back room?"

"Nope."

Clement had moved to the door, and covered C as he entered. "Clear," said C through my earpiece a few seconds later. "There's nobody here."

I looked down to the guy kneeling in front of me. "Where's the girl?"

"Not here, brah."

"She was."

"Just for a few minutes," he said.

"People are starting to come out into the halls," announced Alanson. "Think about wrapping it up."

I nodded without thinking about it. Something was off here. "Where is she?"

"No clue, brah. And that's the honest truth." If the young man was lying, he was psychopath level good at it. I believed him. He also didn't seem particularly surprised for someone who recently had the door blown off of their apartment. Alanson was right. We needed to get out of there. We'd figure out where we went wrong once we reached the safety of our hideout.

"Exfil," I said. "Move now." Kim planted herself at the door, back to the wall beside it, covering the room while the rest of us exfilled.

In the hallway, two or three people milled around, and at least another who had been poking their head out disappeared back inside at the sight of us. The lights came back on, forcing me to take a second to remove my night vision goggles.

"We've got a problem," said Alanson. "Police are inbound. Multiple vehicles."

Shit. That was a hell of a fast response. "You sure they're coming our way?"

"Yep," said Alanson. "They'll be on your block by the time you can get out the door."

Shit shit shit. Butler was going to have my ass for this. Funny that that was my thought right then. Not going to jail, but how me going to jail would look to Butler.

"Ditch anything illegal before you hit the door," I said, stopping as I did so to dump my stun stick and an auto-injector of sedative down the trash chute. I considered chucking the beanbag gun, too, but that wasn't illegal. Just unusual. If the police caught us, we'd have to answer for it, but they were hard to come by and we had at least a chance of getting them back. Kim had more illegal stuff than the rest of us, and it took her a few seconds to ditch everything. If the police were thorough, they'd eventually find it. Hopefully they wouldn't be.

True to Alanson's report, flashing blue and red lights reflected from the buildings lining the street as I burst out the door. I considered running for it, but we had nowhere to go. I set my beanbag gun down on the ground and put up my hands. No sense risking them taking it as a real weapon and firing at me.

Within a few seconds, four vehicles stopped in the street in front of the building, lights still flashing. A pile of officers poured out of them, all shouting, to the point where I couldn't understand the orders beyond getting down on the ground, which I did.

CHAPTER 10

Butler

ALANSON FILLED ME in on what happened, so it didn't surprise me when I got a call from the police station telling me that some of my employees had been arrested. Those were their words. My employees.

"I don't have any employees," I said. I wished that were true. But even though they did work for me, there was nothing official. It's not like I gave them health care or a retirement plan or anything. I paid under the table, which might seem sketchy, but makes sense when you're hiring people to do borderline illegal things. Or, in this case, not so borderline.

I heard murmuring on the other end, like somebody was having a conversation with their hand over the microphone. A few seconds later, a woman's voice came on that I recognized.

"This is Donato. Cut the shit, Colonel." I guess we'd gone away from using first names now. "We've got your boys. And girl. You going to come down here and discuss it or not?"

"You going to let them go if I come in right now?" It was two thirty in the morning, so I really doubted it.

"No. That's not how this works."

"Then I'll see you around eight." It was a calculated move. I hadn't done anything illegal—well, other than conspiracy, but they couldn't prove that. Yet. So they couldn't *make* me come in. I had to drop off Frankie, and my lawyer wasn't the kind of attorney that answered calls at this hour. Whatever was going to happen, I'd be better prepared if I got four hours of sleep before I engaged.

It sounds callous, but I went back to the rental home and took a nap. I told Alanson to take one too, though I don't know if he did or not. He might have been too keyed up. Either way, I got my rack time, a quick shower, and headed to the station around 0800. I left Alanson at the house, and I left a message with Stoddard's answering service to meet me at the station, which she might do and might not, but it was worth a try.

Nobody arrested me when I walked in the front door, which I took as a positive sign. I scanned the room for Donato, and when I didn't see her, I looked for Kinlaw, since he was the only other person I knew. After maybe thirty seconds, a dark-skinned officer approached me. "Colonel Butler?"

"That's right."

"Come with me." She led and I followed her back to the interrogation room area, which I remembered well. She opened the door to one of the rooms and gestured for me to go in. "Have a seat. Someone will be with you in a minute."

It was more than a minute. At least fifteen. Part of me thought they might be making me wait on purpose, hoping to soften me up. It's the kind of thing I would have done if I was on the other side of this. Eventually the door opened, and Donato came in. That, too, was positive. At least I thought so at the moment.

"Sorry to keep you waiting." She said it with no trace of a smirk. She might have meant it.

"No problem. You're busy."

"Just got in," she said. "When you told me last night you weren't coming until morning, I went home and got some sleep."

I stifled a laugh. We thought the same way. "What can I do for you?"

She walked over and took the seat across from me. "You know exactly what you can do."

I had some ideas regarding what she wanted from me. Most of them were rude or anatomically impossible. I glanced at the two-way mirror. "We alone?"

"Absolutely not." No flinch, no inflection. Someone was watching, and she wanted it that way.

"Then I'm not sure I want to answer questions. Especially if I'm under suspicion."

"Should you be?"

"Usually," I said. "But go ahead—ask something specific. I'll try to answer."

"Did you order the four people we have in custody—McCann, Castellano, Clement, and Kim—to unlawfully enter a residential building and assault one of the apartments there?"

"I did not." That was true, technically. It had been Mac's idea. I hadn't *stopped* them when I probably could have, but that's not at all the same thing. At least I didn't think it was, from a legal standpoint. I really hoped Stoddard showed up soon, but I didn't want to refuse to answer without her. Not yet. I might learn something from the questions, and I'd rather be answering them from Donato than anybody else.

"Did you know about it?"

"I mean . . . I knew they went out. I don't know exactly what they did."

"I told you to go home, Carl." Back to first names. That was good.

"You did. Obviously we didn't. Sorry about that." I wasn't being a smart ass—it was the truth. I really was sorry. But my purpose in saying it was to confirm Donato's statement for anybody else watching—her boss, maybe. Let them know that she'd done the right thing.

"We have you on camera dropping Frankie off at a public transit stop."

I *did* learn something. They were watching me closely if they picked that up. "He needed a ride."

"Would Frankie say that if we asked him?"

"I can say with certainty that I have no idea what Frankie might say in any given situation."

"We can't find him."

"I haven't seen him since I dropped him off." So far, I hadn't had to lie. That was good. I didn't want to, if I could avoid it.

"He didn't make it back to his apartment."

"Is he the reliable type? Maybe he had something else to do."

She paused and studied me. We weren't getting anywhere, and she obviously could see that wouldn't change unless she did something about it. "I didn't peg you for a man who liked to waste time."

"You've got me wrong. I'm happy to chat until my lawyer arrives, at which point she's probably going to insist that I don't. I've answered everything you've said honestly. How about I ask you something?" I pressed on, not giving her a chance to say no. "How did you know to show up at that building when you did?"

She snorted. "You think you're subtle? You show up that morning asking about a girl. You think she's there. It would have been a surprise to me if you *didn't* try to take matters into your own hands."

I noticed that she left out me calling her about it after our morning meeting. I wouldn't bring it up. It might put her in a bad spot with her superiors. Probably didn't help me, either.

"Yeah. That makes sense. What else were they supposed to do?" I made sure to use *they* and not *we*. So far, I wasn't under arrest, and I wanted to keep it that way.

"Minding their own business and letting the authorities handle it was right there."

"Were you going to? Handle it?"

"I asked some questions. She wasn't there, and nobody knew where she went."

I wanted to tell her that that wasn't what Frankie had said, but that would be giving away too much. "You believed them?"

"Did you find her there?"

"Honestly? I don't know."

She considered that, and while she did, the door opened, and her partner ushered in Maxine Stoddard. A younger man in a nice suit trailed behind her. Probably a criminal defense attorney, if I had to guess.

"Questioning my client without his attorney, Officer . . . ?" She paused, waiting.

"Donato. We're just chatting. He's not charged with anything."

"Not charged is good. Is he not suspected?"

Donato thought about it. "Not yet. But get back to me later and I might have changed my mind."

"He's free to go then?"

She thought about that, too. Donato wasn't the type to rush into an answer just because someone asked a question. Another reason that I liked her. "Yeah. I don't have any more questions. None that he's going to answer, anyway. He's free to go."

"And the others?" I asked.

"Oh, no. They're staying."

"What are the charges?" asked Stoddard.

"Disturbing the peace, for starters."

"That's a blanket charge that could mean anything."

"Exactly," said Donato.

"And it's a citation. A fine. Nothing you can hold them on."

"I said for starters. Possession—and use—of a class three explosive is on the table."

"Meaning you can't prove it," said Stoddard. I just sat there, watching the two of them spar, neither blinking.

"Meaning I haven't proved it *yet*. I haven't proved the assault and battery and destruction of property yet, either. But I suspect that won't be long."

The two women stared at each other for several seconds, neither of them speaking. It started to become so uncomfortable that I almost said something myself. Thankfully, the door opened, saving me from my own impetuousness.

"Donato. Can I see you for a minute?" It was her partner.

"Excuse me," she said.

"We'll wait here," said Stoddard, though the flatness of her tone made it sound like we were doing Donato a favor.

"Should we go?" I asked, once Donato had left.

Stoddard held up her hand to shush me, and then pointed to the two-way mirror. Her confidence from the other day that nobody was listening in had apparently disappeared. "We'll want to stay for what comes next."

"What comes next?"

"Based on the look on the face of the officer that interrupted us, that was bad news. It might be unrelated, but it also might be their case falling apart."

I'd missed that look. I was slipping, or maybe I didn't know what to look for. Stoddard was the best that money could hire in her field of law. That wasn't criminal, but it still didn't surprise me that she caught something I didn't. "We should definitely wait for that. Who's your colleague?"

"David Westmore. Criminal defense." He held out his hand to me and I took it. It made sense for him to be along, though with Maxine's instincts and gravitas, I wasn't sure I actually needed him. It probably meant they'd bill me double.

Turns out we didn't have to wait long. When Donato returned, I *didn't* miss the change in *her* attitude. She was pissed, almost stomping as she walked back over to us. "Your friends are free to go."

"What happened?"

Donato turned and headed out without answering but reconsidered and stopped in the door. "I don't know what you did, Carl."

"I didn't do anything. I promise."

She studied me, probably looking for guile. But I was as surprised as she was, though not nearly as upset at the outcome. "Okay. You got lucky then."

"I was due." I smiled, trying to soften the disappointment in losing her case.

She didn't quite crack, but I thought maybe I saw a hint of her lip turning up. "Same advice as before applies."

"Go home?"

"I really recommend it."

"I think I might do it this time."

She left, leaving Stoddard, Westmore, and me to find our own way out.

"What do you think happened?" I asked Stoddard.

"Let's talk outside." She opened the door and held it for me.

The city had come alive in the time I'd been inside, traffic now congesting the street, a parade of pedestrians streaming by. Despite the crowded sidewalks, there was no mistaking two young men standing off to the left at the bottom of the stairs. They stared at us, one of them talking to the other in words I couldn't hear. I wasn't armed. Standing on the steps of a police station, that didn't seem like a *major* problem, but I didn't want to approach them. But one of them stepped up and called out, "You're Butler."

"That's right," I said, slightly more at ease. People recognized me often enough, though I didn't think this was that. Something in the guy's set told me he wasn't an immediate threat.

"Jinks."

"Ah. I've heard of you."

"Thought maybe you had. Can we talk?"

"Absolutely."

"You sure this is a good idea?" Stoddard whispered to me.

"I am not," I admitted. But I walked down the stairs toward the young man. He had light brown skin with freckles and a short haircut. Both his hands were in his pants pockets, but not in a way that looked suspicious. More like casual. Not a threat, but not scared, either.

"What can I do for you?" I asked.

"I want you to pay for the damages to our apartment."

I studied him for a moment. "Yeah? Why would I do that?"

"Because I told the cops that we didn't see anything last night. Your friends are probably being set free right now." That seemed a bit suspicious, but he acted like it was the most natural thing.

"Thanks. Can I ask why you did that? I mean . . . I appreciate it, but I have to say, it's a bit unexpected."

"Two reasons. First, we don't snitch."

"Fair. What's the second?"

"Because I get the feeling that we're caught up in something we don't understand, and that doesn't feel like a place I want to be. This is me washing my hands of it."

"I can understand that." He could be lying, but he seemed sincere, and regardless, I didn't want to crap on his gesture.

"So . . . about the damages."

"You got a number?" I asked.

"Nine hundred."

"Nine hundred and we're good?"

"Six-fifty for the door. It needs a new jam as well."

"Makes sense," I said. That seemed more than reasonable, and if we needed to negotiate, it wouldn't be about the amount.

"Two-fifty for my boy who took a beanbag in his ribs."

"Doctor?"

"Nope. That's his payday for taking one for the team."

I reached into my pocket. "There's a thousand on this stick. You answer one question for me and it's yours."

"Depends on the question."

"Of course. You said there's something going on that you don't understand. What led you to that thought?"

He considered it. "Those your lawyers up there?"

"Yeah."

"Nice suits."

"They're not cheap."

"I should have asked for more money."

"Probably," I said. He was stalling, thinking about what to say, but I wasn't in a rush. I had to wait for Mac and the crew, regardless.

"You know when something seems too easy? Probably means something's off?"

"Sure."

"This was too easy."

"What was?"

"Guy approaches me. Says he'll pay me fifteen hundred. All I gotta do is put on a show with my crew. Bring in this girl, let her hang for about fifteen minutes, and then sneak her out the back. At the time, I figure it's some kind of sex thing, you know? Either she's gotta lose a tail so she can be with somebody without anybody knowing, or they're playing some kind of freaky game."

I raised my eyebrows.

"Hey, I don't judge," he said. "At least I didn't until your boys showed up in the middle of the night with an arsenal and blew the fuck out of my door. At that point, I start to wonder if maybe there's a connection."

I handed him the stick. "One more question?" He didn't respond, but he didn't walk away, so I pulled out my device. "This the girl?"

He looked at it, looked back at me, and nodded once.

"Thanks," I said, and then I had another thought. "Frankie . . . he's one of yours, right? He was talking to this girl before she came."

"That so?"

"I dropped him off last night. Cops said he hasn't been back."

"Ain't seen him."

"That like him? Not showing up?"

Jinks shrugged.

"He was fine when he got out of my vehicle," I said. I hoped that Jinks believed it. I didn't think he'd be a problem, but I didn't want to give him any reason to be. He didn't respond, though—just turned, rejoined his friend, and the two of them walked off. Stoddard and her partner came down the steps and stood next to me.

"What was that about?"

"I'm not sure. But I think it means that there's more going on here than we understand." I didn't say it out loud, but it made me wonder about the whole situation. If maybe we were the targets, and if it had anything to do with the intruder at my place. I needed to keep Stoddard out of it. "Can you pretend that you didn't see any of that?"

"Any of what?" she asked.

I stifled a laugh. "Exactly."

CHAPTER 11

Butler

I T TOOK ABOUT three hours before we made it back to the rental house. Donato hadn't been lying—they released Mac and the team—but they took their time out-processing them. It might have been a product of an overtaxed system or might have been a sign of Donato's displeasure. For what it's worth, I didn't love how it went down either. More, I liked her, thought she had her stuff together. In another situation, I'd like to think we'd have got along and worked together. But shit happens.

With plenty of time to think, I'd been sorting through all the possibilities that led to us assaulting that building. If I believed Jinks, then the evidence pointed strongly toward a setup. I couldn't see it any other way. Someone had wanted us to see the girl entering that place—which meant they had to know we'd be looking. If I followed that rabbit trail, it meant that they'd staged the scene we'd seen from the hacked traffic camera in hopes that somehow, we'd see it. Perhaps they'd staged other things, too, in order to have a better chance of us picking up on it. If I believed that, I had to also allow that they'd planned to get us here to the city in the first place. And I had to consider that the girl—Janie—might be in on the whole thing. And that . . . that was a pretty big conspiracy theory. The kind that I'd have once dismissed as ridiculous.

Back before I knew better. One thing I knew almost for sure was that Frankie was involved. He'd been in contact with Janie, he'd given the critical information that led us to green-light the attack. And now he was missing.

Jinks hadn't been open with his thoughts on Frankie, but that felt somewhat natural. He probably saw Frankie as a subordinate and wouldn't want to share team business with an outsider like me. If he was the leader that Donato had implied—and my meeting with him hadn't done anything to make me doubt that—he'd deal with Frankie internally. If he found him. Frankie would know that, so I had to allow for the possibility that he was avoiding Jinks intentionally. That was the *best* possible view of it. A more pessimistic one was that someone had prevented him from making it home. The police knew where I'd dropped him off, which meant that somebody else might have known as well. It was a big department. It would certainly have leaks. Or someone else besides Ganos could have hacked the camera feeds. I couldn't rule anything out at this point.

But thinking about it was getting me nowhere. There were too many variables, and without added information, I'd be guessing. Without access to Frankie, Janie was the center of this. If we could find her, that would solve a lot. But barring that unlikely occurrence, I needed Ganos's help. And I needed to talk to Janie's mom.

Alanson was standing on the porch, waiting, when we arrived. "There's something you need to see," he said, as Mac and I approached.

"Sure. How soon? I've got a few things I want to get working," I said.

"You're going to want to see this first. I found something when I went back through all the drone footage from last night."

"Can I see too?" asked C.

Alanson looked at me for approval. "No reason for him not to."

"Sure," I said, and all of us piled into the kitchen where Alanson had a few tablets rolled out on the table.

"I was going back through it, looking for anything I missed in real time. I focused a lot on when the police showed up, trying to see if I could find someone in the area tipping them off or something."

"Donato said they were already watching themselves. I'm not sure if I believe her or not. She could have had an informant." Now that I thought about it, it actually seemed likely.

"I don't know if she had an informant, but look at what I found." Alanson pointed to the biggest tablet which was paused on a scene looking down from above on the street outside the target building. Mac and his team were at the door. "I'm going to run it at full speed."

We watched about three minutes of video. Lights flashed from one end of the street as Mac came out, and then we watched as the police pulled up and Mac's team surrendered. "Okay," I said. "I didn't see anything."

"Flash from the roof of the building across the street from our target," said C. "Could have been optics on a weapon catching the light."

Alanson stared at him. "You're good. Check it out." He scrolled the scene back about thirty seconds and froze it. "This is where the police first turn onto the road—they're down three blocks." He pointed to another tablet that showed the police. The time stamps were almost identical. "Now watch when we go frame by frame and focus on the building across from the building our team entered."

He clicked through one frame at a time, and this time I saw the quick flash. Alanson stopped there.

"I can just see it," said Mac. "The outline of a person."

"Any way to enhance it?" I asked.

"Unfortunately not. There was no light up there, and I didn't have the drone focused on that direction. That we picked it up at all is happenstance."

"That's it?" I asked, when the shadow had disappeared.

"Yep. Twelve frames. Nothing before, nothing after," said Alanson. "Trust me, I checked."

"Maybe they bugged out when the police showed," said Mac.

"That was my take," Alanson agreed.

"If that was really an optic from a weapon . . . could have been a night sight . . . doesn't have to be a rifle . . ." C's words trailed off.

"Go ahead. Finish that thought," I said. He was the closest thing to an expert that I had on this sort of thing.

"I was thinking that if I wanted a clean shot at someone coming out the door of the building, that's where I'd have set up."

"You think this was a shooter?" I asked.

"Could have been," said C. "Maybe they got spooked by the police and left without doing the thing. Wish we could have gotten a better look at what they were carrying. Then I'd be able to give you a better take."

"They'd have had to have been there for us, right?" asked Mac.

"Not a hundred percent," I said. "But yeah, probably. If not to take a shot, then to observe and report. The timing, the location. It fits with what Jinks told me—that someone had planted the girl as a story. Could have been bait to get us to the location."

"The location I get. That could be a plant. But how could they know when we'd be there?" asked Mac.

"How did the police know?" I asked in return. "Something leaked." I didn't want to say it, but I couldn't help but consider the new members of our team.

"Another thing . . . why not take a shot on our way in? The shooter had to have had a clear line. Our backs were to them." Mac had moved on from the timing thing quickly, and I wondered if he had the same thoughts I did about a potential leak in our team. If so, glossing over it was a good move on his part.

"I don't know." I thought about it for a bit. The idea of a shooter on the roof brought us even further into conspiracy-town. But there we were. Still, if someone wanted to kill one of us . . . or all of us . . . there were plenty of opportunities. They could just shoot me on my way into Moop's. Why go to all the trouble of a complicated setup like this? The others let me have time to think, seemingly content to wait for whatever I came up with. But nothing came. "I want to call Ganos. See if she can revisit what she found initially about Janie and see a potential setup in it. Depending on what she says, we might want to go talk to the woman who started this."

"Long drive," said Mac.

"Do we have a reason to stay here?" I asked. "Why not head back to our home turf? We're done looking for the girl, right?"

Mac didn't look so sure. "We might be. But there's a chance

that we're taking too much of this on the word of some people we don't know. If we think about Janie . . . we know she was here. If there's more to this than meets the eye, then sure, maybe she's a willing participant. But maybe that means she's in even more trouble than we first thought."

While I was thinking about it, C added, "We've got this place for four more days. It was the shortest rental term I could get."

I nodded. "Guess we might as well stay another night. But check with the mom and see if she's heard something."

"Roger," said Mac. "Let's set up whatever we can here on the perimeter," addressing the others. "If that was a shooter, someone might track us here and try to take another shot."

"I sure hate it for them," said C.

I didn't know what Mac and the team had planned, but I'd have bet good money that it would be excessive. And probably expensive.

"Do me a favor, boss," said Mac.

"Yeah."

"When you call Ganos, tell her she might want to bug out."

I stared at him. "Why?"

"If somebody is coming after us . . . or you . . . then she's a target too."

"Nobody is going to go after Ganos," I said.

"Do I need to remind you what happened on Taug?"

I started to respond but stopped. He had a point, and it seemed really important to him. "Okay. I'll warn her."

IT TOOK ME an hour to get in touch with Ganos. After all, it was before noon, which was some of her prime sleeping time. She insisted on audio only, claiming she had couch head, which I think is like bed head, but if you didn't make it to bed. Why she slept on a couch in her own home, I didn't know. I didn't even know if she had a house. I knew her general vicinity, but it wouldn't have surprised me to learn that she lived in a secret cave complex or something. She did a lot of work to keep information about herself private.

I started by explaining everything that had happened and what we had learned about Janie.

"Weird," said Ganos, when I finished. She left it at that.

"On a scale of one to ten, how likely is it that she staged something for you to find and made it look real?"

"On a scale from one to ten, you want to know how likely it is that a teenager and a low-level drug dealer fooled me. On the net."

I could tell from her tone that she thought it was a dumb question, but I had to know. "That's right."

"On a scale of one to ten . . . zero. There's no chance."

"None?"

"I didn't just pick off one message. The girl had an entire online history, both public and private. To invent something like that would take . . . I don't know. A lot. Same with Frankie."

"But it's possible?"

"Anything is possible. But highly, highly unlikely."

"Okay. I need another favor."

"It's your money," she said. "I'm happy to take it for services rendered."

"I need you to do whatever you can to find Janie and/or Frankie again. Anything you can get that gives us a hint of their location would be really useful."

"With what intent? You want to apprehend them again?"

"Just talk to them. Preferably Janie, but if not her, Frankie." Either of those two things would go a long way toward helping me figure out what was going on.

"I'll do what I can. It'll be tough unless they contact somebody or walk around openly in public. If they don't want to be found? Like finding a one in a field of lowercase Ls."

"Thanks. One other thing." I almost didn't want to say it.

"What's that?"

"Mac says you should bug out."

"Mac said that?"

"He thinks that someone might have deliberately come after us, and that if that's true, that they're likely to come after you next."

The line went quiet for a few seconds. Then she spoke, her mouth away from the microphone. "Hon! Get the go bags. We need to run."

"Really?" I expected her to tell me she could take care of herself. I did not expect *this*.

"Yeah. Mac can be overprotective. But he's also usually right. If we bug and it's nothing, we haven't lost much. If someone *does* find my place and comes here? Well . . . I'll leave them a nice surprise."

"Okay. You know best. Be safe."

"Will do. This is going to slow me down on your project by an hour or two. My mobile rigs are good, but nothing like being tied to a hard fiber line."

"It's fine. Get it when you can."

I didn't know if her finding Janie or Frankie would be the thing that broke this open. But we needed *something*.

But more than that, I wanted Ganos to be safe. She could take all the hours she needed.

And I could just stew until then.

CHAPTER 12

Mac

B UTLER AND I viewed things differently. He tended to not see the danger in a situation until it had bit him in the ass. I think it's because deep down, even though he would tell you he doesn't, he wants to see the best in people. But right now, having been set up the night before, I saw the entire world as populated by shitheads who meant us harm. Maybe they wouldn't come after us, but I didn't plan on waiting to find out. We'd be ready. The rest of the team saw it my way—I didn't have to ask. They'd been soldiers, and soldiers always fortify the position when they have time.

Setting up a defense of our expensive rental property presented challenges. We couldn't simply install security systems and hope they worked. Anybody who wanted to hit us would have us under observation, and they'd see what we put in. They'd use that intel to help them circumvent our defenses and nullify our element of surprise. But this game had levels. They'd *expect* us to set up security, so if we did nothing, that would seem suspicious in itself. It was all about deception. We had to let them see some of it while installing more than they'd account for. Thankfully, we probably had more toys than they'd reasonably believe. Because of course we did.

The initial stage was easy: setting up perimeter sensors and cameras to give us early warning. It was the barest minimum defense. Expected, and easy enough to counter, but when they *did* counter it, we'd know, so in that regard it still served its purpose as early warning. And going out to set it up gave us a reason to be in the woods, which allowed us to put in less obvious defenses. I don't want to give away *all* my secrets, but let's just say there were improvised landmines involved. Allegedly.

ONE THING I learned during this mission was that I had to get smarter on the drone stuff. We had an expert, and I'd rely on him, but I still needed to know more in order to manage the entire fight. For instance, what we could expect to see, but also what we *couldn't*. I trusted Alanson—he'd earned that—we'd been in fights, and he'd kept his cool and performed. But I didn't know how good he was relative to others in his field, or if the other side might have somebody better. I couldn't expect him to be the Ganos of surveillance, but I was still learning what tier below that he was. Hopefully, he was self-aware enough to know, but in my experience, that's a tough thing to expect. It helped that he was an older guy—sometimes they have less ego about stuff. But you never know until you're in the thick of things.

I huddled up with him to learn. Mostly about drones, but also about him. "What kind of shape are we in?" I asked him.

"Right now, I've got a standard pattern up with the outer band at three klicks. It's mostly a deterrent. Anybody who's looking will know our drones are there, but at the same time, there's not a lot they can do about it."

"They can't take them out?"

"They *can*. But if something takes down a drone, I'll know it."

"And that alone is information," I said. It was the same as the perimeter sensors.

"Right."

"And they have to be a lot more careful in their own drone use." Alanson was talking as if we were already in a fight. I liked that.

"How come?" I asked, on cue.

"The bigger the drone, the more the capability, right?"

"That makes sense."

"I don't care if my drones are seen, so I can fly whatever size I want. But what happens if the other side flies over us? We see it. They don't want that."

"We have stuff that's hard to see."

"And so do other people," Alanson agreed. "But invisible drones sacrifice performance. They're either small or something they can disguise. So . . . be on the lookout for loitering birds."

I chuckled, but Alanson didn't smile. He meant it. "Can we take their stuff down?"

"We can. In fact, we have a huge advantage in that because we're the target. That means their drones have to come to us. The closer they get to us and the farther they get from their own base stations, the easier it becomes to jam them. Conversely, because we're centrally located, and my base stations are nearer, it's much harder for them to jam us."

"We have that capability? To jam."

"Yes. But we shouldn't use it. Not now."

"Save it," I said.

"Right. If I took out your eyes twelve hours before an attack, what would you do?"

"Find new eyes."

"Right. Plus, you'd know not to rely on those same systems again. I'm banking on the fact that most people probably wouldn't expect us to have jamming capability. It's illegal—you can't mess with the frequency spectrum. This isn't stuff you can easily buy."

"How'd we get it?"

"Mostly made it," said Alanson. "You never know what you might need."

"We going to get caught?"

"Out here? Probably not. Especially if we do it in the middle of the night. There isn't much to interfere with. Drone frequencies don't interact with the broadband that enables our communication devices. Our one worry is if they're flying on some non-standard frequency or frequency hopping."

"Can they do that?"

"The military does. Commercial stuff works on a few specific channels, and that's where I'll focus initially."

"Won't it take down our stuff, too?"

"Normally, it would. But I've modified all my frequencies from the standard."

"Will others think of that?"

"Maybe," Alanson admitted. "Depends on what they think of our abilities. That's where it gets complicated. But I'm ready for it—as ready as we can be. We'll be scanning the frequency spectrum for signals and comparing it to the baseline I've already mapped."

"Can we do that now without tipping our hand?"

"Yeah. Scans like that are passive. It's the encroaching drone signals that are active."

"Anything up nearby that's not yours?"

"Nothing close."

"So . . . if they're watching us, they're not using drones."

"Or they're using something too sophisticated to be spotted. Remember, on Taug, we got fired on by something big that we never saw. But I also wasn't scanning the frequency spectrum at the time because I wasn't expecting the attack. Now I am."

I nodded. "Okay. I'm going to leave you to it. Last question. If I want to drop enemy drones, how much heads-up do you need?"

"Everything's charged and ready. I'll be scanning constantly. You call, I'll flip the switch, but it's not magic. Things aren't going to fall from the sky. We'll definitely degrade them. Might even completely blind them. But it'll be a continuous fight, and some stuff might sneak through."

"Understood. Thanks." I felt better. He seemed confident without being cocky, and that made *me* more confident. I needed that. Because I had no idea what was coming at us, and wasn't quite sure what to do next.

One thing I *could* do was to call Judith Strand. She picked up right away.

"Hi Mac. Have you found anything?" Her voice had so much hope in it that I didn't want to answer.

"We've come up blank so far." It wasn't the total truth, but somehow "we illegally assaulted an apartment where we thought they were holding her and got arrested" didn't seem like the right kind of thing to share. "I'm sorry to say it, but we might be at a dead end. That's why I was calling—to see if you've heard from her?"

"No . . . no, nothing." She sounded deflated, and I hated that.

"Okay. We're going to keep at it for a bit. Hopefully, we'll turn something up soon."

I found Butler to give him the update. He made a hmmph sound that could have meant a lot of different things.

"A girl can't just disappear," he said.

I didn't respond because my thoughts about that were too negative. She absolutely could. People disappeared all the time, and most of the ways weren't intentional and weren't pleasant.

I WAS ASLEEP when the attack started. That probably sounds like bad business, but we didn't *know* somebody would come, so we couldn't all stay up all night. We'd be tired tomorrow and worthless by tomorrow night. Alanson had given us all a class on how to monitor the sensor network, and we'd split the night into four shifts. C had another mission.

The alarms tripped during Clement's shift, just after 0200. He'd woken Alanson, who was sleeping nearby for just that purpose. Alanson verified the contact and woke me thirty seconds later. I'd taken forty-five seconds to get up to speed, and then I'd woken Butler.

Now we all stood in a loose circle around the equipment in the situation room. We had the windows blackened, and the only light came from Alanson's monitors and equipment. Let the enemy think they caught us sleeping. Alanson hunched over his stuff, trying to figure out what he'd lost and what he still had as well as launching more of his drone fleet from its pre-positioned spots on the roof.

"What have we got?" Butler asked a little too early. He was on edge—we all were. Clement was strapping on his body armor. Kim had hers on already and was checking some remote controls that were probably detonators. I really hoped this was just a probing, and we didn't need to use her stuff. We were isolated, but that would still wake up the neighbors.

"Best guess is nine of them," said Alanson. "Using facial distorters. At least two are armed."

"If two are armed, they're all armed," said Butler. He didn't mean that as intel. That was guidance telling us to treat them like combatants. We were officially at war. "Where's C?"

"He's in position but catching some shuteye."

"Get him up," said Butler.

"Movement inside the perimeter," C said into my earpiece, as if he sensed us talking about him. "Three bogeys. Dark clothing. They've got long guns. Best guess is projectile."

"Hold for now," I said. "There are more out there." The last thing I wanted was him taking a shot at these three only to be surprised by another group.

"Three groups of three," confirmed Alanson.

"How close?" asked Butler.

Alanson pointed to one of the tablets that showed three heat signatures from directly above, closing in on the tree line behind the house, which was about fifty meters from the back porch. As we watched, they stopped. In combat terms, fifty meters was *really* close.

"I can take them," said Kim. "If they start moving again, I'll lose that chance in a hurry."

"What have you got?" asked Butler.

"Explosives in the tree line," said Kim.

It was dark, so I didn't see Butler roll his eyes, but I know he did. I also knew he'd use the explosives. "If they start to make another move, execute. Are these the same three C has eyes on?"

"My group is headed to the front of the house," C said.

"Okay. That's six of the nine."

"That we know about," I added. Others might be coming in another wave.

Glass shattered downstairs. Nobody had reached the house or even been within throwing distance. That probably meant a grenade launcher. I was sure we were going kinetic before that happened, but now I *really* knew.

"Gas masks." I gave everyone five seconds to get them on, and then I looked to Butler.

He nodded.

"Drop the enemy drone coverage," I said.

Alanson flipped three switches and then watched his scanner. "I think . . . not seeing anything else. They're down."

"Movement," said Kim.

"Engage. C, you're clear to fire. Clement, on me. Alanson, call bogeys." I headed for the stairs with Clement on my tail. We had a firing position on all four sides of the house, but I didn't know which ones we were headed to yet. If I didn't get a call before we hit the bottom of the stairs, we'd trust C to take out the three up front and Kim to at least delay those in the back with her explosives. Clement and I would take the sides.

As if on cue, the house shook, and another window shattered in the back. Might have been another grenade, but smart money said that the force of Kim's explosion got it. Hopefully, she got more than glass.

"Two down, one gone to ground. Scanning for more targets," reported C. Surprise sniper, motherfuckers.

"Keep your eye on that one. He's not going to stay stationary forever." I motioned for Clement to go left as I went right and sprinted to my firing position. As I'd expected, gas fogged the air and made things hard to see. The masks had been a good call. We'd piled sandbags up to the bottom of the window to keep anything from penetrating the siding. That's how I'd have engaged someone popping up and shooting from a window—I'd shoot through the house below it. The enemy would too.

"Nothing moving in back," said Kim. "I think I got them. Either that or they shit their pants and don't want to move anymore."

Good. Even if they still presented a threat, it wasn't an immediate one.

I popped up to scan my sector. Theoretically, Alanson would see anything moving, but cameras weren't perfect.

"Clear," called Clement, meaning he'd manually swept his side. Targets could still be lurking outside our sensor range, but with nine of them, they'd have been planning to breach the building. Make sure they got us.

I picked up a heat source back in the treeline and fired a three-round burst at it. It disappeared, but I couldn't tell if I hit them or if they had ducked behind something. "Contact," I called.

"I've got them," said Alanson. "Ten meters into the treeline. Two heat sources . . . no, three."

"Kim. Any explosives?" I asked. She had something on this side, but I didn't know the exact location.

"Not close enough," she said. "It would shake them up, but that's it. If you can get them to shift to your right, they'll walk into it."

I didn't respond. There was no time for recriminations. She'd improvised the best she could. Sometimes the enemy doesn't co-operate.

The window above me exploded, and glass rained down. I ducked my head away from it instinctively, though my mask would have protected me. I'd have to watch sliding around on the floor now. I popped up and fired off three single shots in the general direction of the enemy, not taking time to aim. It wasn't a good tactic, generally, but we were winning, and I wasn't go-ing to over-expose myself and let them get me when we had better options. I needed to keep them pinned down and focused on me.

Ducking down, I tried to imagine for a second what they'd be thinking. I mean . . . beyond, "Oh, shit, what did we walk into?" They probably expected to execute a surprise attack.

Well . . . surprise.

Bullets tore up the windowsill in front of me, throwing up splinters. More ripped over my head and fucked up a bunch of stuff in the room behind me. We were definitely not getting our deposit back.

"In position," called Butler. He was still upstairs and would have shifted to the same side of the house as me.

"Third target down," said C. Three kills, and not a change to the inflection in his voice the whole time. Just a confident whisper. Dude was cold.

"I'm going to draw their fire," I said. I didn't need to give any other instructions. When I did, Butler would engage from the higher angle.

I popped up and got one round off before the world lit up around me. My shoulder burned, and I found myself spun away and on the floor.

Fuck. They'd been waiting for that.

"One down," said Butler.

"Two," called C.

I reached up to my left shoulder, and my hand came away bloody. I didn't want to announce that I was hit—it would throw off the plan. Hopefully it wasn't too bad. I needed to think for a second. If the initial call of nine was correct, the guy in front of me and whoever survived Kim's explosives were all that remained. Though there were certainly more, somewhere. Command and control. Mitigation team. But we'd fucked this bunch up enough where I didn't think that they'd commit more assets—at least not right now. We'd also made enough noise that even out in the middle of nowhere, the authorities would be here soon.

"We want to capture this guy or take him out?" asked C.

"Anything moving in the back?"

"Negative," said Kim. "Either I got them or they're down and not getting up."

Someone could have survived back there. We could question them if they were conscious. That was a risk, though—they might all be dead. We had one for sure alive on my side, but I didn't know if they'd surrender or go down fighting, and I didn't want to expose myself to find out. I only had a few seconds to make the decision. Whoever was still out there was realizing how fucked they were. They wouldn't sit still long. Then it hit me.

"Blow the explosives."

"Which ones?" asked Kim.

"All of them." Even if they didn't get the guy, I'd rather they were blown than still in place when the authorities got here. We could explain a lot. Not that.

A deafening roar erupted, and the house shook so hard that I worried we might have cracked the foundation. A second later, I yelled, "Cover me," and dove through the window. I tucked into a roll as I hit the ground. Hopefully, my last bogey was disoriented from the huge blast. If not, they'd get one shot at me before C or Butler drilled them. My money was on C.

I sprinted for three seconds and then dove to the ground. Another second, and I rolled left, then got up and sprinted another three seconds toward the woods. My shoulder must not have been too bad, since I barely noticed it. Just a constant burning.

Nobody fired.

I still wasn't taking any chances. I rolled left and then rolled left again. I counted to two and jumped up and started sprinting again, allowing myself four seconds this time. Still no fire. If they were sighted on me, they'd have definitely fired by now. One more sprint and I'd be to the wood line and some cover.

I didn't want to move, which was stupid. Yeah, I was on the ground, but that was only an illusion of safety. But it's hard to make your brain believe that. "What have we got?"

"No movement," said C, still whispering into his throat mic.

"Concur no movement," said Butler.

"My side's still clear," said Clement.

"I've got no movement on the property but you," said Alanson. "Police have been dispatched. ETA seven minutes."

"You alive?" I yelled.

No response.

"You've got five seconds to answer or I'm going to have my sniper put a bullet in every heat source he can see."

"Fuck you!" A man's voice, about twenty meters from me.

"Boss?" There were too many variables here, and I needed help. Part of me wanted to shoot the guy so only our side would be able to tell the story to the authorities. Another wanted to get answers from him.

"I think we—" Butler never finished his sentence. A single shot cut him off.

"He was raising his weapon," said C.

"Roger," said Butler. Didn't even question it. That said a lot about his opinion of C. "Sweep the area. Check the enemy bodies. We've got five minutes to learn everything we can before the authorities get here, and then we've got to surrender. Move fast. Move now."

I got up and hustled into the woods to find the three bodies there.

CHAPTER 13

Butler

I WAITED HALFWAY UP the drive for the police to arrive. I didn't have my hands in the air—that would show too much guilt—but I made absolutely sure that they were visible and away from my body. Showing up to a residence in the middle of the night had to be a tense situation for any responder, and I wanted to make it as easy for them as possible. Whatever happened, we were *not* getting into a violent confrontation with the authorities.

Alanson told me that it was a single vehicle coming, but when it turned into the drive by itself, it still surprised me a little bit. Obviously they weren't responding to the actual situation, but to something they thought was smaller. If we'd still been in the fight, a single patrol car with two officers wouldn't have even slowed it down, let alone stopped it. If they didn't know what happened, then that gave me a lot of options on how to play it. It would have been less complicated if they'd shown up in force and arrested us. I preferred this way, though. I didn't relish another trip to jail.

The vehicle stopped about twenty-five meters from me, and I tried not to turn away from the bright lights in my face. Both doors opened. One of the occupants came forward while the other stayed behind their car door. They didn't have a weapon out, but they were in position to provide cover, so they were being at least a little cautious. Smart.

"Good evening, Mr. . . ." The approaching officer paused, waiting for me to fill in the information.

"Butler. Carl Butler."

He stopped a couple paces away, close enough to talk without raising our voices, but not close enough where I could touch him. "The military hero?"

"That's right," I said. I shy away from that title—I don't buy into it, and it makes me uncomfortable. But while half the galaxy thinks I'm a hero and half a villain, law enforcement tends to fall distinctly on the hero side. Rural law enforcement, even more so. In this situation, I wanted to use that to hopefully mitigate any trouble.

"Well. It's an honor to meet you. I'm Officer Jameson. My partner is Officer Sikorski. This, uh . . . this a rental property?"

"That's right."

"We've had some noise complaints. Couple of the neighbors say you've been shooting at Tannerite bombs."

I almost laughed. I forgot where we were or at least hadn't fully understood the implications. Not only did they not know what happened, they had their own pre-made alibi ready for me. It was a shame I couldn't use it. Because someone on the other side knew what happened here, too, and we had nine bodies in the woods. If I lied now, someone would call in an anonymous tip about the bodies, and we'd be caught trying to dispose of them. "I'm afraid it's more serious than that."

Jameson didn't react. "How's that?"

"Officer Jameson, this is going to seem unreal, but my friends and I were attacked by a group of highly trained armed assailants. I'm afraid you're probably going to need some additional manpower. It was pretty bad."

Silhouetted in the lights of the vehicle, I couldn't make out his face—just the steam from his breath in the cold morning air. But the fact that he didn't answer for ten or fifteen seconds gave me a hint at what his expression might be. "Is everybody okay?"

"Well . . . not exactly."

"Should I call an ambulance?"

"I don't think we need one. You're going to find nine bodies in the woods, but they're dead."

Jameson's hand went toward his sidearm, where he rested it but didn't draw. So far, so good. "Let me get this straight. You and your friends were attacked by nine armed professionals."

"Yes."

"How many of you are there?"

"Six. Five plus me."

"Your people okay?"

"Mac got clipped in the shoulder, but it was a graze and we've treated it. Everyone else is uninjured."

"I take it your people are armed," said Jameson. His calm demeanor given the ridiculous situation I'd sprung on him impressed me.

"All the weapons are inside the house. The five members of my party are on the porch, currently unarmed." I didn't mention that I'd had to almost yell at Mac to enforce that order. I had no idea what Jameson might do here. I think in his place, I might back out completely until I could get some serious reinforcements. I hoped it didn't come to that.

"Ski." Jameson didn't look back, instead keeping his eyes on me.

"Yeah?" Ski had a deep baritone voice.

"Call back to dispatch. Tell them to wake the captain and for her to give me a call ASAP."

"On it."

"This might be a few minutes," said Jameson.

"Of course. You don't run into this kind of thing every day." I tried to keep my tone light, which was hard to do right after a firefight, even though my own part in it had been pretty minimal.

"Do *you*?"

"Do I what?" I asked.

"Run into this kind of thing."

A fair question. "Not every day. But it's not the first time."

"I guessed that. I mean . . . if six of you took out nine of them without a casualty, you've got to be pretty good at it."

I liked Jameson a lot. He made his question seem casual, but he was fishing for information. He wanted to know if we'd truly been attacked or if we'd murdered people, but he phrased it in such an innocuous way that I could provide information without going on the defensive. He'd either been trained or had a lot of natural talent for interrogation. "Someone has targeted my life a few times recently. My head of security tends to get a little paranoid, and a lot over the top with his preparations. So we were ready for an attack. I think the assailants planned to take us by surprise in the middle of the night. They didn't."

"You were expecting them."

"We were prepared for the possibility," I said. There was a

difference, and I wanted it on the record. "We have to be," I added. I was playing it up for Jameson, trying to make it seem more exciting than it really was. I didn't know how much sway he held, but another person on my side would never hurt.

His device chirped, and he looked at it. "Stay right where you are."

"Of course," I said, as he moved back to his vehicle to take the call.

A TEAM OF folks, some police, some not in uniform, descended on us within an hour of Jameson's first arrival and had been working for a while by the time the sky started to lighten. They had seated my team on the driveway in a circle with a single officer watching over us, but with orders not to talk to us. The air fogged with every breath—it was the coldest part of an already chilly night— but they'd brought us jackets and blankets. They hadn't forbidden us from talking among ourselves, but we kept quiet. Kim, C, and Clement were dozing, as if sleeping while seated and in custody happened every day. Mac stayed alert—I don't know how given that none of us had slept much—taking in everything. Alanson appeared awake, but what he had on his mind, I had no idea.

I nodded off a bit, but paid attention enough to see three different teams working in different parts of the woods. Probably each with a set of bodies. Another team had entered the house with my permission. We were in an odd spot with that, where I don't think refusing would have been helpful. I didn't own the place, so they could contact the owner for permission to search it if I said no. It seemed premature to involve the landlord. That would be a matter for lawyers and insurance companies, given the damage.

Somehow, I doubted that the standard rental contract covered bullet holes, let alone percussive blasts.

When a tall woman stepped out of the passenger side of an arriving vehicle, every officer in eyesight turned to look at her. Even without a uniform on, there was no doubt this was the boss. I considered standing to meet her, but decided instead to let her come to me on her own. She might want updates from her team first. That line of thought blew apart when I saw who got out of the back seat.

Officer Steph Donato.

What was she doing here? We were definitely not inside of city jurisdiction. But here she was, in uniform. She looked around, taking in the scene, but her eyes stopped when they fell on me. She asked something to the captain quietly, and when the captain nodded, Donato headed my way.

"I didn't expect to see *you* here," I said.

"The local department reached out looking for volunteers to pull some hours. This is my day off, and when I saw what it was about, I had to get in on it. You've got a knack for trouble, don't you?" She had a hint of a smile on her face, as if she might somehow find that trait endearing.

"Oh, I don't know."

Mac snorted.

"What?" I asked, not at all serious.

"You think this is related to what your people did in the city?" she asked.

"Not directly. Do you?"

She walked away without responding. I didn't know if she was holding a grudge or not, but her presence here definitely added another element to an already complicated situation.

The captain took her time before getting to us, going around to each group and getting an update. I appreciated that. She wanted all the information before she questioned us—at least I assumed she'd question us. Maybe she was deciding whether to bring us in. The first thing she'd do, if she really wanted information, was to separate us. But if she did, I'd instructed all of my people to clam up until they got attorneys, so that probably wouldn't work for her. I didn't really need to think it through—I had no control over what came next—but I can't help it. That's how my mind works.

In the end, she called me over to her, effectively separating me from the others. We stood by her vehicle with nobody else in earshot. I didn't know if that was by accident or design but assumed the latter. Always safer to be wary.

"I'm Captain Emery. Chief of Police for Dunwood County."

"Jameson is yours? He's a good one."

"One of my best. Thanks. I'm going to be honest, Colonel Butler . . . I'm not sure where to begin."

"I gave the true story to Jameson. I assume he relayed it."

"Yeah. To hear him tell it, you're almost like some sort of super spy and were attacked by a black ops team."

"I don't know about that. I'm no spy. To be a spy, I'd have to be working for someone. I'm not."

"Nobody?"

"Not officially. Though someone did ask us to find her daughter."

"Right. Janie Strand. Officer Donato filled me in on that." She glanced to her left, and I followed her eyes to where Donato stood, about thirty meters away, staring at us.

"She still pissed?"

"Oh, I don't know. Her opinion is mixed. She likes you, but she thinks you're using your status to get away with things."

"Oh, I'm definitely doing that."

Emery stared for a second and then snorted. "At least you own it."

"We were looking for a missing girl. I'm not going to apologize for that. But this?" I gestured around. "This I have no idea about."

"Yet you were prepared for it."

"Sure."

"*Very* prepared."

"My chief of security is a bit over the top," I said, echoing what I'd told Jameson.

"You have sandbags under the windows."

"Which saved lives," I said. Of everything we did, sandbags seemed like a weird place to draw the line.

"I don't have a bomb team, but when the feds get here, I bet we're going to learn that those explosives weren't Tannerite."

"You're bringing in the feds?" I asked, intentionally dodging the question.

"No choice. I don't have the resources to handle this. And there's the potential that something else is going on. You want to tell me what that is?"

"If I knew, I'd tell you," I said.

"Shame you didn't leave anyone alive to question. Convenient, too."

It was a bullshit accusation. She was basically saying that we'd killed everybody on purpose to avoid them talking. But I wasn't even going to give her the satisfaction of denying it. "I'm going to need my attorney, aren't I?"

Emery took some time with that. "Probably. But not yet. I apologize for that last remark."

I nodded once. "No worries. For the record, we didn't kill anybody that we didn't have to. There was one guy left alive, and my team gave him the chance to surrender. He went for his weapon instead, even knowing he was covered."

"Any thoughts on that?"

Now that I said it out loud, I *did* have a thought. It was almost like he wanted to die, which . . . no way. Unless something worse waited for him if he lived. I'd have to come back to that, though. I couldn't lose focus on Emery, who, despite being mostly friendly, definitely wasn't my friend. I had that effect on a lot of people. Donato was still staring as if to confirm that. "Not yet. But I'm still considering. I need that one thing that breaks it open, you know? The piece that makes it all come together."

"How about this one? You told Officer Jameson there would be nine bodies."

"Right. That was our read from the start when they breached our first line of sensors." There was no sense holding anything back about the hardware we'd put out. They had either found it or would soon enough.

"What if I told you there were ten."

I didn't know what they'd found, but suggesting that they may have counted multiple parts of the same body due to Kim's first explosion seemed a little morbid and a lot self-incriminating. Couldn't rule it out, though. Not everybody had experience with that kind of detonation and what it does to a body. In the end, I settled for, "You sure?"

"Nine we can't identify. One we can. Or, I should say, Officer Donato was able to."

Oh shit. The first thing that came to mind was Janie. That somehow she'd been here and got caught in the crossfire. But it didn't account for us only ever seeing nine heat signatures.

Emery gestured to Donato, and she walked briskly over to us.

I couldn't do anything but stare at her. Eventually, I found words. "Who was it?"

"Frankie."

Huh. I paused, not responding. I'd been so focused on Janie as an outcome, I hadn't considered Frankie. The way Donato glared at me told me she thought we killed him. And I couldn't rule that out, if he'd been part of the assault force. We hadn't seen faces. It definitely hadn't been deliberate. Suddenly, I felt like I needed Donato to believe that. "You saw me drop Frankie off—or at least you know I did. I dropped him in the city."

"And now he's dead," said Donato.

I glanced at Emery to see if she might interject, but she was content to let the two of us talk. Smart. If people are going to give you information, you shut up and take it. "If we'd wanted Frankie dead, we didn't have to bring him back."

"I considered that," said Donato. "But you might have done that to throw us off the trail."

"That would be a hell of a complicated conspiracy."

"Says the guy who had a rental house fortified with sandbags and surrounded by a security system that would make a bank blush. Not to mention the explosives, weaponry, and drones."

"Fair point," I allowed. I was stuck. I didn't know how to get her to believe me, and for some reason, it seemed important that she did. How had Frankie gotten there? And how had we missed the tenth heat source? Unless there *was* no tenth heat source. "Can you check the time of death on Frankie's body?"

"What? Why?" asked Donato, but then her face registered understanding. "You think he was dead before he got here?"

"Easy to check. Body temperature alone should tell us. A body loses one degree C about every one and a half to two hours. Maybe more in this weather."

Emery, who had been listening intently, made a quick call. "We'll know in a minute."

We stood there awkwardly after her call, nobody talking. I decided to fill the space with witty banter. As one does. "So . . . you take on this kind of extra work regularly?"

Donato looked at me like I was an idiot, which was fair. "First time."

"What do you know about extradition between counties?" That one got a hint of a smile before she squashed it. Thankfully, Emery's device buzzed, and we went quiet, trying to listen in on the other end of the conversation. I couldn't make it out, but it didn't matter since she immediately shared what she learned.

"Estimate on the time of death on the identified person is nine to eleven hours prior to the other bodies."

"So if we split the difference and call it ten, then he died at about sixteen hundred yesterday," I began.

"And you dropped him off thirteen or fourteen hours prior to that," finished Donato. "Doesn't mean anything. You could have revisited him." But her tone said that even she didn't believe that.

I decided to leave it alone. "So that leaves why. Why would someone bring an already dead body on a raid?"

The two women both thought about it. Donato answered. "To frame someone for your death."

"I don't follow," said Emery. I thought maybe I did, but it was better to let Donato put forward the theory. Coming from me, it might sound self-serving or overly convenient.

"*If* Colonel Butler is telling the truth, then the group that attacked here probably expected low resistance—expected to leave everyone on the premises dead."

I didn't love the emphasis she placed on *if*, but I liked where she was going.

"They could have planned to leave Frankie's body behind," continued Donato. "Depending on the time before someone found him and the level of forensic analysis, we might have believed he died in the attack."

"Why would that matter?" asked Emery.

I jumped in. "Because when you ran his ID and called in the name to Donato's station, or somewhere like it, you'd have learned that Frankie's crew had a reason to want revenge on my people. At least plausibly."

"*Very* plausibly," said Donato.

"But also very wrong," I added, still feeling the need to set things straight with Donato. "Because Jinks and I settled things. There's no beef. Unless he was lying, and I really didn't get that impression."

Emery nodded, while Donato looked at me sharply.

"You talked to Jinks?" she asked. It was the first time during the visit that Donato seemed surprised. I wasn't sure, but it seemed to lighten her mood a bit.

"Technically, we should probably categorize it as *he* talked to *me*. But yeah, we talked. He gave me some very useful information that probably led to some of what happened here. I paid for his door."

"Now you have my attention," said Emery. "Care to share the details of that discussion?"

I looked at Donato, who nodded. I wasn't sure if that meant that I could trust Emery or that Donato herself wanted to know. I'd think that through later. "Yes. I'll share. Jinks—"

"He's a local gang leader," added Donato, clarifying for Emery. "Reasonably decent human and nominally Frankie's boss. Though I'm wondering if that was still the case."

It's definitely not the case *now*, considering Frankie's current status. But that didn't seem wise to mention.

"Jinks told me that he realized that they'd been caught up in some-thing bigger than he knew, and that he wanted out," I said instead. "Long story short, they were paid to make it look like they were keeping Janie Strand at their apartment. Put two and two together, and that was because somebody wanted to get us to that location." I didn't share the part about the potential sniper across the street. I might decide to give that up later, but for now, I thought I could get by without it, and I didn't have enough of a read on the two other people in this conversation to trust them enough to share everything.

"They baited you into action so that you'd get arrested."

"Maybe," I said. I didn't believe it, but that could have been one of their desired outcomes.

"So how does that lead to . . . this?" Emery gestured around at everything.

"When we thought it through, my security team surmised that if someone was working at a deeper level to get at us in the city, that it stood to reason that they might continue. So, we prepared."

Donato nodded, but I noticed a small frown. "I do worry about Jinks, though," she said.

"How come?" I asked.

"If someone wanted to set you up in the city, but Jinks refusing to testify thwarted that . . . and that same group was willing to send a team to try to murder you . . . then it stands to reason that they might want Jinks to pay."

My gut said no way, but I took a few seconds to consider it. Better not to let preconceived notions get in the way of logic. "I think Jinks and his folks are good."

"How can you know that?" asked Donato. The concern in her voice felt real. This wasn't an interrogation. She was looking for reassurance.

I had to come clean. "Because whoever 'they' is didn't want to set me up to be arrested. They wanted to kill me. They lured us to Jinks's apartment with that intent, but ironically, you being tipped off—or focusing on us . . . whatever happened that brought you to the scene—scared them away."

"And you know this . . . how?" asked Donato.

"I can't tell you that without incriminating myself in other— *minor*—crimes."

"Minor like kidnapping?" asked Donato.

"Minor like . . . hypothetically . . . flying drones inside of city airspace," I said. The hypothetically probably didn't cover me legally, but I was trusting Donato not to make a big deal of what would only be a citation and a fine.

"Well, you've certainly made a mess out here," said Emery, bringing things back around to the problem at hand.

I listened, but I stayed focused on Donato. I was more interested in her reaction—to see if there was a possibility of us working together going forward. Emery would do what she was going to do, but I didn't have any more business in her county. In fact, if she let me, I'd be leaving it almost immediately.

For her part, Donato didn't give much away. I was going to have to ask her directly if I wanted to know. But I couldn't do that until Emery had her say.

"Should I call my attorney?" I asked, seriously this time. If she was going to bring us in, I'd have no choice.

"Not yet. Currently, I'm leaning toward not holding you. The evidence fits what you've said—everyone who was shot was on the property. Most of them were coming toward the house when they got shot. A couple, the angles were off on the entry wounds—"

"We had one man hiding in the woods," I offered.

"Of course you did," said Emery, without missing a beat. "As I was saying, I think the evidence supports self-defense."

"Thank you," I said.

"*Now,* there *is* the bit about the property damage. That's currently not a criminal charge, but we're documenting it, and if you fail to remunerate—"

"I will have my attorney contact the owner and/or the owner's attorneys immediately," I said. I wanted to make it as easy as possible for Emery to let us go.

"If I was following procedure, I'd probably ask you not to leave the county. But in this case, I find that I *really* don't want you to stay."

"Understood. We'll be on our way as soon as practical."

"Make it sooner than that," she said.

"Yes, ma'am."

"And . . . one more question."

"Go for it," I said.

"Who *were* these people?"

"I have no idea."

And that was the truth.

CHAPTER 14

Butler

W E KEPT MY word to Captain Emery and left town, leaving behind a lot of our gear as *evidence*. We might get some of it back someday, but not the illegal stuff, which was also the hardest stuff to replace. That put us in a bind if we got into another firefight in the near future, which, hopefully, we wouldn't, but I don't love relying on hope as a strategy. At least we were heading home. If someone wanted to come after us at my place, we'd be better off there than playing an away game.

I didn't expect an attack at home, though. Nobody would try something complicated when something simple would work, which meant that they only chose to lure us into a conflict in the city because they'd considered and rejected an attack on my house. I wasn't arrogant enough to think that they couldn't beat us in a fight. Because of course they could. Anybody could beat anyone with enough time to plan and the proper resources. That indicated another reason that they hadn't attacked, and once I started thinking about it, it became obvious. They hadn't come for me here because if they did, it would draw a completely different kind of attention. In the city, they could spin my death as something random—maybe even pin it on Jinks and his crew. If they came at me at home, the story would always be the murder of a notorious military figure. People would notice. *Government* people would notice. It would bring the kind of scrutiny that one would want to avoid if one was killing someone.

That didn't make us safe, but we were at least *safer*. Maybe having failed in their other attempt, they'd take the risk. But probably not, and even if they did, we had pretty significant defenses in place. So all I had to do was go back home and stay there. Forever. Never leave. As nice as that sounded at the moment, it would never work. I'm not wired that way—to accept something because it's easiest. And even if I could force myself to accept it mentally, something would come up where I'd *have* to leave. Or they'd get tired of waiting and arrange something to look like an accident right there at home. Bottom line, if you try to play defense forever, eventually you lose.

We had to go on the offensive. The problem was, I hadn't been lying to Emery. I had no idea who had attacked us, and the police investigation of the bodies hadn't shed any light. It wasn't like I had a shortage of enemies. Omicron probably topped the current list, since I'd messed them up back on Taug, and they knew it. But I'd damaged them before, and they hadn't held a grudge. At least not a "send contracted killers" level grudge. I mean . . . times change. Maybe new leadership had a more proactive view on such things, but I doubted it. No profit in it. Companies are cold and calculating and would kill kittens if it helped them make a profit. But they weren't psychopaths. Either way, I couldn't prove their involvement, and while they topped the list, they weren't alone on it, so it wasn't enough to act.

I still had some open avenues. I'd talked to Donato before we left, and she'd agreed to continue looking into things in her jurisdiction. She'd probably focus on protecting people there, but we promised to keep in touch and share what we learned, so I'd get at least some residual information.

But my best asset was the white panel van sitting in my driveway when we got home. Mac stopped our two-vehicle convoy a hundred meters away and began surveillance of the strange vehicle, but a few seconds later, Ganos stepped out through the back doors. Another person—a huge, dark-skinned man—got out of the driver's door. That was Parker, Ganos's coworker back in the military and now husband. We all loaded up and headed to the house.

"I can't believe you have an actual white panel van," said Mac, as he, Parker, Ganos, and I sat around my kitchen table. Alanson and Kim were outside, working on who knows what, and C and Clement had headed to the store for supplies. Mostly food. It looked like we'd be feeding a bunch of people for a while.

"I can't believe you don't," said Ganos.

It took Mac a few seconds to realize she'd made a pedophile joke about him. "Ha ha."

"Seriously, though," she said. "It's got racks built into both sides for hardware and a high-performance cooling system. It's the ultimate mobile processing station."

"A nerd's wet dream," said Mac.

"How much do you spend on security equipment?" she asked.

"A lot," Mac admitted.

"Think of this as my security."

"Ah. Touche. Well, we're glad to have you," said Mac, in a rare show of contrition.

"How soon before you can start looking into the folks who attacked us?" I asked.

"I already have. With my mobile platform, I can work on the move. As soon as you messaged to tell me about the attack, I started looking for signs. You're not going to like the answer, though."

"There are a lot of ways to not like something," I said.

"This is the worst kind. There's *nothing* out there."

"Shit." She was right. Even bad news beat no news. No news meant you had to assume bad news, but you didn't even have the benefit of knowing what flavor of bad news to expect. "Nothing?"

"These dudes don't exist. The authorities haven't even got names at this point—not real ones, anyway."

"And you know this because . . ."

"Come on, sir. Do we have to have this conversation every time?"

"Yeah, yeah. I don't want to know. Except this time, I do. You're inside the local police's system?"

"County or city?"

"County."

"Yes."

"Wait . . . what about city?" I asked.

"Also yes."

I paused. "Why didn't you say both from the start?"

"It was funnier this way," said Ganos. "Neither have anything on your assailants beyond fake names and records."

"Any charges pending for us? Any arrest on sight orders?"

Ganos laughed. "I didn't find anything, but that might not mean anything. Might be informal and not in the system."

"Since you're there anyway, keep an eye out for anything asking for support closer to our current location. If they decide to arrest us after the fact, they'll have to get help."

"Easy enough. Though with the feds involved, they might just come."

"Tell me you're not inside the feds' systems."

"Okay. I'm not inside the feds' systems."

I almost asked her if that was true, but in this case, I really *didn't* want to know. "If the authorities can't ID the bodies, what are our other options?"

"Fairly simple explanation, really. If you want all your biometric data scrubbed from the galaxy, there's pretty much only one place to go. But that's its own problem."

"Because that place doesn't talk."

"Wouldn't be a very valuable service if they did," Ganos agreed.

"And you're *not* inside their system."

"That would be suicide. So, no. Definitely not. Truly. Not like when I tell you I'm not but I really am."

"I understand. Does knowing that these people got service there tell us anything?" I asked.

"Tells us that they're extremely well-funded. Getting erased isn't cheap. Having a whole team of erased people? Let's just say that *you* couldn't afford it."

"That *does* help." It meant corporations or government. Though one would like to hope that the government didn't use such services. One would be naïve if they thought that, though. On the other hand, it still didn't help, because those were always the likely suspects, and knowing that the team was well-funded barely qualified as news. I guess maybe knowing that for sure made me feel better. That they'd wasted their money. If they killed me, I'd live on forever as a major budget item.

I hoped their stock went down.

Moving to another tack, I asked, "Have you been able to piece anything together on Janie Strand and what started all of this?"

Ganos blushed. Like her face actually turned red. So much so that at first, I thought that maybe she was having some sort of reaction. I'd never seen it before. "Yeah," she said. "About that. They got me."

"What do you mean they got you? I asked you what the chances were, one to ten, and you said zero."

"And I'm sticking to that! There's no way that two kids pulled something like this over on me."

"I'm messing with you. Just tell me what happened."

"That's it—I don't know. But when I went back and looked at it all again, there were anomalies."

"Like what?" I asked.

She considered it. "How do I put this into language you'll understand?"

"I'll pretend not to be offended."

"I'll pretend to care that you were." She paused, then said, "There were . . . tracks. Tracks so faint that you'd never see them unless you were specifically looking, and only then if you were really talented."

"Which means . . . what? It was all faked?"

"That's the worst part. Faked is such a tough concept. The messages were real—at least as much as anything anybody writes is real. But there are some issues with the creation time stamps that lead . . . somewhere. For now, we can't know what it means other than we can surmise with pretty good confidence that it's not at all what it seems."

I snorted. When was it ever? "You say for now. Will we get answers at some point?"

"We . . . I don't know. I'm going to keep working, but the level of skill and effort it took to do what I've seen so far . . . I can't guarantee that I'm going to unravel it."

"That sounds like something we've seen before," I said, referring to a couple of months ago on Taug when we found that someone had been erased from a bunch of different camera feeds, and Ganos told me the same thing.

"I was thinking about that. In fact, that was my *first* thought. That we were probably dealing with the same entity. But that's flawed logic. We're dealing with someone with a similar capability—but the jump from there to it being the same person, or group of people, isn't necessarily correct."

I nodded. It wasn't *necessarily* correct. But that didn't make it a bad place to start. Flawed or not, Omicron, and then Caliber, would be my top two suspects right up until something proved that they shouldn't be. The problem was, I didn't know how to even start proving it. Maybe Ganos did. "What's your next move?"

"Parker needs to get some sleep. Okay if we stay here and he crashes in your place?"

"Seems wise. There's a reasonable degree of safety inside our perimeter, and unless I miss my guess, that degree is going up with each passing minute. I'm sure the team is putting more security stuff in. You mentioned Parker . . . don't *you* need sleep?"

"I'm not driving. If I nod off at the keyboard, we don't slam into a tree."

Not a literal tree. But her job was at least as dangerous. If she made a mistake, bad things could happen. But I didn't have any way to tell her that without seeming like an overly concerned dad, so I left it alone. "Okay. Just take care of yourself."

"I always do."

"And be careful," I added, making it clear those two things weren't the same.

"Sure." She winked. I hated when she did that. "What are you going to do?"

"I want to go talk to the mom. Like you said, something's not right. I'll have a lot better chance of telling if she's bullshitting me if I can look her in the eyes."

"You be careful too."

"I'll have Mac with me. I'm sure we're going to be *extra* careful."

"I'll talk to him, then. I've got a couple tricks that he might like."

"You two seem to be getting along now."

"What can I say? We've bonded over the trauma of having to try to keep you alive. And you know . . . he did save my life back there on Taug."

"Right." I appreciated that she left out the part where the only reason her life was in danger was because we left her unprotected. From how she spoke, I'd like to say that she didn't hold a grudge. But that really didn't seem like the woman I knew.

Then again, maybe I didn't know her as well as I thought.

CHAPTER 15

Mac

BUTLER WANTED TO talk to Judith Strand, which made
sense, I guess. I'll leave the plans to him—he's the chess
player. Checkers are more my speed. On the checkers board
side of things, the problem was that going to see Strand was
predictable. And given that the last time we did something predictable, someone set a trap for us, potentially with a sniper,
well . . . I had my reservations. But when Butler wants to do
something, he's not likely to be denied, so I did the best I could
with it and asked him for an hour to prepare. He didn't *quite*
roll his eyes, but I could tell that he wanted to. Whatever. I
got my hour, and if I ended up being right, he'd thank me for
it. Not with an actual apology, or anything . . . but he'd know.
And I'd know.

Plus, I had use for that hour. I got the team together and assigned work. C would come with us (Butler's eye rolls be damned),
Alanson and Kim would continue their "upgrades" on the defense
system (calling it an alarm at this point was like calling a rifle a
diplomatic tool), and Clement would provide security for them,
Ganos, and her husband. Parker had served, but I didn't know his

capabilities—pretty sure he was a techie like Ganos—so I wasn't going to count on him yet. I'd rather have him helping her, anyway. What she did was at least as important as what we did. Probably more.

I had C start prep work on our route. He knew the deal, so I didn't have to coach him. He'd find alternate routes, cameras, and potential choke points. Anything the enemy might use or that we might. He'd prep the vehicle, too. I didn't tell Butler about any of that. With luck, we wouldn't have to use anything, and he'd never have to think about it. He had enough to think about without having to worry about my things.

Once everyone else had their tasks, I got on mine. I called Sandra and asked if Mrs. Strand had been in to the gym. I'd much rather talk to her there than at her house. Home turf advantage, and all that.

"She hasn't been in."

"Not at all?"

"Hold on. I'll check it again." The line went quiet for a few seconds. "Nope. Not since you left."

"That seem odd to you?" I asked.

"A little. But you know how people are. They get busy or lose motivation."

"Right," I said. But it seemed like a pretty big coincidence that she lost motivation at exactly the same time all this went down. "Thanks, Sandra."

"You betcha. You coming back tomorrow?"

"Probably. We'll see. You free to cover if I can't?"

"Yeah. Happy to have the hours."

"Okay. I'll let you know."

I waited until we were on the road to brief Butler. If Judith's mini disappearance concerned him, he didn't show it. I drove, he rode shotgun, and C occupied the back seat. It was a twenty-six-minute drive to the Strands', and Butler spent the time lost in thought. I didn't ask him what was on his mind. He'd let me know when the time came. He was probably still assessing the situation. That's why he wanted to see Strand—to gather another piece of information so we could make the next move.

Like I said—chess shit.

We reached her neighborhood without any problems. Not that I expected any on the way there, because that would mean they'd have had to pick us up leaving Butler's, which we'd have noticed, given how much surveillance we had on the area. He lived in a small, rural town. Anything out of place really stood out. The drive was mostly rural, too, until the last few minutes when we entered more of a suburb. Suburb was probably overselling it a bit. There were three housing divisions in a consolidated area with some trendy shops and restaurants, about fifteen minutes outside of Dovecoat, which was what passed for a city around here even though it had a standing population of about forty thousand. It was also home to a really cool gym.

The houses in the Strands' neighborhood looked exactly like where you'd expect a doctor to live, big and made of brick, wide roads, manicured lawns. It's the kind of place you'd dream of living, if you were vanilla and didn't mind that there were only five or six different house designs in the two-hundred-plus house development. Like someone decided to sell upper middle-class out of a catalogue. The GPS led us to the address we had on file at the gym, and we pulled up in front of it. There was no name on the mailbox—only a number in the same font and color as the number on every other box in the neighborhood. There was a newish white SUV in the driveway. I didn't know what Mrs. Strand drove, but it certainly fit the profile.

"This it?" asked Butler.

"Yeah. This is what's on her application at least."

He opened his door and I exited quickly, moving around to his side of the car before he headed for the front door of the house. I scanned the street both ways, finding only one person outside. A man three houses down on the opposite side was mowing his lawn, the whir of the electric motor barely audible at this distance. Everything else was quiet.

Butler pushed the doorbell—one of those fancy ones with seventeen different camera angles and communication options. The kind of thing that people who didn't understand security had for security. After a few seconds, a male-sounding AI voice said, "Soliciting isn't allowed in this neighborhood."

Butler kept his voice neutral when replying. "We're not soliciting. We're looking for Judith Strand."

It took about five seconds before the voice responded, "You have the wrong address."

Butler looked at me, and I dutifully checked my device even though I knew I had the right place. We'd looked at commercial satellite pictures and street views of the whole neighborhood before we came. "This is the place," I mouthed.

"Our records indicate that she lives here."

"Your records are wrong," said the voice after the same delay that it had previously. Someone was typing responses for the computer to speak.

"Please. If she's there, or if you know where she is, this is about her daughter. Janie."

"You have the wrong address."

"Is there someone there I could talk to face to face?" asked Butler. His voice was still neutral, but I recognized the signs of frustration creeping in.

Nothing happened for maybe thirty seconds, and we were about to head back to the vehicle when the lock clicked, followed by another one, and then the door opened. A woman who looked to be in her mid-sixties stood there, fit for her age, pale-skinned with naturally white hair. Definitely not Judith Strand. I guess it *could* have been her mother, but they didn't favor each other in anything other than skin tone.

"I've scanned your faces and gotten your identifications," the woman said, holding the door open only partway, making it clear that she was not inviting us in. I didn't know if she'd really gotten our IDs or if she was bluffing. Probably the latter, since she didn't comment on Butler's identity.

"We won't take much of your time, Mrs. . . ." Butler paused, waiting for the woman to fill in her name, but she didn't, so he continued, "As I said before, we're looking for Judith Strand. Any chance that you've seen her?"

"Never heard of her."

"Any chance that she's lived at this address in the past?"

"I've lived here for eleven years. I don't know anybody by that name."

I took out my device and scrolled through my pictures. I didn't have one of Judith—that would have been weird—but I did have one of Janie, since we'd been looking for her. "Ever seen this girl?"

"No. Are you some kind of detectives?"

"We're looking into a missing person situation," said Butler, both answering the question but also not.

"Well, I hope you find her."

"Thank you. And thank you for your time."

Back in the vehicle, we sat there for a moment before taking off. "She might have given you a fake address when she signed up because she doesn't like her real info being out there in the world," said Butler.

"Maybe," I agreed. There were people who did that. But neither of us believed it in this situation.

"Let me message Ganos with what I found out. Maybe she can find a real address."

I started driving, but slowly. I didn't want to stay in front of the house, but I didn't want to get too far only to get new instructions from Ganos. Butler's device buzzed about thirty seconds later, and he picked up with it on speaker.

"Everything I've got says that's the address," said Ganos.

"There's another person living there," he said.

"Send her this," I said, passing him my device.

"It's a picture of the woman who lived there," said Butler. "How'd you get this?"

"Come on, sir. You want me to give you all my secrets? Then you wouldn't value me as much."

He snorted. "See if you can ID this woman."

"Yeah. Give me a minute," said Ganos. Less than fifteen seconds later, she said, "Alexandra Gowens. Retired dentist. Husband has passed away. Lives at the address you were just at."

"I thought Strand lived there."

"Yeah." The anger came through in Ganos's voice, making me glad it was Butler she was talking to. "When you pull up Strand, everything about it leads to that place. When you pull the house deed from the municipal court—"

"When you what?" asked Butler.

"You get Strand as the owner," said Ganos, ignoring him. "It's only when you specifically search Alexandra Gowens that you get her at that address. From an article on a local news site where she was running for HOA secretary."

"She did seem like the HOA secretary type," I said. Clearly I didn't have anything useful to add, but I wanted to be part of the conversation.

"Of course, I never searched for Alexandra Gowens before," said Ganos, ignoring me, too.

"Because why would you have?" asked Butler.

"Right. At the time, I felt like I was going deeper than necessary on Judith Strand. On the net, she absolutely exists, and she and her husband own that home."

"This gets bigger and bigger," said Butler.

"Yeah. You have a picture of Strand? The mother, not the daughter. I can try to find her that way."

"There's got to be one on the cameras at my gym," I said. "We can swing by there on the way back and I can send—"

"Got it," said Ganos. "No need to go by."

I wanted to ask if she'd hacked into my gym. Or if she could set something up so somebody else couldn't do it so easily. But Butler told her that we'd be back in a bit and cut the connection.

"Home?" I asked.

"Yeah. I'm out of ideas for now."

We drove for a bit, away from the houses and shops. Butler didn't even ask to stop at the good sandwich place, which showed how focused he was.

"We might have a tail," said C.

"You think?" I asked.

"Where?" asked Butler.

"Might be," said C. "They've made three turns with us, and they're hanging back. Black SUV."

"That's a little cliché, isn't it?" asked Butler.

"What's in front of us?" I asked.

"Choke point in about a klick," said C.

"Going over the hill," said Butler.

"That's right," C said. "Rock wall on one side, steep drop on the other."

"Any cameras out there?" asked Butler. He hadn't focused on our job. But he knew we'd done it.

"None," said C. "Nothing since we left the built-up area."

"If they block the road on that hill, we're fucked." I glanced over at Butler.

"Yeah. That's where they'd do it. Push our vehicle down the embankment, make it look like an accident."

And he thinks *I'm* paranoid. Thing is, I didn't disagree with him. "What's the play?"

"What did you bring for weaponry?"

In the back, I heard C break out the Bitch assault rifles. "We brought a little bit."

Butler laughed. "Slow down. A lot. Let's bring the vehicle behind us up close before we reach anything in front of us."

I took my foot off the gas.

"If we find a place, pull a U turn. Let's head back at them."

"Here they come," said C. "I think they're speeding up."

I looked in the rearview. He was right. I'd dropped 25 klicks per hour, but they were closing too fast. They'd accelerated. Shit. They were going to ram us. I stomped on the accelerator. C lowered his window, bringing a cold, whipping wind into the vehicle. They were at fifty meters and closing fast.

"I'm going to take them out," said C.

"No!" said Butler. He'd turned in his seat, but I couldn't do the same since I had to focus on the road. "What the fuck was that?" he asked.

"Ganos gave it to us," said C. "It's magnetic, and when it hits their vehicle it sticks and it releases a virus into the vehicle software, rendering it inoperable." Sure enough, the trailing SUV slowed to a stop on the incline and distance built between us.

"Stop," said Butler. "Turn us around."

"You want to go back?" I asked.

"Better than going forward. These guys back here can't shoot us."

"They *can't*?" I asked. "Because if I remember correctly, the people at the rental house didn't have much hesitation in shooting."

"They were going to make it look like retaliation by Frankie's people. Out here, it would just be a shooting."

That seemed like a lot of faith in a theory, but I stopped and pulled a three-point turn on the road. Thankfully, nobody was coming the other way. "You sure?"

Butler shrugged. "I've got a hunch. Besides, there are three of us and only two of them. And I'm wagering we're better armed."

C handed him a Bitch, answering that question.

"Better to face them when we have the upper hand. Maybe we can get some answers," said Butler.

"You're the boss." I accelerated back toward them.

"What are you doing?" asked Butler as we got closer. "You're going to hit them!"

"Just playing chicken." I almost hit the brakes to cede the game when both front doors opened, and someone jumped out of each of them. I slammed on the brakes, bringing the smell of burning rubber in through the open window. We squealed to a halt, coming to rest maybe two meters from the other vehicle. Butler and C were out the door, and I followed quickly. I left the two obvious enemies to them, drew my sidearm, and moved to their vehicle. I looked in the windows, and it appeared clear, though it was hard enough to tell through the dark glass that I poked my pistol and head through the open passenger door to fully sweep the back seat.

"All clear," I said. By the time I turned around, Butler was marching his person—a brown-skinned woman—over to C and his prisoner, who was a light-skinned man with bulging arms. We only had a short time for whatever we were going to do, because we expected another enemy vehicle blocking the road ahead of us, and at some point, they'd get suspicious. Plus, we didn't own this road. A random civilian—or even a law enforcement vehicle— might appear at any second. But I didn't want to say that out loud to Butler because if we let the prisoners know we had a deadline, they'd have an easier time holding out. Maybe they'd figure that out on their own. But maybe not.

Butler definitely knew it, because he immediately started questioning the prisoners. "Why were you following us?"

Predictably, neither said anything. He'd have to separate them to have any chance—neither would want to blab in front of the other. We could threaten them, but for that to work, they'd have to believe it. We could *make* them believe it, but that would mean shooting the first one and then questioning the second. We weren't going to do that.

But it did give me an idea.

"Give me the man," I said. "Face her the other way. I'll question him, you question her."

C complied immediately, and Butler faced the woman away from me as I prodded my guy back down the road twenty meters. What he didn't know—what nobody knew—was that I had no intention of questioning him at all. There wasn't enough time.

"Over the guardrail," I said.

"What?"

"You fucking heard me. Over the guardrail. I'm going to give you ten seconds to run down that hill before I start shooting. I suggest you use them. You're lucky. All I have is a pistol. If you give me any shit, I'll have C shoot. Trust me . . . you'd rather have me."

The guy looked at me for a second, maybe trying to assess whether I was bluffing or not. Whatever he saw, he hopped the barrier, stumbled on the slope, and started scrambling away. After a couple of steps, he got his feet under him and ran as if death itself was on his ass. As far as he knew, it was. Dutifully, I counted down from ten in my head. When I got to three, I counted out loud, making sure that Butler's prisoner would hear me clearly.

"Three. Two. One." I fired my pistol in the general direction of my fleeing adversary, but well over his head. He kept running. "Mine wouldn't talk," I called to Butler. "Hope yours is more cooperative." Yeah, I couldn't shoot the guy. But *she* didn't know that. It also got my guy far away from his vehicle, which we needed. We didn't want them following us when we left.

Butler caught on quickly. He's smart like that. "Look, you can either talk to me, or you can talk to my partner. He's, uh . . . not super patient."

"Let me talk to her," I said, as I moved toward them.

"Hold on," said Butler. "Give me one last chance. Why were you following us?"

She spoke right away. "That was the job. Follow you to this road, and when you got to the hill, close in behind you and force you into the roadblock ahead."

It was nice to get confirmation that we'd read it correctly, but it didn't help us a lot.

"Who do you work for?"

This time she hesitated. "If I tell you, they'll kill me. They've done it before."

I'd come up right behind her by that point. "With them, at least you've got time to disappear. I'm standing right here."

"If I run your biometrics, what am I going to find?" asked Butler. It was a specific question, and it had a calming effect on the woman, who had started shaking.

"Nothing," she said, again confirming what we already suspected. I'm sure Butler had a reason for it though.

"You work for a corporation. How many of you are there?" A statement with a question, though the statement was part conjecture. He wanted to show her that he knew to make it easier for her to talk. The risk was that he'd give her an easy lie if that wasn't the case.

"I don't know how many. There were twenty in my cohort.

There are at least four cohorts. But there might be more—they don't tell us everything."

"Who is they? Who do the cohorts work for?" asked Butler.

"They don't tell us."

"But you know," he said. The calm in his voice, the assuredness. He wasn't asking if she knew. He was stating it as irrefutable fact. He was giving her permission to confirm it.

"Our arm is called Central Holdings. Nobody ever says it, but you see stuff. Hear stuff."

"That's the name of the company?"

"That company doesn't exist," said C, who was looking at his device. "Well . . . there is one. But they make parts for central air conditioning systems."

"Fuck," I said. "You know it's bad when the air conditioner people are sending out hit teams."

"Cold-blooded killers," C added.

Butler ignored us. "Central Holdings. Thank you. Who do *they* work for?"

"Caliber," she said. It was like he'd hypnotized her, and she was responding to everything he said.

"Thank you," he said, still calm, though he had to be seething on the inside. Fucking Caliber. "You need to run. Right now. Down that hill. Don't stop. My man here is a remarkable marksman. You won't be safe from him until you're a thousand meters away. Do not stop."

She hesitated. "Go now?"

"Go," he said.

She hopped the rail and took off, albeit at a slightly less reckless pace than her partner had. Still accomplished the purpose.

"What now?" I asked.

"Grab that thing that you hit their vehicle with, and let's get out of here. We'll head back the way we came and find a different way home."

"Three route options." C offered his device to Butler.

"You pick it. I need to do some thinking."

CHAPTER 16

Butler

W E ARRIVED BACK at my house without further inci-
dent, and while I'd thought the entire way there, I hadn't
solved anything. Based on my interrogation of our captive, Caliber was behind attacks on our lives. But I couldn't trust that with
a hundred percent certainty—the woman could have lied to me.
I hadn't had enough time to really question her the way I'd have
liked. But you worked with what you had, and I *did* think it was
more likely than not that she'd told the truth as far as she knew.
But if I got really into conspiracy territory, I had to consider that
somebody may have intentionally leaked that to her—to her entire
cohort—so that if they *were* questioned, they'd give it up believing
it to be true. They could even pass a lie detector.

I also didn't know their target, which I regretted not asking her
when I had the chance. They'd come at us as a group. Did that
mean they wanted all of us dead, or just me? Or, if I could put
my ego aside for a minute, was it maybe just one of my team? I
couldn't see any reason that would be the case, but I was missing
a lot of information in the puzzle, so I couldn't completely rule
it out.

A big problem was that I *wanted* to believe it was Caliber. That's dangerous, making decisions on information that you hope is right. I wanted to believe it because it fit, and because it answered a bunch of questions. Caliber had the ability to create false trails on the net to lead Ganos astray. They had the ability to create untraceable soldiers. And they had the resources and potentially the motive to come after me. I could come up with a list of reasons they'd want me dead. I'd gotten in their way more than once. But the obvious one was the most recent. On Taug.

Except I'd ended things there on pretty good terms with them. I'd given them the information that they needed to gain an advantage on their competitors. Unless something had changed, they should have been sending me a nice fruit basket for the holidays.

I also had to consider the death of Justin Parnavic. If someone wanted to kill me and make it look like an accident, maybe his accident wasn't accidental at all. I had to table that one for the time being. Pressing that brought in a whole new set of variables via the military involvement that would make things too complicated to even consider. I didn't have enough facts for that. To go there, I'd have to have information so compelling that people had to listen.

So I fell back on what I *knew*. One: There was a team of professionals out to get me or someone near me, and they wanted to make it look accidental. Two: They were using predictable situations—or even trying to create them—to target me. Three: Having left two of their people alive, they likely now knew that I knew what they were up to. I'd had to let the woman go free, and I had no doubt that they'd collect her whether she reported back in willingly or not. She'd tell them what she'd told me, though probably not willingly. She'd probably lie, since telling the truth would probably lead to her death. But they'd get the truth from her, one way or the other. Ironically, she'd have been better off if we'd kidnapped her. But I hadn't thought that all the way through at the time, and there was no use wishing I'd done something different now. That was it. Three things. Not a lot, but I had to do something with them.

Our information had a gaping hole in it: What had the Strands had to do with this? Had that been bait from the start? Despite the complexity of it—targeting Mac at his gym—it seemed . . . likely? But searching for the Strands was . . . predictable. The enemy had used that once already to target us. Even if someone delivered their location on a silver platter, we'd probably be walking into a trap. Our enemy would be waiting for the predictable.

There was a chance I was being blind to something obvious, so I gathered the whole team in the kitchen around the table to talk through our options. They could point out things I wouldn't see myself. Places where I might be predictable. "Here's your chance. You know the situation. Predict what I'm going to do. Give me all of your ideas. Tell me what you think I'll do next, how I'd do it right or how I'd screw it up—I don't care which. Ganos, Mac, you're my main contributors here since you know me best. But anybody feel free to chime in. C, don't hesitate."

Everyone looked at each other, as if wondering what to make of my odd request.

"Well," said Mac. He or Ganos had to start—it's the only way the others would jump in. But Ganos seemed distracted. "You'd consider all of the information."

"Sure," I said, trying to coax him to more. He was being tentative. And too kind.

"You'd figure out what we had, and that it wasn't enough."

"Okay."

"And then you'd do something to try to gain the information that you needed."

"Okay. I'm not sure how much that helps, but—"

"And it would probably be reckless and completely disregard your safety and the safety of the team," he said, cutting me off.

"Ah. Right. That's fair." I'd asked for exactly this kind of feedback, but it still stung a little.

He saw that, and tried to soften it. "Not that that's a bad thing. It's part of your success—you're willing to take risks."

"Yeah."

"Even when you probably shouldn't."

"Yeah. I got it," I said. Now he was just piling on.

"Some people might say that you have a death wish."

"No . . . really?" That seemed a bit beyond reality. Didn't it? "Okay. Let's say all of that is true."

"It is," said Mac. I didn't like this exercise anymore.

"*If* it's true, what's the predictable course of action? Where would I go next? Someone other than Mac."

C spoke up. "The logical thing would be to find Mrs. Strand—or Janie—and go to their location. It's a trap—we know that, and they probably know that we know that. But even so, if we found her and could question her, she could potentially answer a lot of questions."

"Good point. Let's say I wanted to do that. What would that look like?"

"You'd be looking for the trap, and then you'd try to fight through it, or go around it. Get the bait without getting caught," said Kim. They were all getting into the exercise now. It showed in their faces.

"No," said Mac. "It would go a level beyond that."

"How so?" I asked. I agreed with him, but I wanted to hear his logic.

"You'd expect a trap—you're not stupid. You'd have a counter-trap. So, if I was setting you up, I'd set my trap, look for your counter, and flip that on you."

He had a point. That had happened before. I'd seen the first trap but got caught in the second. "So how do we flip *that* on them?"

"We can't," said Mac. "Because what are we going to do? We make a plan, they counter it, so we counter that, and then they counter that . . . and we can never be sure that we're going in with the upper hand."

"It's worked before."

"It's gotten you captured before. And while you were able to turn those situations into something useful, the risk is higher this time. People don't send a sniper to the top of a building if their goal is to capture you."

"Another guy is dead," said Ganos, without looking up from her device. She flipped her device to show us a picture of the archaeologist Whiteman.

Another piece of the Taug puzzle.

"Dead? What are you talking about?"

"Reported ninety seconds ago. Hung himself in his cell," said Ganos.

"That can't be a coincidence," said Mac.

"Doesn't seem like it, does it?" asked Ganos.

"First Parnavic, then Whiteman," I said.

"Then you," said Mac.

"Us."

"Maybe," Mac allowed.

"Okay. Let's say we give up going after the Strands. What are our options? If we stay here and wait, they'll eventually find a way to get at us. A truck hits us on the way to the gym. A gas leak in Moop's blows us all to bits. There are a hundred ways."

"True," said Mac. "We can't take the Strand bait, and we can't sit here and do nothing. So come up with something nobody would expect."

"Is that all?" I asked.

Mac gave me a flat smile that felt a bit like a kick in the pants. But maybe I needed that. I had a spark of an idea, and maybe I just needed his push to fan it to life. "There might be one thing we could do . . ."

"I'm going to regret this, aren't I?"

"Probably. I need to work some things out. For now, I want you all to prep like we're going after Judith. If that's what the enemy expects us to do, let's show them exactly that. Keep them complacent. Don't be *too* obvious. Make them work for it. Take all your normal precautions."

"Wilco," said Mac. "Let's move, people."

"Ganos. If you could stay behind?"

"Sure thing, boss."

I waited for the rest of the team to file out. "Everything okay?"

"Yeah. I'm just . . . we're going down that path again, you know?"

"I do. But this time, I don't think we have a choice. *They* came after *us*. If it hadn't been looking for the girl, it would have been something else."

"Yeah. That's what I'm afraid of. So . . . be careful, okay?"

I didn't respond right away. Because the idea I had wasn't careful. I also couldn't do it without Ganos's help. "I'm going to do the best that I can. But I can't promise you anything."

The corner of her mouth turned up at that. "If you had, I'd have called you a liar. What do you need me to do?"

"I need it to look like we're going after Judith Strand. Which means I need you to find her."

"Sure."

"At the same time, I need a way off the planet without anybody knowing."

"You're not running away, are you? You can only hide so long."

"Nope. I'm running *at*."

She stared at me. "Okay. I'll bite. Running at who?"

"Caliber."

"That seems less than wise. So of course you are. Care to share why?"

"It's my best guess for who's behind all of this. The woman we interrogated said that was who hired her—"

"She might not even be right."

"We've got to start somewhere," I said. "It's either Caliber or it's not. If we go after them, we can confirm it one way or the other. Even if it's *not* them, there's value in knowing that."

She rolled her eyes. "It's a big company. Where are we going?"

That she said *we* made me happy. "Might as well start at the top."

"Corporate HQ?"

"Yep. I want to talk to Zentas himself." Corporations didn't seek revenge. But egotistical psychopaths did. Drake Zentas fit that description pretty well.

"Isn't there a restraining order?"

"On both of us. Yeah. The court put it in place after the events on Eccasis, as part of my settlement," I said. "But I don't think it's very serious."

She snorted. "Sure. We need . . . what? Invisible passage for . . . how many? You, me, and Mac?"

"The whole team. Just to be safe. We'll do what we can locally to make it look like we're still here."

"Okay. Any idea where to start? I'm sure there are smugglers who get people off the planet, but I don't have any on speed dial."

"I had someone approach me wanting to work together—someone who might have those contacts. Elizabeth Young of Meridian Resources." I handed Ganos the card I'd gotten at Moop's.

"A random person approached you offering to help. That doesn't seem suspicious at all." I could hear the eye roll in her tone, even if I didn't see it on her face.

"That's why I'm handing it to you. Reach out to her for help and see what happens. Best case, we get the help we need. Worst case, it's a trap, you see through it, and we've got another lead we can use."

She hesitated. "You're counting on me a lot here."

"I always do."

"I missed the ball with the stuff between Janie and Frankie."

I nodded, let it sit for a couple of seconds. I couldn't deny it. Ganos wouldn't accept that. She'd screwed up, and we had to acknowledge it. But then I said, "Which is why I'm extra sure you won't miss anything this time."

She let that sink in for a few seconds. "Right. I won't miss. We'll need fake IDs in addition to transportation if we want to do anything other than walk around once we reach the other end. Probably multiples, if we're being smart."

"Can you get those?" I figured she could.

"They're available. But they'll need to be quality, or they'll flag in any number of systems and make us discoverable to the wrong sorts of people."

"You think they'll be looking for us on another planet?"

"You think they won't?" asked Ganos. "Do you want to underestimate them again? Because personally, I've learned *that* lesson."

She had a good point. There was no sense doing the unexpected just to get caught by the mundane. "We need to disappear. Caliber did it. They've got invisible people after us right now."

"Caliber has unlimited resources. You don't."

"You can't put a price on peace of mind," I said.

"Oh, you absolutely *can* put a price on it. Just don't yell at me when you see what that price *is*."

CHAPTER 17

Butler

I'VE NEVER LIKED Talca. It was centrally located—close to a lot of gates—so I'd flown in there maybe forty or fifty times, and it always struck me in the worst way, the ads for defense contractors and other heavy industry blaring from every flat surface. But I'd never flown in via a container ship. Elizabeth Young passed Ganos's tests, and Meridian Resources had come through. I'm sure I'd owe them in the future, but if I ended up having to pay, at least that meant that I *had* a future.

Surprisingly, the trip wasn't bad. Sure, we started out boxed up in a container, but once we cleared the Ridia orbital facility, they allowed us to move around in our own segregated area of the ship. We didn't interact with the crew, and they didn't interact with us. The accommodations were passable, if not fancy. We had plumbing. Pretty important on an eight-day trip.

About six hours out from our destination, we loaded back into our container, and someone outside came and sealed it up. It sounds bad, but while it was cramped, we had comfortable chairs, good air, and refreshments. Not all human smuggling happens in such nice conditions. We got the deluxe version.

The worst part came after we arrived at the docking facility. We couldn't see what was happening, but there's no mistaking the feeling of a moving ship coming to a stop. Nobody came to get us. Academically, we knew we'd have to wait as the ship cleared customs and inspections. But it's one thing to know that and another to sit there wondering what would happen if nobody came to let you out. Sure, they probably wouldn't get paid, since we had to message Meridian that we'd arrived safely. Which *sounds* good. Right up until you're there and realize that them not being paid doesn't help you at all if you're stuck in a container. On the bright side, at least we didn't see any of the Talca ads for morally suspect corporations with names that people knew but operations that nobody did.

The team each coped in their own way. I sat and thought. Probably too much. I tried to doze but had only sporadic luck. Ganos fidgeted and scrolled on a device that she couldn't connect to the net, because that would be an easy way to get caught. Mac paced. Alanson read a book—an actual physical copy. He'd brought a whole bag with him. Kim, Clement, and C slept. Parker had stayed home. He was Ganos's partner, but not part of our team. After nine hours and twenty minutes of container time, the hidden speaker in the wall finally came to life.

"We've cleared station customs. Strap in. We'll be transferring you to a cargo shuttle."

We couldn't ride the passenger section of the space elevator down because we'd never officially arrived. A closed station like the arrival terminal in orbit around Talca has a discrete number of people aboard, and they're tracked. Ganos could probably have done something to alter that, but she deemed it more risky than prudent, and when *Ganos* says something is risky . . . well . . . that's like an infantryman telling you that you swear too much. You should probably listen.

We rode down in our container, which meant twenty-six hours with nothing other than a couple of portable toilets and a pile of snacks. From there, I don't really know how it worked. We shook and shifted several times, and we definitely moved via ground transportation—probably a bot truck—at some point. The door finally opened from the outside, but whoever opened it disappeared before we opened our side. We stepped out into a warehouse filled with identical containers stacked eight high. Our container was on the bottom, so we exited onto the concrete floor in dim light. It was night, and we were alone. Someone probably had a camera on us, but we'd accounted for that, and all wore the facial distorters that Ganos provided. We had crates of equipment and weapons, but none on our bodies. The laws on this part of Talca didn't look as kindly on armed people as my home on Ridia did. That had to be killing Mac. But the last thing we needed was to go through all of this trouble sneaking onto the planet just to get arrested because of a random security scan.

Three vehicles waited outside in a mostly empty lot, the keys already in them. They were registered to a fake company called Gymsalia, which was something that Ganos had developed a while back in case we ever needed it. We loaded up our gear and ourselves and headed out of the city. Or, at least as close to out of the city as one could get on this part of Talca. More accurately we went out of the city with all the warehouses and tall buildings and into the city with large apartments, a few crowded housing areas, and slightly shorter buildings. But that had its advantages. With millions of people jammed into a small area, we had unending traffic and a crowd to blend into. With the rampant gig economy, temporary rental space existed to fit any need.

Our new company headquarters was a two-story facility with a faux-brick exterior set in an area of multiple such building complexes providing short-term space close to the business hub but away from the ultra-high prices of the inner city. Not that this was cheap. We had offices and a conference room on the first floor, apartments on the second along with six valuable parking spots out front.

Mac and Alanson did a walk around the perimeter while the rest of us went inside. I let Ganos claim her space first, since she needed it more than anybody else. The rest of the team would fill in around her, and eventually, someone would tell me where they wanted me. Mostly I stayed out of the way, letting everyone else do their jobs. I grabbed Mac when he came back in from getting the lay of the land.

"How is it?"

"It'll do. It has a built-in security system, but it's laughable. It works as camouflage, though, since it has cameras. Ours won't stand out in this compound. Only two entrances, and the one in back is pretty secure. It's only meant as an exit. It would take explosives, or a really invasive system override, to breach it from the outside."

"Let's hope it doesn't come to that. We want to get in and out. We can't be getting into a gunfight here. If we go to jail, it's going to be a lot harder to get out than it was on Ridia." With all the defense industry here, nobody was going to cut us any breaks by perceiving us as heroes.

"If someone comes at us, it's better to be in jail than dead," said Mac.

I wasn't so sure that one didn't equal the other, given what had happened to Whiteman, but Mac was already in a negative mood and I didn't want to add to it. "We're in a bad spot already. Having to set up under an alias, we've got a lot more risk if someone *does* detect us. They won't hesitate to kill us, because they can spin it as us doing something underhanded."

"That's why we've got our exit off planet already set."

"How good do you feel about that?" I asked.

"Not good yet. But I'm going to have C and Alanson check it out tomorrow to make sure that it's everything that we paid for."

"I appreciate that. Don't leave Ganos by herself."

"Never again," said Mac. His eyes told me I hadn't needed to say it, and I understood. He'd been there too. He knew. "Alanson will be with her most of the time, Clement will be with her all the time."

"Good." Alanson could help her with some of her work. He didn't have the same skills, but he had more than the rest of us, and a lot of what they did worked in parallel. Clement was a fighter and provided a different kind of security. The kind that punched you in the face if you got too close. "Where's that leave us for Alanson's capabilities elsewhere?"

"C has been learning. He'll bring some of that stuff along on our mission. But we can only do so much with surveillance here on Talca anyway. Almost none where we're going—they'll have scanners."

"That's fine. I'm not entering that building to try to mess with its technical stuff. No way do we win that. I want the softer target."

"You've got a funny idea about soft," said Mac.

He was probably right about that.

MAC DIDN'T LET me do anything the next day. Said that I was too recognizable and that if even one person identified me, it could screw the whole mission. He took the team and worked ingress and egress routes until everybody knew them by heart, and they checked our escape plan and our backup escape plan. I sat in our fake headquarters, waiting for someone to kick down the door. Ganos said we weren't impossible to find, but to find us, somebody really smart would have to know where to look. That *would* happen—I had no doubt. They might have started looking already. We'd left decoy information back on Ridia—check-ins from different locations, interactions on the net. Everything we could. But it wouldn't last forever, and we'd already been gone eleven days. We were on a clock. What we had going for us was that it was a *big* galaxy, and we could have gone anywhere. And when we departed Ridia, we left four trails. The three decoys were easier to find than the real one, and any one of those would take a lot of time to run down.

None of this made me relax. I was anxious to get the job done and get out of here, but Mac's caution made sense. We only got one shot at this. To pass the time, I put together a thousand-piece jigsaw puzzle. Mac brought it, maybe thinking that it would give me something to do and keep me from interfering. It barely worked. Clement helped from time to time, when he didn't have other duties. He had a very good eye for color variations.

Finally, the next morning, Mac said it was time to execute.

CALIBER HEADQUARTERS HAD its own building. All thirty-seven floors of it. It sat on a corner and had entrances on two sides, both at street level. There was a third entrance at the top to service the landing pad, which would have been ideal since our ultimate destination was the executive area on floor thirty-six, but my resources had limits.

I'd wanted to enter by myself, but Mac was having none of that and came with me. I took it as a bit of a win that he'd acquiesced to this plan at all. It had everything he hated in it. Namely, me walking into enemy hands. I *did* have a plan to get out, but as he correctly informed me, no plan survives contact with the enemy. I held my breath as we passed through the scanner and into the lobby. We'd come during the morning rush to blend in as much as we could, and nobody pulled us out of line. Not that I expected them to, since we weren't carrying anything that would trigger a sensor, we had very good fake IDs, and we had our faces electronically distorted. I still worried though. We were inside, now, and couldn't know if we'd triggered something silently. From the moment we showed up, someone might be working on a plan to ensure our downfall.

If they hadn't, they'd start in about one minute when I walked up to the lobby reception and announced myself. I had a very straightforward plan. I'd walk up and ask to talk to the boss. Okay—it really wasn't much of a plan. But I wanted to talk to Drake Zentas, and asking gave me as good a chance as anything else. He'd stepped down as CEO after the scandal I exposed a couple years back on Ecassis, but still kept his role as Chief Asshat. And he hadn't really given up the other role, either. Someone else's name was on the CEO office door, but Zentas had a bigger office down the hall and—I was certain—a bigger voice in the direction of Caliber. Calling him the shadow CEO would have been more accurate if he stayed in the shadows. He had, for a time, until things calmed. Now it was barely even a secret that he ran things.

Generally speaking, you didn't walk into Caliber headquarters and get to see Drake Zentas. In fact, Caliber did their best to hide when he would even be in the building. Surprise, asshole. Found you. And I was betting that I was the one person who actually *could* walk in and see him. The novelty of it might have been enough to make it happen. Butler walks into a building after disappearing off of his home planet. I had to think that someone would want to know *why*. That there was an equal chance that they'd walk me into a locked room—well, that kept things interesting.

We'd find out soon enough.

But I wasn't stupid. Well . . . not totally, anyway. The minute I walked through the door, we'd started the other part of our plan by announcing my presence on Talca and broadcasting news of my meeting with Caliber officials to the press. That way, if I disappeared, it would at least be a lot harder for people to cover up. Not that that would make me feel better if I found myself face down in a shallow grave with a knife in my back, but you take whatever security you can. They'd at least have to think about it before they attacked me. But announcing my presence also started another clock. Now that everyone knew my location, if I *didn't* get Caliber to stand down—or if I was wrong and it wasn't them—that clock ended when whoever was out to kill me got the assets in place to do so. Hopefully, we'd be on our way off the planet before that happened.

Lot of hope in this plan.

Five different people worked at the reception desk—four at terminals and one floating, who might have been a supervisor. Of the four, two were women and two men, and I studied them to decide which one's day I was going to ruin. I didn't want the easiest one to manipulate. If I did, there was a pale, underweight woman who looked like she might jump at her own shadow. I also didn't want the hardest one. That was the other woman—a dark-skinned lady in her fifties with a stare that looked like it could see through to the back of your head. I wanted someone in the middle—someone I could manipulate but who would then have enough of an ego to go to his boss and insist that he was making the right decision.

I might have been overthinking it. Regardless, I got in the line of my guy. The two people in front of me moved through fast enough, and when I approached the counter, I studied him for a second. His nametag said Charles, but I bet he went by Chuck. Or Chaz. Definitely not Charles.

"Carl Butler to see Drake Zentas." I said it like it was the most common thing in the world.

"Mr. Zentas isn't in today," he said, barely looking up. A rehearsed line. Apparently people did come in asking to see him.

"Yes he is."

He looked up at that. He hadn't signaled security yet, which meant he thought he still had things in his own arsenal of administrivia to deal with me. "Sir." His tone was that of someone dealing with a child. "He's not here. And even if he was, you don't have a meeting with Mr. Zentas."

"He's definitely here. And I do have a meeting. Look on the net. Multiple news sites are reporting about it."

"How is that—" He cut off, now looking at his screen. After a few seconds, he turned to the floater employee. "Julia?"

The woman made her way over, and they conversed in hushed tones, drowned out by the clamor of the busy thoroughfare that was the entry lobby.

"Mr. . . . Butler?" Julia asked.

"That's right. Carl Butler."

"We don't have anything about a meeting."

"So then, Ms. . . . ?" Her nametag only had her first name.

"Katz," she said.

"Ms. Katz. Are you saying I should leave and go out to the media and tell them that I was turned away on your authority?" I looked at Charles with a questioning expression, almost as if to say, "Can you believe this?"

"Maybe we should call upstairs," Charles suggested.

"You won't be the one to get reamed for bothering Mr. Spencer," she said, mostly under her breath. Spencer had to be the next level up. The person in charge of the people at reception. Probably seven degrees away from the one who would finally make the decision, but baby steps.

"You could call an escort to take me up to thirty-six," I offered with a fake smile to egg her on. While I'd have preferred to keep it as quiet as possible, the more noise I made, the faster word would reach the top. I couldn't come back if I left, so I'd make as big a scene as necessary. If Zentas learned of my presence and decided not to see me, there was nothing I could do. But I doubted he would. He had too much ego for that.

"That's not going to happen," she said.

"Then call who you need to call. Or do *I* need to make a call? Katz. That's with a z at the end?"

She held out another fifteen seconds, and then she shuffled away to make a call. Hopefully we could cut through the next few levels of management and get to the top. I kept one eye on the elevators, as anybody who could get me access would certainly come from a higher floor. Mac, too, had his eyes there. Probably for different reasons than me.

A tall man came out of one of the doors maybe a minute later while I still stood at the reception station. He immediately focused on me and started walking with a purpose. I'd have bet a lot of money that it was Spencer. If Zentas was Chief Asshat, this guy was at least somewhere in the asshat chain of command. This was going to be fun.

"Mr. Spencer," said Julia, hurrying over to where I was standing. "This is—"

"Shut up," said Spencer. Yep. Asshole. "I know who he is. What are you doing here, Mr. Butler? Or should I call you Colonel?"

"Either is fine. Your people have told you why I'm here. Either make that happen or get the fuck out of here and take the consequences." I could be an asshole, too. Especially to assholes who deserved it.

He recoiled a bit. Whatever he expected from me, that hadn't been it. Society has a set of polite rules, and guys like Spencer made a living out of crossing those lines just enough to make people uncomfortable. I'd obliterated the line because bullies aren't used to being bullied. "What consequences?" he managed, finally, with it coming out weaker than he wanted.

"Let's start with your name splashed across the news all over the planet. News that your bosses are definitely going to see."

We went through two more levels of management, which seemed inefficient, even for a mega-corporation like Caliber. I'm pretty sure the final boss was actually Zentas's personal scheduler. I didn't love it, waiting, as every moment I stood there was another moment that they could be preparing action against me. But I was in it now. No backing out. Finally, an attractive young woman came to escort me to the elevators. No security. At least nothing visible. I signaled Mac to join us, and if that bothered the nameless woman, she didn't let it show. We rode the elevator in silence until the door opened on thirty-six.

We stepped out onto a deep blue carpet. The walls were either polished hardwood or an incredible fake, inlaid with gold accents. I've been in some nice places before, but this was near the top. We definitely weren't on Ridia anymore.

"Right this way," said the woman. She led us down the hall, our footfalls not making a sound on the expensive carpet. We took a left and then stopped as she put her palm to a pad and opened a set of double doors on the right side. It opened into a conference room with floor-to-ceiling windows on the far side that provided a wonderful view of the city. It had a huge table that looked like it might be granite, a dozen expensive chairs down each side.

"Nice view," I said.

Mac skirted around the woman to check out the room, even though it was clearly unoccupied.

"If you'd wait here," she said.

I noted that she didn't say Mr. Zentas would join us, and since I felt like asking at that point gave up what little power I had, all I said was, "Sure."

She closed the door behind her, effectively locking us in. Mac moved toward the door, as if to check it. I waved him off.

"It would be funny if we made it all this way for this to be an expensive prison, wouldn't it?" I asked.

"Hilarious," he said.

I watched the doors, ready for anything. When they opened again, we could be facing security, a team of lawyers, or even law enforcement.

They let us wait. An hour went by. Maybe nobody would come at all. Maybe they were just softening us up.

Finally, the doors swung open.

CHAPTER 18

Mac

C ARL FUCKING BUTLER."
Zentas walked in, arms spread, like either he wanted a hug or he owned the place. Which . . . I guess he did. I hadn't spent a ton of time with the guy, but I'd have known him anywhere. Preferably hanging from the end of a rope out of a flying vehicle. I moved to the side wall and put my back to it. I knew my role here.

Butler moved toward him, but not far, giving it the minimal amount of effort. He did take Zentas's offered hand, though. "Drake."

"Violating the restraining order, I see. Or maybe I'm violating mine. What happens when we both move toward each other? I'll have to ask my lawyers."

"I hardly think it matters," said Butler. "Nobody here to enforce it."

"As you say. Have a seat. If I'd known you were coming, I'd have had lunch prepared." *You had over an hour, asshole*, I thought. "I've got the best new chef. She used to work at Nobuki."

I didn't know high-end dining, but even I'd heard of Nobuki. Fancy. I wondered if this guy was showing off out of habit, or if he had a purpose. This meeting had a lot of history behind it, and both players operated on multiple levels. Me? I just wanted it over with. To walk out of here and go home. I didn't see what we had to gain here. Even if Zentas was behind the attacks on us, we weren't going to physically stop him. Sure, Butler was a good negotiator, but I didn't think he'd talk this guy out of what he wanted to do.

"I'm sure she's great," said Butler.

The door opened, and a bronze-skinned twenty-something-year-old woman in a dress that was a little too flashy for the office came in, pushing a cart.

"Drink?" asked Zentas.

"It's eleven in the morning," said Butler.

Zentas held out his hand. The woman poured whiskey from a crystal bottle with no label into a heavy glass, took two spherical ice cubes out of a cooler with tongs and dropped each into the drink. She brought it to Zentas. "It's five o'clock somewhere," he said.

"Sure," said Butler, and we all waited while the woman repeated the procedure. Butler sipped at his drink. "Oh, that's good."

"Of course. When I heard who was here, I broke out the expensive stuff."

"Is this the twenty-five year?"

"Good taste buds. It is. Have a seat. Can I get you one?" Zentas looked at me.

"I'm good," I said. I'd leave it to Butler to play the games. I wasn't smart enough for that. Not in this room. But here's what I know about a room full of smart guys: Punch them in the neck, and they stop talking. That, and that they always underrate the chances that someone might punch them in the neck.

I'd wait for my opportunity.

Zentas took a seat in the middle of one side of the table, facing me. That might have been random, or maybe he didn't want me at his back. Probably the latter. I didn't have a weapon, but I could easily kill him from behind. Not that that was the plan. Yet. I decided to call that plan B.

The two men sat face to face on either side of the table, neither taking their eyes off the other. I really just wanted them to fight and get it over with, but of course they wouldn't do that. Butler would have kicked his ass. On the other hand, I bet Zentas was the kind of guy who fought dirty, maybe went for the eyes. You can never be a hundred percent sure with a fight.

"You wanted to see me," Zentas said, finally. "I imagine it must be pretty important."

Butler studied him a bit longer. I'm not sure if he was trying to gain some sort of information or just making the rich man wait. "I want to know what you're up to."

"Running a mega-corporation? Creating an environment for cutting-edge R and D? You're going to have to be more specific."

"I'm talking about how you killed Parnavic."

Zentas didn't react at all. Almost like he didn't hear it, except that there was no way he didn't. Dude was cold.

"And Whiteman."

Still nothing. It didn't seem to bother Butler—he didn't let anything show. But we were losing. If Zentas sat there and said nothing, then we'd wasted a trip. Worse, we'd exposed ourselves for nothing.

Maybe Butler understood that too, because he continued, "And the team that you sent to kill me."

Zentas sat silently for fifteen or twenty seconds before finally speaking. "Oh. *That*."

Well shit. Was that an admission?

"Yeah. *That*."

"What do you want to know?" asked Zentas, as if they were discussing the weather instead of murder.

"Why'd you do it?"

"Tell me you didn't come all the way here to ask me a question you already know the answer to."

"Somebody tries to kill me, I want to hear him say why. Humor me."

It was more than that, of course. He'd made it personal, but in truth, he and I both had recorders. Tiny things with almost no metal that we were able to sneak through the scanners. For an admission to be useful, Zentas had to say it explicitly.

Zentas sighed as dramatically as a teenager talking to their parents. "Fine. You know about the technology find on Taug."

"So what? So do a lot of people."

"Two fewer, now," said Zentas. Shit—he really was cold. Parnavic and Whiteman were real people. Or had been. Even if one of them had been a piece of crap.

"But dozens of people know about it," said Butler. "What good does it do you to kill a few? Unless your plan is to hunt down every soldier who went to the site."

"That would be difficult, even for me," Zentas admitted. "But it's not about *knowing*. Come on, Carl. You're smarter than that. It's about telling."

"Everyone talks."

"Sure. But nobody listens. Except to a few people. Some soldier puts some wild ass theory out on the net, we discredit it. You'd be amazed what bots can do on social media. Make the guy seem crazy. Conspiracy theories arise all the time."

"Parnavic would have filed official reports by now."

Zentas shrugged. "Filed them to the wrong people, apparently."

"Apparently?"

"There's more than one way to keep someone from talking."

"Bribes," said Butler.

"Ugly word. I prefer investments. But yes."

I started sliding surreptitiously toward the door. Butler said that they couldn't harm us inside the building, that it would be too obvious. But I knew a villain monologue when I heard one. When the bad guy tells his nefarious plan, he doesn't intend for the hero to get away to tell the story. Butler would sense it too. He had to. Hopefully, he'd stall long enough for me to get into position. I was unarmed, but I'd fix that when the first person came through the door with a weapon. They'd have to be careful because they couldn't afford to hit Zentas. I had no such restriction. That would cause the hesitation that I needed to take someone down. From there, I'd play it by feel. Either shoot our way out or take Zentas hostage.

They probably thought they had us. That helped. Like I said before, people rarely account for someone simply punching them.

"I'm surprised you'd admit it," said Butler, in a voice that seemed anything but surprised. "The Strands. They were part of it?"

"One part. Yes," said Zentas.

Shit. I'd known that to some degree before we came, but hearing it confirmed . . . yeah. I'd fucked that one up pretty royally. I owed Butler a drink . . . a lot of drinks. But for now, I had to make sure he got out of here to enjoy them.

"Why'd you take this meeting?" asked Butler.

Ego. Obviously.

Zentas turned his palms up. "Call me nostalgic. Maybe I wanted to see your face one last time."

"There's still time. Maybe we can work this out," said Butler.

"What? You tell me that you won't talk, and I take you at your word?"

"Sure," said Butler. "I could keep quiet."

"You're not the kind of guy who lets things go."

"Why do I care who gets the tech?"

Zentas snorted. "Even if I believed that you'd be willing to let me exploit the find, no way could you turn your back on the murders."

"Whiteman was a piece of shit. You find a way to make it right with Parnavic's family, I can come to terms with it. I'm sure you can be creative, given how much money you stand to make."

"So now I'm supposed to believe that you're for sale."

"Everyone's got a price, right? I've done it before. Ask your own people. I walked away from Taug for a payout."

"Money to the dead assistant's family," said Zentas. His people had briefed him about Ramirez's daughter. Of course they had.

"And I stayed completely out of it after that," said Butler.

"Leaving it in the hands of Parnavic, who you believed would ensure that nothing fell into the wrong pockets."

"That was never a guarantee. I can walk away from this. Make me an offer. Tell me what you'll do for Parnavic's wife and kids." On the surface, the words came across like a desperate plea, but Butler didn't sound remotely desperate.

Yet Zentas seemed to actually be considering it. I don't know how he could be. In my mind, anything that he did for the family would be an open admission that the death hadn't been an accident. But they were smarter than me about this kind of thing. Maybe they had ideas. "You're good," said Zentas, finally.

"I try," said Butler.

"You almost had me. For a second there, I was actually thinking about it."

"That's because it's a good offer. The best one you're going to get."

"You think so?" asked Zentas.

"Given the alternatives?"

"Which are?"

"That I burn your entire company to the ground. And this time I make it stick." Butler said it not as a possibility, but a certainty.

Zentas actually laughed. "The ego on you."

I had to bite my tongue at that one. The ego on *both* these guys. Except I was pretty sure Butler was faking it for a purpose. Not that he *didn't* have an ego. Just that he had it in check right now. I did want him to finish up. We had what we needed on recorder, but it didn't do us any good unless we got out of there since we couldn't transmit.

Butler gave an exaggerated shrug. "Don't say I didn't warn you."

"You obviously had some plan when you came here. I don't know what it was, but I can tell you what you accomplished."

"What's that?" asked Butler.

"You got another guy killed." Zentas looked at me. It wasn't subtle.

I immediately started calculating the odds that I could beat him to death before somebody could get into the room and stop me. I'm not great at math . . . but they weren't zero.

As if he could read my mind—and honestly, it was a pretty open book right then—Butler put a hand up to hold me back. "You're not going to do a thing to us. Everyone in the galaxy knows we walked in here. We're going to walk out."

"Absolutely. Wouldn't dream of it," said Zentas. "Thanks for that, by the way."

"For what?" asked Butler, seeming for the first time to be legitimately confused.

"For letting—as you put it—the entire galaxy know your location." He paused, maybe wondering if he needed to elaborate. He did. At least for me. "You're a man with a *lot* of enemies, and you've been in here long enough for them to get into position. When you walk out the door and someone kills you today, well . . . it could be any one of them."

So that was the plan. Okay. Assuming we did make it to the door, we had something for them. We'd exposed ourselves by coming here. Of course we had plans to make it out.

"Ah. So you think you're in the clear," said Butler.

They'd know we had plans, of course. That much wouldn't surprise them.

"I think you're as good as dead. Now, if you'll excuse me, I have a business to pretend not to run."

And that was it. It would come down to whose plans were better. We'd had more time to put ours together, but still, I didn't know our odds.

But, again, they weren't zero.

When the door opened for Zentas to leave, I tensed, ready to put a wristlock on whoever came through. I held up when it was the woman in the tight skirt who had led us in. Zentas stopped to address her.

"Please see these two gentlemen to the front door. Don't let them out of your sight."

"Yes, Mr. Zentas."

That was inconvenient. Not the part about not getting jumped. I was fine with that, though it would have at least gotten things over with. But the escort limited us.

"Right this way, gentlemen," she said, as if it was the most natural thing in the world. To her, maybe it was. All she was doing was escorting somebody to the door. Maybe she didn't know that it was to our death. Or planned death, at least. It was a good move by Zentas. She'd control our pace on the exit, and she'd make a horrible hostage. Not that I was planning on taking a hostage. But I wasn't *not* planning on it.

We were about to play a high-stakes game. We had our recordings. If we lived, we won. Zentas had to *really* believe in his side. I started to think about what that might look like, preparing myself to react. We'd talked it all through—me and the team— but it didn't hurt to review. We had to deal with immediate threats first. Someone popping us right as we left the building. A sniper on a roof across the street. Someone walking down the sidewalk. Right now, Zentas could be letting people know the exact moment we'd hit the door.

That's why our plan had three stages. Survive the exit. Disappear. Get off the planet. Stage one carried the most risk, so we'd gone way over the top with that part of our plan. I couldn't contact C, Ganos, or the others. I had to trust that they'd done their jobs. We'd know soon enough.

We entered the elevator ahead of the woman, who followed us in. She pressed the button for the ground floor as easy listening music played softly from a speaker. "We got some good information," I said, flashing Butler my device.

"No, we didn't," he said.

I frowned. "How do you figure?"

"He had something jamming recordings."

I glanced at the woman, but she stared straight ahead at the closed door. Butler was clearly fine talking in front of her, but I didn't want to be so blunt as to mention that. "You sure?"

"Go ahead. Play it back."

I checked my device. Nothing. He was right. Of course he was. He always is when it comes to that kind of thing. "What now?"

"Nothing changes. Do your job."

"Roger." I wasn't saying anything else. Maybe the woman wasn't listening. Maybe she was. But they'd learn my plan only when I started executing it.

We reached the lobby in silence, and Butler and I headed for the door without waiting for the woman to show us the way. She hurried to keep up. She had her orders. But we weren't letting her set the timing. Our people would be watching. Unless somebody had taken them out. If that had happened—if we'd lost the pre-fight—then this was about to be the shortest trip ever.

Outside, horns blared, giving me my first indication that at least part of our plan had worked. No traffic was moving in front of the building. Ganos had turned all the lights red, creating gridlock, making it harder for anybody to get to us by vehicle. The enemy had only an hour or so to put things in place, so delays mattered. Our team had been in position before the traffic jam started.

We reached the revolving doors and slid left to the standard door beside it. The door that was normally the entrance. Anything we could do to switch things up.

Through the door, we sprinted left. If everything had gone to plan, our team had cleared away any threats from the front of the building, but we weren't hanging around to find out. C had worked counter-sniper in the area, so we probably didn't have to worry about someone putting a bullet into us from long range. *Probably.* But even the best professionals can miss something.

I got out ahead of Butler, which wasn't difficult since he has a bad wheel. Three people occupied the sidewalk between us and the corner. Two women and a man. I had about two seconds to assess them as threats before we reached them. It's amazing how your mind can slow things down in moments like that.

The lone woman wore an expensive business suit with a skirt, hands visible, looking at her device. The man and woman, standing together, were dressed more casually. No visible weapons. His hands were visible, one of hers wasn't. Probably not a threat, but I couldn't rule them out. Not in the time that I had. It would suck to put our entire plan together only to have it derailed by someone touching a stun stick to one of us as we ran past.

Not happening.

I shifted direction slightly and shoulder-checked the man hard enough to throw him into the woman, knocking her off balance. The guy yelled, first in surprise, and then in anger, but we blew past him, and I didn't look back. There would be more people around the corner. Probably innocent civilians.

I reached the silver hovercar—the most common color and model in the city—about three steps ahead of Butler. Both doors opened automatically, and I turned to scan the area while Butler dove into the back, joining Clement there. Two men came running toward us from the direction we'd come. They weren't going to reach us. I piled into the front seat. The signal in front of us immediately turned green. It had been red for quite some time, so nobody expected it to turn green except for Kim, who was driving, and she sped off before anybody else could react.

I put in my earpiece to give me comms with the rest of the team, and turned in my seat, trying to get a last glimpse of the two men who had chased us. One was talking, definitely on a comm. Passing the word of our temporary escape, most likely. I didn't like that, but it told me that our planning hadn't been for nothing. Butler sometimes thinks I'm paranoid. I bet he didn't now.

We took a right onto a street with almost no traffic. Immediately after we did, the signal behind us turned green. I couldn't see it, but the backed-up traffic from the other side of the intersection would have surged forward, completely swallowing the one-way road behind us. Good luck if anybody was following, unless they randomly happened to be at the front of that particular intersection.

You'd think that you couldn't hack an entire city's traffic grid.

You'd be wrong. You probably *shouldn't*. But that's more of an ethical discussion than a practical one. Ganos told us that she could do it, saying something about getting in through the EMS computers, and we'd believed her. I think her exact words were, "The security is complete shit. It's amazing that nobody's done it before." She also told us that it would draw massive attention after the fact, and that the authorities would track her down within a couple of days. Good thing we didn't plan on being on the planet when that happened.

We made another signal-light-assisted turn onto another one-way street. How Ganos and Alanson had figured out how to keep some roads mostly clear and others completely gridlocked, I didn't know. It made me rethink everything I ever thought about traffic. But only for a second.

"There's a drone up." Alanson's voice across the comm. He was somewhere on top of a building, watching the route and scanning for exactly this. Drones were illegal in the city. That didn't mean somebody wouldn't use them—*we* were going to, if we needed them, so why not others.

"Could be a police drone," said Butler.

"Could be," Alanson responded.

"Splash it anyway," said Butler.

"Roger. Launching counter-drone now. Thirty seconds, if I get it first try." Alanson had his own drone that held a single-use EMP charge. He'd fly it near the other drone and then trigger it, killing them both. Hopefully, they wouldn't do too much damage when they crashed.

I looked back at Butler. "You sure about that?"

"No," he admitted. "But I'm not taking chances."

"Concur," I said, glad that we were on the same page.

"How long until we do the switch?" he asked.

"Twelve blocks," said Kim.

"Roger. Alanson, you've got about two minutes. Let us know when it's done."

"Wilco."

The net stayed quiet for a bit, and so did we. Clement watched our tail, I scanned up front, looking for threats so that Kim could focus on the road. Butler was probably running odds or something. Not that I'm complaining. Those thoughts in his head had saved my ass often enough. Got me into a lot of trouble, too, now that I think about it. We'd call it a wash.

If we got out of this.

"Splash," said Alanson.

"Roger," said Butler. That ended the drone threat for now.

A minute later, we made another turn, this time into two-way traffic. "Switch coming," said Kim.

We readied to exit the car. The plan was for three of us to jump out and switch to a vehicle driven by C traveling the opposite direction. Kim, who was mostly unknown, would continue on in her vehicle. Before too long she'd abandon it and melt away into the city. As a newer team member, she had the best chance to avoid attention. We'd link back up with her later, once we'd lost any pursuit.

We stopped in the middle of the street, drawing a chorus of honks from behind us. C was driving a blue car, wheeled, not hover, and stopped in the lane closest to us in the other direction.

"Go!" I said. Butler and I exited one side, Clement the other. He had to run around the car, which drew even more horns.

"Get outta the fucking road!" a man yelled.

I'd have flipped him off, but I was keeping my head down, making it as hard as possible for anybody to identify me. Within a few seconds we were in the other vehicle and moving again. In theory, we should have been clear then.

Theory isn't worth much in combat.

CHAPTER 19

Butler

WHEN WE TRANSFERRED to the car driven by C, I felt safer. That lasted about a minute and a half. Right up to the point when Clement announced, "We've got company."

"How?" asked Mac.

It was a reasonable question, but the wrong one. We didn't have time for how. "Are you sure?" I asked.

"Police vehicle. Just turned on behind us. A hundred meters back. Ran the signal. Lights on."

There were three possibilities. One, it was someone working for Zentas out to get us. Two, it was legit police who were going to stop us and potentially take us in for . . . something. We'd definitely violated multiple laws. Or three, they weren't after us at all and had randomly turned onto the same street. I had to decide quickly what to do about their appearance on our tail, and two out of three reasons for their presence were bad. But if I acted against them and it was number three, we'd be buying ourselves trouble we didn't have to.

"Ganos. Flip the next signal right behind us. Alanson, if the police car runs it, take it out." It didn't solve the problem completely.

Police in their normal duty might run that light to get to an emergency. But it was the best we could do. We were almost to the highway that would take us out of the city, and we had to be sure nobody followed us.

We went through the intersection, and I really hoped that the police vehicle wouldn't follow. But of course it did.

"Drone inbound," said Alanson.

I turned to watch. A small drone slammed into the hood of the police vehicle, which turned hard to the right and crashed into a parked car. The lights went out, the vehicle incapacitated by the virus program that the drone carried. Well . . . if we weren't in trouble with the police before, now we were. Though it would be hard to connect our vehicle to the drone since we had no control over it. I doubted they'd see it that way. The real problem was, if they *had* been after us, they now had a description of our vehicle. The virus would have shut down comms from their vehicle, but they could call it in on their personal devices.

Thankfully, Mac had a plan for that. I'd pushed for only one vehicle switch. He'd insisted on two. Seemed pretty smart now. C raced six more blocks and then pulled to the curb on the right side. We jumped out and hopped over a guard rail, half running, half sliding on the steeply sloped cement. I took a few running steps on the flat ground at the bottom before I fully regained control of my momentum, and then I followed C to a new vehicle, this one a silver utility. Part of me hoped that the police *did* have a line on the blue car. Maybe they'd find it and turn it back in to the rental agency. Might save me and my fictitious company some money.

Within a minute, we were back on the road and headed out of

the city. All we had to do now was get to the rendezvous point and link up with Kim, Alanson, and Ganos.

Of course it couldn't be that easy.

"Police are entering the building I'm on top of," said Alanson.

"Get out of there," I said.

"Already moving. There's a chance they traced one of my drone signals."

"Roger. Ditch everything you can." It was reflexive. He didn't need my instructions. He knew the drill.

"Going dark," he said.

WHEN WE REACHED our destination three and a half hours later, Ganos was already there, and Kim had checked in. She was about twenty minutes out. We hadn't heard from Alanson. He didn't know our current location—we hadn't told him or Kim, planning to give them the information when they called in. All he knew was which road to take out of the city, because what he didn't know, he couldn't spill. At least we had that going for us. But I didn't want to leave him behind.

C pulled our vehicle into a warehouse, and we disembarked. There are a limited number of ways off a planet. Almost all of them go via orbital platforms, and all of those were known, tracked, and run by the government. You could smuggle things through them—we'd proven that on the way in. But that wouldn't work again. Too many people with too many resources were looking for us now, and they'd focus on those obvious choke points. That left us with one of the few other options: a ship that left from the surface, which is a really expensive option. Escaping a gravity well is never cheap.

We'd chosen a private launch facility, and not one of those closest to the urban center. Those were more regulated and might draw the attention of Caliber and their eyes. This one was . . . more discreet. It serviced mostly rich people and people who wanted to avoid attention and would definitely take another significant chunk out of my net worth. But with our lives on the line, I'd pay whatever I had to pay.

"What about Alanson?" asked Ganos.

"That's a tough one." I'd made tough decisions before. Even sacrifices. But we were a smaller team now. It hit harder. But if we stayed on Talca, eventually Zentas's people would catch up to us, so we had to go. "I think there are three possibilities. The police have him, Zentas has him, or he's on his own and unable to call."

"I hope it's the third," said Mac. "Shit all we can do about the other two." He was right. If someone had him, we'd have to go after him if we wanted him back, and in doing that, we'd expose ourselves.

Ganos didn't look so sure. I couldn't read Clement to see where he came down on the issue, but regardless, I needed to explain it.

"I hate leaving anyone behind. If we had even fifty-fifty odds of retrieving him and not ending up captured or dead ourselves, we'd be planning how to do it. What do we rate our odds at here?"

"I don't know," said Ganos. "Ten percent?"

"Less than that," said Mac. "Maybe five. Too many people looking for us, and the longer we stay here, the bigger their advantages get. If they have him, they'll use him as a trap, and they have us way outgunned."

I nodded. "Agreed. I don't ever want to leave someone behind, but I don't see another option."

Mac shrugged. "That's why you get the big bucks. To make the hard decisions."

Clement nodded. Ganos hesitated, but after a few seconds, she nodded too.

"Okay then. It's settled," I said. "We'll give him a little longer, and I'll do what I can to keep him safe here once we're gone."

Thankfully, I wasn't without allies on Talca. I hadn't talked to her in a while, but I used one of my burner devices to call Karen Plazz. She wouldn't recognize the caller, but she was an investigative reporter for the *Talca Times*—one of the most respected news organizations in the galaxy—so I assumed she got unrecognized calls all the time. How happy she'd be to receive mine, I didn't know. We'd first met on Cappa, and we'd had an up and down relationship since then. Probably because I tended to try to use her to accomplish things and she wanted a good story more than she wanted my friendship. But she was what I had, so I called.

As expected, she picked up. "Karen Plazz."

"This is your friend you met on Cappa. Don't say my name—there's a good chance that someone is scanning comms on the planet looking for me."

The other end remained silent for a couple of seconds. "Hang up. I'll call you back in sixty seconds from a secure line."

True to her word, my burner buzzed a minute later. "How secure are we?"

"Secure enough," she said. "It's not my first day on the job. How are you, Carl?"

"I'm in trouble." No sense in sugarcoating it. She'd see through it anyway.

"And you want my help. You can't see me, but right now I'm making my surprised face. Oh. Wait. Not at all surprised. You only call when you need something."

"I'm really sorry about that."

"Are you, though?"

"I don't have a ton of time," I said.

"And that answers that question. I saw that you were here on Talca. I'm guessing that didn't go well?"

"If you consider a psychotic billionaire trying to kill you as not going well, then I guess we can say it's not going well."

"Zentas?"

"You know any other psychotic billionaires?"

"You'd be surprised," she said. "You have any proof?"

"My word. Mac's word. Zentas basically confessed."

"Not good enough," she said. "If I try to run with that, Caliber's lawyers would bury me."

"I figured. But I was hoping you could help me out with something else."

"To refresh the slate, I don't owe you one anymore, Carl."

I breathed out a deep breath. I had to decide how much to tell her, but if I'm being honest, I think I'd made that decision when I decided to call. "I've got a bigger story for you."

"I'm listening."

"There's a moon called Taug. It orbits—"

"Ridia 5," she said. "I'm aware. I keep up with your exploits."

"Okay. Well, what you don't know is that while I was there, we discovered what we think was an alien ship."

The line stayed silent for a couple seconds before she finally spoke. "A UFO?"

"Technically, it wasn't flying—"

"Carl."

"I don't care what you call it. Whatever it was, it had technology beyond anything in the galaxy."

"I've heard about that. Rumors and conspiracy theories. All the typical crazies."

That fit. Like Zentas had said, they didn't have to kill everyone. Just lose them in the noise. "Except it's real."

"You're sure?" she said in a tone that suggested she thought I might be one of the crazies.

"I saw it."

She considered it for a moment. "Anybody else see it?"

"Mac."

"He's not going to be a great source, since he's going to confirm whatever you say. Sorry."

"A soldier named Barnes. She's dead. Lieutenant Colonel Parnavic. He's dead."

"Lot of dead people. That does seem suspicious."

"Alanson," I added, seeing my in. "He saw it. He's missing."

"That's better than dead, at least. The military was there. Was there an investigation?"

"There was. Or at least, they told me they were starting one. I don't know what came of it, but Zentas suggested that he'd had them bury it. It's in Caliber's best interest for nobody to hear about it, and they have the connections to know who to bribe. They're probably exploiting the ship right now. We don't have a lot of time before it's too late."

"You want me to send a team to Taug?"

I considered it for a second. I hadn't thought of that possibility.

"I don't think so. Too dangerous. Caliber will try to stop them. Probably violently."

She stayed silent for a bit. "Tough situation. I believe you, Carl. As farfetched as it is, I believe you. But that's the problem—*because* it's so farfetched. So unbelievable. The best I could do without proof is to run something about the rumors, talk about how maybe there's something to them. Not sure what that will accomplish, though."

"Might do more harm than good," I said. What I didn't say was that it might paint a target on her back. She knew the risks in this business. "There's another story. The cover-up. Someone in the government—someone in the military—knows about this and is specifically suppressing it."

"Still goes back to evidence. I can look into the investigation with the military, but if they buried it, they'll work hard to keep it that way. If you had a specific *name* of the person doing the cover-up, I could at least shake the tree, see what fell out. See if I could get them to meet, get them to slip up and give me something. You have a name?"

I didn't. Parnavic might have. If he'd had it, maybe someone else on his team did. If they'd share it—that was a different question. Certainly not officially. But maybe if I got them face to face. But that would mean a trip to Taug. "I don't have a name. Where's that leave us? What do you need other than a name?"

"Video. Show me the site."

I nodded to myself. If I'd been thinking, I'd have gotten that when I was there the first time. Someone had to have taken pictures, but like before, that line of thought ended with Parnavic's death or with someone in his former organization. I had to make a decision. I had a way off the planet and a fast ship waiting to take me home. Ridia 5 wasn't that far out of the way. "Can you get a camera to Taug?"

"I thought you said it was too dangerous."

"I'll find a way to make it less dangerous."

She hesitated. "You're going there?"

Of course I was going there. "I'd rather not say."

"I'll get someone there as fast as possible. They'll probably send someone from Ridia 2, so they'll beat you there. You know. Hypothetically."

"Right. One last thing. I need a favor."

"Remember when I said I didn't owe you any favors?"

"Consider this a pre-payment for the favor you're going to owe me after I get you this massive story."

"Maybe. What do you need?"

"I'm going to send you the file of a guy named Alanson."

"The one who went missing?"

"Yeah. There's a good chance that he either got arrested or that Zentas has him. Either way, he's in danger."

"From the police?"

"Whiteman died in prison."

"The archaeologist? You're saying that wasn't suicide?"

"I can't prove it. But yeah, that's what I'm saying."

"You're full of all kinds of great stories that I can't use without proof."

"I want you to try to find Alanson. If you do, he can confirm what I said about the alien ship. He might even have footage. Guy is a walking camera. But mostly I want you to keep him safe."

She thought about it for a couple of seconds. "Yeah. I can do that. No promises, but I'll shine some light around and at least make it harder on whoever has him."

"Thanks. I'll send the file."

"Okay. Carl?"

"Yeah?"

"How about you? Do you need help? I have some contacts that might be able to get you some protection here."

For a second, I considered it. But we had to get moving, and I didn't trust that *anybody* could keep us safe on Talca. "I think I'll be okay. But I do have to go."

"Okay. Be safe."

"I'll be in touch."

DESPITE THE INDICATION that I gave to Plazz, we weren't necessarily going to Taug. Part of that was deception—I trusted her, but she could slip. More significant, going to Taug was a somewhat predictable move, making it dangerous. I needed to assess our pilot before I made a decision—see if they could get us there safely. And before I did that, I needed to check in with the team again, see if they were on board. They'd followed me into danger on Talca, but that was a *known* danger with a plan they believed in. Taug presented different risks altogether. I needed them to make up their own minds. Ganos, in particular, had already shown some reluctance, and given her previous experiences on Taug, this was asking a lot.

But I wanted to talk to everybody together, and our launch window came before I got the chance. No matter what else we did, we had to get off planet. We strapped in while we pulled four Gs, so we didn't have the opportunity to talk until we rendezvoused with our charter ship in orbit. The pilot met us and got us situated in comfortable chairs in the passenger compartment, and we took off. Either way, we were headed for the Ridia system, so I had some time before I had to inform him of our final destination. We'd elected for the non-sedation trip, but we still wanted to get there as fast as possible, so he'd be doing his initial acceleration at two Gs before later slowing to a more comfortable one point one. The specialty chairs would help with all of that.

Breathing a bit labored because of the Gs, it still only took five minutes to run down my conversation with Plazz to the team, and then I filled them in on my plan for the moon around Ridia 5. I gave them all a few minutes to sit with it, and then I leaned over toward Ganos—at least as much as one can lean at two Gs.

"How are you feeling?"

"Not a fan of Taug," she said, clearly understating the look on her face.

"I think that's very reasonable. If you don't want to go, I'll make arrangements. It's no problem whatsoever."

"You going to cancel the mission if I don't go?"

"No. I don't think so. Not if everybody else is in."

"You don't have another tech. So that pretty much settles it, right? I've got to go."

"We'll definitely miss you if you're not with us. I'm not going to lie about that."

She snorted. "Miss me. You'll get yourselves killed in the first fifteen minutes."

We might do that anyway.

I let Ganos have the time she needed to think. Part of me *wanted* her to say no. To head home to relative safety. But the selfish part of me knew we always had a better chance with her along. That part of me wanted her on the team.

That part of me is an asshole.

"I'm in," she said, finally. "One condition."

"Name it."

"You don't leave me alone. Ever. Not for even a minute."

My instinct was to say yes without reservation, but I took a few seconds to think it through. We didn't have a huge team, and losing Alanson meant we were down a team member. I didn't know what help I could expect from the military. At the same time, I couldn't deny her request. If we couldn't protect her, we shouldn't bring her. The only way I could keep someone with her might be to bring her along wherever we went. And if we got into the shit, that would hardly be safer. "How do you feel about rolling out?"

"On a mission? Like to the alien crash site?"

"Yeah."

"With all of you?" She knew that and was buying time to consider it.

"Of course. Nobody left alone."

She sat there for a good bit without speaking. Mac, who was seated at her other side, was no longer hiding his interest in the conversation. I'm not sure if Ganos noticed that, but she turned to him. "What do you think?"

"You had basic. You know how to use a Bitch."

"I mean . . . not *well*. I know you point the shooty end at the other guy."

"We'll train you up. It'll be okay." He didn't mean that we'd put her out there on the front line. He couldn't. But Mac doesn't lie, and his confidence seemed to buoy her. If I'm being honest, it picked me up a little bit too.

"Okay. I'll do it," she said.

"Great. Glad to have you aboard."

There wasn't a lot of drama with the rest of the team. C joined immediately. Clement asked about compensation, which was fair. He was basically a mercenary at this point, so I had no problem with him making sure the financials made sense. Kim nodded her agreement.

That left the pilot. This one was more complicated. It wasn't if he'd agree as much as if I determined he could do the job. I waited for the two G burn to end, and then I got up and knocked on the cabin door. The pilot stepped out, a tall guy, pale skin, blond hair, and perfect teeth. He looked like he stepped off the cover of *Pilot Model Weekly*. That's probably not a real thing.

"What can I do for you?" he asked.

"What's your background?" I asked.

"What do you mean?"

"I mean what did you do before you started flying expensive charters?"

He studied me, understandably cautious. "What's that matter?"

There was nothing to do but be honest with the guy. It was his ship. "I'm considering a change to our itinerary, but it's one that might present a challenge."

"If you don't tell me what the challenge is, there's no chance I'm taking it on. And since this is my ship, you might as well lay it out."

I liked that. He was confrontational, but that's the kind of thing we needed. After all, we were headed for a confrontation.

"I'm thinking about a stop on Taug. A moon orbiting Ridia 5."

"Never been there. But I've been to other moons around 5. I'm sure the orbital mechanics are somewhat similar. But that's not what you're asking, is it?"

Perceptive, too. Another good sign. "It's not. The catch is, someone may want to stop us from getting there."

"Someone's after you?"

"Yeah. That a problem?"

"No. I kind of figured that when you wanted to meet in flight and not on an orbital station. Not really something people do if they're okay being seen. How bad is it?"

"Someone wants us dead."

"Like an ex?" he asked.

"Like a multibillion-mark corporation." I half expected him to stop the ship and drop us off right there in cold space. Or at least consider it.

"Okay," he said after a few seconds. "Good to know. Should have mentioned that up front. It'll change the way I do things."

"How?"

"Space is big. You'll never see another soul out here. But the mechanics of space in the modern world actually put us closer together than you might think. Flying through gates, there are natural routes. They change as things in the galaxy move, but at any given moment, there's an optimal path. We can offset that a bit. Lower the odds that anyone tracks us."

"We got away clean. Nobody knows we're on this ship."

"Sure. Probably not. But maybe we'll play it safe anyway."

I nodded. Not that I had a choice—as he'd said, it was his ship—but I didn't hate his plan. Given that he took the whole situation in stride, it seemed best to just ask him his thoughts on the rest of it. "What do you think about Taug?"

"You asked my background. I flew for the military."

"Transports?" I asked.

"Ground support."

"I knew I liked you." Ground support pilots were a different breed. Almost more grunt than pilot. They'd saved my ass more times than I could remember. "So we're going to do this."

"I can't do a forced landing against opposition. I don't have chaff or any other countermeasures."

"I just need you to get us down to the military base. I'll get us clearance to land."

He shook his head. "*I'll* get us clearance. If you're as hot as I think you are, we don't want to give any indication that you're on board until you walk down the ramp."

"Fair enough." I reached out my hand and he took it.

"Brad Sanders," he said.

"Carl Butler."

"Oh. Well fuck me."

CHAPTER 20

Butler

I STOOD BY AS Sanders called for clearance, listening in as he talked his way into a previously unscheduled landing at the same facility I'd departed about two months prior. It wasn't that I didn't trust him. Okay, it was a *little bit* that. Taug, for its part, hadn't gotten any more appealing in the interim, still all gray and brown and barren with most of its facilities underground and those on top lacking any sort of aesthetic appeal. The surface landing pad immediately lowered us into an underground facility. Mac took Clement and disembarked first to ensure that we were clear. I watched via camera. It seemed like overkill. Even if anybody knew we were coming and beat us here, they couldn't jump us as we got off our ship. Too much security. They'd attack us later. But I wanted to see who showed up to greet us. That might tell me who knew we'd arrived and indicate how we might be treated.

Nobody came. No military liaison, nobody from any of the corporations. Not even a cargo specialist or fuel handler from the port. I couldn't draw any conclusions from their absence, since we hadn't been scheduled to land. They might simply be off duty or at work on another pad. Still, the deserted landing pad did make me glad that we had an arsenal at our disposal and people who could use it. Hopefully, it wouldn't come to that, but if we had to shoot it out, I'd prefer to do it while we still had a ship we could escape in. We wouldn't have it for long. The pilot had been accommodating, but he drew the line at sticking around on the ground. I didn't blame him. If I didn't have to, I wouldn't have spent any more time on Taug either.

We headed to the only hotel on the moon, as it didn't seem prudent to show up at the military base carrying a dozen footlockers full of weapons and equipment. C found a motorized cart somewhere while Mac and Clement discussed security—who would stand fast at the hotel and who would escort me to the base. I stayed out of their way. Sometimes I make fun of Mac for being cautious or paranoid. Right now, it was good business. Because if Zentas or his people predicted we'd come here, who knew what might be waiting? They could be anywhere. Part of me wondered if my house would be standing when I made it back to Ridia 2.

We got rooms, and Mac assigned them. They doubled up in a couple of them and left a couple of others empty as deceptions and workspaces. Kim and Ganos moved in together, which met the promise that I'd made to Ganos. I didn't worry about the others. Mac would handle it.

With that settled, he and I set out for the military compound. I expected him to bring another security person, but he said he had it covered. We stopped at a checkpoint that hadn't been there on our last visit, manned by a skinny private with a sidearm in a holster on her right thigh.

"ID's, please," she said.

Mac glanced at me, but what was I going to do? I took out my retired ID card and showed it to her, unsure if it would get me through. They'd upped their security, which made sense, given how things had gone on our last trip with Ganos being kidnapped. I did wonder if Parnavic had instituted it or if they'd put it in place after his death.

The private stepped aside and allowed us to pass.

"How long has this checkpoint been here?"

"A few weeks," she said. I wanted to ask if it came before or after Parnavic's death, but I couldn't think of how to phrase it without it sounding weird, so I let it go.

"Thanks. Is the new commander on the ground yet? I'd like to meet them."

"Not yet, sir. I think later this week. But they don't really tell me much."

"Thanks again."

We reached the front door of the headquarters without further hindrance, only to find that they'd installed a guard there too, inside the double doors. A big corporal sat behind a small desk. He stood when we entered.

"Colonel Butler for Sergeant Major Davenport." I didn't like to advertise my presence or throw my weight around, but everyone would know soon enough, and we were in a hurry. The corporal went to the comm and made a quick call, and the sergeant major appeared not long after.

"Sir. Mac. Didn't expect to see you two back here." The big man gave away nothing with his demeanor, which was neither welcoming nor standoffish. He could have been noting the weather for all the emotion he showed.

"We didn't plan on it. Can we talk in your office? I've got to ask you something."

"You should probably talk with Major Xavier, sir. She's acting commander. At least until Colonel Exley arrives in three days."

Exley. Not someone I knew. That happened more and more, since I'd been out so long now. "She's welcome to be there, but I need to talk to you." I'd met Xavier. If I talked to her, she'd let me talk her into anything. In theory, that was exactly what I needed, but I wanted Davenport there for his experience and the counsel he'd provide her . . . and me. If I knew anything, it was that sergeants major—and especially this one—wouldn't buy into anything unless they truly believed. He'd be the first one to call bullshit. We needed that. Because as good as Mac and I were, we could still fall into a groupthink trap.

Davenport thought about it for a few seconds and then nodded. "Okay. I'll get her. We'll all meet together."

Mac and I sat on a low sofa in the sergeant major's office. He sat behind his desk, and Xavier closed the door behind her, then leaned back against it.

"There's no good way to say this, so I'm just going to put it out there. Lieutenant Colonel Parnavic's death wasn't an accident." Davenport and Xavier glanced at each other. I'd expected shock, maybe denial. They showed neither. "You don't seem surprised to hear it."

"We've talked about it," Davenport admitted. "There are a lot of things that didn't add up. You have proof?"

"Nothing definitive that I can show you. But someone admitted it in front of Mac and me."

"Who?" asked Davenport.

"Drake Zentas. He runs Caliber—well, their parent company."

"The mining company?"

"Right."

"And he admitted it? Why would he do that?"

"Because he thought we were dead men," Mac said. "Turns out, we're harder to kill than he thought."

"So you came out here to bring the war to our doorstep," said Davenport.

I hadn't thought about it that way, but he did have a point. "If we had any other way out, we wouldn't have."

"So lay it out. You're here for a reason. What is it?" Davenport didn't seem angry. He just wanted to know, to get it over with. I could relate.

"We can't bring Parnavic back. But the same people who killed him want to kill us. The only way we put a stop to that is to expose everything."

"And you think you can do that here?" asked Xavier.

"Tell me this," I said. We'd only get one shot at this, and I wanted as much information as I could get before I played my only card. "You mentioned that some things didn't add up. What kind of things?"

Davenport studied me, maybe deciding how much to share. I did my best to give him my most trustworthy look. Whatever that is. Mostly I just hoped for the best. "The investigation stopped. They sent a colonel out here to do it—"

"Tackleroad," said Xavier.

"Right," continued Davenport. "Colonel Tackleroad. The first day or so, it all seemed legit. He was digging in, getting witness statements. All the stuff you expect. But then something changed."

"He got a message," said Xavier.

"Yeah. Encrypted. His eyes only. After that, his attitude changed. He stopped asking good questions, started rushing through things. Finished his report and told us we weren't to talk about it. Which—you've been around soldiers. Might as well tell them not to wake up in the morning as to not talk when there's bullshit afoot."

"How did Parnavic react?"

"About how you'd expect. He smelled a cover-up. He was pissed."

"And his flight went down right after that?"

"His flight *out to the site* went down," said Davenport.

"Which should have triggered *another* investigation," I said.

"It did. I have the results," said Xavier. "It stuck to the crash itself. The officer assigned—a major—said anything else was beyond the scope of his orders."

"Did you tell him what you thought? That there was more to it?"

Xavier shook her head. "No way. He wouldn't have listened to me. Someone had clearly read him the riot act before he got here. Anything I said, he'd have reported back somewhere. I figured it best to keep my mouth shut. Look for a better opportunity."

"And here you are," said Davenport.

"I don't know if I'm a better opportunity," I said. "Might be nobody will listen to me, either. We don't know how high up the cover-up goes. But I do have an ace in the hole. We have a major news organization that is willing to run the story."

"What's the catch?" asked Davenport. I didn't mind his skepticism. He was right. There was a big catch.

"We need physical evidence of the site. Video."

Xavier snorted. "Which is directly against our orders."

"You have orders not to take video?"

"We have orders not to go out there at all. They came right after the crash. I asked why—in the most respectful way that I could—got some bullshit about it not being safe. As if us being there caused the crash or something. At least that was the implication."

"Who gave the order?"

"Brigade. Came to me through Ops, but they assured me the old man had issued it himself."

"You talk to him? The Brigade Commander?" I asked.

"No, sir. Ops told me he didn't want to talk to me about it. To just fucking do it. Her words."

Xavier could have insisted. I almost said that—that any commander can talk to the commander at the next level—but I let it go. It might have helped show the true origin of the order, but her stint as commander was temporary, and she'd done the best she could. And she'd probably read the situation right. Who knows? If she'd pushed it, maybe she'd have ended up like Parnavic.

That the conspiracy seemed to run in the military and not just Caliber . . . that didn't sit well with me. No way did I believe that anybody in the chain had caused Parnavic's death. It was hard enough to believe that they were sweeping it under the rug, but they were. It couldn't be widespread, though. Too many people in the military will do the right thing, consequences be damned. But it only took a few who were dirty. Once that happened, it became hard to report a problem with any confidence. You might be talking to someone corrupt, or you might be talking to someone influenced by someone corrupt. For example, the Ops officer who told Xavier to let it go might be clean. She might have received an order that felt legit and passed it on. Might even have thought that she was doing Xavier a favor, giving her good advice to let it go.

Most of the time, there was still recourse. Take it higher up the chain or take it to the inspector general. But this . . . we had no idea how far up the chain it went. Caliber might have politicians putting pressure on the military at the highest level. That pressure might be personal or professional. The military legitimately needed resources, and the government held a lot of those strings. Whichever it was, we didn't have time to figure it out. Caliber held the alien crash site, and with the military out of the way, who knew what they were doing there?

But maybe we could figure *that* out.

"Can we get pictures of what's going on out there?"

Xavier shook her head. "No satellites."

"Still?" I found that suspicious.

"We've got comms stuff up, but they haven't sent us replacements for the picture takers yet."

"That's half your mission on this moon."

Xavier didn't respond, but her countenance said that she understood that obvious point. "That's high on my list of things to bring to the new boss. Maybe she'll have more pull."

"When does the new commander arrive? Seems like it's been a long time. I'd have expected a replacement by now."

"There's some bullshit going on with that, too," said Davenport. "We had a guy slated. Nothing official, but I got the name through backchannel. Then he was pulled, and we didn't hear anything for a while—not until they announced Exley."

I considered that. It could be a coincidence. Assignments

changed. But I didn't believe in coincidence—especially not in this situation. Someone might have wanted Exley here specifically. I'd been put in that spot, back on Cappa—sent to meet an agenda. She might not be dirty, but she might have been specifically chosen by someone higher because they knew she'd do what they wanted. She could be clean, but a certain kind of clean. "I think if we want to act, we have to do it before she arrives. She might be coming with very specific orders."

"If we were smart, we'd wait for her to arrive," said Davenport. He said it to me, but that was a hundred percent for Xavier's benefit.

"Yep. That's one way to look at it," I said.

"Book solution," said Mac. We were all on the same page with that.

"Right. By the book." Davenport let that hang for a minute, and then looked at me. "You're here for a reason. You want something. What's your pitch? What do you want, and what does a win look like?"

"That's a good question. If we make the situation public via the media, Caliber has to answer. We expose what they're doing. Obviously they're not going to admit to murder. But the more eyes we get on them, the harder it becomes for them to disappear with whatever's out there at the site."

"So we'll screw them over," said Davenport. He was leading me down a path, but I couldn't tell where he was taking me.

"Exactly."

"Revenge is fun. I like sticking it to people as much as the next guy. But it's not a great basis for a military decision."

I nodded. Here it was. My real pitch to get him on board. "It's not. But when you think this all the way through, it's not about the corporation at all. It's about the military. You can see it. The orders. Something up there." I let that hang for a couple seconds— the nebulous distinction that somebody at higher headquarters was screwing up. It was a concept as universal as the command structure itself. Somewhere, right now, a squad leader—a leader at the lowest level—was ranting about those bastards at platoon. "You said it yourself. The bullshit investigations. Orders that don't make sense. Failure to get you new equipment to fulfill your primary mission. Somebody, somewhere, is complicit in that. I don't know if it's a politician, an officer, or some combination. But you can see it as well as I can."

"Sure," said Davenport. "We see it. But what can we do about it? We don't know who is involved, but whoever it is, they're going to continue to bury the evidence. They have to. And they might bury *us* with it. Me? I don't care. Go ahead. Give me an excuse to retire and take my pension. But the major here . . . she has a career."

Xavier was taking it all in, listening to her advisor, who was providing her absolutely sound counsel.

"I'm not going to sugarcoat this," I said. "There's risk. If we go and we lose—if we fail to expose this, or if we're wildly wrong— then you can expect the heat." I turned directly to Xavier. "You might even get fired. They won't prosecute you, but like the sergeant major said, it could be the end of your career."

Mac looked at me like I was out of my mind. We'd come here for help, and I was giving her reasons *not* to help. But I wasn't done, and I think he knew that too, because he didn't say anything before I continued. "But you have to decide what kind of career you want to have. Decide if when you see something that you know is wrong whether you'll do the easy thing and turn a blind eye, or whether you'll step out and shine a light into the dark corners. Because if we *are* right—if we *win*—we'll use the spotlight on Caliber to expose the people in the military who helped them. We'll be making the organization a better place. Don't get me wrong. Not everybody above you is going to love you for that. But some of them will. The good ones."

Nobody spoke for what seemed like minutes but was probably seconds. Xavier broke the silence. "Sergeant Major? What do we do?"

"I'd offer to do it behind your back," he said. "But you're not that kind of officer. You're going to own it. And because of that, only you can make the call."

I couldn't fault the sergeant major's logic. He was doing exactly what he should.

"If I say yes, what does it look like? What specifically happens?"

"We'll need as much force as we can generate," said Mac. "We'll do an assessment, but we probably load up in every combat vehicle we can muster and make a drive. A long one. We can task the intel people to determine what the bad guys have, but without satellites, we're probably going in blind."

"You think they'll fight us for it?" asked Davenport.

"You think they won't?" I asked.

He grunted. They already had, once. Of course they'd fight. They couldn't afford to let us win.

"Who leads it?" asked Xavier. It was a shrewd question, but I didn't know how she wanted me to answer. It might be that she wanted someone else—like me—to do it. To keep herself out of it, if not from a responsibility standpoint, at least physically. But it could also be a test. If I said I'd lead it, she might take it as me making it personal instead of sticking to business. I didn't know her background. On my previous visit, she hadn't been as important. But even without knowing, I'd have bet a lot of money that me leading gave us a better shot at winning. Some would call that ego. Doesn't mean I was wrong.

"It's your call. My team and I are at your disposal. You know your people better than I do. I've led a few combat missions in my day. Mac has been in the shit. Castellano is a quality sniper, and he's got the kit with him. The other two I haven't fought too much with, but they're solid."

"You have Ganos with you," said Xavier. "She's not a combat soldier."

"Yeah. But last time we were here, and we left her back here to do her thing, it didn't go well. Because of that she's coming."

"That was in her hotel room. What if I put her in my headquarters?"

I couldn't hold in a snort. "You let Ganos on a computer in your headquarters, it probably gets you fired faster than launching a combat mission."

Xavier shrugged. "In for a deci-mark, in for a mark. If we do this, I don't think we want to leave uncommitted assets."

"Okay. But it's going to be her call."

"I'll talk to her," said Xavier. "Her field is more in my background than leading an assault. Sergeant Major, who do we have who can lead in a firefight? Because that's not me. I haven't been shot at before, and I don't think learning on the fly is a great idea. I want the team that gives us the best chance to win."

Davenport responded without hesitation. "Kirkland. Lieutenant. New guy. Didn't go out on the last mission, but he's been in combat before. He's good."

I nodded. If Davenport said a lieutenant was good, the lieutenant was more than *good*. Xavier was good too. A lot of people in her spot would have taken the lead because they felt like they were supposed to. *Had* to. It took a lot of humility to say that you couldn't do something. Knowing where you're weak is at least as important as knowing where you're strong.

"What's your role going to be?" she asked him.

"If we go"—Davenport paused, making sure to acknowledge that this wasn't settled—"then I'm going with. Not in a lead role—not initially. But I want to be there. See things firsthand. I'll jump in as necessary."

"Lot of pressure for a lieutenant, leading with guys like this along." Xavier indicated Mac and me. "Is he going to understand how to handle that?"

"I've got some experience riding along behind a young leader," I offered. Anything that might make it easier for her to say yes. She was leaning that way, and I didn't want her to reverse course.

"Is that true? He can do that?" She looked at Mac.

"Yeah. As long as things are going well. The LT gets in over his head? Well . . . you don't let people die if you have the ability to stop it." Mac was never going to lie when it came to combat, and he had it spot on. I could work with a junior officer right up until the moment where I couldn't. Hopefully Kirkland could work with me too. We wouldn't know until the shit hit the fan. But I could handle whatever came.

She considered it. "Sergeant Major, let's look at a roster. See what our team looks like, how we're going to organize. Sir, I'd be happy to have your input on that. We have air assets—not much, but some. I'd love to see how you planned to integrate them."

"Sure," I said. If this was a test, I could pass it. The last time I tried to fly out there we got blown out of the sky—and so had Parnavic—but we might find a safe way to employ aircraft. "I lost my drone guy. If you've got somebody, I'd love to talk to them."

"Sure. You do that, I'll talk to Ganos. See how things go. Not everybody is going forward. It might be safer for her here."

"If you offer her the keys to your network, she'll at least have to consider it," I said. "Whatever the two of you work out is good by me."

She nodded. "Okay. Let's meet back here in two hours. We'll make the final decision then."

"Great." I said it, and I meant it. We'd got the best result I could have hoped for. But given that the outcome had me going back into combat against unknown odds, I might have been better off if I hadn't been quite so persuasive.

CHAPTER 21

Mac

THEY SAID THAT we'd get back together in two hours to talk about the plan. Maybe they needed that much time for the officer shit. My work . . . it would take as long as it took. You could never plan for all the things that would come up once you got started. You just got to work and kept moving until you were done. But the first unexpected thing that showed up kind of blew my mind.

I had headed to the armory to check out every piece of equipment I could get eyes on. As one does. Ganos found me there.

"Mac." She was leaning on the door, looking even smaller than her normally tiny self. As if part of her was missing. It looked like being back on Taug was putting her through some shit. I understood that. Butler would too, if he was paying attention. But I'm not sure he was.

"What's up?"

"Can we talk?" She nodded her head outside, and I followed her out into the larger supply room that encompassed the armory. It had rows of boxes stacked on metal shelving that stretched to a low ceiling, like a cheap warehouse store with no signs on the shelves. I checked the row beside us to make sure nobody would overhear.

"What's up?"

"I don't know what to do."

"And you think *I* can help?" It was flattering, but not quite believable.

"Yeah. Maybe. It's about the mission."

"XO asked you to stay here and work?" Xavier was technically the commander, but only temporarily. Ganos knew what I meant.

"Yeah. Offered me access to their network." She almost grinned. "Not very smart."

"Except it probably is. Given everything that's happened, you think Caliber would hesitate to go after the military network?"

That actually made her pause. "I didn't think about it that way. Two months ago, they wouldn't have. Now? I was thinking about this from an offensive standpoint. What I could do to them. I wasn't thinking about what they might do to us."

"Does that change anything?"

"It should," she said. "But I don't know. If they get into our network, they could really fuck with your plans. On the other hand—" Her voice trailed off.

"It means splitting from us."

"Yeah. Last time, that didn't go so well."

"It didn't. For the record, I'm really sorry about that." I'd never said those words to her. I didn't feel guilty. Not exactly. But I didn't feel *not* guilty. Looking back, I could see why I made the call. I knew the call that I'd make now, if it was mine to make. But it wasn't. Butler had promised her, and even if he hadn't, I'd still want her to make her own decision. Making the right one for herself might be the only way she'd get her mind straight.

"Thanks. It wasn't your fault."

I wasn't sure I believed that, but it was nice of her to say. "Thanks."

"What do I do?"

"Now?" I asked. "With this mission?"

"Yeah."

"What do you *want* to do?"

"What's that matter?"

"Butler made you a promise. We're not leaving you."

"It was a stupid promise. He felt guilty."

Probably true. Also irrelevant. At least it would be in his eyes. "But he made it. You know he won't go back on it."

"He'd let a decision stand even if it hurt his chance of winning? That doesn't sound like him."

"Fair. But you're wrong. For anybody else? He wouldn't. He'd look anybody else in the eyes with that super sincere thing that he does, and he'd tell them why he was backing out of their deal. For the good of the mission." I paused. "But for you? He'll never mention it." I was as sure of that as anything in the galaxy at that moment. I'd spent enough time drinking with the man to know some shit.

"That's pretty fucked up though, right?"

I shrugged. "He's put you in a lot of bad spots in the past. Most accidentally, some intentionally. In the end, we've all got to be able to live with ourselves. This is how he manages that."

She considered it for a bit. Hopefully she was thinking about what *she* needed to do to live with *herself*. But I couldn't say that.

I'd be pushing her too hard. "I'll ask again," she said. "What would *you* do?"

I considered how to answer her question. I couldn't tell her what to do, but if I refused, she might take that as a betrayal. She'd opened herself up by coming to me, and I couldn't shit on that. "I'd consider what I was basing my decision on. I'd make sure I had that right, and once I had that down, I'd use it to make the decision." I held up my hand to stop her when it looked like she was going to interrupt. I had to get this out. "What are you basing your decision on?"

"What *should* I be? Or what am I actually doing?"

"Both. Talk it out."

"What I've always done . . . and this probably isn't right . . . but it's been fuck the consequences, how can I cause the most chaos. Do the most damage." She paused, but I didn't interrupt. I wanted her to continue. "What I'm doing now is thinking about safety. I almost *died*. I've always been aware of the consequences of what I do, but I always saw the worst case as ending up in a dark cell somewhere. That feeling of impending death . . . that was new."

"Sure. Having your life on the line is—forgive me for saying this—a life-changing experience."

"No. I get it. I don't think I did before, but now I absolutely get it. But you guys . . . you deal with this crap all the time."

I shrugged. "This is going to sound like I'm full of shit, but . . . you get used to it. It's like anything else."

She snorted. "Not sure I want to get used to facing death."

"Beats the alternative." I realized when I said it that I'd fucked up. She would ask me what the alternative was, and when I told her that the alternative to facing it was hiding from it . . . she'd take it personally. So I pushed on before she could ask. "You said what you've always done, you said what you're doing now. But I get the feeling that you're not satisfied with either."

"I guess I'm not. But I don't know what would fix that."

She was so close. I wanted her to get there herself, but she needed a push. Thing is, I'd be pushing her to do what I wanted, and I wasn't sure if that was what was best for her or what was best for *me*. This level of self-awareness was a new thing for me. I didn't like it very much. I preferred the simple approach—have problem, punch problem. But I had to help Ganos, even if it meant circling back to the same point. "You mentioned it. How *should* you be thinking about it?"

"That's just it. I don't know. I know how Butler would think about it. How you would. You'd think about what gives us the best chance to win, and you'd do that. Fuck anything else."

I nodded. "That's a fair assessment most of the time."

"And for you, that's cool. But that's not me. I want to *win*, but I also want to stay safe. Maybe I'm selfish."

I shook my head. "Nope. That's a pretty healthy way to think about it. But I think I've isolated your problem."

"What's that?"

"You're looking at the boss and me as examples. That's absolutely *not* healthy. Butler has a bit of a death wish. Or, at a minimum, doesn't give the possibility of dying enough credit."

"Sure. I can see that. What about you?"

"Me?" I chuckled. "I've got no fucking clue what might happen, so I don't let the fear of it get in the way."

"I don't understand."

I considered how to simplify it. "If I've got two choices, how do I know which one is more likely to get me killed? If I start thinking I've got all the answers, well . . . that's pretty arrogant. Say I'm in a firefight and my choices are hiding in my hole or charging at the enemy. On the surface, hiding in the hole seems safest. But what if that gives the enemy a chance to beat us and mop me up later? In that case, it only *appeared* to be the safest."

She thought about it. "You're saying that not knowing makes it easier to decide, because it doesn't matter."

"Not quite. It definitely does matter. I'm saying that I can die in my hole, or I can die charging the enemy. I can't know which is safer, so I might as well do what gives me the best chance to win."

"Can you guarantee my safety if I come with you?"

"No. But I'm going to try really fucking hard."

"And what if I stay back here? Is that any safer?"

I shrugged. "Who can say? It *seems* like it would be. But maybe they expect us to roll out and they're waiting to launch a frontal assault on the headquarters. The enemy can be unpredictable."

She thought for a minute, and this time I gave her space to do it without interrupting. "So, I can die either way. That's comforting." She clearly wasn't comforted.

"I don't want to lie to you about it," I said.

"No. No, of course not. What you were saying—about knowing that you could die either way . . ."

"Yeah?"

"So that means I should take the action that lets me take the most bad guys with me."

I hesitated, unsure if she was pulling my leg and misunderstanding on purpose. "That's not *exactly* what I said."

"It kind of is."

I thought about it some more. Maybe it was. Maybe it wasn't, but that was what worked for her. I shrugged. "Fuck it. I guess that's it."

"Okay. Good talk." She turned and walked away.

"Where are you going?"

"To get logged in. I'm going to fuck some stuff up."

She didn't say thanks. Maybe she didn't owe it—maybe I didn't earn it. But she stood taller now than when she'd walked in, and if we had Ganos with her attitude back . . . I'd take that over all the thanks in the galaxy. I didn't know what she could do to help with the upcoming mission. I sure as shit didn't know how she did it. But I knew one thing:

I liked our odds better with her in the fight.

OUR PLAN WAS pretty basic. We formed two platoons, a total of thirty-seven personnel in nine vehicles, and we were carrying everything in the arsenal. Rockets, anti-air missiles—shit that nobody had pulled out on this rock for ages. Including starburst anti-missile rounds. Lots and lots of starburst rounds. We also had a ten-person reserve team in a flying troop transport. It wasn't a combat ship, but it could move and get into almost any location, so used correctly, it could either refit us or exploit an opportunity.

I spent most of my time on the distribution of personnel. We had soldiers, sure. But not all soldiers are created equal, and with our makeshift team, that stood out even more than usual. A good number of our team were survivors of the battle from our last stint on Taug—combat vets—which helped. It didn't resolve the leadership issues, though.

We didn't have a lack of leaders. Exactly the opposite. We had too many. Don't get me wrong. We need officers. Specifically, we need *one*. You know—to do officer things. Once you have more than one, they become counterproductive and get in the way of the actual work. Especially with a small unit in a straightforward mission like this. Ideally, Butler would have led the whole thing, and barring that, I'd have taken Lieutenant Kirkland. I didn't know him, but Davenport said he was good. And if a sergeant major says a lieutenant is good, that means the lieutenant listens. I'd take that.

But we had Butler, Kirkland, Xavier, and another lieutenant named Early. A timid guy who seemed smart, but book smarts weren't high on my list of qualifications at the moment. And that was before you added Davenport, who brought his own set of issues. He said he'd hang back, but who knew how that would go when the shit hit the inevitable fan? As the unit sergeant major, if he stepped in, everyone would immediately listen to *him*. He could blow up any plan at any time if he got a wild hair up his ass. So could Butler, for that matter, but I'd been with him long enough to know that he probably wouldn't.

Xavier took charge of the reserve team—the one that would fly—which helped in that it got her out of the mix, but presented a challenge in that I had to send somebody with her who I knew could handle her and make sure the job got done. I didn't *expect* her to fuck it up. But by virtue of being a major who, by her own admission, hadn't seen a lot of combat, she had the *potential* to fuck it up. I could have put C with her—I trusted him—but I *really* wanted him with us. Having one guy I could totally count on would mean a lot. Butler helped me out, suggesting a sergeant named Walthes. They'd spent time together in combat situations on our last visit, and if Butler knew anything, he knew people. So I sent Walthes with Xavier.

I assigned each of the lieutenants to lead the platoons and then assigned myself to Early's. Functionally, that meant Kirkland led one platoon and I led the other, though I wouldn't tell Early that. I'd keep him close to me, and he could lead in name. That sounds complicated, but it's nothing new. You pair your weaker officers with your strongest noncoms and trust that the noncoms have enough tact to make it work or enough balls to step in and take over in an emergency. Preferably both. I put Butler with Kirkland. Normally, I'd have wanted to keep him close to me, but I had to take Davenport. I put C with Butler. I told Butler it was because I wanted someone with sniper capability who could think on his own on Kirkland's team. I told C the truth: that he was there to protect Butler. Again, that sounds overly complicated. I could have told everyone the truth. It was better my way. Not my first rodeo.

Once I got the big pieces in place, I walked around and talked to all the soldiers on the mission, getting a feel for them. I paired weak with strong, cocky with cautious—anything that I could do to take this ragtag group and make them into a more effective fighting force. If the officers were aware I was doing it, they didn't say anything. That's fine. They had their jobs, I had mine. They'd appreciate it later, whether they noticed or not.

We had the personnel, the equipment, and the plan.

All that was left was to do the thing.

CHAPTER 22

Butler

W ITH THE MISSION launching early the next day, I stayed in my room. Nobody needed me walking around, getting in the way. Mac would take care of setting the team up, and he'd do a better job than I would. I'd figure it out quickly once we got ready to go. I had another task. The battle we were about to fight on Taug—and I had no doubt that it *would* be a battle—was only one of the fields of conflict. The other, which was arguably more important, would be fought at a much higher level.

Zentas wouldn't be sitting still. Even if he hadn't predicted my trip to Taug, by now, he knew I'd arrived. He had too many eyes and ears not to. And he'd be setting forces in motion to try to stop me. On an isolated moon, he could only use what he already had here or could get here in short order. So he'd use what he *could*: influence on both political and military leaders. At some point, I fully expected Xavier to get an order to stand down and not listen to me.

Zentas and his people had used my predictability against me, and that was a good tactic. But I could use theirs against them as well if I could get specifics. If I knew *who* Zentas would use—who he'd act through, who he'd bought—then I could start piecing together a counter. Ganos was my best shot at that, but I'd promised her some things, and I'd follow through on them. Still, I wanted to find her and see where her head was at.

She wasn't in her room, and she didn't answer her comm, so I finally contacted C, who had the current shift staying by her side. "Where are you?" I asked.

"Standing outside a secured area in the headquarters. Ganos is inside, but I couldn't go in."

Huh. I hadn't expected that. "What's she doing in there?"

"They gave her access to the military network. I think she's on one of their computers."

I didn't respond. Couldn't, really. The Mother help them. "I'm on my way," I said finally.

I picked up Kim as an escort—or rather, she picked up me as I left my room, because I'm sure that's what Mac told her to do—and headed over there. After a brief conversation with a zealous defender of secure areas, I talked my way through the locked door and into a room packed with computer hardware. Four techs each sat in front of multiple monitors. One of them was Ganos. I'd be lying if I said I knew what they were doing, but whatever it was, they were doing it with intensity and focus. Nobody even looked up when I entered.

"Ganos . . . could I have a word?"

"Kind of busy," she said.

We'd have to do this with an audience. Okay. "What are you up to?"

"Oh, you know. Working the net. Fighting against the forces of evil and disinformation. Like I do."

"Right. I thought you were going with us on the mission."

"That's settled." She didn't take her eyes off her screens, and her fingers kept flying. Apparently, that was all she had to say about that. Part of me wanted to question her, to make sure she understood the ramifications of her choice. But she was grown, and she knew what she wanted. That her decision happened to fit my needs . . . well, that was secondary. At least I could tell myself that.

"Could I offer some suggestions on ways that you could best attack said forces of evil?"

She kept at her work for a few more seconds and then stopped and faced me. "Sure. What've you got?"

"I assume you're doing whatever you can here on Taug to maximize our chance at winning."

"That's a good assumption."

"I'll leave that to you. I'm interested in something off Taug."

That seemed to catch her attention, her fingers slowing. "Like what?"

"Zentas will be working everything in his influence to get us shut down. He'll be—"

"You can save some time here," she said, interrupting. "I don't need to know all the details. Tell me what you want me to do."

In anybody else, the impatience would be annoying. In Ganos, it encouraged me. She wanted in this fight. "I want to know who Zentas is talking to. Who he and his people are trying to influence, and what they're saying."

"Impossible," she said.

"You've repeatedly told me nothing is impossible."

"I lied." She paused, thinking. "I *didn't* lie. I can break into everything Zentas is doing. I just need you to get me onto a

Caliber system at the executive level, unsupervised for twenty-four hours."

"Any chance that the back door we opened last time we were here gives you access?"

"None," she said.

Then I had an idea. "You're saying that to break into Caliber, you'd need to be inside Caliber."

"It would help. Greatly. Yes."

"And right now, you're inside the military network."

"Right." Her face lit up. She understood. But I needed to be clear about what I wanted.

"You can work this from the other side. You can't get at Zentas, but you can get at people in the military who might be involved."

"If they're stupid enough to use a military-issued system or device."

"They might be," I said. A lot of people didn't carry a second device for personal use. Maybe those doing illegal or unethical things would. But maybe not.

"People *are* dumb about that kind of thing. What do we want to know?"

"Names. Anybody—especially at a high level—that has contact with anybody associated with Zentas, Caliber, or any of their subsidiaries."

"Just names?"

"Can you get more?" I asked.

"Won't know until I try."

"If you can get specific conversations or find anything incriminating, that would be a big fucking bow on top."

"I'm on it. We done here?"

"Yeah. You sure you're good?" I had to ask.

"Yep."

"Just one more thing, then." I took the palm gun out of my pocket, reset the biometric coding to factory settings, and slipped it to her. "Just in case."

"Is this—"

"You'll have to code it to your hand. It's got a very short range, but in here? Should be fine."

She nodded. "Thanks."

"You're welcome. Of course." I stood there for a few seconds, but with nothing left to say, I finally left her to her work.

KIM ESCORTED ME to my room, where in theory I'd get some rest ahead of our mission. I'd get almost none after we launched, and we'd be at it for a long time. In practice, I lay awake, thinking through everything I could control and quite a few things that I couldn't. Eventually I gave up and logged on to my system, since I hadn't checked it in a couple days. Comms in transit are rarely reliable.

One message stood out immediately. A name I was *not* expecting. General Serata.

Butler,

I hear that you're on your way to Taug. Don't do anything you're going to regret. And before you say anything, yeah, I know who I'm talking to and that you rarely have regrets. I get it. You're going to do what you're going to do, and you probably won't be talked out of it. But there's more going on than you know. I'm on my way there so we can meet face to face. At least wait until we talk.

Serata

Well shit. There was a lot to unpack there. Serata's short note said a lot, but there was a lot that it *didn't* say. Our history together made it even more complicated. He'd been my boss, my co-conspirator, my savior, and my betrayer. Some more than once. Even the opening line spoke volumes. *I hear you're on your way to Taug.* He'd sent this before I arrived. If he knew, others did too. I'd assumed that, but this confirmed it. How many knew? I couldn't be sure. Enough. Zentas, certainly. But it got more complicated. Xavier hadn't received orders to ignore me—or, if she had, she'd kept a straight face about it, which seemed unlikely. I'd previously believed that meant that senior leaders hadn't learned of my arrival yet. But Serata's message showed that they had. So why were they staying silent? And why was Serata—a man as retired as I was—coming personally to see me?

And what did he mean by *Don't do anything you're going to regret*? It wasn't casual and lighthearted. Not from Serata. Was it a warning? Was there an *or else* silently pasted to the end of it or was it just sound advice? Or was it the opposite of what it appeared? What I might regret . . . that was nebulous. Could be anything. Maybe I'd regret not acting when I had the chance. The *at least wait until we talk* would seem to mean wait. But the concession that I was going to do what I was going to do . . . that meant something too. I leaned that way . . . that I should continue the mission. If Serata wanted to issue a threat, he'd have issued it. He'd have spelled out the *or else*. Unless he didn't. Maybe he believed it to be pointless.

That made it my decision then. Because he had that right—nothing he said changed what I intended to do. But it did change how I thought about things. Zentas knew where to find me. He wanted me dead without evidence pointing back to him. There was no better place to accomplish that than in combat on a remote moon. The same people who covered up things in previous investigations on Taug could do it again. They could control the flow of information from a place like this. If I died here, he would win.

With all that I lay back down on my bed, unable to sleep with everything turning over and over in my mind.

I WAS IN a headquarters. It wasn't a specific one that I could recall but had that generic look that all military buildings share. Tile floors, cement walls, everything shined or coated with clean paint. I had a lot to accomplish and not a lot of time to do it. I didn't know the exact deadline, but something in my mind told me two days. The building was empty, dark in a lot of places. I was the only one working, because it was a task I had to accomplish on my own.

I walked the halls, unsure where to start, or really even the details of the task. Just that it was important, that it had to be done and soon. I turned a corner and ran into two lieutenants and a sergeant with some gear on the floor, laid out as if for an inspection.

"Maybe we can help," said one of the lieutenants. I was unclear of my own rank, which seemed strange, but he spoke to me like a peer. Like we knew each other, even though I didn't recognize him.

"What have you got?" I asked.

"They're going to want this from you," he said, indicating some of the gear. I didn't immediately recognize it, but it had the orderly straps of something soldiers would wear. His words rang true. I *did* need this. It wouldn't finish the task, but it would get me closer. I still didn't have a complete grasp on what I had to accomplish, but I knew that much.

An alarm blared throughout the building. I didn't recognize it at first, didn't react to it . . .

I woke up in a bed, confused about where I was. The alert on my door chirped again. At some point I had fallen asleep, still in my clothes. I checked the time. Had I overslept? There's not much that's more embarrassing than being late to the SP of your own mission. I still had two hours. I padded over to the door and hit the intercom. "What's up?"

Kim's face showed on the screen. "There's a reporter here to see you."

I stood there, confused for a second, still recovering from my dream. Reporter. Right. From *The Times*. The person that Plazz had promised. I hit the button to open the door.

A dark-haired woman, short, with a light tan, stood a pace back, decked out in cargo pants and a loose cotton blouse. Boots on her feet that were functional, not stylish.

"Colonel Butler. I'm Miranda Chastain."

"Call me Carl."

"Okay, Carl. They sent me here to . . . well . . . to . . . I was told to meet up with you and that you'd give me more information. But you arrived and nobody told me, and then I found out, but I wasn't able to reach you. I didn't know what to do, so I came here."

"Sorry about that. People tend to protect my time. Come in."

Kim glared at her, and then at me, looking like she might step between us. She saw Chastain as a potential threat.

"It'll be fine," I said.

Kim didn't look very sure about that, but after a couple seconds, she stepped back.

I closed the door, offered Chastain the only chair, and took a seat on the edge of the bed. "Sorry. Not the best place for a meeting."

"I've been in worse."

"I'm sure. Nobody from your organization told you why you're here?" I wanted to mention Plazz to help establish a rapport but held off. Maybe she'd kept her involvement quiet.

"No. It was strange. Very hush hush, as if to even talk about it would somehow ruin the story."

I wasn't sure what that meant. Did they think she was a risk to spill the information, or that there were other leaks? Or maybe they didn't believe me, and they didn't want to sound like they'd bought into my conspiracy theories. "Well, however it worked out, I'm glad you're here. Has anybody given you a brief?"

"No . . . it's more of the same. The guy in charge—Mac—said that if I wanted to go along with you, they'd need to *kit me out*." She made air quotes with her fingers around the last part. "Said I needed body armor and a protective suit at a minimum, but he offered me a gun. I think he thought he was being nice."

I laughed. "You probably read that right. Mac wouldn't offer a weapon to just anybody."

"I'm honored?"

"Did you take it?"

"I didn't. I'm not comfortable with that. And speaking of not comfortable, that brings us to the present. I'm very uncomfortable not knowing what's going on."

"Fair. Especially because you have a decision to make. The story is out there." I gestured vaguely to something outside of the underground compound. "On the dark side of the moon."

"If that's where the story is, that's where I'm going."

She was young. Thirty maybe? I didn't know how much experience she had, but she had a hard look about her. Something in her eyes that said she'd seen shit. But being in tough places . . . well . . . combat is that, but it's more than that, too. It's its own special breed of bad. "You sure? It's likely to get violent."

She met my eyes, unwavering. "Nobody told me what was going on, but I know who *you* are. I've done my homework."

I forget about that sometimes. That a lot of my life is available for study. "Have you embedded with a combat unit before?"

She bit her lip. "I have not."

"How do you feel about it?"

"That's kind of a loaded question, right? If I say I'm excited to do it, you think I'm either lying or nuts, and you keep me off the mission. If I say I'm worried about it, you've got your reason to leave me off. Either way . . . no mission."

She had a point. My gut said don't bring her—keep her safe. But selfishly, I needed her. Once again, I was reminded of my propensity to be an asshole. But what can you do? "I want you along. You reporting on this is kind of the point. If you don't go? Well . . . we'll still film it and get it out, and maybe that'll do. But you give it credibility that we don't have any other way."

"I'm not going to lie for you. No matter if you embed me to get me on your side or not."

"Exactly. That's the point. It only works if you report the unbiased truth."

"You seem pretty sure of yourself."

"I've never been accused of a lack of confidence," I said.

"I mean you seem sure of what's on the other end. That it's important."

"Because I am. I've seen it."

She considered that. I half expected her to break out a camera and try to interview me on the spot. "What are my choices?"

"Ride along. See the whole story. How they try to stop us from getting there. The likely battle."

"Are you going to win?" she asked.

"Maybe. We wouldn't be going if we didn't have a chance."

"Is it safe?"

I snorted. "Absolutely not. Your other option is that I put you with Major Xavier. She has the reserve, and unless we need her sooner, she'll fly out to the objective and meet us there. It might be safer, but it's not without risks. On the downside, you'll miss part of the story."

"I'll still get the critical part of the story?"

"I think so. Yes. That's how I see it."

She considered the options. "What would you do? If you were me?"

"I can't answer that. I don't have the right perspective. I'm biased. I'd rather be on the ground with a weapon in my hand, regardless of the odds. Just feels like I have more control."

"I definitely don't feel anything even close to having control."

"I suppose not," I said. "But you've got to decide right now. I've got to go meet the team, one way or the other."

"No pressure."

"Sorry." I wasn't really. Just felt like the right thing to say.

"I'm going with you."

"You sure?" I asked.

"Yeah. I think despite what you say, *you're* the story."

"I really hope I'm not."

"Probably wise."

SHE MET ME an hour later by the departure point, decked out in her new kit. Mac had everybody organized with the soldiers lined up by their vehicles in two platoons, and I walked around to do a quick check on the soldiers. To a person, everybody understood the mission. They didn't all have the *why* of it, but they knew the location of the objective and potential ways someone would try to stop us. That was enough. In a perfect world—a world with nobody shooting at us—it would take us between ten and eleven hours to get there. We could give more details once we got close. For now, it was more important that people in each of our nine vehicles knew what to do if they got separated or lost radio contact. They did. While I'd slept, Mac had prepared.

I spent a few minutes at my own vehicle, met the driver, Dixon. She wasn't a combat soldier by training, but she'd flown in on my ship and survived the last battle of Taug. That made her a combat soldier in every way that mattered. I used my last five minutes to find the lieutenant in charge of my platoon. That was easy to do, since he was hovering around on the edge of my perception, in case I needed him. Or possibly to keep tabs on me to make sure I didn't screw up his unit. I'd have felt that way in his situation, which I'd have told him if I thought he'd believe me. He wouldn't. To him, I was beyond old. I couldn't possibly relate, even though

I'd probably been in firefights more recently than he had. That was okay. He had a job to do, and I'd let him do it as long as he could. But I had a change to his personnel load plan.

"Kirkland." I called without looking at him to make sure he knew that I knew he was watching me. I didn't want to start our relationship with him thinking I was an idiot.

"Yes, sir."

"You ready for this?"

"Yes, sir."

"I've got one change. I want the reporter, Chastain, in the vehicle with me."

"Sir, I've got you and Castellano in vehicle three. The reporter in vehicle four." That made sense. He'd be in vehicle one.

"I'd like to be able to give her context on things as we go." That wasn't my only reason for having her in my vehicle, but it was all he needed to know.

He hesitated, maybe not sure how much he could push it with me. "If I put the reporter with you, that's two non-combatants in the same vehicle. I'd rather not."

"*I'm* a combatant. Think of me as another one of your riflemen." I wasn't, and he wouldn't, but what are you going to do?

As expected, he hesitated before responding, but he finally concluded, correctly, that he didn't have a choice. "Roger, sir. I can put her with you."

"Thanks. We'll be okay. Trust me." I understood his plan. He wasn't wrong, but we had different ideas about the mission. In his mind, it was about getting to the objective and defeating whatever was in the way. We needed that. But in my mind, it did us no good to get there without the person who would broadcast it to the world. And I had information that the LT didn't have. Mac had put C with me for a reason: To protect me. Mac hadn't said so, but I wasn't born yesterday. That made the reporter safer with me. I'd be watching out for her; C would be watching out for me. That meant C would be looking out for her. It's the transitive property of bodyguards. You can look it up.

CHAPTER 23

Mac

THE MISSION STARTED out well enough. They usually do. Things usually don't fall apart until you hit the first thing that's unexpected. And you always hit something unexpected. With a mission like this, where we had very little information, hitting something unexpected was the only thing I truly expected. Ironic. We'd been following the main road to the mining area for about an hour and had just completed a short stop to set up a comms repeater, when I gave the signal to go off-road. Kirkland's platoon would take the right side of the road, I'd take the left, and we'd move cross-country. I expected the enemy to mine the road. It's what I'd have done in their shoes. It's simple, it's cheap, and unless someone saw you as you emplaced the mine, it was virtually anonymous. Virtually, because a good explosives team could figure some stuff out after the fact. But we wouldn't be doing that here, and from a personal perspective, anything after the fact of me being blown up did me zero good.

The problem came from the terrain off-road, which beat the shit out of us with bumps, forcing us to slow down. If it was just personal comfort, I'd have ordered everyone to suck it up and drive on. But we risked breaking an axle or some other catastrophic accident that would knock out one of our vehicles. We had no recovery assets—no tow trucks—and with only nine vehicles, losing even one hurt. We had a plan for it, of course. We could transload personnel and jam into eight vehicles. But we couldn't afford the loss in firepower.

Lieutenant Early slowed the formation while I considered our options. The slower terrain would turn our ten-hour travel time into more than twenty—and that was if the terrain didn't get worse, which it would in places. We had to get back on the road—at least for a bit. We'd reach alternate routes once we got another hour out, which helped, but for now we had the one main artery. What we needed was satellite imagery—old and current—so that an analyst could do an evaluation of any changes and point to areas that had potentially been disturbed. What we *had* were a handful of drones that I didn't want to risk before we got to a fight.

"What do you think about sending a drone to look at the road ahead for possible disturbances?" I asked Early. I did it partially to maintain the illusion that he was in charge and partly because I actually wanted his opinion. I didn't think he was a fighter, but he did strike me as a thinker.

"We put it up now, it's a risk," he said. "They might take it out. But it's going to be a risk whenever we use it, and if they take it down now, even that gives us information. But mostly . . . what choice do we have? We need to use the road."

"Roger. Let's give the order." He confirmed what I had already thought, but that was valuable. Two people who think differently both coming to the same conclusion gave me more confidence.

"I'm going to up the scans for enemy drones—make it active

instead of passive," said Early. "It'll give away our capability, but I think that's a minor concession for the value. I think if they want to attack our drones, at this point, they'll most likely use drones of their own."

"Concur. They'll assume the capability anyway." I would, and the enemy had people at least as experienced as me.

Early gave the order and . . . yeah.

That's when shit went sideways.

It took maybe fifteen seconds until we got the call. "Enemy drone. Altitude fifteen hundred. Distance nine hundred. Ten o'clock."

It took me a second to process. Dealing with enemy drones wasn't my day-to-day pastime. It was to our left front, but the key number was fifteen hundred meters altitude. That ruled out a lot of smaller drones. This wasn't a handheld—it was bigger than that—meaning that, in theory, we should be able to see it or hear it or both. Except we were on Taug, with a sky that got gray at its lightest and with a thin atmosphere that carried less sound. Still, we had to try. "Visual scan left front. Call it if you see it," I announced over the platoon net. "You think it's armed?" I asked Early on internal.

"No idea."

Me either. We probably wouldn't know until it shot at us. All we could do was prepare. Our left flank vehicle would have the best shot if the drone fired from its current location. We had starburst rounds that could intercept rockets if we fired them in time. They'd also be the most likely target. "Red 2, have a starburst ready. Don't hesitate."

Less than a minute later, a streak ripped toward us from above and to our front left. Sometimes I hate being right. I didn't see the return fire until the starburst flared, a small puff of orange turned into a blazing sun of an explosion as the enemy rocket flew into it and detonated.

Maybe being right is okay.

"Enemy drone is breaking station," came the report across the net. It probably only had the single armament. That's not uncommon with drones, and payloads would be even lower in the thin atmosphere. It also meant that they didn't have eyes on us anymore unless they had something else up that we hadn't detected. Which probably meant there was no mine on the road coming up. They'd want to engage us right as we hit a mine, or, at a minimum, observe us as we reached it.

"Let's get our drone over the road right now. Lead us through."

"Roger," said Early. "And let's engage whatever they send next as soon as we pick it up. Fire a SAM at it."

"You think? We don't have many," I said.

"I do. We let this one fire at us. If we fire at their next sortie, maybe we catch them by surprise. And if we take them out, it buys us some time since they have to re-launch and make the flight. Some of these drones aren't fast."

"Roger." The kid made sense. Maybe I'd have to reevaluate my stance on book smarts. His plan would make them react to us instead of us reacting to them, which was hard to do since they knew our objective. "Let's pick up speed for now. Make as much ground as we can while we're unobserved."

WE GOT OUR chance to try Early's plan about an hour later when our active scan picked up another enemy drone. We only had shoulder-fired SAMs, so we pulled a fast halt, all vehicles stopping together on command. This time, the streak of fire went away from us, up into the darkening sky, blossoming on the other end as the proximity detonator went off and fired hot metal through the atmosphere. No secondary explosion, but I picked up a smudge diving for the surface. We started the platoon moving again.

"Red 2 on me," said Early. We raced toward the crash site, bouncing hard as we went off-road. I wanted to tell him to slow down, but we *did* need to get there. Anything we could do to identify remnants of the drone would help us in future encounters. We crested a low rise and found a rising column of smoke a couple hundred meters in front of us. The wreck itself was obscured.

We were about fifty meters out when the world exploded. Something thwacked into our windscreen, spiderwebbing it. The driver braked without order, and we slewed to the left, the back end of the vehicle sliding around. I slammed forward into my restraint belts. We sat there for a few seconds, none of us speaking, taking in what had happened.

"That was unexpected," said Early.

I considered that for a second, and then I burst out laughing. The more I saw of this kid, the more I liked him. Unexpected. Ha. Perfect understatement. But we *should* have expected it. We'd gotten lucky. Twenty or thirty meters closer and we'd have cracked more than our windscreen. They hadn't been targeting us—at least not with any sort of observation. If so, they'd have waited until we got closer. Likely, when they lost touch with their drone, they detonated the rocket it carried to destroy the remains. The remainder of the airframe was burning. We wouldn't be getting near that any time soon, but we could still call it a success.

I called Butler's platoon and told them to take the lead and continue on while we assessed the damage to our vehicles. Once they cleared the road and didn't find any mines, we could move faster behind them, so we'd catch up presently.

As I said, we'd been lucky so far. We'd need that to continue. If I knew one thing about combat, though, it was this: It wouldn't.

CHAPTER 24

Butler

W E TOOK THE lead when Mac stopped to reconsolidate for a minute after taking out an enemy drone. Our platoon. Not me personally. We had two vehicles in front of us, one behind, and we took a slightly slower pace, so the other platoon could catch up once they were ready. We didn't want to get too far ahead. When the enemy finally presented itself as more than a random drone, we'd want to be able to bring our full firepower to bear on them. The attacks along the route, whether by drones or something else, were annoying, but ultimately helpful. They allowed us to defeat smaller forces in detail instead of having to deal with everything they had all at once. Assuming they didn't take too many of us out.

Big assumption.

Mac had expected the drones. We'd run into one on our last visit to Taug, so it made sense that the enemy would use the same tactic again, but they'd miscalculated. Firing on a military formation isn't the same as attacking a couple of rental cars, regardless of the talent of the people inside the vehicles. The technological capability difference approached an order of magnitude. Off-the-shelf civilian stuff was nice, and in the right circumstances and with surprise, it could cause trouble for a professional force. But not in a protracted and well-planned fight. Granted, Caliber had access to stuff beyond the off-the-shelf. Hell, they manufactured a lot of what the military used. But they couldn't use it all if they wanted to maintain plausible deniability. We'd see how much that mattered here presently.

"There's a disturbed spot in the road. Nine hundred meters." Mac's drone operator announced it across the company net. It might be nothing, but we had to react. We didn't have the right technology to spot mines with a high level of confidence, but at the same time, the enemy probably didn't have a ton of people with experience putting them in. You didn't go out every day and mine a road. We'd just splashed an enemy drone, so that increased the odds of a mine here. They'd employ them together. With the enemy drone down, the situation got a lot less dangerous—we could assess and remove the mine without being observed. That extra level of safety created a good chance for me to assess how Kirkland approached a problem.

Essentially, he had two options. He could take us off-road and go around the suspect area, or he could stop, approach the mine, and try to remove it. Those two options, however, came with a lot of different levels of thought. Going around it off-road would be faster, and thus preferable. But the enemy knew that too, so they might have set a second attack on the most likely bypass route. But we *knew* that they knew, so we could counter-plan to try to exploit their plan to attack us as we bypassed. Like a chess game, the iterations of plan and counter could go on indefinitely.

Or it could just be a mine in the road.

The art of it came from figuring out the right level of thought.

If we planned for the enemy to have a secondary attack set up and went out of our way to counter that, and we were wrong, we'd waste a lot of time and energy for no reason. That could give the enemy the initiative to attack us in a different way at a time of their choosing.

We faced a simple potential mine, but it presented a lot to think about for a colonel, let alone a lieutenant. It came down to how well you knew your enemy, and here, we simply didn't. We didn't know their tendencies, because we hadn't fought them in this type of situation before, and we didn't know their resources. Both mattered. Kirkland's first test came with how he gained information to improve his decision. I'd have preferred to do this in a training environment—on a simulator or during an exercise—but we didn't have that luxury. It's weird to think of a combat situation as a test, but I preferred to know Kirkland's capability now, before things got harder.

"Slowing the pace," said Kirkland. "Drone operator, get me a look out to the right to see if there's anything waiting for us if we bypass. Look for secondary disturbances or any enemy forces."

So far, so good.

"Sir," said C, leaning over to me. He had a large tablet in his hand with a map pulled up. He pointed to a spot on it. "This is where they'd put a sniper team."

I looked at it for a couple of seconds. The basic terrain fit it, though C knew more than me about sniper placement, so I'd defer to his expertise on the exact location. "Call it in."

He looked at me, hesitating for only a second before getting on the net. "One, this is Three. Most likely enemy sniper position is at the grid I'm sending you now."

The net went silent for a few seconds. Kirkland was probably receiving and processing the information. Maybe he knew it was a test, maybe he didn't. The fact that the information came from someone in my vehicle made it more likely that it was. If this was a training exercise, it would have been a bright warning light. Nobody gives you information in training that doesn't matter. Here, we didn't have the answers to the test any more than he did, and he'd know that.

"Roger," he said. "Drone operator, add that grid to your search pattern. We'll wait to see what the drone picks up and reassess after that."

We rode on, slowing even more. We couldn't get too close to the site of the initial disturbance, or we'd miss the chance to bypass altogether.

"No disturbed ground to the right," said the drone operator over the net. "Difficult to tell if there are snipers at the templated position. There's a lot of cover and concealment there."

We had to make a call. It was time for me to step in. I found Kirkland's channel and contacted him privately. "Talk me through your thought process. Quickly."

"There's more risk to the right. I want to set up a covering position and send someone to look at the disturbance on the road, potentially reduce it, but the other platoon has our only EOD guy. We've got your woman—Kim—but I don't know her skill level."

"She's good, but I don't know her mine clearance skill set." I should have asked her before now, but my mind had been going in too many different directions. Kirkland should have asked too, but it was a minor oversight. "Your call."

"We go right," he said. I didn't care what his answer was as much as I cared about how he gave it. There was no right or wrong—not that we could definitively say before choosing, anyway. What mattered was his confidence and how that came across to the platoon.

"Give the order," I said.

"We're swinging to the right," he said over the platoon net. "We'll move into a wedge as we get off-road. Vehicle four, stop and fire a rocket at the templated sniper position. If somebody *is* there, let's give them something to think about." He had a good delivery, no doubt in his tone. Really good. The platoon made the turn together and picked up good spacing despite the terrain restrictions. Not bad for an ad hoc unit. To our front, the rocket Kirkland ordered exploded, throwing dust and detritus that would challenge the vision of any sniper even if it didn't hit them directly. We all held on tight for the next five minutes as we passed, scanning for heat sources. We didn't find any. More important, nobody shot at us, and once we'd cleared the potentially mined area, we moved back to the improved road, and Kirkland sent the route information to Mac's platoon so that they could follow our track.

Still, I worried. Because it felt *too* easy.

Everything we'd seen so far, we had expected. A drone attack—maybe a second that we thwarted—and a potential mine on the obvious route. On the surface, we should feel good. Our estimate of the enemy was confirmed. But it didn't feel good. Not to me. The enemy should have been doing more to stop us. I couldn't help but let my mind go back to Serata's message. In its own way, it was like the lieutenant facing the decision about the mine in the road.

Serata's message hadn't changed my actions—we still launched our mission. But he'd known it wouldn't. What was his real purpose? Him telling me that he knew I was coming here meant that the enemy knew too. Was that his way of warning me? Maybe he was being observed and thought he could sneak that warning through disguised as an innocuous message, trusting that I'd see through it and discern the truth. But for that to work, his observers would have to fail to see through the deception, which seemed . . . overly hopeful. Which Serata wasn't.

It was enough to drive a man crazy.

There were too many variables, and too many innocent lives involved. If it was just me, I'd have ridden it out, even knowing it was a trap. I'd spring it and try to adapt and overcome. I'd done it enough times that I probably had an irrational belief that things would work out. But here, even a win would come at a massive cost to some of the people involved. I wasn't their commander. Those days had passed. What right did I have to ask this of them?

I could stop our assault, but to do that, I'd have to turn the whole unit around. Xavier might argue, but what choice would she have but to comply if I insisted? But if I did pull us from the mission, that was the end. I'd get no more chances to stop Caliber, and I probably wouldn't make it off Taug alive. If they hadn't known when I'd arrived, they'd certainly know when I was leaving. They could kill me a bunch of different ways. If I died before we got back to Ridia 2, they could cover it up. To do that, they'd have to kill Mac too. And probably Ganos, C, Clement, and Kim.

Either way, people would die because of me.

Once I got to that spot in my thinking, it became a lot easier. Whatever I did, people would die. I might as well try to win. To put one set of lives over the others would be disrespect to the ones

I tried to protect. I'd be disrespecting their decisions to serve in whatever capacity they'd chosen to serve. It's hard to think that way, to get past the human cost. We never wanted to spend lives recklessly. But neither did we want to fail to do the job out of excess caution.

So we'd continue. Into the obvious trap.

CHAPTER 25

THE TRAP, WHEN it came, surprised me in both timing and composition. We continued on the road and off, being cautious when it made sense, but not overly so. We kept our drones up, avoided disturbed areas on the roads, drove off two more larger drones of theirs, destroying one and causing the other to lose link and fly off in a harmless direction. We fired three more rockets at suspected positions. Eventually, they put up smaller drones—too small to be armed, which meant they could observe us but not shoot at us. We couldn't afford to waste our limited SAMs on something unarmed and hard to hit. They stayed too far back to allow any sort of ground-based EMP to be effective, and none of our drones had that capability, creating a bit of a stalemate. I missed Alanson.

Our two platoons had linked back up together, and by the time we got within ten klicks of the objective, almost ten hours after we departed, I'd almost started to doubt myself. Started to wonder if I'd been overthinking, giving the enemy too much credit. Sometimes a weak enemy was just that: weak. Not a deception, but rather unable to do better.

They continued to observe us, so they knew our location. We were almost close enough that it seemed like they planned to de-

fend from the terrain right around the dig site. They could do that.
We'd defended from there on our last trip, using the high ground
with the good cover, and we'd been successful. Maybe they'd do
the same thing. If that was the best they could do, I'd count us
lucky. It wouldn't be an easy fight by any stretch of the imagina-
tion, but we could win.

Of course it wasn't that.

The drone operator's tone warned me first, slightly altered from
his usually stoic broadcasts. That tone announced a problem even
if his words hadn't made it obvious. "Enemy heavy battle mech,
one point five klicks."

Well . . . shit.

We didn't use heavy battle mechs against people. We used
them on planets with non-intelligent, dangerous life. They were
near indestructible and had ridiculous firepower. Specific models
had different capabilities, but any of them were more than a match
for two platoons in light vehicles. The lack of attacks along the
way made sense now. They'd observed us, they knew what we
had, and they could afford to let us come because they had us
wildly outgunned. I'd known we were running into a trap. With
a hundred guesses, I wouldn't have come up with this. Perhaps I
should have. Caliber manufactured this kind of hardware, after
all. But as far as I knew, *nobody* had ever used an HBM in a fight
against humans.

Another one for the history books. Might be a short chapter.
Might be my last.

"Get us a picture," said Kirkland across the company net. "We
need to identify the model." He wasn't wrong—we wanted all the
information we could get—but it wasn't like we had battle plans

drawn up for different types of HBMs. It wasn't part of any plan ever. "I'm going to send you the picture, sir," said Kirkland over a private channel.

"Roger," I said. Kirkland actually had something I didn't here. Hope. He didn't have the experience to know that we faced an impossible task. I didn't tell him. Hope has value. Especially when you don't have anything else. I almost told him to slow our advance to give us more time to make a decision, but before I could say that, my vehicle slowed. Mac's platoon was in the lead—he'd probably come up with the same solution I had.

"What are you thinking?" Mac called me privately as the picture showed up with an initial analysis.

It was a Mark 41g. A basic model, but the seventh iteration of it with all the improvements that came with years of field testing. Six meters tall, five meters wide, and seventeen meters long, propelled by two sets of heavy treads on either side that had redundant capability that made a maneuver kill much more difficult. To stop it, we'd have to knock out both treads on the same side, and even then, it would only slow it down in this terrain. On a positive note, it didn't have anti-missile defenses since it wasn't designed to face enemies that had them. On the negative, it made up for that with a wedged front and near-impenetrable armor. Even the treads had protective plates shielding them from the front and side.

It made up for its lack of missile defense with offensive capability, boasting two independent computer-aimed heavy pulse turrets, two heavy projectile weapons, and four rocket launchers. For a second, I thought that maybe we could draw its fire and run it out of ammunition. That would stop everything except for the pulse guns, which would be powered by the machine's virtually unlimited nuclear reactor. But even that slim hope slipped away as I read the basic load. It carried 220 rockets and even more projectile ammo. At least the rockets were unguided. That was *something*.

But not much.

"We can't run it out of ammo. We'd be dead before it Bingoed, even if we gave it one fast-moving target at a time." The rockets would struggle against a fast-moving vehicle in a crossing pattern that varied its speed, but the HBM's AI would switch to pulse guns and burn up the target that way. But that did give me a thought. The enemy mech wasn't operating independently here. It had that capability—you could drop it in an area and it would kill. But on Taug . . . Caliber had to have at least some control. *They* were here, and if they didn't maintain that leash, an undirected killing machine would target them too.

"We could go around it," said Mac. "One platoon to each side, staying out of pulse and rocket range. They'd have to be big loops. But if we did that—"

"It could only chase one of the two platoons."

"Maybe the other could use the time to get to the objective," said Mac.

"Assuming there's nothing else defending there." For all we knew, they had a second mech. But if they did, we were all dead anyway, so there was no sense in worrying about it.

"I think we have to make that assumption," said Mac, probably coming to the same conclusion I had.

"And assuming that the mech doesn't fall back, keeping itself between us and the dig site." To say nothing of the fact that we'd basically be sentencing half our force to death unless they could outrun the mech, which was a *big* if in this terrain.

"I'm betting they don't want to bring that monster too close to their own operations. But they may have another force waiting up there to defeat us in detail. I'll send a drone up to take a look."

No sooner had he said that than a report came across the main feed. "I've lost all drones but one." The net went silent for a few seconds. "Correction. All drones down."

I didn't know what the enemy had used to take down our eyes. It didn't matter enough to waste time trying to figure it out. They were gone. The enemy clearly had a plan to engage us at this spot, and they were going all out. "What's the enemy drone situation?" I asked. If they were throwing everything, attack from the air probably came next.

"Small, low altitude," came the quick response.

"Roger. Watch for the bigger stuff. Engage as soon as they're in range." That was technically Kirkland's call, but I didn't have time for any more training wheels. We had to act, and we had to act quickly if we wanted to survive.

I flipped back to a private line with Mac. "Go ahead and execute your plan, but don't worry about trying to get to the objective immediately. Buy time, preserve the force."

"What have you got?"

"I'm going to see what Ganos can do." It was our best bet. The HBM was connected to Caliber, and it was designed for use in a non-competitive cyber environment. Maybe they'd fixed that, but maybe it was vulnerable. We almost certainly had a better chance that way than we did in a direct firefight.

I flipped my comms to the satellite net and called back to headquarters. Nothing. I checked the connection, hoping it was a problem with my personal comms, and I could use another line.

No signal. We were still talking internally, so we weren't being jammed. Which meant they'd taken out the comms satellite. Because of course they did. We'd checked it constantly the whole way here, and we'd been able to talk fine. They'd waited to take it out until we really needed it. But I'd expected it. They'd taken out satellite comms during the last battle on Taug. That was their problem. *Too predictable.* Last time, they'd got us, because I hadn't thought that they'd attack government infrastructure, and the loss of comms had crippled us.

This time, I knew better and had an alternate plan. Fool me once, shame on you. Fool me twice, and I'm a fucking idiot. Not today. I switched to the manual relay net. We'd dropped repeaters every fifteen klicks from the time we left base.

"Ganos," I said.

Nothing for a second, and then a beautiful sound. "I'm here. We've got a small delay."

"We need help." I hung on, as our vehicle pulled a hard right and accelerated, starting Mac's plan. I wasn't listening to that part of the net at the moment, so I hadn't heard it. "They've got a Mark 41g heavy battle mech. I need to see what you can do to stop it."

"Fuck." As usual, she summed it up succinctly.

"Exactly. Can you do it?"

"I don't know. This is going to surprise you, but I've never tried to hack a battle mech."

"Can it be done?"

"Anything can be done. It'll be fun to try. We're on pretty good footing with the cyber war. They haven't been able to shut us down. We haven't been able to shut them down. This will be a new line of attack."

I slammed into my restraint belts as our vehicle hit a bump that felt like it might rip the front end off. At least *she* was having fun. "Fast would be good."

"On it," said Ganos.

I cut the connection. No need to stay in communication. She'd either get it or she wouldn't, and the more we talked, the more likely the chance that the enemy would discover our means of communication and attack it somehow. Better they didn't know about it in case we needed it again, which we would, if only to call forward Xavier and her flying reserve after we won. *If we won.* I took five seconds to consider if she could help us now, but we couldn't risk it. The enemy would surely be ready to shoot her down.

I tuned back in to the rest of my comms but couldn't immediately make sense of it as three people talking on three different nets bled together on my headset. I flipped my private net to talk to C. He'd have been listening, and unlike Mac and Kirkland, I wouldn't be distracting him from important work.

"Which platoon did the mech follow?"

"Ours. But not directly. It's taking a diagonal route, closing on us but also falling back toward the objective."

"That will buy us some time," I said.

"That's one way to look at it," said C, though his voice didn't contain any of the despair that would have been warranted given the situation. Which reminded me of our other passenger. I found Chastain's private channel.

"How are you doing?"

"I'm . . . I don't know."

"Scared?" I asked.

"A little. You?"

"Sure. But I'm focused on our next move. That helps."

"I don't really know our next move."

And that was the problem. The less she knew, the more the un-known would play with her mind. We were in a shit situation, but our minds could make it even worse than it actually was. Which made me think about the soldiers along for the ride and in the same situation. We needed to fill them in—to give them hope, so they didn't turtle up in despair. I flipped to the wide net.

"This is Butler. Clear the net." I waited a few seconds for the other channels to go silent. I had all the ears now. "We're working on taking down the mech—we've got a plan. Our job here is to keep it busy. Do *not* become decisively engaged. Stay out of range if you can. Fire at it if you have a shot but move immediately. Target the treads if you can, but don't take unnecessary risks. Delay, and then delay some more. More to follow once I know it. Out."

I immediately flipped to Kirkland's private net and gave him more detail. I didn't have much beyond Ganos was working on it, but he needed to know everything I did.

"Roger, sir. We'll keep it occupied for as long as we can. Give her every chance. But it's gaining on us. We're almost in range—"

A crunch-whump drowned out the last part of his transmission as the moon erupted in front of us. Rocks and dirt pelted the vehicle in an avalanche, cracking against the windscreen and outer hull. Our driver swerved—maybe out of training, probably out of instinct. A rocket had exploded directly in front of us. More whumps, a little more distant, but the closest one had been so loud I couldn't count them. All I knew for sure was that we weren't the only target.

Ganos needed time. I didn't know what chance she had, how

well Caliber would have defended that line of attack, but I knew that much. Another explosion sent us up onto our two right wheels. We hung there for a second before slamming back down, jarring my teeth. That rocket had been holy shit close—that's a technical term. We wouldn't survive in our vehicle much longer. Hitting a fast-moving target with an unguided rocket is hard, but they had a *lot* of rockets. Eventually, they'd get us.

"We need to abandon the vehicle." I flipped back to Chastain's private channel, but before I got there, the driver responded.

"I can make it!"

I flipped back. "Slow the vehicle, and we're all going to bail. I don't have time to explain."

Maybe she didn't agree. Maybe she did. Either way, she was a soldier, and her training kicked in. The vehicle slowed.

I didn't have time to brief the reporter individually, so I spoke to our entire vehicle crew. I could have broadcast to the whole platoon, but I didn't want to risk contradicting Kirkland. For now, I had to keep myself and my crew alive long enough to figure out what he'd given for orders. This is why you never want to go into combat with a messed-up chain of command. Hopefully, I'd have time to reflect on our stupidity later.

"On my mark, open your door and bail out. Move immediately away from the vehicle." The mech would target it, whether we were in it or not. "Your instinct is going to be to run. Don't. It will target movement. Find a hole and get in it or find a rock and get behind it. Whatever cover you can get, take it, and then stay there. Hopefully, the mech will pass us by if we don't look like threats." I didn't mention that *hopefully* was doing a lot of the work in that sentence. "Go. Now."

I hit the ground and rolled, doing my best to absorb the impact imparted from the still-moving vehicle. I say rolled, but it was more bounced. I kept forgetting about the low gravity and its effect on standard movements. I finally came to a rest and checked to make sure all my limbs still worked. It took me a second to orient myself, and I glanced around to discern the locations of the rest of my team. I wanted to find Chastain. I'd given her instructions with the rest of the crew but wanted to stay close to her. The urge for her to run would be high.

Our vehicle sped up. "Dixon!"

"I can make it!"

As if to punctuate her statement, three rockets slammed into the ground around the vehicle almost simultaneously, obscuring it in a cloud of dust and debris. Dixon streaked out the other side, still accelerating. How she came through that, I didn't know, but I couldn't focus on her any longer. I had to find Chastain. Everyone else would have to take care of themselves.

I pushed myself up into a crouch and synched my heads-up display to give locations of personnel, which I'd had disabled when we were inside our vehicles. Multiple lights blipped on, which meant others had abandoned their vehicles. A wreck burned about eighty meters away—hopefully they'd gotten out *before* that happened.

I found Chastain on my heads-up, which helped me find her visually. The ground shook as more rockets hit somewhere. Close, but not close enough to matter. Chastain was about twenty meters away, prone, which was good. She was in a slight depression—she'd done what I told her—but it wasn't deep enough to provide cover.

"Chastain. You've got to move. To your left, thirty meters, there's better cover. I'll meet you there."

"You said not to move."

"I know."

"That it targeted movement."

"I'm going to move first, so if it's got us locked, it will target me." The mech certainly had multiple independent targeting systems, but I didn't know how many. There was at least a chance that my moving would protect her. I wasn't *completely* lying. "I'll move on three. You count two more and then go. One. Two. Three."

I pushed to my feet and sprinted in a crouch. I'd covered about six steps when bullets ripped the ground all around me. I probably should have kept running, but instinct kicked in and I dove for the ground, sliding in the dirt instead of bouncing this time. The bullets stopped, and for a second, everything felt still. I waited for pain to register, but other than a throbbing in my knee where it had hit the ground, it didn't come. Nothing sharp or hot. I probably hadn't been hit. Adrenaline messes with that, but my suit hadn't registered any punctures.

I took a second to gather myself and assess the situation. Not like I wanted to get up and run again anytime soon. Obviously, we were inside the mech's projectile weapons range now. I'd probably gotten lucky that its algorithm hadn't deemed me worthy of a pulse blast. That might mean that those weapons had other targets. Chastain was down again, short of her cover, but I didn't know whether she'd been hit, shot at, or went to ground when the mech targeted me. My heads-up still showed her as alive.

"Chastain." I called her on a private net.

A rocket whizzed by. It took me a second to realize that it

came from the wrong direction, and I turned to follow its path. It slammed into the mech a couple seconds later, flame blooming low on the side of the beast. Someone on our side was fighting back. That was either really brave or really stupid.

"Chastain," I called again.

"Yeah. I'm here. Sorry, I messed up my comms for a second."

"You okay?"

"I . . . I think so."

"Can you move? We still need to get to cover."

The net stayed silent for a few seconds. "I don't think I can get up."

I didn't know if *couldn't get up* meant she was injured or if she couldn't mentally make herself do it. Could be either. I wanted to ask, but I didn't want to make things worse if it was mental. If she'd been a soldier, I'd have yelled at her, counted on her conditioning to kick in. As a civilian, that might shut her down further. "Can you crawl? Let's crawl," I said, not waiting for her to respond. "It's not far."

"Sir, it's C."

"Go C."

"I'm hit. Not fatal, but it's in the leg. I can't put weight on it."

I took a second to assess his location. About forty meters away. He'd left the vehicle and gone in a different direction. "Give me thirty seconds to get Chastain to cover and I'll come get you." Thirty seconds was optimistic, but we all needed some optimism at the moment.

"Negative. I've got cover. I can ride it out here. The mech is chasing two vehicles."

"Roger," I said. I could reevaluate once I got Chastain set. If C said he was good, there was at least a chance that he was.

"I'm going to fire at it. Draw it off of you so you can get the reporter to safety."

"No way," I said.

"Let me do my fucking job, sir." He didn't change his tone. He didn't have to. He'd said the words that hundreds of soldiers in hundreds of situations had said before him, and they brooked no argument. He saw it as his job to protect me, and this was the only way he could do it. As much as I wanted to countermand that, doing so would be the utmost disrespect. I'd be saying he couldn't do it. His job. That probably sounds like a lot of macho bullshit. That I was going to let respect cost someone his life. But it's not that. It's not some bullshit code. He was making a choice, and I couldn't belittle that.

"Roger. Switching to her private channel now. Linking you in."

Chastain was moving by the time I got back to her. Barely. She was hugging the ground and occasionally scooting forward a few centimeters. She didn't know how to low crawl. Another oversight on my part on a day where I'd had too many to survive. This wasn't going to work, and I didn't have time to teach her.

"Go now!" said C.

"Chastain, up! Let's run."

She did, and I did. Behind me, a volley of rockets hit, not close enough to affect me. That was probably the end of C. I ran for cover, intending to grab Chastain and drag her along with me. If C was going to sacrifice himself for us, we were fucking going to live.

The world flashed and exploded and then went dark and quiet. Distantly, I knew that my helmet had done that to protect my vision and hearing. Very distantly.

I was flying, tumbling in the air, unsure which direction was up or down or sideways. My vision came back, and I saw the stars, the dirt, and then the stars again. Without sound from the outside, my heart pounded in my ears, a drum counting quick beats until the end.

I don't know how long I flew.

I hit something solid, and everything went black.

CHAPTER 26

Mac

THE PLAN HAD our two platoons splitting with us going to the left. We did that, and we executed it pretty well for a unit that hadn't spent any time training together. It only took us a few seconds. It was the best plan we could manage in a pretty shitty situation. That made it a good plan. Right up until it wasn't.

The mech followed the other platoon.

I hadn't thought it all the way through, but in the back of my mind, I think I expected it to follow us. I don't know why. Had the mech done the right thing, it would have been a good plan, as it would have taken the mech away from Butler and his reporter. Granted, we'd have had a mech following us with extreme hostile intent. That would have been somewhat less good. But at least we'd have known what to do. Now? Our most important assets were in danger, and we were running away from the fight. Why couldn't the mech have done the right thing and chased us? Fucking uncooperative enemy.

Now I had to make a decision. Everyone had heard the plan. I didn't know my team well, so if I changed it now, I didn't know how they'd react. At least a few would have been happy to see it go after the other platoon. Feel lucky. But at least some of them would feel like I did.

Shitty.

While I dithered thinking about our bad luck, we drove directly away from the fighting. I could stick with the plan and head for the final objective, or do what I wanted to do: scrap the plan, do a one-eighty, and try to chase the mech down from behind to save the other platoon. Turns out I didn't care much about *supposed to*. I wanted the win, sure. And to win, someone had to reach the objective. But I wanted to save the team more. If we didn't do something to help the other platoon, they were dead. Maybe they were dead either way, and we'd just be rushing to join them.

But that's combat. You can what-if shit to death, but in the end, you've gotta trust your gut and go. Now I had to convince Early.

"Hey boss." I called him on a private channel. I couldn't do this in front of the troops.

"Go Mac."

"What say we turn around and chase down that mech. Snipe at its treads from the rear."

He didn't respond right away. My request probably surprised him. "Plan was to split so it couldn't target all of us."

"It was. Plans change."

"You think we can do it?"

I almost made a smart-ass comment. That of course we could do it—we just turn the steering wheels. But Early and I didn't have that kind of relationship. He needed honest advice. "I'm not sure. But what I am sure of is that if we don't do something, a lot of people are going to die over there."

"Yeah. Maybe it will be focused on them enough where we can get in some good shots."

"Exactly," I said. Early probably didn't know how many independent targeting systems that mech had. I didn't know *precisely*. But it sure as shit had enough to shoot at them and us at the same time. If I was a good noncom, I'd have told Early that. Given him all the information before he made his decision. But I wanted what I wanted, and that was back in the fight, trying to save Butler and C and the rest of the team.

"Let's do it," said Early. He switched to the platoon net. "Let's turn it around. Go at this thing from behind and see if we can do some damage. On my lead." He told Jameson, our driver, to slow and make a turn to the right. It was messy, but the rest of the platoon followed. Not exactly a maneuver you practice even in a cohesive unit. There aren't that many situations where you make a turn and head in the opposite direction unless you're running. But that's rarely organized.

And that's how we ended up chasing after a giant mech. One of my less intelligent moments in a career full of them. Maybe my therapist was right, and I needed more than one go-to move. I'd worry about that if we survived. Right now, we had to figure out how to engage.

We had two turret-mounted weapons in the platoon—both heavy projectile—but those would do fuck all against the mech. We had some grenade launchers, which would make a lot of noise and a nice explosive show, but not much else. That left the rockets. We had eight disposables, which weren't guided, and six with trackers that the shooter could guide to a specific spot. In theory, if targeted perfectly into the back of the tracks, those *might* slow it down.

The problem was that the operator had to keep the crosshairs on the target for the three to five seconds it took the rocket to fly to impact. Hard to do from a moving vehicle. Harder to do at a moving target. Hardest to do as a big fucking mech hurled hot death at you. Like shooting at a tank, the theory definitely beat the actual experience.

Either way, we had to get closer. The mech continued to move away from us, but not *directly* away, and engaging the other platoon caused it to change course occasionally, which slowed it a little. That gave us the chance to catch up.

"We need to race up, get well inside our rocket range, and then stop and engage," I said to Early. Maybe he knew that already, maybe he didn't. We were beyond niceties at this point.

"Roger. Jameson, can you go any faster?"

Jameson responded by speeding up. A few seconds later we hit a bump that threw us into the air and jarred my teeth together. A second later we slammed back to the surface. Our wheels spun for a second before digging in, causing us to sway to one side until Jameson got it under control, barely avoiding a spin that would probably have flipped us. Hopefully we hadn't broken an axle. In a sane world, we'd have slowed our pace to fit the terrain. Sane had left the discussion.

It took us a few minutes to close on the mech, though hurtling cross country at an unsafe speed, it felt a lot longer than that. The dirt trail kicked up by its tracks acted like a pointer, but we could make the mech itself out visually now, steadily growing larger.

"We're at one point seven klicks," said Early. "Now?"

"Closer," I said.

"Its pulse weapons probably range eight hundred meters. Its

rockets probably double that," he said. It was as close to pushback as he'd given me. It was also a valid point.

"Our rockets aren't much good past two," I said. "And with the mech still moving away from us, it'll be out of range almost as soon as we stop if we're not close enough."

"It's firing in the opposite direction," he said. "Rockets, and it also looks like heavy projectiles." As if to make a point, an intense light streaked away from the mech toward Butler's platoon. A pulse blast.

"We might only get one shot at this," I said. "Let's get as close as we can and volley fire. Everything we've got at the treads." Realistically, that meant five shots—one from each vehicle. The only way to get off more than that simultaneously would be to dismount. If we hit the treads, we might get a mobility kill. That would leave a giant, pissed-off mech stuck in one spot, shooting anything that came near it. But at least then we could run.

"Roger." Early flipped to the platoon net. "Stop when I do. Fire Slider missiles at the treads. Vehicle four and five, target the left tread. Two and three target the right. Make it count."

The kid was cool under pressure. Goes to show you never know about these things until you're in it. Some people seemed great until shit hit the fan, and then they fell apart. Some rose to the occasion. If Early could stay cool now, each second ticking off like a minute as the mech continued to grow in our cracked front window, I'd put him up against anything. We got within a klick of the mech, and I tapped Early on the shoulder to signal him to stop.

"Stop now. Fire at will," he said.

I waited for us to skid to a halt, undid my restraints, and popped up through the hatch. We had a gunner, and this was her job. I didn't know her, but I'd bet a lot of money that I had more experience firing a Slider than she did, and like I said, we'd probably only get one shot. I'd apologize to her later for taking her spot. If we survived.

The mech didn't immediately fire at us, which was nice. Everything slowed—not really, but in that way that happens where you're processing things faster than what seems possible. The LT said fire at will, and I was ready, but nobody else had fired yet, so for a split second I wondered if I should fire first and hope that would trigger everybody else, or if they were slower to get ready and I'd be out of synch with the rest. I wanted to mass fires. It might not help, but then again, maybe it would.

A burning light ripped away to my left, so I pulled the trigger. I locked the crosshairs on the back of the right track, the one spot that didn't have armor, and started counting. *Five.* It was a small window, and the mech was moving, and I didn't know if the rocket would adjust enough or miss by half a meter and burst against the armored back to the left of the target or the tread protector on the right. *Four.* Another rocket whooshed away, this one to my right. I only caught it with peripheral vision. *Three.* Another rocket. I wasn't sure if that was four or five, if maybe two had fired at once. I stayed locked in on my target. *Two.* A fiery explosion erupted low on the back of the mech, spreading upward and engulfing it. Then another and another and another, and the mech was gone, replaced by fire and smoke and dust and chaos.

I held my breath, waiting for it to clear. In retrospect, we should have been running, but in that moment, it was impossible to turn away. We'd taken our best shot.

The stiff wind carried the smoke away.

The mech wasn't moving . . . but it wasn't inactive, either.

It fired a salvo of rockets, and a couple seconds later the vehicle to my left disappeared in a hail of explosions, five separate impacts compressing my chest. Something pinged off my helmet. A rock, or shrapnel.

"Fuck! Get us out of here!" Good news: we'd killed its mobility. But not its firepower.

We started forward and pulled a hard turn. I held onto the turret ring, trying to keep my feet while trying to keep my eyes on the mech at the same time.

Another salvo of rockets tore up the moon's surface exactly where the vehicle to our right had been three seconds prior. Sparks flashed from our wingman's chassis, but they kept moving, accelerating away from the mech like us.

We hit a smooth spot in the terrain, and I called for a second Slider, which the gunner passed up to me. I wouldn't be nearly as accurate from the moving, bouncing platform, but maybe I could blind its sensors for a few seconds, buy us more of a chance to escape. We hit a bump, and my ribs slammed into the turret ring. Ow. That was going to leave a mark. I fired, this time keeping my reticle center of mass. Less chance that I missed, and all I wanted to do was make noise and smoke to blind the thing and let us get more distance from it.

The mech started to turn, faster than something that size should be able to, one track reversing, the other moving forward, and before my rocket reached it, I was staring at the front of the thing. My missile hit the bottom slope of armor, shunting the blast down into the dirt of the moon's surface. Shit.

It took a second to register. The front of the mech. It had turned.

On its treads. "No mobility kill!" I shouted across the platoon net. "Spread out and speed up!"

I dropped down into the vehicle. It took me a few seconds to wrangle myself back into my seat with the vehicle bouncing around and weaving left and right, Jameson probably trying to throw off the mech's predictive tracking. I turned to look out the back window, the armo-glass not seeming nearly as comforting as it had before.

Dust kicked up from the back of the mech as it accelerated forward. Toward us. From our distance, I couldn't tell how fast it was gaining speed. Too fast, if I had to wager.

Why it turned away from the other platoon I don't know. Maybe it had eliminated enough targets and now saw us as more valuable prey. Who knew the algorithm it used? I didn't. I didn't know much right then. Only one thing, really.

We were fucked.

CHAPTER 27

Butler

"COLONEL BUTLER."

"Hey. Come in."

I lay in the dark, two different voices in my head somehow coming from two different places. Both women, one muted, the other louder, as if it were inside my head with me. It took me a minute to figure out where I was, what I was doing. More than a minute, maybe. The voices weren't helping. One of them—the one in my head—went away.

I opened my eyes. That helped with the darkness a little, but not much else. My head felt like it had gone a few rounds with an anvil. I had a metallic taste in my mouth. Even my tongue hurt. "Ow."

"Oh, thank the Mother, you're alive." The voice was distant and muffled, like she was talking underwater. I slowly turned my head, trying to find the source of the sound. I didn't have to go far. Chastain knelt beside me. "Can you move?"

It took me several seconds to figure out why the sound came through muffled. At first, I thought maybe I'd damaged my hearing or lost function in my helmet. But a check showed my gear still working. Credit the military for that. Our helmets weren't the best technology in the galaxy—far from it—but they could sure take a beating. I found Chastain's private channel in my heads-up and connected us. She probably hadn't known how to do it.

"I'm okay." That might have been true. My heads-up flashed a concussion warning. Yeah. Thanks for that. Probably could have figured that one out on my own. I could move my hands and feet. That was a start. We'd work on a more accurate assessment once I had a better understanding of the situation and how I got there.

Oh. Shit. The mech.

"The mech," I said, my brain still taking a bit longer than it should to get things to my mouth.

"It turned around and went the other way," she said. "I think we're safe for now."

It started to come back to me. Except it didn't make sense that the mech had turned away. Unless it had destroyed all the targets in our platoon. But we were still here, so that couldn't be it. "How long was I out?"

"It blew you up into the air about eight minutes ago."

I didn't remember that, but a concussion will do that to you. If I was only out for eight minutes, I'd probably gotten lucky—might be only a minor TBI—traumatic brain injury. Not that any injury to the brain is minor. I'd get checked, assuming we ever got back to a place where they could take a thorough look. For now, I had to fight through whatever ailed me. Better concussed than dead.

"How long after that did the mech turn around?" Even as she answered, I started piecing things together from my heads-up, trying to figure out who was alive, who wasn't, and everybody's locations. Our platoon was scattered over a couple of kilometers. A complete mess.

"Almost right after it blew you up. It kept coming for maybe thirty seconds—right at us. I thought I was dead, but I hid in a depression and tried not to move, and it never fired at me. It stopped, and after a little bit it turned and headed the other direction."

I had a feeling that Mac probably had something to do with that, but if so, I couldn't help him from here. The best I could do was gather what was left of our unit and then assess our situation. Kirkland. He'd know if anybody did. His name still registered in my display as alive. Then again, mine had probably not gone gray, and until a minute ago, that hadn't meant much. Someone being technically alive doesn't always mean they're intact.

I took a few deep breaths and a few more seconds to gather myself. Whatever the situation, me sounding anything other than calm and confident would make it worse. When I spoke, I used the platoon net.

"Kirkland, this is Butler."

"This is Kirkland. Glad you're still with us, sir." His tone was exactly what it should be. Calm, in control. No audible relief to hear me. Just another day. I could see now why the sergeant major had spoken highly of him. The mark of a good leader is how they handle pressure, and it didn't get much higher stress than this.

"I was out for a minute. I've got the reporter, Chastain, with me. She's okay. What's our status?"

"Still assessing, but best estimate is nine effectives, three of those walking wounded. One operational vehicle. One that we can potentially repair by cannibalizing the wreck of another. Needs a new wheel. Four personnel need evac. One critical that needs it now."

I didn't make him elaborate on that over the net. I knew what he meant. We weren't getting evac—not with that mech still in the area. That soldier wasn't going to make it. Nine effectives—half our platoon. A catastrophic loss, though somehow still better than I expected given what we'd been up against. I checked my heads-up for specific names. Dixon, my driver, was grayed out. Her staying at her post and leading the mech off probably saved my life. Castellano and Kim were still lit. I switched quickly to C's channel, still keeping an ear on Kirkland on the platoon net.

"You okay?"

"I'll live. LT has me down as one of the evacs. Broken leg. But I think I can splint it. I won't be doing a forced march any time soon, but I can make a go of it if we've got a vehicle. The low gravity helps."

"Sir." A female voice broke in on a private channel. "This is PFC Ruiz. I'm treating Castellano. Sorry for calling you on a private channel."

"Don't be. What is it, Ruiz?"

"I heard Castellano say that he was going to stay in the fight. He's high as fuck." She hesitated. "Sorry, sir. That's a technical term. I just shot him up with morphine for the pain. He has a broken femur. He's not fighting anyone. Not today."

"Roger. Thanks, Ruiz. Good looking out." I meant it. Sometimes, you had to protect soldiers from themselves. Though if that mech came back, it wouldn't care at all about whether we were combat-ready or not. Of course, if the mech came back, we were all dead anyway.

I probably needed to focus on that first. It was hard, my brain being scrambled as it was. I tuned back in to Kirkland, who had said something that I missed. "Say again."

"Roger. Working on consolidating our unit. Ruiz, Parrow, and Odhiambo are in your area. Link up with them as you can and try to make your way to the rally point."

"Wilco," I said, though I didn't know if I'd follow through and do it or not. I had to check in with Mac and see if there was anything we could do to help him out. I couldn't imagine what that could possibly *be,* given that Chastain and I were on foot and all of our heavy weapons except the single rocket launcher that lay on the ground ten meters from me had likely been destroyed with Dixon and the vehicle.

"Mac," I said, trying to reach him on a private channel.

"Little fucking busy," he said.

"Roger. Glad you're alive."

"Back at you." The line went quiet for a few seconds. "What the fuck?" He said it distantly, as if to himself and not me.

"What is it?"

"It stopped."

"The mech?" I asked.

"Yeah. Watch yourself. Last time it did this, it was chasing you and then turned and started chasing us."

I pushed up to my feet and maxed out the magnification on my helmet. It took me a minute to find the mech. A quick reading marked it at one point seven klicks away, and even from there it sent a chill down my back. Engineered death. No dust trail meant it wasn't moving. I didn't look away, in case what Mac said came to pass. But I had another thought.

Ganos.

I switched to the manual network. "Ganos."

No response. I waited, wondering which would come to life

first. The network or the mech. Beside me, Chastain stood quietly. This had to be a lot for her.

"Ganos," I said, trying it again.

"Where were you? I tried calling you for like five straight minutes."

"I got blown up by a mech and knocked out." I put my best deadpan tone into it.

"I've locked down the mech," she said. "I was calling you to tell you that we almost had it and to be ready."

Whoo. I gave a silent fist pump and looked up to the darkness above for a second. It's hard to explain the feeling of utter relief I had at that moment. I needed to tell Mac, and Kirkland. And . . . I had another thought. "Can you control it?" I could envision myself riding on top of the monster, right up to the dig site.

"That's not how this works. I've got it locked down. *Nobody* can operate it. It can't even operate itself. As far as the mech knows, it's completely non-functional. They'll be trying to reboot it, but I'm blocking that for now."

"Can you hold them off?"

"Not forever. We caught them by surprise to get as far as we did. Guess they weren't expecting me to go after their toy. Whoops. Their bad. Small-brained assholes."

"How long?" I now had visions of the mech coming back to life before we could get away from it.

"I can't say for sure. Probably an hour. At least thirty minutes. But whatever you need to do, if I were you, I'd get on it."

"Roger." I let the line go dead but pulled it up again. "Ganos."

"Yeah."

"Thanks."

"No problem."

"Mac." I called him on the company net, so literally everybody who still had comms could hear us. "The cyber team has the mech locked down for now, but we don't know how long. Thirty minutes to an hour is the estimate."

"We've got to take it out before it comes back to life," he said.

"Concur. What've you got for combat power?"

"Three vehicles operational. Still getting a handle on casualties, but we've taken losses. We've got some rockets."

"I can take it out." A new voice on the net. A woman. "This is Dae Kim. Get me to the mech. I've got explosives and shape charges. They'll work better than rockets."

"You sure you can take it out?" I asked.

"Pretty sure. I'm your best shot. I know *that*."

"Roger. Kirkland."

"On it," he said. "Kim's near me. I'll pick her up and we'll get right to the mech. I sure would appreciate someone coming to cover us while she works though."

"En route," said Mac.

"For the rest of the company, let's consolidate our two platoons. Bring your people to mine," said Kirkland. "We're working on a second vehicle, but right now all we have is the one moving Kim and me to the mech."

"Roger," said Mac.

"Did you hear all that?" I asked Chastain.

"I did. So, what do we do? You and me?"

I considered it for a second. Kirkland had things under control, and for the moment, they didn't need me. If I tried to insert myself, I'd have to divert critical vehicle assets to pick me up. C wasn't far, and there was a fire team with him. I could link up with them. That was the smart thing. Stay out of the way and keep Chastain out of the way.

But I wanted to be there. And when I thought about it, I wanted Chastain to be there. She had a story to tell, and the closer I got her to it, the better she'd tell it. "Are you up for a jog?"

CHAPTER 28

Butler

T HEY BEAT US to the mech, but not by much, since running in low gravity isn't that taxing once you get the hang of it. Up close, even in its catatonic state, the massive machine gave off an aura of destruction that made it frightening to approach. Yeah, it was dead, but it could come back. It was like being next to a tranquilized lion—you did *not* want to be around when that thing woke up. Mac didn't care. He was on top of the mech with two thermite grenades, measuring to find the optimal place to set them.

Kim had a schematic of the mech pulled up on a tablet. Even incapacitated, mechs like this were hard to kill because their important squishy bits sat deep inside, insulated against threats. But she'd said she could do it, and she knew better than I did. When there's an expert available, it's best to let them do their job.

"How is this going to work?" asked Chastain.

"Once Kim sets her charges, Mac is going to drop those two thermite grenades. He'll set them on top of the mech, they'll heat up to around 1100 degrees Celsius, and they'll melt their way straight down until they reach the dirt beneath the mech. Kim is going to set two charges: A shape charge underneath the mech that will shoot hot metal up through the softest part of it and a cutting charge on one of the tracks that will render the vehicle immobile."

"Why two charges?"

"In case the first one doesn't kill it, at least it won't be able to move."

"I assume we'll be well gone," she said.

"That's the plan. The unit is reconsolidating, gathering the wounded to a spot where they can get evac and the dead in a location where we can retrieve them later. After that, they'll prepare to continue the mission."

"We're going to keep going?" I didn't sense fear in her voice. More curiosity.

"Yeah. The only way this works is if we go on. If we quit, they win."

"Got it. I wish I had satellite access. I'd go live right now."

"Record everything you can while we're here," I said. "We'll get you to an uplink as soon as we can."

"I will. How much time do I have here?"

"Not long. Maybe five minutes. We'll need to back off once the charges are set, and then Kim will come back and inspect the damage. So maybe another five for that."

"Okay. I'll get to it then." Chastain moved apart from the rest of us and began recording. I'd have liked to hear what she was saying. Hell, I'd have liked to have told her what *to* say. But this only worked if she reported her own truth—exactly what she'd seen. She'd have her own spin. I *thought* that it was pretty clear cut, that Caliber would come off looking extremely bad. Using mechs against humans was a pretty damning story. But still, I'd have felt better if I could have dictated the narrative.

She'd trusted me so far. Now I had to trust her.

When Kim touched off the explosives, dust blasted out into a large cloud that the wind quickly whisked away. Honestly, it wasn't that impressive, over in a second. That's the reality of explosive charges. Sometimes it's more about placement and how they're directed than the absolute size of them. When the dust cleared, the vehicle listed a little to one side. Part of the protective plating was blown off, hanging by a handspan of twisted metal. The track behind it was gone, leaving a two-meter gap, and one of the drive wheels was canted almost ninety degrees out. That thing wasn't going anywhere.

Now we had to hope that the mech had made Caliber cocky and that they didn't have too much else waiting for us.

There was that fucking word again. Hope.

WE DEPARTED FOR the objective with five operational vehicles and twenty-four people who could fight. Carrying the wounded on top of that forced us to overload for a bit, but we couldn't leave them near the mech in case it came back online. About four kilometers later, we stopped and established a good evac point. C was injured and high, but he still had his rifle, and he could secure them for a short time until Xavier could get there and take them back to base. Davenport was another evacuee, but he was in no condition to fight. I offered Chastain the opportunity to go with them and start broadcasting what she had. She'd already been through a lot, and I wouldn't have blamed her if she wanted out. Instead, she sent a stick full of recordings back with C and stayed with us. Selfishly, that was good. She had more to see. Mac insisted on cross loading vehicles so that he could take C's place with us, which worked since we now formed a single platoon under Kirkland's leadership.

Having Mac at my back was never a bad thing.

WE DIDN'T KNOW the enemy's remaining capability, but they had some. Something had taken down our drones and taken out satellite communications, and it wasn't the mech. Worse, we didn't have much left to our attack. I hadn't shared it with anybody else—not even Mac—but in my head, once we assessed the enemy strength, I'd consider making the call to pull back. Yes, I wanted to win, but I didn't want to throw away more lives as part of a lost cause.

With about thirty klicks to go to the dig site, I expected enemy drones. We'd seen them previously, and once they knew we'd beat their mech, they'd want to wear us down as much as they could. We had two remaining drones, and we put them in the air out in front of us. That was a risk—the enemy had taken down our previous sorties. But at this point, we had no choice but to throw what we had at them. We drove cautiously, staying spread out, moving slowly. Nothing that would present a good target.

Ten minutes, then twenty. We drove on. It felt like the entire unit was holding its breath, waiting for the other hammer to fall. When the drone operator called in, it almost came as a relief, even though I expected the worst. I think we all did. But her voice didn't have that tone . . . the one that cries out warning.

"Shots fired, two point four kilometers ahead." By my map, that put them right at the dig site.

"What are they shooting at?" asked Kirkland. Good question. We hadn't come under fire, and we were out of range of most of what we'd expect them to have for armament.

"It was small arms," said the drone operator. "It's stopped now."

"I wonder what that was about," said Chastain.

"Don't know," I said.

"Bet they had a change in management," said Mac.

"What do you mean?" asked Chastain.

"Anybody fighting us out here is a merc," said Mac. "Might be someone at the top gave them an order that they didn't like, so someone decided to change it. Kinetically."

I considered that. "You've got a point. Might be they liked their payday a bit more when all they had to do was let the mech take care of us."

"What's that mean for us?" asked Chastain. "Does that mean they're going to fight to the death or give up?"

"Depends on who got off the first shot," said Mac.

"They've spotted one of our drones," said the operator. "Someone is pointing at it. I can't tell what . . . there's a flag. Someone is waving something . . . it looks like a t-shirt." The broadcast paused. "It's white!"

"Sir . . ." Kirkland's voice came in via a private channel. "Beyond my experience here. What do you think?" I appreciated that he had the wisdom to know his limitations. I wished that I had a confident answer for him. We could both see what it looked like—a surrender. But we'd need to play it safe. I linked Mac into the conversation.

"Set up overwatch with our longest-range weapons. We'll take two vehicles in to see what's up. If it looks even slightly shady, we bail and the overwatch lights them up."

"Roger," said Kirkland.

"Tell me you aren't planning to be part of the forward element," said Mac.

"Would you believe me if I did?" I asked.

"That's it. This is how I die. My epitaph will read, 'He followed a man who didn't know when to lay back.'"

I laughed, and before long, Mac was laughing too. His heart wasn't really in the protest.

"Something I should know about?" asked Chastain.

"Inside joke," I said.

KIRKLAND SET THE overwatch element fourteen hundred meters from the enemy position. We paused there, and then Mac and I moved forward with another vehicle on our left flank. I did talk Chastain out of coming along, but only by promising her that we'd get her forward immediately after we verified that it was safe.

"What are the odds that this is a trap and somebody starts shooting at us?" I asked Mac.

He thought about it. Odds making was serious business with him. "Thirty percent."

"That low?" I asked. I'd expected him to say fifty-fifty. That was the standard answer when we didn't know. Fifty percent. Either they would or they wouldn't.

"It seems overly complicated. If they wanted to engage us, they could have taken down our drones and waited for us to get in range. Gain surprise that way."

We reached seven hundred meters before I saw movement. I

upped the magnification in my optics, but it was still hard to make out through the windshield. "Gunner, what've you got?"

"Soldier still waving a white flag. A second one behind them, maybe a meter back. Looks like both are unarmed."

I verified the assessment with the drone operator, who was back with Kirkland in overwatch. "Roger. Two out front. At least six more personnel present."

"Armed?" I asked.

"Can't tell."

I looked at Mac. He shrugged. "Driver. Keep going," I said.

We stopped about forty meters from the two personnel in the open who still appeared to be unarmed. I could make out five others. I didn't *see* any weapons, but they were behind cover, so that didn't mean anything.

The site itself seemed mostly unchanged since our last visit. A cave gaped in the rock of the hill, support beams reinforcing it. Two cranes and a heavy hauler sat nearby, parked askew down the slope, unmanned as far as I could tell.

"Now what?" asked Mac. "We walk out there?"

"What could go wrong?" I asked.

Mac sighed and opened his door. If I wanted to expose myself, he'd force his way in front of me. We walked forward about ten meters, out in front of our two vehicles. We both had our Bitches and, more important, we had two gunners with heavy weapons right behind us. If someone took a shot, they'd . . . well . . . they'd avenge us, anyway.

I flipped the speaker in my helmet on. "Come out from behind cover. All of you."

The leader lit up in my display. They'd opened their comms,

allowing me to connect to them. It would also make me vulnerable to a cyber-attack if I accepted. I studied the flag bearer for a few seconds. Big, with broad shoulders, and taller than me. It didn't *feel* like a trap. It was like Mac said: too complicated. It wouldn't really help them to hack my helmet. The rest of our team could still open fire. In a close-up battle between a hacker and a bullet, I'd bet on bullet. I connected. "Who am I talking to?" I asked.

"Wiggins," said a female voice. "The rest will come out from behind cover when I have assurances that you won't fire on them."

"I'm Colonel Butler. Retired. What happened here, Wiggins?"

"Me and some . . . most . . . of the others decided that we didn't sign on to fight against the military. We had a bit of a disagreement with our leadership on that . . . the violent kind of disagreement."

I considered her words. She made it sound like they were just out here doing the right thing. I didn't blame her. It sounded a lot better than *we expected the mech to take you out, but now our own asses are on the line.* I found that I didn't care. They'd surrendered. We could move past the motive behind it. "What am I going to find here? Are there any holdouts?"

"None who've voiced it." Not quite what I'd asked, but she couldn't know for sure. They'd shot people. Not likely that others would be completely open about their feelings if they disagreed with that. But nobody was shooting now.

"What's your strength?"

"Seventeen effectives. Three bodies." That she'd calmly admitted to murder said something about her. What, I wasn't sure, but it did help me trust her.

Pragmatism over emotion. I could relate.

"What about inside?"

"Four. Company people, not from our team. One scientist, one excavation expert. Two others."

"Armed?"

"I didn't see anything. Maybe pistols."

"They going to be a problem?" I asked.

"Maybe. But if it's them or us . . ."

"It's them," I said, completing the saying. "Any reinforcements coming?"

"We've been promised them, but I don't know if they're coming. We haven't heard from anybody. And we've been asking for days."

I thought through the whole situation. Seventeen—of what had been twenty. Even with just small arms, dug in here, they could have caused us a lot of problems. We might not have been able to dig them out, and we'd definitely have lost people trying. Wiggins had done us a major favor. "Roger. You've got my assurances. Bring your people out. Have them lay down their weapons. I promise that you all make it back to base unharmed. Might take us a minute. Transportation is limited."

"What happens after that?"

"All I can promise is that I'll do my best for you. You don't have control over your own contracts—you go where you're sent—so I think we'll be able to wrangle some leniency."

"Roger. But there are the three dead."

"I'm not going to lie. That's a problem." I figured enough people had lied to her for one lifetime.

"Nobody else had anything to do with that. That was me." She was lying. One person surprising and taking out three didn't seem likely. But if she wanted to take responsibility and try to shield the others from guilt, I wasn't going to argue.

"We'll get you a good lawyer," I promised. "You knew that they were going to engage government troops. There's an argument to be made that you're a hero."

She snorted. "I'm no hero."

"I hear that. None of us are." I called Kirkland and told him to bring a team forward to secure the prisoners.

The four people inside gave up quickly once we told them that everyone outside had capitulated. Our team consolidated on the objective, and I took Chastain into the cave. The door at the back of it—a hatch, really—stood open. Mac went first, moving quickly while Clement covered him. Once he called all clear, I led Chastain through, the light from her camera display glowing against her facemask. I took mine off, demonstrating the livable oxygen level. I didn't know how it worked, but the fact that it *did* work was one of the most important takeaways for Chastain. After a few seconds filming me and recording herself, she took hers off, too.

Inside, she stopped to narrate for several seconds. I gave her the time she needed. This was why we came. In my mind, the structure resembled a buried spaceship. Chastain would call it what she wanted. As long as she got the video out, her opinion and mine didn't matter. Experts—professional and amateur, real and fake—would analyze it to death. Some people would believe it, some wouldn't. But nobody would be able to erase it, and some parts, nobody could dispute. It had no detectable power source, and it had been there in the ground for hundreds of years, yet still it had perfect lighting and ventilation throughout its chambers that remained intact.

That's why Caliber wanted it—why they took illegal actions to get it. If they could discover how it worked, the potential profit was unlimited. And they'd been working on it. They'd excavated three new compartments since I'd been there previously, and still, much of the wreck was buried.

Chastain stopped in every room. Mac hovered, off camera, keeping security, but also making sure that nothing disturbed the recording. I'm sure if I checked, Clement and Kim were stationed somewhere back along the way providing an extra layer of protection. Kirkland and his team remained outside, securing and logging the prisoners while they waited for the exfil aircraft to return.

In theory, I should have been celebrating. We'd won. We'd made it to the objective, and the enemy had surrendered. Soon, Chastain would be broadcasting the results to the galaxy.

Something nagged at me, though—I'm sure Mac would say something always nagged me. But it couldn't be this easy. Maybe I was tired. Maybe it was the concussion and the headache nested behind my eyes. Maybe I was letting my cynical nature taint the success. I do have that setting. But I've dealt with it long enough that I've developed some self-awareness. I tend to recognize that mistake when I'm making it. Still, I couldn't quite trust myself. I fell back a bit and signaled Mac over.

"This was too easy, right?" I asked.

"It didn't feel too easy when that mech was about to kill me."

"Fair," I said. That had been unexpected and more than a challenge. "But after that . . . nothing."

"Their mercs quit on them. One of the perils of the business." Mac said it matter-of-factly, no emotion, and I didn't know if he believed what he was saying or if he was playing devil's advocate to help me work through my thoughts. But if I asked him, it would ruin it.

"Something Wiggins—the enemy leader—said is bothering me. They asked for reinforcements, but they didn't come. *Why?* Caliber knew we were coming here. Sure, they had the mech. But they could have brought more—made absolutely sure they stopped us."

"Maybe they tried."

Huh. I hadn't considered that. That's why it helped to talk things through. If they had tried and failed . . . or tried and been too late . . . that would make more sense than what we'd seen. Interplanetary travel had hiccups sometimes. Mercenaries refused contracts or were too far away. There were lots of explainable reasons that allowed us to reach this point. Any one of them could have been true. So much so that I almost started to believe it—that we'd won and that was that.

Almost.

I'd have continued to think about it, but Chastain came over to me, her camera now off.

"I'd like to interview you."

"Here? Now?"

"Yes. I think it would provide context."

I'd planned to get involved, to talk about all the things that Caliber had done. Killing people, trying to kill *me*. We didn't truly win until we got the word out about this, and more specifically, about what Caliber was doing to try to suppress it for their own gain. But if I talked now, I felt like it would taint her product. It would be easy for a Caliber propagandist to spin this as me being bitter toward them since, well . . . I *was*. Better to let her tell the story, get it out there. I could add to it later, once people digested the first round. "If I talk, it's going to come off as biased. There are a lot of preconceived notions about me out there in the galaxy, and people are going to look at me with their minds already made up."

"Anything is better than me narrating. Reporters aren't exactly the most trusted profession."

I had a thought. "What if I could get you someone else? A scientist."

She looked around, exaggerating it for effect. "You see one?"

"Professor Seibring is outside with the prisoners. He was here working with Caliber. That would provide some credibility, right?"

She studied me. "Depends on what he says. You think he'd be honest?"

"I can be pretty persuasive. Let me try."

I could directly ask him to do the interview, but if I did, I gave him too much power. He'd know I wanted something and could use that as leverage. Instead, this needed to be about what *he* wanted. A way out. I needed to convince him that what he really wanted was what *I* wanted.

But first I'd start him off with some intimidation. Get him on his back foot. Fortunately, he was already a civilian thrust into the unfamiliar situation of being on a battlefield, so I had a head start in that regard. We'd taken the standard action of separating him from the other prisoners and not talking to him. But he wouldn't know that was normal. By now, his mind would have concocted all of the worst possibilities.

I didn't know much about the professor. A quick search said he'd worked in academia for a long time before making the jump to corporate life. Probably for financial reasons.

I had Mac send for him, had Clement escort him in to see me alone. Clement didn't rough him up—that would be over the line—but he wasn't exactly gentle, either, guiding him by the arm in a way that let him know who the boss was. We weren't going to hurt him. But we didn't have to assure him of that fact, either. Clement deposited the man in front of me and left. Mac stayed, a couple steps away within Seibring's line of vision, looking menacing. Not on purpose. That's Mac's normal demeanor. I let Seibring stand there in silence until he started to fidget.

"What do you want from me?" he asked, finally. His voice didn't exactly scream panic, but he could get there with a little push.

"The question is, what do *you* want from *me*?"

"You can't keep me here."

"Can't is a pretty nebulous concept, isn't it? I definitely *can*. I can also release you outside and abandon you on the surface of Taug." I let that sit for a few seconds. "But I'm probably not going to do that."

"If you do, you'll—"

"I'll what? Get in trouble? I promise that I've done much worse things to much better people than you, and I'm still here. And that's assuming that anybody ever acknowledges your presence on Taug. The soldiers with me didn't put you in their records, and I have a feeling that right now Caliber is doing everything in their power to distance themselves from this operation. It's quite possible that you don't officially exist."

He stood there, probably trying and failing to come up with a good comeback. That was a shame, because I had several more prepared if he did. I got tired of waiting for him to speak again, though, so I took the lead. "I'll dispense with the threats. I'm not going to leave you out here or have you killed. You have my word on that. For you, there are exactly two options, and they're not negotiable. Option one: I put you in cuffs and we take you back to base and charge you with multiple crimes. I say that you had full involvement in Caliber's actions on Taug, and that you were part of the team that knowingly and willingly attacked government forces." I paused to let it sink in. "That would be treason, so we're clear."

"That's a lie!" he said.

"Maybe. But maybe not. You'd say anything at this point to save yourself. A fact that won't be lost on prosecutors. Or a jury. You're here. You weren't restrained when we arrived. Right now, my best hacker is searching for the financial arrangement between you and Caliber. She'll track down all of your travel, to see if you came willingly or if you were on a prison ship." None of that was true—I hadn't set Ganos after him yet. But he didn't know that. And I *could*.

"I didn't know that Caliber was going to attack coalition soldiers!"

"That's a good story. I'd stick to it for your defense. Maybe someone will believe it."

"I came to work on a scientific find."

"And exploit it for Caliber's profit."

"No! Well . . . yes. But that's not why I came."

I hesitated. He seemed earnest. Maybe there was another way to get what I wanted. "Why *did* you come?"

He stared at me. "Are you kidding? This is the discovery of a lifetime. I've worked my entire career in this field, and there's been nothing even *close* to this. Yes, I had to work for a corporation. No, that's not ideal. But that was the price if I wanted to study the find."

"What did they promise you?" I asked.

"Access. And I guess I thought that if I was here, I could control it. Do good with the discovery or at least limit the bad. That might have been naïve."

"A bit," I said. "So . . . what now?"

"You've got the guns. You tell me."

"There's a way out," I said, throwing him a lifeline.

To his credit, he didn't immediately grab at it. "What's the catch?"

"No catch. We make you the good guy. You go on camera with a reporter, and you give a guided tour of this place. You answer every question she asks about this structure, and you do it with a smile and to the best of your ability. You answer questions about Caliber and what they were trying to do here. You answer anything that Ms. Chastain asks you."

He shook his head. "The press? That doesn't do me any good. There's no credit in that. I need to publish. Get peer reviewed. If I go on camera, I'm giving everything away."

Huh. I hadn't considered that as a motivation. I guess I don't understand academia. But I do understand people, and I believed him. I also didn't care about his credit. "This story is going out with or without you. If you don't want to be part of it, I'll put you back with the prisoners. Either way, it'll be news all across the galaxy within twenty-four hours."

He considered it for longer than I would have expected. "Caliber will—"

"They'll be pissed," I said. I left out the fact that they might try to kill him. We were both in that boat if we didn't cripple them. "Consider this as turning state's evidence via the media."

"What are my requirements if I do the interview?"

I kept my face neutral at that. Smiling now would only mess things up. We'd come to an agreement—he'd do it. Now we were just haggling over price. "We want the truth about the ship and Caliber. We're less worried about the truth about you. Make yourself likable. Be the scientist explaining this once-in-a-lifetime discovery to the galaxy."

"And after that . . . what? Prison?"

"Did you shoot at any soldiers?"

He frowned at me. "No."

"Did you order anyone to shoot at soldiers?"

"No."

"I'm asking you to tell the truth on camera. If you do, then I will include those two facts as part of the truth that *I* report."

"Why should I believe you?"

He had a point. I would absolutely lie to him. It happened that I *wasn't*, but he couldn't be sure of that. I wanted to ask him what choice he had. But if I did that, I risked him refusing to talk. You can't ever rule out someone being a stubborn bastard. I mean . . . look at *me*. "You're small time in this. Caliber orchestrated it, and they're going down for it. Your decision is whether you're riding the ship with them or not."

Still, he took his time. "Okay. I'll do it."

Now I smiled. "Good man."

CHAPTER 29

Butler

THE RIDE BACK was a lot smoother and faster than the ride out, since I went by air. We'd gotten everything we needed from the crash site. Professor Seibring started slow on his interview, maybe trying to hold back his secrets. I was going to step in, remind him of his obligation in a less than subtle way, but Chastain didn't need me. She asked leading questions, and more and more he opened up. It's nice to work with people who are good at their jobs. He gave her a full rundown of the system that they'd excavated that he believed controlled the creation and flow of oxygen, explaining what he thought each piece did. They hadn't taken it apart yet—he didn't understand it well enough for that and didn't want to risk ruining it with no way to re-create the technology.

He explained that they hadn't yet uncovered the power system, but that readings indicated it wasn't much farther down—readings that didn't match the signature of any known form of power generation. He spoke as if that was an even bigger discovery, and given how much Chastain had gotten him to open up, I had no reason to doubt him. Others would dig into it soon, regardless.

He'd mentioned peer review in our negotiation. Once this became public content, he'd definitely get that.

Now all we had to do was get Chastain to a terminal with off-moon access, and we'd be good to go. We hadn't even had to shoot anybody in the face. That alone felt like a win. I was riding high enough that half of me expected Caliber to launch an anti-air missile at us on the way home. Part of that is my pessimism. Another part is just good business—evaluating the worst possible outcome and preparing. To mitigate the risk, I had Chastain make me a copy of all her footage. She'd balked at that, wanting to make her edits before letting the public see it, but I promised that I wouldn't use any of it except in an emergency. She still wanted to interview me for the story, get the bigger perspective, so I had some leverage, and I used it to get my way. I gave the copy to Kirkland, who was returning by ground.

Caliber hadn't quit. They couldn't. They'd keep trying right up until there was no hope. Sure, we held all the cards at the moment, but they'd try to change the game. Serata coming was probably part of that. If they couldn't shoot us down physically, maybe they intended to do it politically. Mac wasn't talking, lost in his own thoughts and scowling at anyone he didn't know who tried to come near us. Chastain was busy going over her footage and making notes. Xavier was with us too, but she had her own pressures to deal with, so I couldn't confide in her.

I never thought I'd miss having an aide. I'd always said I didn't need one, and in some respects I didn't. I could make my own arrangements, take care of my own needs. But having someone, even someone inexperienced, that I could bounce ideas off of as a sounding board . . . I really could have used that. Especially when I learned that Serata had landed an hour prior. He wanted something—or someone did, and he was the messenger—and I didn't know what. So when we arrived back at base, I did what so many people before me had done in difficult situations.

I ran away.

I took my time getting off the ship, letting Xavier disembark first and greet Serata, and once they were engaged, I grabbed Mac and slipped away to get a checkup for my concussion. It set an example for soldiers by taking that injury seriously, and more importantly, in this case, it made an unimpeachable excuse for my delay.

That bought me half an hour, as they gave me a physical exam and then a CT scan to rule out more serious injury. In the end, they told me to cut down on physical activity for a couple of days and avoid situations where I had to concentrate. I told the doctor's assistant that I'd do my best, and she believed the lie. I used the time to think through my upcoming interaction with Serata.

If it had been anyone else, I'd have had to consider that he could be trying to cover up Caliber's crimes. Zentas had a lot of influence, and he could have pressured whoever he owned in the government and/or military to intervene. But Serata being here—specifically him—negated that. He couldn't be bought. If Serata came here to cover something up, he'd only do it if he believed it to be the right thing to do. He had his own moral code . . . even if some of it was a bit warped.

He also knew me. He knew that if he showed up and told me to drop everything I found against Caliber, I'd dig in. Shit, I'd double down. He wouldn't try that. Instead, he'd try to manipulate me, change my mind, but only within the boundaries of the possible. Things that I'd potentially accept. Nobody knew those boundaries better than he did, so he'd know that me letting Caliber off the hook was off the table.

I couldn't avoid him forever, so we headed toward headquarters with Mac walking in front of me. Like before, he glared at everyone who came from the opposite direction like they were a potential threat. Once, he stopped a civilian contractor and put him against the wall for a quick pat-down search. I almost asked if that was necessary, but held it in. He'd done it, so in his mind, obviously it was. Clement walked behind me, and nobody got by him. Anyone in a hurry could find another route.

We entered the front door of the headquarters to find Serata there, standing in a group with Xavier and the new commander, Lieutenant Colonel Exley. Serata had probably flown in with her, which added yet another layer of complexity to the whole situation. Was she in league with him, or was he here to keep an eye on her? Or did they simply share a convenient ride?

The general excused himself and ambled toward me. I took a couple steps to meet him, but he covered most of the ground. He was the one who wanted something. He shook my hand and pulled me in for a hug at the same time, and I returned it. We'd greeted each other the same way dozens of times, but this time it held no warmth. He was here to do a distasteful job. I knew it, and he knew that I knew it. In a weird way, I had to credit him for understanding the difference. The hug was for show. We were at odds, but nobody else needed to know that.

"We need to talk," he said.

"Yeah." It was a simple response, but Serata would be able to read a lot into it. No "yes, sir." No emotion in it. A flat acknowledgement of fact. I pulled back from our embrace. "Major Xavier."

"Yes, sir?" She'd been watching us, because of course she had. Her new commander was here, but that was a sideshow. We were the main attraction.

"Can we borrow a place to talk?" The only space I had was my hotel room, and I wanted to keep this in a more businesslike setting.

She glanced at her new boss. Meeting the new commander was always a bit awkward, and my request made that worse. Couldn't be helped, though. "You can use my office," she said. "I'll be with the new commander anyway."

"Use *my* office," said Exley. "I insist. It would be an honor."

"Thanks, Tabitha," said Serata, accepting before I had the chance to protest.

"I'll meet you there in a couple minutes," I said. "There's someone I need to talk to first."

If Serata wanted to challenge that, it didn't show in his face. "Sure."

We separated from them and Mac glanced at me for instructions. "Ganos," I said. He led the way, clearing a couple of soldiers out of our path as we headed to the secure area where they'd set her up. Kim was there, outside the door, guarding it even though it was locked. That she'd gotten here this soon after we returned meant Mac wasn't relaxing. I hadn't expected him to. She rang the buzzer, and Ganos herself answered.

"Heard you were here." She handed me a piece of paper with five names on it. Military names. "Thought you'd need this."

"Thanks. How sure are you of this?"

She shrugged. "Depends on what you mean by sure. I'm sure that these people had contact with Caliber in ways that they probably didn't want known. I haven't looked into financial arrangements. Yet. That's a different kind of operation. Best not done from military hardware."

"This everybody?"

"Probably not. Others might have been smarter."

I nodded. "Thanks. I'll come back and find you once I'm done."

She disappeared back inside, and Mac and I headed to the commander's office. "She seem off to you?" he asked.

"I don't know. A little?" But my mind was already moving forward to Serata, thinking through the possible permutations of that conversation.

Mac went into the office before me. Maybe he expected Serata to try to kill me. He wouldn't. He'd have people to do his dirty work for him. I waited in the hallway without saying anything.

Serata was standing when I went in. I moved past him and around behind the desk. "Coffee?" I asked. I'd been in the office before on my previous trip and knew there was a machine. "I'm having some. It's been a long day."

"Sure." Serata took a seat at the small table. I almost sat behind the desk to set the tone, but I dismissed the idea. I made two coffees and took a seat across from him, pushing his over the table.

"You got here quick," I said. I preferred to get started with minimal bullshit, but some amount was unavoidable.

"You took a detour."

"Talca?" I was legitimately curious at his choice of words. I didn't understand how it was a detour.

"When everything went down on Ridia 2, we expected you to come straight here. It took time for word to get to me and then to get everyone on board with a plan to meet you here. But then you didn't come directly, so we caught up."

"Hold on." He'd caught me off guard with more than one part of that. He'd said *we*. *Who was we?* But that wasn't even the biggest flag. "You know what happened on Ridia?"

"That Caliber tried to kill you? Yes."

I considered what that meant. If I was taking the worst possible meaning, it meant that the "we"—and with Serata, that probably meant government entities—were complicit. But if that were the case, I wouldn't have made it off of Ridia 2 alive, so there had to be more to it. I decided my only option was to let him explain. But I didn't have to hold in my anger about it. I was fucking furious, but I kept my voice level and cold. "And did nothing? No warning. No help."

"They didn't know until after it happened." So *we* had turned to *they*. Convenient. "After the ambush at the rental house. But something like that happens . . . it sets off alarms all over the place. It takes a minute to work its way up the chain, but it gets there."

"That's convenient. Finding out once it's too late to do anything about it."

"You came out of it okay."

I had. If you didn't count the concussion. Or the blood on my hands. But I didn't want to let him control the conversation, so I changed directions. "Who are you working for?"

He stared me down for a second, maybe taken aback by the insolence of the question. But he wasn't my boss anymore. "Who do you think?"

"I think it's the government. Probably via the military, but not only military. But I'm going to need to hear you say it."

"That's correct," he said.

"If the government wants something from me . . . and you wouldn't be here if they didn't . . . this is a strange way to start."

"Come on, Carl. You want all the information. You're not going to make a decision until you get it. This is me telling you the truth."

At one point in my life, that would have got me. I'd have taken that truth as a sign that he had my best interests at heart. He didn't. The people who sent him *definitely* didn't. I was a tool that they'd use and discard. "And I'm saying that the *truth* here is pretty convenient. *They* sit back, see who wins, and then deal with the winner."

"It happened the way I told you—the timeline of when people found out. There's evidence. You're going to have to take my word for now. I don't have it here. But at least trust that I made them show it to me. Like you, I had to know the truth."

I considered it for several seconds. Not because I needed time, but because I wanted to make him sweat before I conceded. He was telling the truth—or the truth as he believed it—and it would have been hard for anybody to make him believe a lie. He could read people the same way I could. Probably better. "Okay. Let's say I accept that. What else don't I know?" I had things to confront him with, to poke holes in his story, but I wanted him to say everything he had to say first. Maybe I'd learn something.

"There's a *lot* you don't know."

"I'm sure."

"There was a power struggle inside the military about the commander of Taug once Parnavic died."

"Once Parnavic was murdered," I corrected. I couldn't help myself.

"Possibly."

"Probably," I said.

"Okay. Probably."

"And definitely covered up."

"The investigation was rushed. Yes. And a new commander was assigned. Someone who was likely to keep the status quo here."

"Someone influenced by Caliber."

"Probably not?" That he questioned it made it more believable. "But probably someone beholden to someone influenced by Caliber. Or maybe another layer removed. Honestly, I don't know. Yet."

I fingered the list of names in my pocket. I hadn't decided yet if I'd give that to him or not. "But that commander got derailed for Exley, who is—"

"Someone who will do the job right. Which was more complicated than a swap of orders. To simply remove Robinson—the original commander—would have warned the bad actors that leadership knew something. Instead, he got orders to a higher priority job elsewhere, and nobody was immediately slotted as a replacement."

I nodded. If that was the case, the solution made sense. Make his removal look like a promotion. "Which left Xavier in charge."

"And gave you time to get here before orders came."

"You're saying that not only did they *let* me come, they *wanted me* to?"

"That's exactly what I'm saying. If they wanted to stop you, all they had to do was tell Xavier to detain you upon arrival. They didn't."

"They wanted me to run directly into whatever Caliber had waiting," I said.

"Come on, Carl. Think it through. You knew this was too easy."

"It didn't feel easy when a heavy mech was trying to kill me." It was Mac's line, but it fit.

"A failure in intelligence. Didn't know it was here."

"Now who needs to think it through?" Of course he'd say that—or someone would say that to him.

Serata slid me his device. The screen was open to a picture of a bunch of soldiers in a troop transport. Close to a hundred of them.

"What's this?" I asked.

"One of the two companies of mercenaries who the military intercepted when they entered Ridia system."

"You're telling me that the military detained a corporate transport."

"Yes," he said.

"That's illegal."

He shrugged. "Okay. Maybe they'll sue. Somehow, given everything that's happened, I doubt it."

"Caliber was sending a couple hundred soldiers to bolster their position?"

Serata nodded once. "How much chance would you have had against that?"

If he was telling the truth—if the picture was real—then we'd have had zero. We hacked the mech. You can't hack an infantry company. I didn't say that out loud. I didn't need to. Serata knew what I was thinking. "Give me a second," I said.

I needed to assess how likely this scenario was. That the government had known about Caliber and then decided to use me as an instrument to do something about it. I *wanted* to believe it. That's the thing, though. If Serata was trying to manipulate me, he'd give me something that I wanted to believe. I had to take my ego out of it, see it objectively. "Why not deal with it themselves?"

"Let me answer your question with a question. Who—government, military, or other—is influenced by Caliber?"

I almost pulled out the list, but it wasn't time yet. "I don't know."

He studied me, maybe sensing the lie. "There are multiple people involved. Right? Some maybe that we suspect, but definitely some that we don't."

I was starting to get the picture. "You're saying that they wanted *me* here because they knew I wasn't compromised."

"That you couldn't *be* compromised. Without knowing who in the military is involved, it would have been difficult—if not impossible—to find *anybody* who couldn't potentially be reached. Not bought, necessarily. Not even involved. But someone who could be swayed by a superior telling them it would be best to go one way instead of the other?"

"Okay. I get it." I wasn't sure I believed it completely, but the thesis was sound. There were very few truly independent actors in the military. I certainly hadn't been. Back on Cappa I'd *thought* I was. But Serata had known exactly how to pull my strings, had used me even without my explicit compliance. And here we were again. "But if that's true . . . it sounds an awful lot like they used me. And put me and my team at significant risk to do it." I left out the word *again*.

To his credit, Serata didn't turn away from that. He met my eyes unwavering. "That's true. And that's why I'm here."

I seriously doubted that that was why he was here. It might have been *one* reason he came, but not the primary one. He was here because he—or more likely, the government—still needed something. I was too tired to play games, so I decided to get to it. "What do you want?"

"Excuse me?" he said. Maybe I offended him. He'd been my superior, and I'd always treated him with deference, even after we both left the military. Maybe he was buying time, thinking through how to respond. Or maybe he hadn't understood me.

"You wouldn't have come all the way out here to talk to me unless you still wanted something."

He smiled. "Ah. Right. That."

I smiled back, at least as fake as his. Probably more. "That."

"I want to make you an offer."

I kept my face flat. Didn't respond. If he wanted to make an offer, he could make it. I didn't have to make it easy.

"What if your trip here was official?"

I didn't respond immediately, but this time it wasn't intentional. He'd lost me, and it took me a second to catch on. "You mean post-dated. Like we planned it from the start."

"Right."

"To what end?"

"For an official action, the government would reimburse all your expenses—you and your whole team."

"It's not about money," I said. But truth be told, I'd spent a *lot* on our trip, especially getting on and off Talca. I could say that money didn't matter—and it didn't, when I had it—but I'd run through a good chunk of my net worth. I didn't want to let on to Serata, but he could probably read the half-truth from me. He was good like that. And he'd certainly done his homework and had the help of a nearly limitless staff, who would have looked into every aspect of my life.

"Of course not," he said with no hint of duplicity in his voice. "But it could help."

"What else?"

"What else do you want?"

"I don't know. Just seeing what's on the table."

"How about being cleared of your crimes on Talca?"

"What crimes?" I smiled.

He laughed. "Well played. Okay. Clearance of Ganos's crimes on Talca."

I didn't respond.

"Clearance of *Alanson's* crimes on Talca."

"Who?" I asked.

"Come on, Carl."

"Where is he?"

"He's in a minimum-security facility on Talca, awaiting the outcome of further investigations."

"Minimum security?"

"Basically, a hotel he can't leave."

He knew exactly what to offer. I cared what happened to my people. "And by further investigations, you mean if I do what you want."

He shrugged. "I haven't told you what *we* want from *you*."

"I have a good idea," I said.

"Do you?"

"You're not going to ask me to cover up Caliber's actions. Because you know that's a waste of time. There's no price."

"I do know that. Took me a minute to convince . . . certain people . . . of it."

"Which means you want me to protect . . . someone? Not Zentas. Someone . . . in the government or the military."

He smiled, more genuine this time. "Sometimes I forget how good you are at this shit."

"It took me a while to figure it out. Why you came. Other than the fact that someone thinks you're their best chance to convince me."

"For the record, I told them that that was true at one point, but probably not anymore."

"I don't know. You got me alone in a room. I'm not sure who else would have been able to accomplish that without handcuffs."

"Fair enough," he said.

"Who is it?"

"Who is what?"

"Who do you . . . *they* . . . want me to protect? I want a name."

"I don't have one."

"Then no deal," I said.

"Carl, will you fucking *listen*?"

This time I smiled. I was being a dick, pushing him, and it had finally had the intended effect. He'd lost his composure. Unless I missed my guess, this was where he threatened me. Hopefully, he didn't pop me in the face. He was a lot bigger than me and still in good shape.

After a few seconds where I didn't respond, he continued, "There's no specific name because we don't know all the names yet."

"Then I'll ask again. What do you want?"

"It's simple. You leave it to us."

I snorted. "Right. I leave it to you—*them*—to cover up. Pass."

"Hear me out," he said without pleading. He was back under control. "Have you gone on the record with the news yet?"

"Not yet. Soon."

"Good. What I *want* you to do is stick to Caliber. Don't mention complicity in the government or military."

"I'm not going to—"

"Immediately following the report going public—*the same day*—the military will publicly announce that they've discovered internal corruption in conjunction with Caliber's actions here on Taug, and that they'll be conducting a full investigation."

"Will they? Conduct a legit investigation?"

"Absolutely. What you're doing by not mentioning it is helping the institution keep trust with the people. When military leaders come forward on their own to admit that they have a problem, that's much better than being seen as reacting to somebody else's accusations."

I considered it. He had a point. Sure, they could still cover it up later, wait for it to blow over. Serata would say they wouldn't, but I knew how little that was worth. And he hadn't played his last card. The threat hadn't come yet, but it was there. If I didn't do business with him, my team could still disappear on Taug. So could Chastain. That would be a drastic step, for sure, but bad things happened. Thankfully, the list of names in my pocket gave me some control. I could let the military do their investigation and then check my names against their results. If I didn't like what I saw, I could release it to the press.

I let my shoulders sag. If I caved too easily, Serata would suspect something.

"Chastain—she's the reporter for *The Times*—will have questions. There's no way she doesn't ask me about government involvement."

"Can you put her off? Talk around it?"

"Maybe. Off the record, I can tell her the military is going to make a statement. But it harms my credibility."

"You'll figure it out. You always do."

"I probably can."

"But . . . ," said Serata, correctly predicting that I had more conditions.

"I want more."

"Never doubted that. Spell it out."

"A soldier named Dixon sacrificed her life to save mine. She's a hero. I want her treated as such."

"Done. Even if there's no other deal, I'll make sure that happens. And we'll do what we can for everybody harmed in this action. Posthumous promotions, if they're eligible, so their families get more money. We've done it before. You know the drill." He met my eyes. He meant it, and I appreciated it. They deserved that, regardless of the politics and bullshit.

"Nobody interferes with the report from *The Times*. No suppression of it by any means. That means no removing it from the net, but it also means no government pressure on *The Times* to bury it or retract it. We tell the full truth about what's here on Taug."

"Deal," he said. Whether he had the authority to back it up, I couldn't know. I could only take him at his word. "Caliber will pressure them as well, though."

"Caliber goes down."

"Define that." His quick request for clarification meant that he'd clearly anticipated my request.

"*Real* punishments. Expulsion off of Taug. Cancellation of all government contracts—"

"Expulsion off Taug, yes. The other . . . we can't do that. You know that." I did know that. Caliber was a major arms and ship builder. Replacing them would take time if it was possible at all. They had illegal influence, sure, but they also had plenty that was legal. Lobbyists, campaign contributions, supply contracts.

"Jail time for those involved in the murders."

"They'll scapegoat people."

"Jail time for Zentas."

He almost laughed. "Carl. Let's live in the real world."

"I'm fucking tired of the real world. In the real world, nobody suffers consequences for their actions. Nobody rich. No corporation. Fines won't do it. They don't mean anything beyond a cost of doing business."

"Zentas isn't going to jail."

"He tried to have me killed."

"Which we can't prove," said Serata.

"Okay. But we can charge him."

He rolled his eyes. That was fair. I *was* living in a fantasy world.

"Fine. Then I want his private army dismantled. I'll provide information on how they skirt the system and create off-the-grid assassins."

"That . . . that might work. Though things like that are notoriously hard to shut down. You find one nest and they relocate somewhere else."

"Protection for my team. Every member. Chastain, too. Caliber has proven that they'll kill people. I want that stopped."

"What's that look like? In practice?" he asked.

"I don't know. Short of dismantling them completely, they'll always be a threat."

Serata thought about it. "We'll come up with something. It's a fair ask. Maybe it's government protection."

"What, you hide us away with fake identities?"

"If you want."

"I don't. But I'll ask the team."

"We'll work it out. Anything else?"

"If all we get for Caliber are fines—"

"And expulsion from Taug."

"I want the biggest fine in the history of the galaxy," I said. "Something that will really hurt. I want it to hit their *share price*. I want every shareholder—everyone connected with Caliber in any way—to feel this."

"That's ambitious," he said.

"Sure."

"I can't guarantee the size of the fine."

"Promise me we'll ask. That we'll *try*," I said.

"Okay. I promise. Anything else?"

"One more thing," I said. "They owe me."

"What even is that?"

"I don't know," I admitted. "But I'm doing them a favor. Everything I've asked for—none of it's guaranteed beyond the reimbursement of expenses. Right? Once I pass up my shot to make it a big deal on the news, if the government doesn't follow through, there's not much I can do."

"I suppose that's true. Yeah." It wasn't, but I hoped he believed it was.

"I want them to know they owe me one."

Serata considered it. "I can't speak for the government on that. But I'll give you this. *I'll* owe you one. If they don't follow through—even if they do—if you need something, I'll do my best to make it happen."

It was the best I was going to get. "Deal."

CHAPTER 30

Mac

O NCE BUTLER ENTERED the room with Serata, they wouldn't come out for a while. I love Butler, but he can talk. And Serata is just a bigger version of Butler. Put the two of them together, and I could have gone for a shower and a nap, gotten in a workout, and still made it back before they noticed. Add to that the fact that they were in the commander's office, and . . . well . . . I didn't *relax*. That's not happening any time soon. Maybe never again in my life. But I felt secure enough to leave Clement outside the door to ensure their privacy so that I could take care of business.

I'd sent Kim to watch over Ganos. We'd left her alone during the mission because we had to. Now that we were back, I wanted her covered. Butler thought this thing was over, but in my experience, it's never truly over. Not since the simple days where I was a grunt on the battlefield. Good times, those. You knew who your friends were, and more important, you knew your enemies. They were the people trying to shoot you in the face. And once you beat them, they stayed beaten. Here, dealing with politicians and corporations and double dealing, someone would take a shot at you in the shower if they thought they could get away with it. Which was a shame. I really wanted a shower. Combat is dirty work in more ways than one.

I needed to talk to Ganos, but with her protected, that could wait. C was alone. He'd been evacuated early on the medical flight, which probably meant that he was in the hospital. I suppose technically I was alone, too, but if somebody wanted to come after me . . . well . . . bring it on, assholes. Not that I thought I was invincible. Anybody can be killed. But I still had my Bitch. If they wanted to take me out, they were going to earn their paycheck trying. It's a whole different story when your target fights back.

I didn't realize my error until I stepped through the door in the medical facility. It's never the threat you prepare for that gets you. Instead, I found one of my own making staring at me from three different faces. I recognized two of them. All three of them recognized me. I'd been at the facility before, not too far in the past, and . . . well . . . I'd been slightly less than professional. Now I needed help finding C. I *hate it* when I have to face the consequences of my own past actions. In my defense, I'd only been a dick because someone from my team had been critically injured, and the staff wouldn't tell me anything. Somehow I doubted that they saw it the same way. If I'm being honest, I probably didn't see it that way either. More like I'd *mostly* been a dick for that reason. Some of it was just my natural propensity to be a dick. Either way, medical people have no sense of humor, and I doubt they'd forgiven me. But there was nothing to do but get to it, so I lowered my head in an attempt to look contrite and walked up to the main counter.

"Excuse me. I'm hoping you can help. I'm looking for Castellano. Probably came in a few hours ago. Broken leg."

The sergeant looked at me, almost glaring, but not quite. Maybe she was buying my humble look. I had at least a bit of hope. She checked her screen. "He'll be sedated for another eight hours while the healing accelerators work."

"Thank you," I said, forcing myself to smile. "There's a chance we may need to leave Taug in the near future. Is there someone I could talk to about that?" I appreciated that they had him on accelerators, but we might not *have* eight hours. It wasn't a specific threat, but I didn't *feel* safe. And I really didn't want to leave C behind if we had to make a hasty exit. We'd already abandoned one team member back on Talca.

"I can get his doctor, if you'd like."

"Thanks. That would be very helpful." Okay. I'd gotten through that much. I'd only interacted with one doctor on my last visit. What were the chances that it would be the same—

"Security," someone said behind me.

I turned to see where it came from. Dr. Dickless. Because of course it was. That wasn't his real name, which was kind of a problem, because I didn't actually *know* his real name. But it was most definitely the same guy I'd insulted—and maybe threatened—on my last visit. Butler had pulled me out of that one. Butler wasn't here now. I had to ask myself: *What would Butler do?* He'd definitely run away.

No, wait, that was me. Definitely my subconscious inserting itself. I could stay. What were they going to do to me? I still had my body armor and rifle. If worst came to worst, I could fight my way out of here.

No, that was me again.

Shit. I was really not cut out for this kind of thing. It's hard to suppress your nature.

"Doctor," I said, doing my best to sound contrite and probably failing. "I really want to apologize for my behavior the last time I was here." Okay. That didn't sound like Butler, but it least it was a step in the right direction.

It seemed to have the right effect, as he at least stopped looking around for armed guards to help him. Now he looked directly at me, with all the confidence of a rabbit looking at a wolf. If intimidating him would have gotten me what I wanted, I'd have had no problems. "What can I do for you?"

I noted that he ignored my apology. And that he was talking from across the room. But at least he was talking. Baby steps.

"You treated a man who worked for me? Castellano?"

"I did."

"I understand that he's still sedated."

"That's correct."

"There is a chance that we might have to leave Taug sooner than expected. Is there any chance that he could be ready to go?"

"How soon would he need to move?"

"Uh . . . two hours?" I didn't really know, but that seemed the soonest we could go. Butler would be in there talking for almost that long.

"Absolutely not." He started to turn away.

I didn't rush over, grab him by the stupid white coat, and start shaking him. That's progress. "It's just that . . . we've pissed off some pretty dangerous people. It might not be safe for him here."

He turned back to give me a condescending look. "He's in the medical facility. There's no place safer." Now he was trolling me. That was the stupidest thing I'd ever heard. Okay, not the *stupidest ever.* But at least the stupidest in the last few hours. Maybe since that time when someone suggested that we launch an assault on a mech. What can I say? The bar for stupid things in my life was pretty high.

The old me might have popped off a few rounds there in the waiting room. You know, to show the good doctor exactly how safe he *wasn't* here in his medical facility. The old me probably would have gotten arrested, forcing Butler to come talk his way into securing my release.

I missed the old me. The new me smiled. Given the response on the doctor's face, the new me wasn't any better at that than the old me. But I tried. And then I channeled my inner Butler. How hard could it be? "Let's say that hypothetically we had to go. No other option. What would it take for him to move in two hours?"

He stared at me the way that teachers sometimes had back in math class, that look somewhere between anger and pity. "I'm not releasing that patient for twenty-four hours, no matter what."

"Okay. Thank you for your time." I turned and walked to the exit, keeping a measured pace and betraying no emotion until I was sure that the doors had closed behind me. Even then, I outwardly kept my composure. The doctor's words had settled it. The new me had failed. When it was time to go, I'd have to get Clement and break C out by force. We'd probably need to kidnap a nurse to keep up his medical treatment on the way, but we'd burn that bridge when we got to it.

Maybe some people aren't meant to change. I wondered what my therapist would have to say about *that*. Can a person fail out of therapy?

I PUT THAT behind me and headed back toward headquarters to check in with Ganos and prepare her to move in a hurry in case we needed to. Butler hadn't left things well with her, though I'm not sure he realized it. He was focused on other things. I could clean that up for him. The Mother knows he'd cleaned up enough of my messes. I passed two people outside the headquarters—at first I thought they were a couple, all huggy and kissy, a tall, pale man and a medium-height woman with deep tan skin—but there was something missing. There was no real feeling there. I don't know why I knew that, but I did. They were faking it. Since I was the only one in the corridor with them at the moment, I didn't know why they'd bother. I didn't see any weapons, and I got past them without issue. It nagged at me a bit, but I had bigger fish to fry, so I continued into the headquarters.

Kim was still waiting outside the vault door in the intel section. "She busy?"

"Don't know." There was a keypad and a buzzer to the right side of the door. I'd been inside there before, but only with intervention from the sergeant major. I doubted they'd let me back in now, no matter how sweet I talked. I hit the buzzer.

A short corporal answered the door. "Hi, Sergeant Mac."

"Hey." If I could have remembered her name right then, I could have maybe talked my way in, but my memory deserted me. I've never been good with names. "Is Ganos there? I need to talk to her."

"Sure thing. Hang tight."

Ganos arrived maybe a minute later.

"You have time to talk, or do you need to get back?" I asked.

She studied me. "I can take a few minutes. Thanks for asking, though."

"You want to walk?"

"Yeah. It would be good for me to stretch my legs. Can we walk to the mess hall? I don't remember the last time I ate."

"Sure. They don't bring you food in there?"

"I don't know. They might. I get pretty focused."

I waved for Kim to follow behind us but give us some space. "How are you doing?"

"I'm good."

I stopped, forcing her to stop with me. "Seriously. How are you?"

She took a deep breath and let it out. "I'm . . . okay. The panic came a couple of times, but I was able to mostly get it under control. I don't think anybody in there knew what was going on. Butler gave me a gun. That helped."

I started walking again, slower this time, letting her set the pace. "Good. You really should talk to someone, though."

"Like you?" she asked.

I laughed. "Absolutely not. When we get back. A professional."

We walked in silence for a bit before she spoke again. "You think I should?"

"Yeah. I don't know much, but I know that bottling shit up isn't good."

"From personal experience?" she asked.

I laughed. "Maybe. Don't tell anyone."

She mimed zipping her lips. "Your secret is safe with me."

We had almost reached the mess hall when I stopped. "Hey. Thanks."

She scrunched up her face. "For what? Of course, I'd keep a secret. And . . . uh . . ." She dropped her voice to a whisper. "It's not really a secret."

I laughed again. It was good to laugh. "Seriously. Thanks for saving our asses out there. With the mech. I don't know how much you know about our end of that, but it was a close thing. Wasn't sure we were going to make it out of there."

Her shoulders sank. Not the reaction I expected. "From what I hear, some didn't. We were too slow."

"Don't beat yourself up. None of us expected to face that."

She nodded. "I know. But still."

I got it. I really did. No matter how good we did—and she'd done beyond good and into the almost impossible—it was easy to beat ourselves up for the ones that didn't make it. But that way lay madness. "Seriously. You saved us. Me and Butler, Kim and Clement. C is going to recover. Everybody who lived through this has you to thank."

She almost smiled. "I guess."

"Was it hard? Taking it out? I don't know anything about that kind of thing."

"They weren't expecting us to go after the mech, I don't think. We got ahead before they reacted, and by the time they realized what we were doing they were stuck playing defense. And I had help. When they shifted focus to try to keep us from killing the mech, we got into their other stuff and started shutting shit down. After that, they couldn't keep up."

"Well, I'm glad we had you with us. Without you, this is an entirely different story."

"Right. The story. Do me a favor and keep me out of that."

"Of course."

"Tell Butler, too. I was never here."

"People saw you," I said. I wanted to heed her wishes, but we couldn't put that back in the container.

"*Here*. Sure. But here is nowhere. Butler is going to broadcast shit to the entire galaxy. *That's* the story. Whatever he says it is. The little voices here will"—she put out her hand and blew on it—"scatter like dust. I'll reveal my piece of it in my own time, to my own contacts. When it'll get me paid."

"Sure. I'll tell him." I gestured to the entrance to the mess hall. "You good here? Kim will stay with you."

"I'm good. You go. I know you've got things to do."

"If you need me—"

"Go!" She smiled. "You've changed."

"You think?" I asked.

"It's good. See you soon."

"Right. Be ready to go in a hurry. Things could still go south."

"Always ready. And hey—in case I don't get to tell you later—"

"Yeah?"

"If you ever need anything, just write a note in front of the camera at your gym."

I stared for a second, unsure if she was fucking with me until she cracked a smile, and then I laughed again. Though I noticed that she didn't say she was kidding. "Will do." I headed back to find Butler. I didn't know about Ganos's assessment about me changing. But she's super smart, so maybe she was right.

CHAPTER 31

Butler

I TALKED TO SERATA for a good while after we agreed to our deal, catching up about the old times. He had nowhere to be since his flight wasn't leaving for ten hours—the crew needed rest. He offered me a ride home, but I passed. I said I didn't want him to have to go out of his way to Ridia 2, which was true, but mostly I wanted my own space. An hour or two of catching up was great. Beyond that, we'd end up getting into real issues and things from the past, and nobody wanted that. Besides, since I'd cut my deal with the government, I could afford my own flight.

Mac was waiting for me outside the door, because of course he was. There was something comforting about his consistency. "How'd it go?"

"We made a deal."

"Good."

"Don't you want to know what it is?"

"I trust you," he said. "I'd like to get out of here. There's something off."

"I told you, I cut a deal. It's over. We won."

He shook his head. "Ain't over. This shit'll never be over until we're dead or they are."

I paused and looked at him. He felt strongly about it, and I don't ever want to discount that. Too often, there's a reason for our gut feelings that our conscious minds haven't parsed yet. Plus, if I ignored him, that was just tempting the universe to kick me in the nuts. Not that I'm superstitious or anything. "Okay. I hear you. We can leave as soon as I do my interview with Chastain. That's pretty critical."

He glanced in both directions. Something really did have him spooked. "Do it quick, okay? I already got us a ship."

"Oh?"

"There's one on the ground that'll do. Not a luxury ride by any stretch, but it'll beat riding in a container."

"Good. I'll hurry. Did you check on C?"

"They've got him sedated. You're probably going to have to get involved to get them to release him."

I gave him a look. "What did you do?"

"I didn't threaten them. I didn't do anything. I asked, and they said no. I didn't make it any worse."

"But they remembered you from last time." He looked embarrassed, so I let it go. "I'll talk to the commander, have her make a call. It shouldn't be a problem. We can pay for a medical suite to monitor him on the trip."

"I checked in with Ganos, too." That was good. I hadn't given her much time, what with Serata arriving and everything I had to do.

"How is she?"

"This place is hard on her." She wasn't the only one that it was hard on. Mac had his scars from here, too. We'd talk about that, but it could wait until we were safely ensconced on our ship and on the way home.

Chastain was set up in a conference room that the unit loaned her. She didn't like that I put a couple of limitations on our interview by not talking about the military and government involvement. But if she wanted, she could put that in herself as editorial content. Serata and I had agreed that *I* wouldn't talk about it, but we'd also agreed that nobody would interfere with her report. I stuck to the spirit of the agreement and didn't suggest that to her. After all, it was her job. She had the skills, and she could make the decisions. Or her bosses could. It would be naïve to think that a story this big wouldn't get a *lot* of editorial oversight.

To make up for not talking about the military, I piled on Caliber hard. I shared everything I could prove, and theorized some things that I couldn't. I blamed them for the shootout on Ridia 2, for trying to kill me on Talca, and for their direct attacks on the military on Taug, including use of a heavy mech. Part of me worried that Zentas would buy the whole thing out, and it would never see the light of day. But I had my copy of the footage. If *The Times* wouldn't run it, I'd release the unedited footage for free on the net. And I'd have Ganos do it in a way that made sure it didn't get suppressed.

WITH THAT FINISHED, we gathered up the team to head for the hanger—everyone except for C, who would meet us there. Mac and Kim walked up front, Ganos and I behind them, and Clement brought up the rear. Mac stopped almost as soon as he got outside the door of the headquarters, putting out a hand to hold Kim back.

The rest of us stopped naturally behind them, me awkwardly in the doorway as it tried to close.

"What is it?" I asked.

"Back inside." He turned to Kim. "Get EOD."

"What'd you see?" she asked.

"I don't know," he said. "Something is off—it's been off for a while. And it just dawned on me what: two people were outside the headquarters earlier."

"That's not a lot to go on," she said. I agreed.

"I might be wrong. But I want it checked."

Clement kept watch on the door, and Ganos buried her head in her device. I pulled Mac aside, keeping my voice low. "Are you okay, brother?"

"I really don't know. I'd say that I'm not myself, but . . . I don't really know who I am anymore."

I nodded. I understood. I really did. "You've been working pretty much nonstop for the last six months. Even before that. When we get home, you'll take some time off. Relax and figure it out." I left unsaid that he'd get help from a therapist. He had one already, and I didn't need to harp on it.

"I wasn't kidding, earlier. They're not going to stop coming after you. You know that."

"Yeah. We can hope that this news stops them. Or at least slows them down for a while. But that's probably wishful thinking."

"You need me."

He was right about that. They wouldn't stop. But that didn't mean he didn't need time off. "I do. But I've got a feeling that people will be coming after me for a long time. We can let someone else handle it for a bit. You come back when you're ready."

"I *have* been promising Cassie that we'd take a vacation together."

"Do it. Somewhere off world."

"Remove all temptation to check in, huh?"

"Exactly."

Kim returned, three soldiers in tow, one of them strapping on protective gear as she approached. How she got them to respond that quickly, I'll never know. The other two carried a sizable drone between them—a high-end bomb drone with all of the sensor suites. It probably wouldn't find anything. Mac was right—they wouldn't stop coming after me. But that didn't mean it would be there on Taug. Still, we could spare the time for Mac's peace of mind.

"If you all could step back around the corner, please," the sergeant who was strapping on her gear said. "If there's something out there, we might set it off. This area won't be safe."

I almost said something, but she was just doing her job. Someone said bomb, the bomb squad came. I moved back around the corner, out of the line of fire. I was ready to let it go, but apparently Mac wasn't.

"You want to bet on whether there's something out there?" he asked.

I hesitated, sure he was fucking with me. "What are the odds?"

"Give me two to one."

"Seriously?" I looked at him. He wasn't joking. "Okay. How much?"

"My fifty to your hundred."

"Deal." I offered him my hand and he shook it. "I feel bad taking advantage of you."

"Don't," he said. "I trust my gut."

"I trust that my gut is going to be full of fifty-mark liquor, courtesy of your gut."

He laughed.

"Holy shit." Someone around the corner said it. One of the bomb team. The tone . . . I knew that tone.

"You want to pay me now?" Mac asked.

"I will never make a joke about you being paranoid again," I said.

"Yes you will."

"I probably will." But his point hit even closer now. They would *never* stop.

RIDIA 2 WAS . . . I almost said nice, but it's not really anything special. It was home, though, even changed as it was since we left. The changes involved a bomb team checking my house before I got back to it and a rotating security detail in the area around the clock. Serata had come through on that, perhaps with a little bit of overkill. I could imagine him laughing about it in his living room that *wasn't* surrounded by armed guards. We had never found out who had tripped my sensors back before the whole adventure kicked off, but if they were still out there, they'd have a tougher time getting at me now. Me? I just wanted to rest and enjoy the footage of Caliber leaving Taug with their tails between their legs and watch their stock price tank. It was down eighteen percent, and not looking like it would recover any time soon. I'd hold out hope that Zentas went to jail, but I wouldn't hold my breath.

Chastain's story went out in a week-long set of special reports that kept it in the public consciousness. From there, others picked it up, and not just news organizations. Scientists, business outlets, talk show hosts . . . even social influencers were running clips of the technology and talking about it. It wouldn't last. Nothing ever does. Something else comes along and takes over the news cycle, pushing the current *big thing* to the back burner. But it was out there, and while I'd never be done with it, nobody could put it back in the dark, either.

The military held up their end of things too. The vice-chief of staff made the announcement of corruption in the military herself and said there would be an investigation with public results. I'd watch that and make sure they didn't skimp on those results. I still had my list of names.

Ganos disappeared almost immediately, taking only a bit of time to huddle with Mac and talk before Parker showed up to get her. Kim and Clement left together, which left just Mac, C, and me at my house. Alanson had been released from custody with a protective detail to get him off of Talca. Mac wanted to wait for him and make sure that security was set before he left on vacation, and C was going to stay for a while to cover me in Mac's absence. I had the space, and it made Mac happy that I'd have one of my own people there and not just the government-provided folks. We probably didn't need to worry. Serata had come through on security. On everything else, too.

WE NEEDED TO talk, Mac and I, so we did what we always do. We sat down with a bottle of talking juice—in this case, good whiskey. C sat with us, though he still didn't drink. I trusted him anyway.

"So," said Mac, after the second pour.

"So," I said.

"What now?"

"We definitely don't go looking for any missing teenagers."

Mac snorted. "Yeah. Not my best decision."

"It worked out," said C.

"This time," said Mac. "Next time . . . who knows?"

"Is there going to be a next time?" asked C.

I wanted to tell him no. I really did. Let him believe that there's an end, keep him from becoming as cynical as Mac and me. I couldn't. Not in good conscience. The bomb that Mac found had proved beyond a shadow of a doubt that we'd always be in danger. There was no *normal life* for me. "Probably. Yeah. If you want off the bus, this is probably the last chance you get."

C thought about it, which was good. I didn't want him staying based on emotion. Finally, he said, "I'm in."

We drank in silence for a bit. We were into our third glass when Mac started up again, as if the conversation hadn't even paused. "Okay. But what do we *do*? What do our lives look like?"

"For you? You've got to figure out what works. For me, it's hanging out here, working out just enough to stay functional, and a lot of time with books and movies."

"And then what? Wait for whatever blindsides us next and pulls us back into some shit?"

I shook my head. "It's like you said—it's not over. I don't know what has to happen for it to ever *be* over."

"We could kill Zentas," Mac offered.

"Sure," I said, as if murder were the same as taking out the trash. "But does that end things, or does someone else just take his place?"

"I don't know," he admitted. "But it would feel pretty good."

I laughed. It would at that. "Here's what I think: there's no rush. We can sit back and rest for a while. They'll still be there for us when we've recovered. We can decide then."

He stared at his drink for a few seconds, as if maybe the answer was in there. Maybe it was.

MAC FINALLY LEFT on vacation six days later. It made me laugh that he had to take a security person with him.

Me? I did what I said and took some time to myself. I reflected on what had happened, those we'd lost. Dixon, my driver, stuck with me especially. I reached out to Ganos, had her track down the family and secretly funnel some of the money the government paid us to them. It wasn't much. It wouldn't bring back their daughter. I knew that firsthand. But it was all I could do, and maybe it would help me sleep at night. Probably not.

And then, one afternoon, maybe three weeks later, I got off my ass and decided to live. Stop feeling sorry for myself. I got out my device and sent a message. Donato responded almost immediately. That seemed like a pretty good sign.

The End

ACKNOWLEDGMENTS

Like all my books, I had a lot of help on this one. I'd like to thank my early readers, P. K. Torrens, Ernie Chiara, Jason Nelson, and Dan Koboldt. Each of them helped me shape the story into what it is now. Any problems that still exist are absolutely my fault and no reflection on their great work.

I'd like to thank my agent, Lisa Rodgers, for her continued support and advice in general, and specifically for her insightful thoughts on this book. I'd like to thank the entire team at Harper Voyager for putting this together and bringing it to market, and especially David Pomerico, my editor, for his support of my vision for this series. His trust in me is going to allow me to finish the series on my own terms and bring the Carl Butler saga to the close it deserves.

Most important, I'd like to thank my wife, Melody, for her continued love and support. Between the time I started writing it and the final product, we moved houses. There's no way that happens without a great partnership and a lot of hard work on her part. Thanks for everything, honey. I love you.

ABOUT THE AUTHOR

Michael Mammay is a retired Army officer and a graduate of the United States Military Academy. He has a master's degree in military history and is a veteran of more wars than he cares to remember. He lives with his wife in Georgia. He is the author of the Planetside series, *The Misfit Soldier*, *The Weight of Command*, and *Generation Ship*.

ABOUT THE AUTHOR

Delve into the Planetside series from acclaimed science fiction author
MICHAEL MAMMAY